"That all of these characters seem so true—from what they eat and wear and drive to how they act and think and feel—is a testament to Smiley's extraordinary talent (and extraordinary application)."

—*Minneapolis Star Tribune*

"Smiley tells not only the story of an American family, but also the story of America itself. . . . The way the characters interact with history is indivisible from the way they interact with each other, which is inextricably bound up with family dynamics and the mystery of human personality."

—*Chicago Tribune*

"A literary historical panorama. . . . The power of Smiley's project ultimately lies in her ability to situate her readers here, on the edge of a new world."

—*Milwaukee Journal Sentinel*

"Radiant. . . . Beautifully crafted."

—*Pittsburgh Post-Gazette*

"Bold. . . . Satisfying. . . . Insightful. [Smiley] is superb when it comes to summing up a character's hopes and insecurities. . . . She is an endlessly sensitive explorer of . . . liberty and the abandonments it entails. . . . *Golden Age* is a welcome reminder of her enormous talents as a storyteller."

—*Financial Times*

"Compelling. . . . Familial relationships are explored with biting intelligence, great narrative skill, good humor and generosity of spirit. . . . Her humanely realized characters are what make these novels so addictive. . . . *Golden Age* reverberates with shocks and surprises."

—*BookPage*

"Timeless in the rapture of its storytelling and the humanness of its insights. . . . Readers will be reading, and rereading, Smiley's Last Hundred Years far into the next."

—*Booklist* (starred review)

JANE SMILEY
Golden Age

Jane Smiley is the author of numerous novels, including *A Thousand Acres*, which was awarded the Pulitzer Prize, and most recently *Some Luck* and *Early Warning*, the first volumes of The Last Hundred Years trilogy. She is also the author of five works of nonfiction and a series of books for young adults. A member of the American Academy of Arts and Letters, she has also received the PEN Center USA Lifetime Achievement Award for Literature. She lives in Northern California.

Jane Smiley is available for select speaking engagements. To inquire about a possible appearance, please contact Penguin Random House Speakers Bureau at speakers@penguinrandomhouse.com or visit www.prhspeakers.com.

Golden Age

A Novel

JANE SMILEY

ANCHOR BOOKS
A Division of Penguin Random House LLC
New York

FIRST ANCHOR BOOKS EDITION, JUNE 2016

Copyright © 2015 by Jane Smiley

All rights reserved. Published in the United States by Anchor Books, a division of Penguin Random House LLC, New York, and distributed in Canada by Random House of Canada, a division of Penguin Random House Canada Limited, Toronto. Originally published in hardcover in the United States by Alfred A. Knopf, a division of Penguin Random House LLC, New York, in 2015.

Anchor Books and colophon are registered trademarks of Penguin Random House LLC.

The Library of Congress has cataloged the Alfred A. Knopf edition as follows:
Smiley, Jane.
Golden age : a novel / Jane Smiley. — First edition.
pages ; cm — (Last hundred years trilogy ; 3)
1. Rural families—Iowa—Fiction.   2. Social change—United States—
History—20th century—Fiction.   3. Domestic fiction.   I. Title.
PS3569.M39G65 2015   813'.54—dc23   2015016461

Anchor Books Trade Paperback ISBN: 978-0-307-74482-1
eBook ISBN: 978-0-385-35244-4

Book design by Cassandra J. Pappas

www.anchorbooks.com

Printed in the United States of America
10 9 8 7 6 5 4 3 2 1

This trilogy is dedicated to John Whiston,
Bill Silag, Steve Mortensen, and Jack Canning,
with many thanks for decades of patience, laughter,
insight, information, and assistance.

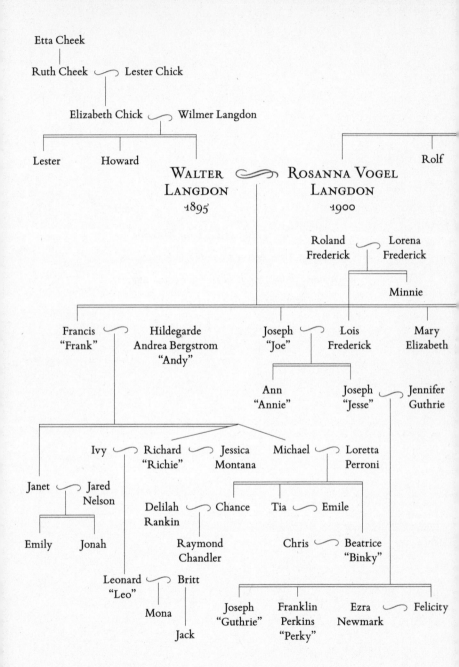

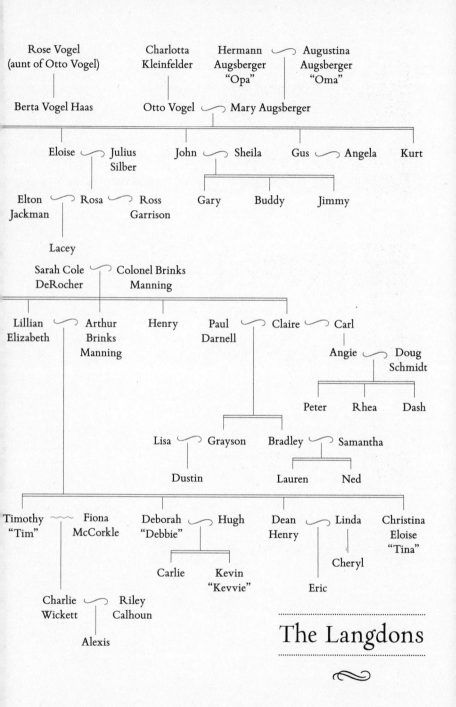

The Langdons

Golden Age

1987

〜

I T WAS FRIDAY. Everyone was somewhere else, doing last-minute chores. The tall young man got out of his little green station wagon, stretched, looked around, took off his sunglasses, and started up the walk. Minnie Frederick, who saw him through her bedroom window, dropped the stack of sheets she was carrying and ran down the stairs. But he was not at the door, and when she went out onto the porch, he was nowhere to be seen. Back in the house, through the kitchen, out onto the stoop. Still nothing, apart from Jesse, her nephew, a noisy dot, cultivating the bean field east of the Osage-orange hedge. She walked around the house to the front porch. The car was still there. She crossed to it and looked in the window. A pair of fancy boots in the foot well of the passenger's seat, two wadded-up pieces of waxed paper, a soda can. She stood beside the green car for a long moment, then touched the hood. It was warm. It was real. She was not imagining things, sixty-seven years old, she who came from a long line of crazy people on all sides, who was both happy and relieved to have chosen long ago not to reproduce. What, she thought, was the not-crazy thing to do? It was to make a glass of iced tea and see if her sister, Lois, had left any shortbread in the cookie jar.

When did Lois first mention him—Charlie Wickett—sometime in January? But Minnie hadn't paid attention, because she was planning her summer trip to Rome. He was Tim's son, Lillian and Arthur's grandson, produced by means of one of those irresponsible high-school romances that every principal was only too familiar with. The baby had ended up in St. Louis. Tim had ended up in Vietnam, killed by a grenade fragment. Charlie now lived in Aspen, said he would be happy to meet everyone, to drive to Denby, and within a week, a reunion had exploded around his coming. They were all heading to the farm—Frank and Andy, Michael and Richie with their wives and kids, Janet, alone (Minnie remembered that Janet had always had a thing about Tim), Arthur and Debbie and her kids (Hugh, her husband, couldn't come because of exams, though). There hadn't been a family gathering of this size since Claire's wedding—1962, that was. Minnie hoped everyone would mind their manners. She knew plenty of farm families who did not get along, but they kept their conflicts to themselves and behaved, at least in public. Families that had scattered, like the Langdons, could end up looking and acting like alien species of a single genus. Frank had nothing in common with Joe (never had), except that, thanks to Frank, the farm was paid off. Frank let Jesse and Joe work the land however they wished. Lillian, whom everyone had loved, had passed three and a half years before, and there was plenty of family gossip about what a mess Arthur and Debbie were. Dean kept to himself, and Tina, the youngest, had taken off to the mountains of Idaho. She wasn't coming (but she had driven down to Aspen, met Charlie, liked him, and issued a bulletin in the form of a drawing that depicted a handsome, laughing kid. How she had gotten the twinkle into his eye, Minnie didn't understand). For once, Henry was coming from Chicago (Minnie suspected that no one in Chicago knew that Henry was a farm kid). Only Claire, who was driving up from Des Moines, was a regular visitor. A big party. Lois was in charge of the cooking, Jen in charge of shopping, Joe in charge of the generous welcome. Minnie had done a lot of cleaning.

Now Charlie appeared on the other side of the screen door, loose-limbed and fit. He saw her, he smiled, and Minnie said, "I thought you were a phantom."

"Oh, I am sorry," said Charlie. "When I got out of the car and realized how hot it was getting, I decided I had to take my run right away, so I ran around the section. What is that, do you think?"

"Four miles," said Minnie.

He said, "Well, I'm not used to the heat yet. But it's really flat, so that makes up for it a little."

She got up and opened the door. She said, "I'll bet you'd like some water."

She took a glass out of the drainer and held it under the tap. Not too brown. Lois had bought some kind of French sparkling water for the weekend, though Minnie was surprised you could get that sort of thing in Iowa. He tilted his head back, opened his mouth, poured it down. She didn't see the Langdon in him the way Frank had when he first espied him in a coffee shop in Aspen last fall, and, supposedly, was convinced the boy was a younger version of himself. Nor did she hear it in his voice (but, then, she hadn't spent much time with Tim). What she saw was grace and a ready smile. His eyes flicked here and there as he drank—he was no less observant than Frank, probably, but he looked like those kids she had known over the years whose parents were indulgent and easygoing, kids who understood that redemption was automatic.

Yes, she was charmed.

She said, "I've made the bed in your room. You can take your things up there and have a rest, if you'd like. Everyone else should be home in a bit. Jen took Guthrie and Perky into town to Hy-Vee, but she should be back any time." He filled his glass again and drank it down. She said, "My name is Minnie Frederick; my sister, Lois, is married to your great-uncle Joe. Gosh, we sound old! I'm the dedicated aunt of Annie and Jesse, also nosy neighbor, retired local principal, and arbiter of disputes."

"Are we going to need one of those?"

"We should know by tomorrow evening."

The smile popped out. He said, "I thought of bringing my protection squad along, but she had to work."

"Your girlfriend?"

He nodded.

"We heard about her."

"You did?"

"You don't know that you were followed, that your license-plate number was jotted down, that your every move went into the photographic memory of Frank Langdon?"

"When was that?"

"Last September. You sold him boots, too."

Charlie shook his head, but he didn't seem disconcerted. He looked at the ceiling moldings for a moment, then said, "May I look around the house? My mom would love this house."

"It's a kit house from 1916. It arrived on the train, and my father, grandfather, and uncles helped put it together. There used to be lots of other houses around, including the Langdon place, which we could see from here, but that one had to be torn down. We had a one-room schoolhouse within walking distance, but that's gone now. In some places, there are a few trees where houses used to be." Minnie made herself stop talking, only said, "But you look around, ask questions if you want. I'm going to clean up in here."

He went through the swinging door into the dining room. She tried to imagine how the place looked to him. Old, though not decrepit. Weighty? Awkwardly set into the tall-grass prairie (maybe a sod hut would be more appropriate)? She had lived here her whole life, except for a few years in Cedar Falls, getting her teaching degree. Her parents had died here, and not easily—her mother had lingered for years after her stroke, with only Minnie to take care of her and Lois after her father disappeared, and then her father returned, full of drunken resolve to get something back that was owed him; Lois had found him at the bottom of the cellar stairs, his head smashed into the concrete. (What had he been looking for? Booze? Treasure? Revenge?) But if every day was spent in the same place, then bad days were overlaid by good ones, your home was just your home, there was no reason for restlessness. Even the story Minnie told herself, that she'd always and only loved Frank, was a dusty remnant now that she had watched him habitually disregard the beautiful Andy, now that she'd realized that the small value he placed on his wife had its source in him rather than her. If Frank had, by some miracle, appreciated Minnie, lo these forty years ago, and loved her, and married her instead of Andy, he would have estimated her, too, at less than her real value. It wasn't in him, whatever it was.

Charlie came back into the kitchen as Minnie was wiping down the sink. He said, "Airy."

Minnie laughed. "Well, exactly. But thanks for reminding me to shut the windows. We can keep out maybe five degrees of heat if we close the place down for the afternoon. Tonight might be okay; your room has a fan, at any rate. No air conditioner—sorry."

"Oh, I don't like air conditioners. My grandmother's lived in St. Louis for almost sixty years without an air conditioner. She believes in wringing a cloth out in cool water, then folding it across the back of your neck."

"She sounds enterprising. You do what you want. There's always plenty of food. You weren't supposed to be here till tomorrow, but I'll tell Jesse and Jen that you'll be coming and going as you please."

And he took her hand in his warm one, squeezed it, and said, "Thanks! Thanks, Minnie. You are great! I hope all the Langdons are like you."

THE OFFICIAL DINNER WAS Sunday at three. Janet was standing maybe a little too close to her cousin Debbie, but Debbie didn't seem to notice. She was saying, "Why would we ever see him again, now that he's seen us roast this hog? I mean, look at the smoke over the house, like a black cloud. Could it be any cruder?" Debbie sneezed. They were in the kitchen—Janet slicing tomatoes, Debbie chopping celery. Through the window, Janet could see the whole family staring at the sizzling pig; of course her dad looked avid, but everyone else was smiling in anticipation, too. Janet had thought meringues and soufflés were more Aunt Lois's sort of thing. Debbie went on, "I mean, I was ready for Tim's doppelgänger, you know? But I don't see it in this Charlie. And that's a relief." Janet did see it, though—the hips, the hair, the vocal timbre. Debbie said, "I admit I was afraid at first, and to you, I will admit why—the comeback of the golden boy." She shook her head. "But this is good for me. I've come to terms with my own issues, which everyone has to do at some point, right?"

Janet did not confess the waves of irrational hope that had broken over her these last few weeks. This Charlie would be something of a resurrection; would she adore him, would she embarrass herself? Her childhood worship of her cousin Tim was family legend. She said, "I hope so." Charlie had turned out to be himself, in spite of his resemblance to Tim. And Janet had turned out to have no feelings toward Charlie other than regular first impressions. She said, "At least he's not some stray product of my dad's youth."

"Uncle Frank had a youth?" They both smiled. "Who said that?"

"My mom," Janet said. "She thinks of that as a joke." Debbie rolled her eyes. Janet said, "Has anyone told Fiona?" Janet remembered Fiona as Debbie's wild and intimidating equestrian girlfriend, much braver than any horsey girl Janet had known at Madeira or Sweet Briar. That Fiona had been at all interested in any boy, even Tim, and had gotten pregnant, was more than a little startling.

"I did," said Debbie.

"How did she react?"

Debbie spun toward her, knife in hand. "She said, I quote, 'How interesting. Oh dear. There's the van. I'll call you.'"

"Did she ever call you?"

Debbie shook her head.

HE FIT RIGHT IN, thought Henry, who was standing on the back stoop, letting the breeze blow the stench from the roasting hog away from him. Extrovert, for sure. Charlie didn't just shake your hand, he patted you on the shoulder, looked you in the eye. From where he was standing on the porch, a little elevated, Henry could see the pattern—the kid would go from group to group, listen first, say something, listen again, his head bent slightly forward. When he was introduced to Henry, he'd said, "Oh, I hear you teach medieval literature! I took two semesters of that, and, you know, it wasn't what I expected." What had he expected? "Well, you can imagine: the first book I ever read was *The Once and Future King*. I thought it would be lots of sorcerers, not so many monks." Charming, but he was not Henry's type. Were he to show up in, say, Henry's freshman lit class, Henry would prod him, treat him a little severely, imply all semester that Charlie Wickett wasn't putting anything past old Professor Langdon. The boy might rise to the occasion—sometimes they did. Minnie leaned out the door and said, "Time to get organized!" Everyone began moving toward the table.

EMILY SAID that she had to go to the bathroom, but it was just so that she could wait and see where her mom was sitting, and then sit somewhere else. The downstairs bathroom door was closed, though, so she went upstairs, and instead of going to the bathroom, she went through the baby's room and out to the back porch. From there she could see over the fields to the horizon, and she could imagine her favorite thing, which was flying. She didn't know how this had started, but maybe from dreaming. Now the dreams and the made-up stuff were mixed up in her mind. She often thought about a myth they had read this year in her school, where a father figured out a way to fly (the book showed giant spreading wings, like eagle wings), but he put the wings together with wax, and when the son got too close to the sun, the wax melted, and the son fell into the ocean. Eli Grissom, who sat behind her in class, pointed out that the son—Icarus, his name was (Eli pronounced it "EYE-carus")—could not have gotten ninety-three million miles in ten minutes, if at all, but in spite of Eli, Emily imagined it almost every day, the wings catching an updraft, the boy feeling himself lifted, the warmth and the brightness all around. It was too bad, Emily thought, that he didn't remember how birds bend their necks and fold their wings and swoop downward— maybe he was so excited that, when the wax started melting and the feathers dropped away, he didn't notice it in time. Emily rested her hands on the sill and leaned toward the window. The horizon was a beautiful thing, she thought.

"THERE SHE IS," said Joe. He cocked his head toward the second-story windows, and Janet looked up. She said, "I thought she was going to the bathroom!" She began to push her chair back, but Joe said, "She'll be fine." Janet looked up again, bit her lip. She said, "Uncle Joe, I should have done what Loretta's done. Emily could have gotten lost in the crowd. She hates being an only child."

Joe shifted his position—his hip was bothering him a lot this year—and said, "Sweetheart, any number's the wrong number."

"Do you really believe that?"

"I really do."

Joe patted Janet on the knee. She gave him an uncertain look, then went back to staring at Emily. There wasn't a time Joe could remember seeing Janet, even as a toddler, when she didn't look like a face outside the window, exiled, staring at the warmth inside. According to Lois, this was all Andy's fault; according to Minnie, it was all Frank's fault. Joe hadn't intended to say what he said—it just popped out. But it was true, and not only with regard to inheritances. He and Lois had agreed that Joe's childhood on this farm, as Frank's much-pummeled younger brother by two years, had been a nightmare, and so he and Lois had decided that Annie and Jesse were enough; but as a result, Annie and Jesse had never gotten a moment's privacy. Joe's always darling sister, Lillian, and her adored Arthur seemed to have hit on the right mix, but Debbie, their skeptical oldest, would not have agreed. Your hog had a big litter, and you were glad, but then there were always those runts consigned to the hind teats, who didn't have much of a chance. Joe had bred his retrievers twice. Thirteen pups the first time, two pups the second time. You are never satisfied, said Lois. The corn crop was too big, the corn crop was too small. Impossible to know what to hope for.

Well, it was Jesse's problem now. Jesse was scientifically trained, and he sank all his dreams into predictive models. When he had gone to Frank and asked for some money to use to trade commodities futures, Frank was proud of him—playing both ends, good strategy, and why not—but Joe himself had been too dumb to think of it.

Still, it made Joe uncomfortable when Jesse talked about "growth medium" and "inputs" and "upticks." He spent his evenings on a computer, and when he walked the fields, it was with soil-moisture instruments and that sort of thing in his hand. If he wondered about the weather, he watched the news, not the western horizon, and he would never in a million years name a sheep or pat a cow. What you needed to do these days, just to survive, was to turn it into an equation. With an equation, every solution was interesting, even the one that put you out of business. Lois set Joe's plate before him, patted him on the shoulder, then said, "Kevvie? You want a popover? I made some."

NOW EVERYONE WAS SEATED, including Emily, who had come around the house and claimed the seat beside Andy. Andy squeezed her granddaughter's hand and spooned some of the pork and the potato salad from her own plate onto Emily's. Emily's head dipped forward and her nostrils flared, suddenly reminding Andy of what had happened sometime before dawn. She and Frank had the guest room of that funny house where Joe and Lois lived, now that they'd let Jesse, Jen, and the two boys take over the big house. The room suited Frank (twin beds, a row of six double-hung windows facing east), and while they were getting ready for the night, he had gotten a little talkative about Charlie: he wasn't entirely wrong, the kid *did* look like him from the back; he had recognized when he bought the boots that the kid had gotten a gene for agreeability from somewhere, but Joe was agreeable, Jesse was agreeable (he smiled automatically when he referred to Jesse, couldn't help himself). He hadn't thought of Tim at the time, but if he had . . . Andy had drifted off to the sound of his voice.

The double-hung windows looked out on the back field, and when a light along the fence line came on, she woke up. There was a fox, triangular head, dark eyes, pointed ears, gray and bushy but small, taking a drink from the dogs' water bowl. The window was open; she could hear lapping. She stared, wide awake at once. The fox lifted its head, looked away, looked at her. She would not have said this to anyone, but she did trade a thought with it before it trotted off— not words, but perspective, the tunnel through the corn, amplified sounds of crickets, the crusty feel of the dirt beneath its paws.

WHEN HIS TWIN BROTHER, Michael, started yelling at their cousin Jesse about farm subsidies, Richie saw with amusement that Loretta's immediate reaction, though her hands were full with Binky, six months old, who was burping or something, was to knock Michael's bottle of Pabst Blue Ribbon off the table, surely an effort to distract him. Richie licked his lips and took a bite of potato salad to hide his smile. Michael and Loretta had been married for almost eight years now, and Loretta had informed Richie that sometimes distraction did work with Michael: The last time he was in California, the Labrador retriever had taken Michael's dirty undershorts and was found rolling on them out in one of the horse paddocks. When Loretta came upon Michael holding the Lab by the collar and taking off his belt, she rammed the corner of a box she was carrying into his side, as if by accident, and when he jumped out of the way, no doubt shouting, "What the fuck fuck this fuck that!" he lost his grip on the dog, who ran off. Loretta said that they ended up laughing about the undershorts. She said Michael had a good sense of humor. Yeah, right, thought Richie. She had also said—with perfect sincerity, as far as Richie could tell—that she and her mother agreed, if you wanted a man with some fire in him, and who didn't, you had to deal with getting burned every so often.

Jesse was shaking his head. "I think you have to accept that farming doesn't fit easily into the free market—"

"Bullshit!"

"The free market doesn't control the weather—"

"Externals can be accounted for, and would be, if the government would allow it. The subsidies are what destroy the market, and let bad farmers keep farming!"

Jesse's good-natured wife, Jen, was breathing a little hard. She said, quietly, "Why do you care? Why is it your business?"

"Because I don't want to pay taxes to keep you in your fucking house if you aren't competent enough to keep it on your own."

Richie reached for another piece of the pork, happy not to be involved, then kissed his own wife of one year, Ivy, on the cheek. Ivy made a face and squeezed his knee affectionately. They were in complete agreement that this reunion would count as one of the four times per year that they had to see his brother, Loretta, and the kids.

The real problem, Richie knew that Loretta knew, was that Michael's mistress, Lynne, had kicked him out two weeks ago, and, worse than that, it had been a surprise—Michael had thought he was set until someone he preferred came along. It was pretty obvious to Richie that Lynne had taken up with Michael mostly to get connected to his Wall Street friends as clients for her remodeling business. Loretta wasn't supposed to know this, of course.

Now Michael got himself together. In their whole life, possibly even in the womb, Michael had been good at getting himself together, though often his initial go-to strategy had been hammering Richie a

few times. Michael coughed and said, "Okay. Okay." Then he leaned
forward and poked Binky lightly in the chest. He smooched at her,
"Peek-a-boo, you!" He held out his arms, and Loretta put their still-
fussing daughter into them. He stood up. "I think we need a little
walk."

Nothing about this persuaded Richie that it would be good to
have a kid.

⌒

THE PERSON Charlie reminded Arthur Manning of was not Tim as
much as his own father, and not his father as he'd known him, but
his father in old black-and-white photographs from the 1890s—he
had short pants and long hair, and had been told to be still but wasn't
quite able to accomplish that; the ghost of a smile fluttered around
the child's mouth, strangely predicting the ebullient Brinks Manning, who spent a lifetime not going into battle, but procuring things
for going into battle, not caring for his son, but making sure that his
son was cared for by kind and amusing nannies, teachers, principals.
There was no one more useful, and in some sense more self-assured,
than a practical young man, and Charlie Wickett was a practical man
who, by his own account, had been solving this problem and that
problem for as long as he could remember. (When is the best time to
escape the house? When Mom is taking a shower. When is the best
time to talk your way into the high-dive class? When they are fed up
with you but can't resist your smile. When is the best time to ask a girl
out? When she thinks her new haircut makes her look bad. When is
the best time to tell your parents you are leaving St. Louis for Colorado? When they are delirious with relief that you actually graduated from college and have a job, even though it is with some sort of
wilderness rafting company. When is the best time to dive out of the
raft? Just above a waterfall that looks dramatic but really isn't—gives
the customers a frisson of excitement and is quite refreshing on a hot
afternoon, especially good if the other rafting guides are coached to
shout, "Hey! Hey! Oh my God!")

Charlie made Arthur laugh, and he made Arthur grateful that he
had missed those early years. After dessert, Debbie sat down next
to Charlie, and she and Arthur did the thing that maybe they were

destined to do: they alternated telling him stories about his mother, Fiona—fox hunting, jumping huge jumps in shows, standing on her horse's back and racing down the hill—but sweeter ones, too, Fiona teaching her horse to push a little tire with his nose, Tim hiding raw eggs all over the house one Easter, playing in his band, the Colts, going to a used-car dealer with his best friend and paying sixty dollars for a ten-year-old Dodge with sawdust in the engine that managed to roll down the hill out of the dealer's yard but got no farther. "And," said Arthur, "those are only the stories we know. They were pretty good at keeping secrets, Tim and Fiona."

"So good we never realized that your parents knew each other," said Debbie.

Arthur had told Charlie that Tim had been killed in Vietnam, but none of the details, and that Tim's mom, Lillian, universally adored (Debbie nodding), had died of a metastatic brain tumor—"She would have loved you"—but none of the details about that. What had Arthur done before he retired? Charlie wanted to know. Debbie looked away; Arthur said that he worked in the federal government, waving his hand as if he meant the Department of Agriculture, certainly giving no details about what he had really done, the agency he had really worked for. All three agreed that Arthur and Debbie should meet the Wicketts.

⤳

FRANK HAD DONE his best. He hadn't said anything impatient, cutting, sharp. He had prevented his foot from tapping irritably under the table. He had spoken when spoken to, smiled when he had to, bounced his grandson Chance on his knee. When he finally fled, he did it smoothly, with a congenial nod, not saying, or even implying, that the clamor of voices was driving him crazy. He strolled as if idly, as if only admiring the straightness of Jesse's rows, out toward the bean field. He put his hands in his pockets and looked west and north, pretending to care about the weather. Twelve more hours and he could leave, whether the others went with him or not. Yes, he was too old to find his origins maddening. Yes, he was too mature to be hurt that Jesse hardly spoke to him. (How many letters had he written to Jesse? More than to anyone else he had ever known, for sure.) Walking along the lilac bushes, remembering his mother, Rosanna, clipping the flowers (they had grown so much that she wouldn't be able to reach them now), he took some long, intentional deep breaths, clenched and unclenched his fists, turned around at last, stared at everyone. Everything was easier to take if he couldn't hear them. It mattered less that Andy was gazing into the trees, that Emily was jumping up and down, that Janet kept wringing her hands without even knowing it, that Richie was practically entrapping Ivy in his bearlike embrace, that Michael was flexing his muscles. Charlie was the prize, but he was Arthur's prize. Charlie was a restless one— huddling with Arthur and Debbie, nodding and laughing, then bouncing from his chair. The person Frank saw in him was not himself anymore, not Tim, not any Langdon, but Arthur, the only truly charismatic human being Frank had ever known, the one who could get you to do whatever crazy thing he wanted you to, not because he had a good argument, or made you an offer you couldn't refuse, but because he wrapped you in a story, filled you with pleasure, dared you to do it. Frank saw Charlie ask Jesse a question, and saw Jesse lean forward, intent upon answering thoughtfully. His mother would have said, "Well, pick of the litter. No two ways about that."

⁓

CHARLIE KNEW that the Highway 61 he was on wasn't the one Dylan meant in the song, but he was glad to be on it—it was much more lost in time than 70, or 80, or 90. He'd already passed Keokuk, gone over a tiny bridge across the Des Moines River, toll ten cents. Iowa made Missouri look very strange. North of the border, towns were flat, with wide streets, grain elevators, and unpretentious storefronts. Houses and barns were close to the road, and fields were neatly planted in corn and beans. South of the border, the landscape was hillier and the houses, with their verandas and even a few columns, were set far up long driveways. He remembered from college that Missouri had once been a great producer of hemp. Charlie was in favor of hemp, but Riley, his girlfriend back in Aspen, was ready to wear hemp, live inside hemp walls, sauté her onions in hemp oil, eat hemp seed for breakfast, write on hemp paper, shampoo with hemp, rappel with hemp (Charlie preferred nylon), and then compost her waste products and grow more hemp.

When he got to Hannibal, he turned off the highway and drove through town; and why would you not leave this run-down but self-satisfied burg when you were eighteen, as Mark Twain had done, and head south, west, east, anywhere you possibly could? He stopped on 3rd Street and went into a café for a Coke, but the cigarette smoke nearly drove him out. At the Langdon farm, only Michael had smoked, and he did it on the back stoop, right beside a bowl of sand for stubbing out and burying his butt. Thinking of Michael made Charlie laugh. He'd acted like the arm wrestling was a joke, at least at first—"Oh, your face is turning red! Oh, your eyeballs are rolling! Okay, I'm going to actually try now!," laughing, sticking out his tongue. But Charlie could feel in his own arm and shoulder and in Michael's grip that Michael was trying harder than he pretended; in the third round, he could feel the jolt of anger that held Michael's arm steady just when Charlie thought he had him. It had crossed Charlie's mind then that he could get a punch in the jaw, but suddenly Michael had smiled, backed off. Later, the other woman, the wife of Michael's twin, came up to him and apologized. Of course, his mom would have called Michael a bully, but Charlie had a lot of experience with bullies—you outgrew them, you walked away from them, or you took them down in an unexpected way, like the time in seventh grade, before he'd outgrown anyone, when he noticed that his customary tormentor, Bobby Rombauer, had just gotten braces; when Bobby grabbed his shoulder that day, Charlie whipped around and smacked him on the mouth, flat-handed. Ouch. Bobby never touched him again.

South of Hannibal, the highway veered inland, through some areas that made Charlie want to stop and get out and run a mile or two, but he knew Mom was expecting him by dinnertime, and dinnertime was six—he could get a couple of miles in before the sun went down at eight, and maybe the humidity wouldn't be so bad by then, anyway. She had been her usual agreeable self about this whole reunion thing. His parents had always been open about his adoption. He was blond, they were dark; he was tall, they were short; he misbehaved, they liked rules and catechisms and confessions and routine.

She didn't say what he knew she was thinking—"You'll do what you want to do no matter what"—she just said, "That ought to be very interesting. Have fun!"

The one he liked best was still Tina, who had come by the shop in April. She was quiet and easygoing; even while taking him and Riley to lunch, she'd been looking at things, and not just the mountains and the clouds, which everyone looked at, but cobwebs and moldings and stray cats half hidden. She was observant, and when she left Charlie her phone number and a sincere invitation to come to Sun Valley for a visit, she'd doodled his own face beside it, a likeness that Riley now kept in her wallet.

It was sunny and getting hot; he drove into range of KSHE and turned the radio up. Some Guns N' Roses carried him across the Missouri River, a beautiful and evocative waterway and, in Charlie's opinion, the true main branch of the river. The bridge was a high one, taking him from the bluffs on the north side to the flatlands on the south side. The afternoon sunlight glinted in lengthening rays on the opaque water. He wondered if he would ever see his grandfather Arthur again. It was uncanny to meet your family as strangers, to look like them, to see yourself in them, but have feelings for them that were only random and new, not conditioned into you. And here he was—this was the oddest thought—alive, speeding through Chesterfield, knowing that in two weeks, when he turned twenty-two, he would have outlived his own father.

IVY WAS in the shower, and Richie was lingering over the front page of the *Times,* when he heard the telltale creak in the fifth step of the third flight of stairs—their flight of stairs—which meant that someone was on his way up, and certainly it was Michael, since Loretta and the kids were back in California; without them, Michael was an early riser. Why sleep when you could get on the motorcycle, zip across the Brooklyn Bridge, terrify everyone on Flatbush Avenue, then get something to eat? Richie hadn't heard the bike, but the window of the co-op faced away from Eighth Avenue, onto the tiny yard behind their building. Always drawn to disaster stories, Richie had just finished reading the article about hundred-mile-an-hour winds, whirlwinds, and square miles of fallen trees southeast of London (didn't they know what a tornado was?). The accompanying picture was of a beached ferry. A British radio announcer had named the storm "Hurricane Ethelred," but so far only thirteen people had died. Michael shook the door handle as if he had a right to come in, and Richie got up from the table. On the way to the door, he picked up the coffee pot. Maybe a cup left.

Richie knew about the stock-market dip—everyone did. He had nothing to say about it. He hoped he could remember that when Michael began babbling. He opened the door. "Fuck," said Michael.

Richie couldn't tell if he was saying this in a positive way or a negative way. He stepped back and Michael strode in. Richie said, "Haven't seen you in a while."

Michael said, "Fuck, I am rich. I am fucking rich."

"Sounds like you're the only one," said Richie.

"I don't mind that," said Michael. "If you could've seen those guys yesterday, just standing around with their mouths open—what does Uncle Joe say? 'Catching flies.' You got some coffee?" He took a cup out of the cabinet and poured out the pot, then pulled out a chair and sat down. "What does the fucking *Times* say?"

"Haven't gotten to the business section yet."

Michael began rummaging through the paper, and found the article he was looking for. "Fuck!" he shouted. "Three hundred thirty-eight million shares! Ha!" He sucked down his coffee as if he didn't even notice that it was hot, and leaned his chair back. His head grazed the window. If, Richie thought, he should lose his balance, he would certainly crack his head on the sill, maybe even break the window and cut open his scalp.

"A hundred points! A hundred and eight, really. You know how many points the Dow fell in 1929? Thirty-eight. So many guys are just completely fucked."

"But not you," said Richie.

"Fuck, no."

He might as well be wearing a T-shirt—Fuck No, Fuck Yeah, Fucked Up, Fucked Over, Fuck Me, Fuck You. He did not talk like this when Loretta and the kids were around. "You have a plan," said Richie, standing up to put some bread in the toaster.

"I went for the delta."

"What's that?"

"Basically, you bet both ways, way up and way down. If the market pisses and moans and piddles around where it is, I'm—"

"Fucked," said Richie.

"God, yeah," said Michael. "But if it jumps or drops big, I win big."

As Michael said this, Richie could almost see the testosterone throbbing through his brother's carotid arteries. He said, "What are you going to do to make sure one of these things happens?" He was joking, but Michael said, "I don't know yet, but I've got till Monday to figure it out." Everyone had a system now. Even his dad had a system, something some guy had explained to him in Aspen, a year ago. Frank didn't use the system, but it seemed like his mom was using the system, in her way, which was to wake up in the morning and say, "I think IBM is about to have an uh-oh day," and then Andy would buy, and then, apparently, IBM would rise, and his dad would say, "I think she's going to turn out to be a genius after all."

Richie, of course, would have to have something to say about the crash, too—Congressman Scheuer would be required to issue a statement about volatility and regulation and why should our nation be beholden to the fat cats—but it was possible that the market would bounce back, and those remarks could be shelved before they were needed. Richie heard the door to their bedroom open, and here came Ivy. When she saw Michael, she gaped, stuck out her tongue, and rolled her eyes, but then she laughed and kissed him on the cheek. She had told Richie over and over that she wanted to see Michael and Loretta as little as possible, but in the end she was always won over. The toast popped, and she buttered it. She said, "You want jam? I have some pear I just got."

Michael said, "Any eggs?"

"There's no such thing as a free breakfast."

Michael said nothing. Ivy got out the frying pan, opened the refrigerator door. Later, Richie knew, she would say that Michael's attitudes were a kind of performance, blond-guy rap. Sure, there was a part of him that was aggressive and inconsiderate, but he was nice to Loretta and better with his kids than, just as an example, their dad had been with them. Michael was a complex person, no two ways about that. She sprinkled in the chili powder and the cumin; she knew what he liked. Richie had told her about the girl at Cornell—Alicia.

He'd told her what he remembered from their sophomore year, that Michael had attacked Alicia, he, Richie, had tried to stop things, and Alicia had stabbed Michael with the scissors in her bag and gotten away. He'd also told her what Michael told him after Richie left Cornell for Rutgers—that Alicia told everyone they both attacked him. Ivy didn't believe either story. They were kids, Michael had a temper, things got out of hand; what was the girl doing, playing them off against one another, anyway? Richie allowed Ivy to give Michael the benefit of the doubt, because didn't he want the same thing for himself?

She said, "You think the computer trading is a problem?"

"Nah," said Michael. "The computers functioned great. I mean, the real problem is people, not computers. It's hard to keep up with them, and you get tired. I'm glad the fucking day is six hours, not eight. Should be four, you ask me, but they haven't thought about that. I mean, we knew this was coming. We knew that volume would pop, and they've spent years preparing for it, so . . ." He shrugged. "Things might settle down on Monday, but if they do I'm fucked."

Ivy cast Richie a glance. Richie raised his eyebrows, their signal for I-will-untangle-this-mess-for-you-later. Ivy set Michael's eggs in front of him and handed him a fork, a napkin.

Michael said, "You pregnant yet?"

"Is that your business?"

"It's not my business, but Loretta asked."

They waited too long to answer. The latest missed period had presented itself only the day before. It had been five days late. Michael said, "Let me try. I have a perfect record." Ivy smiled, thinking he was kidding. "I mean, as an experiment. If I can't do you, then the problem is yours, not Richard's. Down and dirty. Save a lot of medical expense, and if it works, the result is the same, basically."

He lolled back in his chair again, then moved it with a loud scrape. His elbow banged the windowpane, and Richie thought: out the window, three stories, four if he fell into the stairwell leading to the basement co-op.

Ivy scowled, and Michael noticed. He said, "What?" as if truly perplexed. "Okay, I said something. I didn't rape you or go behind Richie's back. I didn't even make an actual proposal. I just floated an idea. I am not blinded by social norms. I can see solutions. So what? It's called thinking outside the box."

"Or joking around," said Ivy.

"All right, joking around. I know you guys got up and left *Beverly Hills Cop 2* because you just couldn't take it."

Richie said, "I like Eddie Murphy." But he sounded so stuffy, and he didn't look Michael in the eye, and he knew that Michael had gotten him again.

1988

H ENRY FOUND the University of Chicago amusing as a monument to wealth. He didn't go there often; however, he did enjoy
the library, not in spite of the fake Gothic feel, but because of it—the
lancet arched leaded windows soaring to the fan-vaulted ceiling, and
warmer this time of year than any cathedral in the world. It was less
than an hour's drive from his apartment down Lake Shore if he went
in the middle of the morning and came back after rush hour. The
snow wasn't bad this year, and he was used to the wind. The bonus
was that he could get away from that letter on his desk from Turner
Klein, which was surely about whether he was making progress on
the panel he had agreed to produce about Philip for the AIDS quilt.
He'd intended to stay away from the AIDS quilt all last summer, and
even into October—he'd thought it would be a tasteless memorial, a
type of headstone in piecrust. Much better, he was vocally convinced,
to build a shining and searing black structure identical to and parallel to the Vietnam Memorial, but he'd ended up going to Washington after all, and had found the two thousand panels laid out on the
Mall strangely affecting, in spite of, or because of, their bright colors and homey shapes. He hadn't broken down, though, until he and
Turner did get to the Vietnam Memorial, and he did touch the name
of Timothy Brinks Manning carved into the gabbro (in his pedantic
way, Henry had told Turner, who was streaming tears, all about gab-

bro, magma, large grains . . .). But when he touched Tim's name, he was thinking of Philip and of Lionel and of Warren, the three AIDS victims he knew best, though only Philip had been his lover. Turner, who was in his thirties, a little panicky and insistent, would not let him get by without somehow seeing to the construction of a panel for Philip, a panel full of words—something severe, he thought, rigorously tasteful, yellow embroidered upon black. How this might be done, Henry hadn't yet figured out.

He had not nursed Philip in the last year—Turner, Philip's ultimate lover, had done that—but he had visited them in New York every month or so and sent them money; he was still sending Turner five hundred dollars a month.

What he was doing at the U. of Chicago was idle work, since he was not doing it in Europe, but it gave him an edgy sort of pleasure. There was that Pope, the evil Innocent III, who had sent Simon de Montfort to Béziers to slaughter the Cathars in the Cathedral. Henry's sympathies were entirely with the Cathars, and he had driven around Carcassonne and Narbonne and the Hautes-Pyrénées several times now, pondering the Cathars at Foix, pondering them at Pamiers and Lavaur, where one of their female leaders was thrown down a well and stoned to death. But through Pope Innocent, he had been reminded of Gerald of Wales, who had met with Innocent several times in order to wrangle himself a position in the English Church, preferably to get Innocent to certify the independence and importance of St. David's Cathedral in Wales, as opposed to Canterbury Cathedral. Gerald (really "Gerallt") had failed, but, out of curiosity, Henry had looked into his many volumes of writings, thinking there might be a subject there for a book or a monograph. He had done the work intermittently and idly, a relief from everything else, but, perhaps because of Philip, the passage that stuck in his mind was not about the exhumation of the bodies of Arthur and Gwenhwyfar, the real Arthur and the real Gwenhwyfar, from the crypt at Glastonbury Abbey in the 1190s. What snagged him was the connection between Arthur's defense of Britain in the sixth century against invading Germanic armies and the Plague of Justinian. He imagined Gerald, who was well traveled and lived into his late seventies, as someone not unlike himself, healthy, active, curious, a man of the Church who wrote about the people he met, the animals he saw, the places he visited. In

all his years of fascination with language, wars, and cultural inva-
sions, Henry had never actually identified with anyone until Gerald
of Wales.

No one talked much about the Plague of Justinian. It had occurred
in the darkest of the Dark Ages, but it was at least as interesting as
the Black Death. It was easy for Henry to imagine Gerald, 650 years
later, standing there as they lifted the mortal remains of the famous
Arthur and his famous second wife. Gerald would have been in his
mid-sixties, simultaneously repulsed and fascinated by the ragged-
clothed skeletons, noticing bits of jewelry and perhaps finery clinging to the bones, thinking: So this is him, what really did happen so
long ago, here they are, exposed to the sunlight of the modern era,
how did they die, what were their lives like? Was he the tyrant that
Henry Plantagenet was? In 1191, Henry had been dead for two years,
and the murder of Thomas Becket was twenty years in the past. Did
Gerald of Wales think of that at once, or not at all? Did he think of it
the way Henry thought of the assassination of JFK, an emblem of his
youth? And it was also true that, if you drove three or four miles past
the University of Chicago, you came to Avalon Park. Supposedly,
Arthur won the Battle of Badon—was that Bath? And he called his
Britain "Avalon"—the Isle of Apples (from the Indo-European root,
ab(e)l). Henry imagined Gerald of Wales turning these ideas over in
his mind, going into libraries, asking questions.

He found a parking spot.

There were two editions of the works of Procopius, the major
historian of Emperor Justinian's reign—an old edition from before
the First World War of the *De bellis* (*Of Wars*) and an edition of the
Historia Arcana (*Secret History*) that was about fifty years old. Henry
supposed it was possible that the U. of Chicago Library would loan
these to the Northwestern University Library—they weren't terribly
valuable—or Henry could buy them on the used-book market, but,
really, he enjoyed this sense of the fan vaulting drawing his gaze as
he walked into the library. The door closed behind him, shutting out
the wind and the cold. Philip had gotten his doctorate from this very
university, and had surely spent hours and hours in this library, but
Henry had never visited him here.

A plague was a plague, no matter what the infection. That was all

Henry was interested in anymore, not friendship or love or student careers or his own advancement, only the nature of infection and its passage around the world by means of things that seemed like good ideas at the time, such as grain storage, such as ships passing from one city to another, such as trade routes opening from China to Ireland, such as conquest, such as vast armies needing food and something to do. The Plague of Justinian (40 percent of the population dying in Constantinople, a quarter of everyone else) made AIDS seem very small, a flutter of mortality, not nearly as large as Philip, thin as wires in his bed, taking sips of water and listening avidly as Henry read an article to him from *People* magazine, oh, back in the early fall sometime, about a family in northern Florida who got a court order so that they could send their three hemophiliac-AIDS-infected sons to public school and promptly had their house burned down. By that time, Philip was past feeling sorry for those boys: however long they lived, it would be longer than Philip himself. What amazed and delighted him were the ideas of the hate-group that threatened the family before setting fire to their house—they thought you could buy a skin cream, like sunscreen, that would protect your child in case an AIDS-infected fellow student touched him, their headquarters was the back room of a beauty parlor, they asserted that head lice were only surpassed in their ability as carriers by body lice (Philip had laughed so hard at this idea that he and Turner had to sit him up and give him water to stop the coughing), and that horses were the original carriers. Henry had stopped reading twice, but Philip gripped his forearm with his own mottled claw until he went on. Then Philip drifted off to sleep, and Turner and Henry sat in chairs on either side of the bed, watching him. Probably that very day, the final pneumonia was setting in, but Philip seemed alert, and Turner could feel no fever. Another thing Henry remembered was that Philip persisted in speaking the Queen's English all the way to the end—maybe one of the last things Henry heard him say to Turner was a grammatical correction, "may not" rather than "might not."

Henry got his pass from the librarian and walked to the elevator. Did the Plague of Justinian look like the Black Death? There were plenty of descriptions of suppurating buboes and black gangrene in the literature. Or did all infections loom, horrifying and gigantic, on the inner eyelids of those who witnessed them, rashes the color of tomatoes, swellings the size of oranges, faces like skulls, never to be forgotten?

JOE WAS OUT EARLY, before the dogs were awake and before the thermometer hit eighty. When he opened the back door, they rolled over and stretched in their pen, and Rocky made his good-natured yawning noise: Glad to see ya, where's my breakfast? They stood up with their tails wagging, and Joe let them out. They loped over to the edge of the east field and started sniffing and lifting their legs. Joe expected he would have to clip them in the next couple of days.

According to Russ Pinckard, the government had three billion, or even four billion stored bushels, so a bad corn crop wasn't going to help anyone, but the farmers sitting around the café taking in the air conditioning, such as it was, agreed that no one knew what was really stockpiled. Jeff Green, who ran the NPPC hog facility between Denby and Usherton, had relied on government figures to decide when to buy feed, and his estimated cost had turned out to be too low by fifty thousand dollars. Jesse said you could gauge the stockpile by the fluctuations at the Board of Trade in Chicago, but in Joe's private opinion, if the quantities themselves were rising and falling the way the prices did, then thieves or ghosts were hard at work supplying and removing tons and tons of corn every hour of every day. At any rate, Jesse had admitted the night before at supper that prices were falling because traders were hedging their positions. "Are you doing that?" said Lois, and Jesse nodded one of those Mom-don't-tell-me-what-to-do nods. So, at least for now, Jesse was betting that a smaller crop would lead to lower prices. Walter the patriarch, Joe's dad, Jesse's granddad, would have been vindicated. But upset.

Lois asserted that either God would provide or the punishment, whatever it was, would be just. However, she was doing some stockpiling herself—two fifty-pound bags of flour, a case of dried beans, and two cases of evaporated milk had appeared in the cellar just this week. She had joined a group based up in Wisconsin that saved the seeds of old-fashioned varieties of vegetables and fruits, and was carefully labeling and saving her best garden seeds—not only tomatoes, peppers, seed potatoes, and squash, which you could justify in the name of flavor, but onions, beets, turnips, carrots, and parsnips, which all tasted the same to Joe. Stashed-away turnips made him think about wartime. Lois wouldn't plant a hybrid in her garden; she still gathered butternuts; she still pretended that her apple and pear trees were all about flavor and pies. She tended them not only with care but with prayer.

Jesse had a soil map of the farm on his computer. Every day or so, he went out with his moisture gauge and his temperature gauge and tested the various soil types, and plugged them into the map. He therefore knew that on the field behind his house, where the soil was loamier, the moisture content was 8 percent greater than it was on the east field, where both dogs were now barking, but 2 percent less than on the west field, where Opa had long kept cattle, sheep, and horses, and for decades had turned their manure under. On the hill behind Joe's house, where everyone had always been careful to terrace if they planted it at all, you could see the soil shading from dark chocolate to caramel just by looking at it; the dust blowing off the brow of the hill was as dry as sand, while on the lower terraces the beans looked like they might survive; but Jesse had mapped it anyway. The map was in and of itself interesting, and Joe liked to look at it and remember what had happened in this or that spot over the last sixty years. Not every event had improved the soil, but every one had deepened his attachment to the farm, like it or not. The savior Jesse prayed to was Frank. He didn't ask him for money (which reminded Joe that his mother had always said that you were never to "pray for goods, only for goodness"), but he did ask him for advice. Frank's most recent advice, handed out yesterday, over the phone from wherever Frank and Andy were spending the summer, had been to sell the place, take the money, move to Cedar Falls, and start a commodities-trading office. Jesse laughed, Jen looked shocked, Lois said, "Good Lord, Cedar Falls! Might as well move to Milwaukee and live with Annie!" Joe thought with an inward shudder of being confined to a fenced-in yard with his two dogs and having to greet the neighbors twenty times a day. And whatever the weather was in Iowa, it was worse in Milwaukee.

Jen's fallback position was that everything would work out because it always had. She was an optimist—the last Guthrie pessimist had been Jen's great-uncle Oliver, father of Donald, who'd gone to the old schoolhouse with Joe and Frank. Oliver had lived to be ninety-five even so; the Guthries saw this as a proof of the power of positive-thinking genetics. Jen was a lovely girl, and very sweet, but she wouldn't have a stockpile in the house—she thought it was bad luck and bad faith. The Guthrie motto was "Do what you want to do, and everything will be fine." Wasn't her second child nicknamed Perky? And a third one was on the way—Jen had driven to Iowa City at the end of June for an ultrasound, and was unsurprised to discover that little Felicity was healthy and already, at twenty weeks, sucking her thumb.

Joe couldn't tell if Minnie was worried about the drought (there, he had thought the word). She kept her thoughts to herself, smiled when you looked at her, and didn't say much. This had always given Joe the feeling that she knew more than she was prepared to divulge. Everyone loved Minnie, including Lois, who was a little afraid of her (but, then, Minnie was a little afraid of Lois). However, should the disaster befall, no matter what it was, anything from a well drying up to the End Times (something Pastor Campbell liked to refer to), you had the feeling that Minnie would sigh and carry on, whether raptured up or left behind, and nothing about either experience would flummox her in the least.

As for Joe himself, he fell back on memories. He knew exactly when the last drought that was this bad had been—1936, the year his uncle Rolf hanged himself in the barn. He'd been fourteen; Rolf would have been a year or two younger than his mother, Rosanna, probably he was not even thirty-five when he did it. Since Joe had turned sixty-six in March, thirty-five now seemed to him awfully young to give up. But he remembered how old Rolf had looked to him then, how desperate, how trapped on Grandpa Otto's farm. He remembered in particular Grandpa Otto standing in the barn doorway, yelling at Uncle Rolf in German about something, waving his arm toward the dusty fields and the wizened corn crop. What had been Rolf's fault or mistake? Joe hadn't known enough German to understand. Rolf's death had overshadowed the fact that on their own farm his father, Walter, had gotten only twenty-three bushels an acre that year for the corn, and sixteen for the oats (though they were then mostly growing the oats for themselves and the animals—

the oats and the straw did get them through that winter, if only just). This year, already on the first of July, the farmers who fed cattle were talking about selling them off—the corn crop could fail entirely. But it never had. In 1953, the year Joe took over the farm after his father died, he got fifty-six bushels an acre and was thrilled; three years ago, he and Jesse were quietly proud of 126 bushels an acre—they'd have settled for 110. Walter would have shaken his head in suspicious disbelief: not going to get ten cents a bushel for that, he'd have said. And Rosanna would've said he was spoiled rotten. Joe stretched his left shoulder, pressed the spot that always hurt with his right thumb, and vowed not to throw Rocky's tennis ball today, even though Rocky brought it to him and dropped it at his feet. Joe kicked it; it rolled away. Rocky glanced at him in disbelief, then ran after it. Snickers was lost in the dusty corn, hunting rats for sport.

Joe picked up the little shovel beside the pen and went in—one mess in the back corner, which he scooped up and tossed out into the weeds (nutrients in dog shit, too). Then he filled the water bowls. Lois had put her foot down about no dogs in the house at night, and no dogs on the new couch, and no dogs alone in the kitchen since last summer, when she happened to come in from the garden and see Snickers, his paws on the edge of the counter and the cooling carrot cake between his jaws. He called the dogs and went inside, pausing to turn the face of the thermometer that was hanging there to the wall. Maybe that was Joe's fallback—the less you think about it, the better.

WHEN RILEY GOT UP to go to the bathroom, she tried to be quiet—if she wanted to get back to sleep, she had to think some blank thought like "blah blah blah" so as to not worry about anything—but she'd made the mistake of looking out the bathroom window, and she saw lightning off to the west. She stood there staring at the brilliant, silent forks that looked like the nervous systems of giants stalking over the peaks. She could hear no thunder, though, since the storm was far away. That was it for sleep. She went into the living room of their one-bedroom; outside the front window, which looked over the town, everything was calm—only occasional brightening reflections of the drama to the west. She sat in a chair in her T-shirt, waiting for the apocalypse. She thought it wouldn't take long—it was already happening in Yellowstone, where hundreds of thousands of acres had burned and the Forest Service was not even close to containing it.

All of this Charlie gathered when he got up, admittedly after nine-thirty, to find Riley sitting over her third cup of coffee. Charlie was a heavy sleeper. His hours at the outfitter's were cut back because of the failure of the tourist season, and no one was rafting because the rivers were so low, but he and Riley had savings from the previous two years, so he was a little lazy lately. The TV was on, and so was the radio. Riley needed to know about any wildfires off to the west. As soon as Charlie said, "Why would there be—" she threw back her head and rolled her eyes about the Forest Service. Charlie had the expert opinion to back him up. The Forest Service had blown it for years, suppressing every fire, by law, by 10:00 a.m. the day after it started. But they'd changed that policy. Now that the Forest Service allowed naturally set fires to burn themselves out, the undergrowth was being cleaned up instead of being allowed to accumulate around the bases of the lodgepole pines, 250-year-old lodgepole pines at the end of their natural life cycle, acting as tinder for the next lightning strike. It was not certain, but why not hope for the best? It was entirely possible, with controlled burns, that the problems would be eased, here in Colorado and elsewhere, without a second Yellowstone taking place. And the pines could be carefully thinned. Yellowstone was a lesson, deserved, but also well learned—

Riley jumped out of her chair and took her cup to the sink. He just didn't get it, did he? In the first place, the Yellowstone fire had started when weather conditions caused controlled burns to get out of *control,* and in the second place, the drought this year was the sign of things to come, that the ecosystem was going through a permanent shift.

Right about then, Charlie actually got himself together. He said, "What happened?"

That's when she told him about the lightning strikes she'd seen. He adjusted his shorts. He was not angry. He recognized that if you grew up in Stevens Point, Wisconsin, if your grandfather was a locally prominent Native American artist who lived on the Menominee Tribal Lands, where your mother had lived until she was twelve, if you studied the Peshtigo Fire in fourth grade, it was much like growing up in St. Louis and studying the Missouri Compromise. Then she said the word, the hot-button word. It was "Hansen." The button that the word pushed was not Charlie's, it was Riley's own button. James or George Hansen or Hanson was a physicist or a climatologist who measured long-term temperature changes on Earth as well as on Venus; according to him, the last ten years had contained some-number of the hottest years in the last number-of-years. Charlie's inability to remember the details was a simmering problem between them. He did know that Hansen had gone to the University of Iowa. Since Charlie had been there, and driven around downtown Iowa City on his way back to St. Louis, Iowa was now fixed in his mind. He'd also thought about his new aunt Tina, in Sun Valley—just Saturday, at the shop, he'd asked Bob how far Sun Valley was from the fires, and Bob had said he thought maybe three hundred miles west, which was safer than being three hundred miles east.

He said a wrong thing: "We probably should have stayed in Golden, but—"

Golden was where the Solar Research Institute was, but the funding had dropped again, and Riley's internship had been canceled in June. Charlie's rafting trips had been so lucrative that they'd decided that the most eco-sensitive choice was for her to move to Aspen, where he had a job in a locally owned equipment store and was closer to the rafting company, while Riley looked for another position. Riley had enjoyed hiking and camping. However, "Hansen" prodded her, made her certain she was wasting time. Here it was, mid-September; graduate programs were starting up everywhere, and she hadn't applied.

She said, "We should have. I regret that every single day."

Charlie hadn't realized that.

But maybe if Riley had not been sitting up since 3:00 a.m., thinking apocalyptic thoughts, staring at the horizon out of the bathroom window for tendrils of smoke rising into the morning sky, she would not have noticed the look on his face that said, Oh, be reasonable, a blip is a blip, we need more data. (That was not what he was thinking; he was thinking, I can't handle this until I have a cup of coffee and something to eat, maybe she'll let me take her out for breakfast in spite of the budget.) The look on her face changed—Charlie could read it—it said, Revelation. Then she said, softly, "I think we're done, baby." And she got up and went into the bedroom. He noted the pale curve of her thigh as she left the room, the bounce of her half-red hair on her neck. She was his first girlfriend, and he didn't want another. She was patient (most of the time), broken in, used to him; he would drive her anywhere; he would try anything she cooked, including tofu, including nettle tea; he loved her breasts and her lips especially. He followed her into the bedroom.

He hadn't made the bed. She had, of course, and perfectly. Now her big old suitcase was sitting on the smoothed-over counterpane. Charlie said, "I'll go with you."

"And do what?"

"What am I doing here?"

"The ski season will begin eventually."

"Not according to you."

"Charlie, you are so much fun."

"I thought you liked that."

"I'm getting old." Her face was smooth, unlined; her hair thick. She looked sixteen.

Charlie said, "You're twenty-two."

"I'm not learning anything here. If I apply to the Forest Service, they will stick me in a fire lookout somewhere, and I will sit there scanning the horizon, and then I will make friends with a deer and a fox or two, and then I will wake up in ten years and be too old to make a difference, and I will have to reproduce and train the kid to make a difference when I didn't."

"It can't be that much of a cri—"

She spun around. Her hair actually lifted as she did so. She barked, "It is."

"I lo—"

She reached for his hand and pulled him down beside her on the bed. She said, "Yes, Charlie, you do, and I love you. But what is the point of that? You tell me. We aren't ever going to have kids. We have a good time together and laugh a lot, but in the larger picture, so what? I don't believe in true love or made-for-each-other. I believe you learn what you can, and you move on. You have to accomplish something."

"I want you to accomplish something."

"Then don't try to keep me here." Her eyebrows shifted toward one another, and a little vertical wrinkle appeared. Charlie knew this wrinkle meant she was dead serious.

He said, "Just admit that we've had a good time here."

He kept holding her hand in both of his. She tried to pull hers away, the wrinkle deepened, but then she actually smiled. She said, "We've had a good time here."

"Then let me come along so that we can have a good time somewhere else. Look. You have a vocation. As far as I can tell, I don't. So I'll support your vocation until mine kicks in." He loosed his hands, so that he wasn't gripping hers anymore, and then she snaked her right arm around his back and laid her head in the spot where she put it when she fell asleep every night—right where the trapezius met the deltoid, right where, she said, his "musk" invaded and overwhelmed her chemoreceptors. She sighed a defeated sigh and said, "Okay."

Charlie said, "Where are we going?"

She said, "We have a year and about ten applications to figure that out." Then, "Columbia?"

Charlie grimaced at the thought of New York City.

"Harvard?"

Charlie made himself sit still.

"Princeton?"

Charlie put his hands on either side of his head and mimicked an Edvard Munch sort of expression.

"Woods Hole?"

Charlie shrugged.

"St. Paul?"

Only then did Charlie grin.

Riley said, "You are truly one in a million, Mr. Wickett."

"I might compromise on Madison."

She said, "We'll see what I get into. And which one is farthest from Stevens Point."

They went back into the kitchen. The radio was playing regular old rock-and-roll, and then Leonard Cohen came on, "First We Take Manhattan." Without seeming to realize it, Riley started bebopping around the kitchen. There was nothing about any fires nearby. At noon, Charlie went out and bought *The Denver Post*. Not much. When he returned, though, Riley was parked in front of the television, staring at what turned out to be footage of the Old Faithful

Inn, in Yellowstone, not of the firestorm itself but of the aftermath—people saying how they had been stuck on the roof ready to die, how they had been watching the fire when, suddenly, they'd had to run for cover, how firebrands had landed all around them, how a fireball had shot down one slope toward the inn but missed it. Everyone was shaken, no one was dead. Charlie stood there until the report was over. She was upset; Charlie was, too. But what a plan gave you, no matter how bad things looked, was a path. And so she only shook her head and said, "Jesus. When is this going to end?" They sat quietly in their little safe spot for the rest of the afternoon, not saying much, and eating leftover macaroni and cheese for dinner.

1989

∾

DEBBIE PULLED OUT Arthur's chair; he let her, though it made him feel stupid. Then she opened the menu for him. He peered at it, turned it upside down, and perused it seriously until she finally said, "Oh, Dad!" and laughed. Once she laughed, he set the menu down. The only thing he liked was French toast, and maybe a slice of bacon. Her mouth opened, and he said, "I do not know anything more about cyanide in the grapes."

She said, "Okay. But—"

"All I know is what I read in the article, same as you. A little cyanide in two grapes out of twenty-two hundred. Not enough to harm—"

"They always say that."

"Yes," said Arthur, "they always do."

The waitress came; Josie, her tag read. Debbie was always friendly. She said, "Hi, Josie. I'll take the Western omelet, and my dad will take the French toast, and we'll split a side of bacon. Thanks."

Arthur said, "I'll take my coffee straight up."

Josie didn't smile, just said, "All righty," and turned away. Debbie's eyes followed her, but she said, "Maybe they blame us for the disappeared."

"Maybe they do," said Arthur. "You throw away your fruit that might have come from Chile. I'm not going to bother." He took an emphatic breath, and this time she believed him. Josie brought the coffee. Arthur took a sip—black and bitter, just the way he liked it.

Debbie said, "Did I tell you Janet called me?"

Arthur shook his head.

"Well, you know that Jared is working with some people on making animated cartoons using computers. So, anyway, he had to be down in L.A. for something, so Janet and Emily went along, and guess what they did?"

Arthur could guess: he would have done the same thing.

"They drove out to Pasadena, where Fiona's stable is—a little northeast of there, really, just below a national forest. I guess the farm had belonged to a movie mogul of some sort. Anyway, the barns are huge and airy, and they have about forty horses in training."

Arthur coughed.

"She pretended to be looking for a horse for Emily. She was very friendly."

"Janet?"

"Well, yes, of course, but I mean Fiona. She led Emily over to a mini that they keep and had her brush it with a soft brush while she and Janet talked, and then Janet said that maybe it was she herself that wanted a horse, not Emily, and Fiona said, 'I've seen that before.' Janet said that she was actually quite personable and almost charming, really."

Arthur decided to play it safe. He said, "Does that surprise you?"

Debbie said, "She said that Fiona was pretty heavy. I mean, you know"—she lowered her voice—"fat."

She looked as though maybe this was the saddest part.

Arthur said, "Maybe she's enjoying life, then."

The waitress set their food in front of them.

Debbie took a bite and said, "Only you would say that, Dad, but maybe."

They ate for a while. Arthur's French toast was spongy and bland, but he forked it in. At long, long last, he asked: "Did she say anything?"

"You mean Fiona?"

"No, I mean Janet."

Debbie nodded.

Arthur tried to gauge by her expression whether the delivery of the news had been a crisis or a celebration, or none of the above. He remembered Fiona as Debbie's friend, her anything-can-happen air, a cocky and observant look on her face. She hadn't been thin then, but she had been quick and well muscled, with thick, dark hair. In fact, he remembered watching her and wondering if she had relatives in the IRA. But that was how he thought about people in those suspicious days. He said, "I'd like to have been there."

"I guess they were shaking hands, because Janet and Emily were about to leave, and Janet just said, 'I have something more to tell you,' and then she came out with it, that Charlie was beautiful and fun and we all liked him a lot, and Fiona said, 'Does he look like Tim?' and Janet said he does, and Fiona said, 'Lucky boy, then.' "

Arthur said, "But I never thought of Tim as athletic—wild, yes, but not with that focus. Charlie seems to have gotten that from Fiona."

"Well, Janet hemmed and hawed, and then she said, 'Did you love Tim?' and you can just imagine how she said it, all the time thinking, 'It was me that really loved Timmy.' And Fiona said, 'He was daring. Not quite as daring as I was, but he came the closest of all the boys I knew. That was exciting. When Deb told me that time in New York that he'd died, it did shake me up.' She gave Janet a little hug, like Janet was the one who needed consoling. Janet left her address and her phone number. We'll see if Fiona gets in touch with her."

"If only to sell her a horse."

"If only to sell her a horse. Janet waited to see if Fiona would ask for Charlie's info, but she didn't."

They ate in silence for a few moments.

"If she got a horse," said Arthur, "she might give Emily a little space."

"It's weird that Janet is an hour or two from the Perronis, since they might as well live in different centuries. I asked her if she'd seen Loretta and the kids at all, and I thought she was going to say, 'Who's Loretta?' "

"What did she say?"

"She just said no."

"I'm sure Loretta would laugh and smack her on the back and tell her to send Emily for the summer, it would do her a world of good."

"I'm sure she would. And maybe it would." Arthur noticed that Debbie pushed the fruit aside—two cubes of cantaloupe, a strawberry, a piece of kiwi, and, yes, two reddish-purple grapes. Arthur ate his. They weren't bad. The way Debbie watched him do it made it seem rather refreshingly death-defying.

NOW THAT Congressman Scheuer was dean of the New York City Congressional Delegation, Richie had gotten used to being called "Richard" or even "Rick," and also to spending a lot more time in Washington. Biaggi was out, so the congressman no longer needed Richie to do what he did so well—hang around with other New York City politicians and their henchmen, making jokes and keeping his ears open. Considering how corrupt the New York Democratic Party was (Michael had a point, there), making sure that no scandal ever appeared in the vicinity of Congressman Scheuer was a full-time job. But the congressman remained good-natured, clean, and classy, and Richie admired him. At the last minute, he got the night off, so he called Ivy, who was home reading manuscripts (she was a full-fledged editor now), which she always did all day Sunday, and suggested that they go watch the Washington inaugural bicentennial fireworks from the Brooklyn Heights Promenade. She said, "Margie lives on Pierrepont."

Margie was Ivy's best friend on the production side. She made sure that no printings came back from the bindery missing the author's name on the title page, or without the essential photo insert of the athlete going for the jump shot or catching the fly ball and winning the World Series. The managing editor, Margie's boss, was out giving birth, so Margie was a little overwhelmed these days.

"What time do you want to order the car service?"

"We can walk. It's right down Flatbush. We can get a car service back. I need the walk."

Did she need the walk? Did she not need the walk? She was five months pregnant, in that golden period, according to Loretta, between nausea and swollen ankles, but Richie was afraid for her to walk—what was it?—almost three miles. He said, "I'm going to be home by six. Let's walk to Boerum Hill, get something to eat, and then go to Margie's."

When she said, "That's a good idea," she didn't sound the least suspicious. Richie hung up relieved, and happy, too. He sorted through the papers he had to take home with him—he was off for the afternoon, but the congressman had to appear at the inaugural re-enactment. He looked at his watch: almost noon. He ran down the back stairs.

Yes, getting her pregnant had been like climbing a steep hill and discovering every hundred yards that the trail had washed out or a tree had fallen over the path, but once she was pregnant, everything changed—they had come to a spacious clearing with a nice view and a luxurious stash of provisions. Richie wanted to linger there as long as possible, because he couldn't imagine being a father. He knew as well as he knew his own name that he would be expected to perform: to change diapers, to comfort the child, to nourish, educate, and bathe. And, unfortunately, one of the books Ivy had read in her long quest had suggested that men could breast-feed if they really wanted to, though she'd dropped the subject after mentioning it four times in two days. Every so often, Richie looked at his hands and wondered how they could perform all of these tasks.

The weather was brilliant, New York in April, perfect weather for the flotilla. Not many babies in this part of Lower Manhattan, but he observed the two that he saw—they were both looking around, old enough to have survived the first few months of parental incompetence. Old enough to be cute. He sped up his walk, and made a face at one as he passed it, and then felt ashamed when it didn't smile. He came to the subway stairs and hustled down them, not wanting to see that baby again.

He had mentioned his anxiety to his mom, and she'd said, in her idle way, "It passes so quickly. If they live, you don't influence them at all. But they do need to earn enough money later for the psychiatrist, or the mind reader, or whoever they choose. So be sure you save them a little something." He laughed, but when he pressed her—when he said, "What if I drop it?"—Andy said, "Oh, goodness, my great-aunt Ingrid was so afraid of dropping Cousin Helga that she left her in her cradle day and night. And look what happened to her!"

Richie said, "What happened to her?"

"That! Well, she died in a car crash up in Wisconsin—where was it?—north of Eau Claire somewhere."

He almost abandoned the subject right then, but he couldn't resist. "What's the connection?"

"She was running away from home! Couldn't stand Aunt Ingrid, ran off with the first boy who ever liked her or showed her any affection. Brakes failed." And Richie left it at that, thinking not of the brakes on the imagined car, but of the brakes on Helga's impulses. It was, of course, easy for his mother to take a fatalistic view, since, as Ivy said, she and his father hadn't done a thing right with any of the children, but never had he felt quite as clearly as he did now, at thirty-six, taking his seat on the train, that he was too young for what was to come.

FRANK WAS SURE he'd left the light on, because he'd fallen asleep reading, sitting with his back against the headboard, his book resting on his knees. The book was one he bought when it was on the *Times* best-seller list, *The Great Depression of 1990*. It had been sitting beside his bed for two years now, and Frank hadn't felt enough anxiety to read it, but here it was, July, and 1990 only six months off. He picked up a few things leafing through it before he dozed: that the fall of the Soviet Union was inevitable (that one looked true) and that if 1 percent of the U.S. population controlled more than 25 percent of the wealth, a depression would be on the way. Then Frank had gotten to thinking about Black Monday, when, briefly, his own son Michael (according to Michael) had been worth more than Frank, and then his head had fallen back. But now the room was dark; he was lying down, emerging from a dream about people at a party at what looked like Bergdorf's staring at him, and he opened his eyes to see a wavering figure in the corner of the room, white. He didn't gasp or anything—he retained the sense he'd had in the dream that if he was patient every strange thing would resolve itself. Then the figure approached, and it was Andy, in the antique silk slip she used as a nightgown, her white hair completing the ghostly impression. He woke up, and she sat on the bed. She hadn't been in his room for years except to clean it when he wasn't home. He thought maybe she was drunk, but she hadn't had a drink now in a decade, and then he thought he should be offended that she hadn't knocked, but he wasn't.

She put her fingertips on his left temple and ran them under the wisps of hair that remained there.

The room was light, and the moon out his window looked like a pale, startled face, glancing downward. He could see Andy perfectly. She said nothing; Frank felt himself unable to speak. He could hear her breathe, in, out, not anxious or quick, and then he could feel his own breaths synchronize with hers. He closed his eyes. Some time passed, and then he felt the covers, which were light because it was summer, rise. He moved over toward the center of the bed, only out of curiosity (he told himself). But when she slipped in beside him, the fifty- or sixty-year-old silk of her gown cool and smooth against his skin, it stunned him how his body curved to conform to hers, and how familiar her body still was, supple, thin. The texture of her skin, too, was familiar. Her arm went across his chest, and he lay still, voluntarily pinned. How did he feel to her? Hairy and paunchy, for sure. She gave off a deep sigh, more like an emanation than a breath.

Frank did not usually sleep on his back, but pretty soon he was sleeping, or something—no dreams, and still a sense that he was in his own room, but the figures from the Bergdorf's party reappeared, staring and smiling. Then nothing. Then his eyes opened, and he was looking upward at the beams above his bed, thinking he was strapped to a gurney. Andy's voice said, "What in the world!" and the bed dipped as she sat up. Frank looked at her, and then sat up himself.

Andy said, "What am I doing here?" She pushed her hair out of her face with both hands, a gesture he remembered from years ago; then she lifted both her shoulders and rolled them; then she opened her mouth as wide as it would go and cracked her jaw. Even when they'd shared a bed, he hadn't seen her wake up since her hair was blond—she always got up before he did. Frank said, "You tell me." Then, "I thought maybe you were making a play for me."

She smiled. She was kind. She said, "Only in my dreams, I guess."

"Well, you turned out my light, put my book on the shelf, sat on my bed, and stroked my forehead. I woke up. I saw you."

"I must have been sleepwalking. Were my eyes open?"

Frank thought for a moment, and said, "I didn't notice. But I think sleepwalkers' eyes are open. There was a sleepwalker in our barracks at Fort Leonard Wood. We would wake up and watch him, and I remember everyone whispering that his eyes were open, and then one of the guys stepped in front of him and waved his hand, but he didn't react."

"What did he do?"

"Twice he went over and sat in a corner of the barracks, curled up in a ball. That's all I remember."

He put the tip of his finger on the hem of her silk gown. The fabric was so fine that some roughness on his fingertip caught and released. Then he sat forward and drew her to him. He was so old, he thought, and then he regretted that thought, because, as always, it was about himself. To muffle it, he said, "I'm glad you came, even if you didn't want to."

She said, "Darling, I must have wanted to." And her good-humored, half-distracted tone struck him as charming rather than as empty-headed. But he didn't dare kiss her. He was so used to demeaning her, both in his mind and to others, that he was almost afraid that she would turn out not to be the Andy he thought he knew, that he'd been married to for forty years. If she was not herself, he thought, then who was he?

HENRY WONDERED if having his sister stay with him all these weeks was what marriage might have been like. Over the summer, Claire had gotten herself hired at Marshall Field's, in the main office, as a buyer of household goods. Supposedly, she was looking for an apartment downtown somewhere, but she'd been staying in Henry's place now since the first of August. Henry, away much of the summer, over in England and France, continuing his lackadaisical but alluring pursuit of the inner essence of Gerald of Wales, had sent her a key. She'd made herself right at home for two and a half weeks; when he got back, *many* things were out of place, and she had concocted a little framed display box, into which she had put a picture of the two of them from sometime during the war (he looked ten and she looked three), along with her lace handkerchief from the 1830s (Henry couldn't remember which virginal great-aunt had made it) and his gold dollar. And then she had placed this display box on the mantel, smack in the middle, not an interesting spot at all. But in the end, he didn't move it, nor did he remove his mother's pink-and-green afghan from the back of the couch. And he ate what she cooked, including the lamb shanks and the shepherd's pie made with ground beef. They watched the nightly news! Henry hadn't watched the nightly news, or even had the sound of conversation in his place, for years, but now they deplored Hurricane Hugo and remembered tornado near-misses and told each other tales about mythic snowfalls. By mutual agreement, there was nothing in their present world west of DeKalb; each of the three times he had referred to Des Moines, she had shaken her head and said, "Where in the world?" in an exact imitation of their mother's most skeptical voice. Claire maintained that, because she had spent her entire marriage listening to Dr. Paul (this is what she called her ex-husband) analyzing his childhood—painful but worth it in the end because of the result, himself—and also because she was fifty years old now, her uprooting had to be thorough and ruthless. She was in Chicago, and she only looked east. When she took him with her to check apartments, it was Henry who was dissatisfied and hard to please.

She got Henry to go with her to clubs. She didn't care if they were gay or straight, and she didn't care if anyone looked at her, though she dressed nicely; she wanted to see what people were wearing, how they did their hair, what sort of accessories they carried. She said it was research, and maybe it was, because maybe you didn't buy so many pink quilts in Chicago as you did in Des Moines. Claire corrected him—you didn't buy pink even in Des Moines, but there was a great demand for moss green. They laughed a lot, and Henry remembered that they had done that as kids—their senses of humor were as ever like two different notes that harmonized, even when no one else thought something was funny.

Claire was now rummaging through his closet in search of something interesting to wear to Buddy Guy's, a club that had opened in the summer. Henry knew vaguely where it was—maybe Wacker, maybe Wabash. Claire maintained that, in the history of fashion, now, 1989, was a uniquely bad year, and might never be surpassed in baggy violet strangeness. Henry, standing in the doorway, said, "I didn't know you had so many fashion rules."

She pulled out a sweater and took it to the window. She said, "No high waists, no pants with front pleats, no fake leopard skin, no lime green." She liked everything in his closet and sometimes asked to be allowed to wear a sweater or a shirt. As her agreeable faux husband, he let her, and she looked good. She put the sweater back—a deep, winy red—and emerged a moment later with an old fedora he had from the forties—an antique when Philip gave it to him. She walked to the mirror and put it on, saying, "And no enormous shoulder pads." The fedora looked raffish (*rif et raf,* Old French, "to strip and carry off") and flattering. She smiled at herself and said, "The buyer for designer wear told me that they train the sales force always to bubble over in delight when a woman comes out of the dressing room, no matter what she really looks like. In our department, all we do is turn on the switch of the KitchenAid or say, 'Yes, the Le Creuset is very heavy,' but we never mention that you might drop it on your toe if you don't watch out."

Henry said, "What were we like as kids?"

"Were you ever a kid?"

"Mama would have said no. She said I rejected the breast as soon as I learned to read."

"Which was at two months old, right?"

"I doubt I waited that long."

They laughed.

They took her car—not "used," but "vintage," as she called it, a silver Datsun 280Z that her older son, who called himself "Gray" now, had talked her into buying for him, but lost interest in when his girlfriend declared it unsafe. Its all-too-apparent lack of safety was why Henry liked it—all options were on the table, including death. That seemed the realistic way of looking at things.

Somewhere around Rogers Park, she said, "There are a couple of places to look at in this neighborhood. You want to go with me? I think there's an open house somewhere, too."

"Why don't you just live with me? I'm getting too old for three bedrooms."

She glanced quickly at him. Through her window, he could see the darkness of the lake. The fedora was pushed back on her head the way you always saw it on gangsters in the movies. She said, "What if I make a mess?"

"I'll clean it up."

"I accept." She said it quickly, as if afraid he would take it back.
"What about your furniture back in Des Moines?"

Claire said, "Hate that crap." Henry leaned across the center console, the shift, and the lever of the emergency brake, and kissed her on the cheek. He was the one who was grateful.

AS SOON as Claire walked into Andy's house in Englewood Cliffs, she saw that if this Christmas visit was to come off, her expertise was needed. Arthur, Debbie, Hugh, Carlie, and Kevvie were expected, as well as Richie, Ivy, and Leo. When Andy had called after Thanksgiving, she'd said that the unaccustomed celebration was all about Leonard Frederick Langdon, named Leonard after V. I. Lenin and Frederick after Friedrich Hayek (according to Frank, a true hybrid), August 14, seven pounds, four ounces. Claire gathered that "Leo" was a triumph of modern obstetrical science.

Gray would come up from Philly for the day with his girlfriend, but Michael had gone to California (Loretta was strict about Christmas), Tina had the shop in Idaho, and realtors like Dean could never get away, so there would be no discussion of the savings-and-loan crisis. Claire bought potatoes, butter, milk, turkey, onions, celery, and bread for stuffing, cranberry sauce, canned pumpkin, shortening for piecrust, and Häagen-Dazs vanilla ice cream. She baked rolls just the way Lois had taught her. She strung Christmas lights, hung ornaments, bought holly and pine boughs. She simmered some cider with spices on the stove, and all the time, Andy followed her around, saying, "Oh, that's a good idea. I hadn't thought of that." Sometimes Frank walked through and kissed both of them on the cheek.

Claire and Henry agreed that the weirdest part was that Henry had been put in Frank's room (Claire in the maid's room, which was sunny and pleasant). Frank was sleeping with Andy. This information had led to raised eyebrows, but nothing verbal. While she was cooking and decorating, Claire decided that she should have been a housekeeper rather than a wife. She didn't mind doing this stuff—she was organized, she liked things to smell good and taste good. Perhaps she was more like her mother than she had ever cared to admit. She was happy each time the front door opened and the bundled-up revelers who came in from the cold smiled, took deep breaths, and threw off their coats, which Andy then piled in her arms and carried to Janet's old room. Frank kissed everyone and even hugged them—he seemed to be wearing an invisible Santa suit. Claire and Henry raised eyebrows a few more times. Then Frank carried Leo, who at almost four and a half months was wiry and bright-looking, around the room, jiggling him a little bit. He showed him off to Arthur, to Debbie, to Kevvie, who gawked uncertainly. Richie hovered nearby, ready to catch Leo, but Frank, possibly the worst father ever, made babbling noises. Finally, Henry and Claire exchanged a glance and laughed aloud.

At dinner, Claire slipped into her serving mode: she carved the turkey, dished up the mashed potatoes, made sure that the gravy was hot, watched the plates passing to see that none of them tilted dangerously. It was pleasant to eavesdrop. Jesse had told Frank that he and his dad had gotten 115 bushels an acre this year, about average, but better than last year (which Claire remembered was seventy-five or something like that). Loretta's dad had been diagnosed with emphysema, then went out that afternoon and branded cattle. Did you hear about those tornadoes in November? One of them had struck a house in Yardley that Dean had finished showing only an hour before; a big one had struck the same day up in Quebec; wasn't that amazing? Someone should make a tornado movie—but how could you? No one would go besides Midwesterners. Noriega had been removed because he was working for the CIA; Noriega had been removed in spite of the fact that he was working for the CIA. Everyone looked at Arthur, who continued to eat without commenting or even turning his head. Ivy was almost back to her pre-pregnancy weight already. Janet had bought a horse named Sunlight; you could ride year-round out there; the stable was three miles from a Neiman Marcus. That boy Charlie was around New York somewhere—his girlfriend was studying at Columbia now. The Dow was around 2,000; it would never hit 3,000. "I remember," said Frank, "when it hit eight hundred. I decided to buy some shares in American Motors."

Andy was sitting at the head of the table, wearing a lovely dark-red sheath. Her hair was swept up behind, and every time she turned her head to look at one of her guests, the candlelight caught her pale skin in a flattering way. Claire had long since gotten over her youthful wish to be beautiful, but just now she appreciated that quality

Andy had, of seeming like a captured wild animal, graceful and taut in every muscle, but yielding to fate at the same time. And then Claire caught Andy and Frank sharing a tiny smile. It was brief and yet so intimate that Claire found herself weirdly embarrassed, and she knew that she would say nothing about it to Henry.

1990

~⌒~

CHARLIE WAS THRILLED with Manhattan. He'd never imagined how wild the city itself was, and if you started at the southwest corner of Central Park, across from Columbus Circle, and ran north through Central Park to the corner of 110th Street and Cathedral Parkway, then down 110th Street a block to the southwest corner of Morningside Park, north from there to 123rd Street, then over to Riverside Park, then followed that park down to where it ended at Seventy-second Street, then east on Seventy-second to Central Park West and south again to Columbus Circle, it was only about nine miles—an easy run. He'd wangled a clerk's job at a luggage store, and had submitted his application to an outdoor outfitters on Broadway. He and Riley were earning enough to rent a much-infested studio on 125th Street, though he told his mom it was on Ninety-eighth Street. Even his mom knew that 125th Street was in Harlem, and though his mom had laughed so hard she gagged when a woman from church said that if you drove through East St. Louis with your windows open, black people (she didn't call them that) would jump on the roof of your car and take you captive, she also had never liked him driving around East St. Louis. New York, as far as she knew (she had never been there), was just like East St. Louis, because, well, it was a thousand miles east of East St. Louis. She vacationed in the Ozarks and was proud that Missouri had all five indigenous American poisonous snakes right within its borders. Iowa was flat, Kansas was dry, Arkansas was hot, and Illinois was damp. That was all she needed to know.

Their furnishings were sparse: a gray futon on a metal frame, two bookcases, a table for a desk, three chairs, some dishes and cooking utensils, and a collection of mouse, rat, fly, mosquito, and roach traps.

Since the reunion, he'd exchanged a few letters with Minnie, Christmas cards with Jesse and Jen, two phone calls with Debbie, and one with Arthur. His mom had written Arthur and heard back, sent baby pictures and one of Charlie's funnier report cards from third grade ("Reads backward with unusual skill, must be prevented from walking the top of the monkey bars"). Arthur had sent two pictures of Tim as a child, but his mom hadn't yet forwarded them. Debbie wrote his mom that Janet had been in contact with his birth mother, but that this woman hadn't shown an interest in knowing more. Charlie didn't remember who Janet was, and he didn't blame his birth mother. His mom said that if she lived in Pasadena, California, it was probably better not to have anything to do with her.

His luggage store, four blocks south of Central Park, had some nice stuff. Charlie was rearranging the counter display for January markdowns when Michael entered. Michael's glance passed over him without a mote of recognition; Charlie shifted his own expression from friendly to professional and went back to the wallets. Lisa, Jackie, and Mark were behind the counter—they'd just been arguing about where Jackie should go skiing over the weekend, and Charlie had been eavesdropping; he hadn't been skiing in New York yet.

Michael went straight to Lisa and said, "Hello, there."

Lisa, who lived with her parents at Eighty-eighth and York, was working here as a punishment for dropping out of Connecticut College for Women after the first semester of her sophomore year. She gave Michael a warm smile. All four of them were good at this, since they worked on commission. Michael set his briefcase on the counter and regarded it. Lisa said, "May I help you, sir?"

Michael flipped the briefcase over and pointed at something along the side. He said, "Do you see that stain? The oil stain?"

Lisa bent down, but she didn't really look at it. She said, "I do, sir. I'd be happy to send that to our repair shop. I'm sure Giorgio could get it out."

"I would always know it was there," said Michael.

"Giorgio is really—"

"I need a new one."

Charlie could practically see Lisa salivating.

"This one is Bottega Veneta," she said. "I'm sorry, but we don't carry that brand. I can show you—"

"I'm sure you can," said Michael.

"—some comparable styles, however. Do you prefer Italian boutiques, sir?"

Michael gave her a brilliant smile, and she matched him; then he said, "This is a few years old. I personally think Bottega Veneta has gotten a little too flashy lately." He surveyed the golden-lit displays along the walls and said, "What's that one?"

Lisa pirouetted neatly and said, "Such a lovely piece. That's an Asprey. Let me also show you the Valextra. They are Italian, but based in Milan. Not quite as . . . baroque as Bottega Veneta." Charlie almost snorted with the pleasure of it. Mark went through the curtain into the stockroom. The wallets were now in a perfect line; Charlie stepped a foot to the left and started coiling belts. Lisa set two briefcases on the counter; they were both brown, the Asprey edging toward cordovan, the Valextra edging toward buckskin. She smoothed her hand over one, then the other. Michael said, "Mmmm." Charlie moved even farther left, caught Jackie's glance, and stepped into the window, afraid he was going to make real noise.

He could still hear them, though.

"That is nice leather."

"The best."

"The English is a little conservative. I hate to look stuffy."

"I totally understand."

"On the other hand, as I get older—"

"I wouldn't worry about that, sir. I really wouldn't."

Pause.

"I am drawn to the Valextra. I've looked at those before."

The Valextra was maybe 30 percent more expensive than the Asprey. Lisa said, "It's a rare piece. It's not for everyone. We sell maybe one a season, but I always think . . ."

She had been working here for two weeks. Charlie went deeper into the corner beside the window.

Outside, a woman passed him, her nose in a guidebook. She

stopped, looked toward the street sign, then opened the door of the shop. Charlie saw Jackie intercept her—they went back out the door. The show went on.

Lisa said, in a regretful, almost lachrymose voice, "I have to tell you, sir, the Valextra is a fifteen-hundred-dollar item."

There was a long pause, and Charlie peeked out from behind the stack of Tumis. Michael had one hand on the Asprey and one hand on the Valextra, and he was stroking them gently with a half-smile on his face. Then he hoisted the Valextra and gave a deep sigh, matched an instant later by Lisa. The curtain to the stockroom fluttered—ah, Mark was watching, too. Michael said, "How much is the Asprey?"

A pregnant pause; then Lisa's voice half broke when she said, "Eleven hundred."

Michael looked straight at her and said, "I'll give you eleven hundred for the Valextra," but he said it cheerfully, with a grin, as if he were joking. Lisa responded, "We don't usually . . . Well, thirteen is as low as I can go. The manager is in Italy, looking at new collections. I don't think . . ."

Another pause. Outside, the confused lady had walked on, and Jackie was talking to someone else, who was bundled in a full-length black down coat.

Michael shrugged, took his briefcase off the counter, gave Lisa one last winning smile, and turned for the door. Lisa let him get there, let him put his black gloves on, let him touch the handle, then said, "Twelve is okay. I can do twelve for you." She put on a regretfully redeemed expression, and Michael strode back to the counter. A win-win situation. Everyone was happy, including Charlie, who knew that they sold the Valextra, full-price, for eleven hundred. Mark came out of the back, looking genial but uninterested, and Michael and Lisa completed the transaction. When Lisa put on her coat and they went out together (Lisa told Mark she was taking an early lunch), Michael still didn't recognize Charlie, but he did smile at him this time.

It was Charlie's job to make the jokes and tell the funny stories, and it was Riley's job to laugh, but she didn't laugh when he told her about Lisa and Michael—she was offended. Charlie had learned to make no assumptions about how Riley might be offended. It could be anything: Ripping off Michael? Lisa going off with him? But of course it was the waste that offended her, getting rid of a perfectly good leather item because of a small stain. And calfskin, at that; did Charlie know how much grain went into feeding cattle? This brought her around to hemp again, as so many things did. Or bamboo! Bamboo was *verrry* interesting, and Charlie heard all about it over the roasted vegetables and grilled goat-cheese sandwiches they had for dinner. The cheese was from the shores of Cayuga Lake, and that was where Riley wanted to go on their first trip out of the city.

HERE WAS HOW Michael told the story: Everyone in their group thought going on the *Jolly Roger* would be fun—just a two-hour cruise around Dickenson Bay, then back to Magnus King's condo on Runaway Bay (Magnus King had started out life as Bruce King, but changed his name when he made his second million; he was up to ten now). The boat had several levels, and everyone wanted to see the view from the top level—it was sunset, the bay was flat. Michael was sitting on the railing with his feet on a cushion. Admittedly, you were not supposed to sit on the railing—you were supposed to sit on the cushions. The boat shifted, he lost his balance, and the next thing he knew was that he was reaching out to grab a lanyard that was hanging there, but it was attached to nothing, and he toppled over onto a white awning that collapsed underneath him, and then he was caught in the huge arms of the black chef who'd been grilling steaks on the poop deck for the partyers. The chef stood him on his feet. He went back to the bar, got himself another rum punch, and ran up the stairs. When he got there, everyone was gone.

Here was how Loretta told the story: Michael was smashed to smithereens. When he originally staggered up the steps to the upper deck, he'd been swaying, and Magnus King had made a joke about him. Loretta was embarrassed, and told Michael he needed to taper off; he told her to shut up, jerked backward, and disappeared. The seven of them looked over the railing and didn't see anything, so they ran down the stairs, but it was a big boat with two sets of stairs, and as they were running down one set, Michael was running up the other set. They searched the lower deck, and then Loretta looked up and saw Michael waving his arm and laughing. She was really happy to see him. But, she said, at that point he had learned nothing.

The next thing, Michael said, was that when the cruise was over, and they had eaten their steaks and sobered up just a hair, they got so impatient with how slow the barge was that ferried passengers back and forth to the beach that Michael handed Loretta his wallet (as always!) and dove into the water, then Magnus went, then Tyler Coudray, leaving all the wives and Zeke Weiner, poor Zeke.

Zeke was happy to stay with us, said Loretta—why would he want to ruin his clothes and get wet and cold for nothing? By the time the five of them got to that crappy beach bar, Magnus, Tyler, and Michael were sitting in Buccaneer Cove with their drinks, out of their minds. Tyler threw up right when his wife got there, and the throw-up sort of spread around them and got on Magnus and Michael, and they didn't even notice. All the wives were pretty fed up, but there was no going home while the Red Stripe beers were being extracted from the ice chest. And it was cold. It was something like California, how cold Antigua got in the middle of the night, and all they had was sweaters.

The miracle, Michael said, was the bwi dog. Not a big dog, not a little dog; brown with a black face.

The miracle, said Loretta, was that they got home at all. There was no public transportation by that time, they had to find their way across that isthmus—

And the dog led them every step of the way, said Michael, down a winding path, through the plants that were growing behind the beach—kassy, it was, prickly and tangled—and the dog just took them. It must have been three miles.

It seemed like a mile, but probably it was only a hundred yards, at least as the crow flies, said Loretta; if they'd been sober enough to look up rather than at their feet (Michael did fall down—not once, but twice), they would have seen that Dalla left the light on in the second-story window, they could have made it; and thank God they got there before the children woke up, it would have been such an embarrassment, their clothes all torn and covered with dirt and bits of plants; Michael had lost his shoes completely, though Loretta managed to carry hers—they were ruined, though.

No, said Michael, the miracle *was* the dog, a dog that gave himself to them, to lead them home, and then lay on the stoop for the rest of the night, even though, when Dalla got up with Chance, Tia, and Binky, she shooed him away.

And well she should, said Loretta, since there is rabies everywhere; we just don't think about it. But the dog wouldn't leave no matter what she did, so she couldn't even take the children out for a swim in the pool. Dalla didn't like the dog at all, and Loretta didn't blame her. None of the adults got up until after lunch, and Michael, when he did get up, kept saying, "What happened, what happened, what happened," and complaining like a broken record that his lower back and his shoulder hurt, until Loretta and Zeke sat him down and told him about the fall and the walk and the dog.

Then, Michael said, he went outside and found the dog and petted him and thanked him, and gave him a steak from the refrigerator, and the dog wandered away with the steak in his mouth, maybe to bury it. Everyone laughed, but Michael was changed; even he said so. He got sober, he let his mom talk to him about AA, he kicked out his latest girlfriend and put the place he'd bought for her in SoHo on the market so that he could buy a bigger place uptown where Loretta could live comfortably, and not like camping out. He would have remodeled the place in SoHo, but they had to be near the schools, and those were all uptown.

Loretta said, Well, finally, he scared himself enough to wake up, but I always knew he would.

What Michael said was, You get to the point where everyone has their hooks in you, not that they always want something, even if mostly they do, but they want to prove you're wrong or you're an asshole, or you've always been an asshole, and even if you have always been an asshole, you can't let them prove it.

What Frank said was, If you don't realize you're an asshole around the time you're thirty-seven, you never will.

What Andy said was, Well, we'll see.

What Ivy said was, Everyone has always taken Michael too seriously; most of his rants and misadventures are jokes and stunts, and everyone like that goes too far once in a while. She could perfectly imagine the thing on the boat, Michael just making hay out of it all, waiting for the laugh and never getting one. Loretta's sense of humor was about as big as the head of a pin, and, maybe because she was raised Catholic, she was really afraid of irreverence; no one blamed her for that, because she meant well, but she and Michael were a mismatch. But Ivy only said this to Richie, as they were pushing Leo in the stroller in Prospect Park.

Richie didn't say anything.

ROSANNA HAD SPENT years regaling everyone who cared and who didn't care with tales of the Langdon children; Minnie had always listened with interest, and sometimes wondered what her mother or father would have said of her. But she was seventy-one now, and Lois was sixty, and if there had been stories, they were lost. For that reason, she wrote down entries in a small diary about Felicity, who would soon be two—nothing lengthy or analytical, only notes about what she had said or done that she would give her someday, to go along with the pictures Jen and Jesse took. One thing she didn't write down, but did think, was that this was the child she wished she had been—not good, not agreeable, like Guthrie and Perky, who were now seven and six—but intent. When Felicity talked, she talked to herself—if you entered the room or interrupted her, she zipped her lip and stared at you, and then, after you left, she would begin again, a dialogue with two or three parts. Twice Minnie had managed to write down some of the lines in her little book—"Please do sit down. Thank you very much. Once upon a time." Minnie supposed that she was trying out phrases, maybe wondering what they meant or consigning them to memory. When she had to communicate, she was good for her age—precise and direct.

Jen had no complaints—Felicity ate well, slept well, was potty-trained, knew how to button her shirt, sat quietly in the shopping cart when they went to Hy-Vee—but she was not a cuddler. Jen seemed surprised that Felicity was restless in her lap and always climbed down after a moment or two. And Jen seemed disappointed that when she made a playful face, the kind that Guthrie or Perky at the same age would have laughed aloud at, Felicity only gazed at her, as if to say, What next? Jen would say, "She was born suspicious. I wonder where she gets that?" Minnie had an answer, but she never mentioned it.

Minnie's pleasure was that Felicity would sit beside her on the sofa in the breezy, oak-paneled living room while Minnie crocheted or looked out the front window at the cornfield across the road, and she would pat Minnie on the leg, rhythmically. She would look into Minnie's face while Minnie sang her a song—"Froggie went a courtin', he did ride." She made an "f" and an "o" sound with her lips. "Sword and a pistol by his side." She made a little hissing sound. Her face had a studious expression. Minnie's diagnosis, as a woman, former teacher, and former principal, was that Felicity was going to do things her way, and she thought that single-minded was the best strategy, even if you pleased few of the people not much of the time. Two, she thought, was the most ephemeral age, the age of incipient consciousness, when personality was first chinking into place. Felicity was her last chance to enjoy this, and so she did, day after day.

ANDY DIDN'T LIKE waking up facing the clock, because she didn't want to know what time it was, for example, now, when it was one-fifty-nine. One-fifty-nine was too early, and as far as she could remember, she'd had no dreams, so maybe no REM sleep. Then, even though she was careful not to move, and did not roll over (she could still see the clock), Frank's arms went around her and he kissed the back of her neck. She said, "I didn't mean to wake you."

"I was awake. I was watching the snow. There's enough of a moon that it sparkles." Frank didn't draw the curtains; his vision was still sharp, and he could make out constellations and passing satellites.

Andy turned over. Frank was solid and warm even though the room was cold. Now that they were sleeping together every night, she'd had to buy lighter bedclothes, and a mattress firm enough to support the weight of both of them in one spot. He slipped his hand around the small of her back and pulled her toward him. She put her leg over his. Frank ran his hand down her thigh and rested it, then jiggled himself so that they were even closer. Andy kissed him on the lips, but it wasn't going to lead to lovemaking. A pleasure of being seventy was that comfort seemed more appealing than passion.

In the last year, he had won her. He had come to Sleeping Beauty and kissed her again and again, and each time, she had awakened another degree, sloughed off another layer of skepticism. It was a surprisingly painful process. In all the stories, the prince went away, sometimes for ten years, sometimes for a hundred years. All the princess had to do was mind her own business, and that was what Andy had been doing for thirty-five years now. Sometimes her business had been trivial, sometimes her business had been misguided, sometimes her business had been useful and informative, and quite often she had been helped in her business by people who did and did not know they were helping her. But Frank, the prince, had been on the scene the whole time, and so she had put a layer on every time he grimaced, every time he left the room, every time he rolled his eyes, every time he looked around the restaurant or the theater or the parking lot or the airport as if he were searching for someone, known or unknown, who might save him from the troublemaking boys, the clingy girl, the unloved wife.

That night she had truly been sleepwalking. It wasn't the first time. As a child she'd done it twice: Once out into the snow in January; Sven, who was only eight to her nine, had heard the door open, looked out the window, and told their parents. The other time, she was twelve—she walked into her parents' room and lay down on the floor between their beds. They were sound asleep, and her father stepped on her when he got up in the morning. But no one delved into the book or the story or the nightmare that had produced the somnambulism. She had done it twice in this house, once to the kitchen, where she woke up sitting at the table; once to the car, where she woke up stretched out on the front seat, staring through the windshield. But Frank had known nothing about those incidents. And so she had been dreaming about something—she liked to think it was one of the children—and had gone into Frank's room and inserted herself back into his life.

The result was that there was this time every day, between ten at night and eight in the morning, when they were alone, sleeping or talking, the lights out. They prepared by adjusting their pillows, straightening the covers, making sure the room was ventilated and cool. They coiled together; then Frank's breaths started ruffling within a few minutes, while Andy thought blank thoughts—the names of islands or flowers or views she had seen of scenes that meant nothing to her, like a beach in Venezuela. Andy preferred dreams that made no sense and referred to nothing. By mutual consent, they did not talk about the boys, the girl, the collapsing investment in the farm, any beloved relatives who seemed to be effacing themselves from the world despite the kind attentions of a recently discovered grandson. In their room and their bed, they regretted nothing, recalled no missed opportunities, acknowledged no loss of beauty or grace. Sometimes, Frank told a joke: Did you hear the one about the guy who went to his doctor, and after a lengthy examination, the doctor said, "I'm sorry to inform you that you are very ill. You have six hours to live." Andy laughed—she didn't have to wait for the punch line. Frank kissed her on the forehead, and when she turned over and pressed her derriere against his crotch, he slipped his arm under her neck, along the line of the pillow. She put her hand in his. She could feel his warmth all along her back, animal comfort.

She fell asleep between "Oahu" and "Patmos" and woke up at seven-thirty-seven from a dream that she was trying to remove a box from the trunk of her car, which she had parked on the grassy shoulder of the Palisades Parkway. As she woke, she was turned toward Frank, who was looking upward, his profile as distinct and alluring as always. She gazed at him in the extra-bright, snow-whitened, Hudson River–inflected morning sunshine, and thought that these long, perfect nights were the best thing that had ever happened to her. But wasn't it also true that they came over her faster and faster, warm, comforting waves that made everything that she got up for in the morning seem trivial and ephemeral? Perhaps, she thought, if you were happy half of every twenty-four-hour period, your punishment was that you sped toward the end of that happiness ever more quickly.

1991

〜

JANET HAD MEANT to leave Fiona's place in the morning and take the 101, because, even though the 5 was quicker, it was much more sinister, and she was not looking forward to hauling the two horses over the Pacheco Pass. She also hadn't meant to have two horses in the trailer, but Fiona had led out this Quarter Horse/Icelandic mix, named Pesky, trotted him around, and had him take two carrots from Janet's hand with utmost politeness; Janet had not been able to resist him. Fiona was straightforward about his soundness issues—an old tendon injury, a little osteo in the hocks—but he was fifteen years old. He was easygoing and petlike; Emily would not have to ride him to enjoy him. But she might ride him. Janet was taking him home on spec. And then there was a little bit of lunch, for horses and for riders, and so here she was, and the radio was on, the highway was desolate, and Iraq and Kuwait were about to be invaded.

Through habit and concentration, Janet thought, she'd trained herself to believe nothing. She was forty now, the Peoples Temple was years in the past, she could watch her one-time-adored Lucas play a lawyer every week on *L.A. Law* and feel only curiosity about how he was aging (well) and whether she might run into him in an upscale supermarket sometime (that would be fine). She saw through Reagan, she saw through Dukakis, she saw through Pat Robertson, she saw through Eugene McCarthy, though she'd written him in in the '88 election. She saw through Freudianism, she saw through Jung-ianism, she saw through M. Scott Peck, and she saw through Joseph Campbell. She saw through money, though she used some of it on horses, some of it on Emily's school, and some of it on their house (a Minnesota-ish house in strangely Minnesota-ish Palo Alto, Califor-nia, spacious but not pretentious, exactly what Jared felt comfortable in). She was happy to be as far from her father and her mother and her fucking twin brothers as she could be (she had lobbied to move to Seattle, but that had gone nowhere—Jared didn't think that com-puter animation had a future in Seattle). Emily was a worry, but now that Janet had Sunlight, her worries were divided, and if she found herself obsessing about Emily, she would consciously shift her atten-tion to Sunlight; with the addition of Pesky, she would probably end up giving the child room to breathe.

And so, how was it that so well-trained a person as herself—also trained by Fiona, at these clinics she took Sunlight to—driving a Ford F-350, a person who was hauling the best horse trailer money could buy (made in Iowa!), was so nervous? Why did she keep look-ing to the north, to the east, to the west, in the Central Valley of Cali-fornia for telltale signs of an invasion by vengeful Iraqis? For a rain of bombs, not nuclear, but firebombs, say, or cluster bombs? How was it that a grown woman who laughed at the very mention of George Bush, the "president," felt a fluttering anxiety every time the radio said the words "Saddam Hussein"?

For a year now, she had been taking lessons in how to be Fiona McCorkle, which was, indeed, what most people did who took les-sons from Fiona, though no one else drove as far for just a weekend. The physical part was hard enough—even mature, overweight, and sun-bleached, Fiona had a grace that you couldn't stop staring at. Her husband rode the big jumps, but Fiona put the miles on the younger horses and the badly trained horses that came to them from other stables. She rode four hours a day, and gave lessons three hours a day, and said that if Charlie Wickett ever came their way, she would be happy to meet him, but it seemed to Janet that she viewed him like a horse that had been in the stable for a while and then gone on to another owner. When Fiona was on a horse, any horse, she settled in, made only the slightest moves, and that horse conformed happily to Fiona's intentions. Fiona said that her nervous system took over the horse's nervous system, and the interchange was in the small of her back—if it remained flexible and alive, supported by her abdominal muscles, then the two of them could float here and there, at any gait, doing anything, and be happy. She offered no advice about any other part of Janet's life; in fact, they didn't talk, as most women did, about husbands, children, clothes, hair, politics, cooking, or books. They talked about horses, flexion, strength, forward motion, tendons, back muscles, bits, and theories of horseshoeing. Was Fiona happy with her husband? Did she have a big mortgage and money problems? Janet had no idea, and suspected that Fiona didn't even know Jared's name, though it was right there on the checks Janet wrote for lessons and horses.

She turned west on the 152. The gas station by the side of the road at Santa Nella, small as it was, looked bright and appealing, and she was sorry, again, that she had passed the 46 without turning left and heading to Paso Robles. You missed both passes that way, but she never took the 46—it was even more barren than the 152, and added to that was the fact that James Dean had been killed there (only anonymous people had been killed on the 152). The reservoir shone flat and dark under the sky, and she started up the grade. She could feel the Ford exert itself. In the trailer, the horses would be spreading their hind legs, dropping their heads, shifting their weight forward. There wasn't a moon, so when the Ford tilted upward she could see sprays of stars rising above the ridge, quiet and still, not at all like bombs or white phosphorus, something she didn't have to know a thing about to imagine and fear. The radio was garbled now, a good thing, so she turned it off. The engine roared. She put down the window. The chill breeze blasted her face, and she wondered if believing nothing was a victory or a defeat, if it was evident in her looks, in her actions, if it led necessarily to suicide, and whether that was a bad thing? As her eyes adjusted, the stars got more numerous. Could you believe that the stars were millions and billions of light-years away, and also believe in life, in horses, in the importance of an odd-looking quadruped named Pesky?

As Janet now remembered, the Pacheco itself was less scary than the thought of it—the intimidating parts of the pass were the rough crags to either side, the roads that turned off the highway and crept over the ridges. People lived back there, and every day this was the easy part of their drive. The Ford was reassuring; plenty of gas, too, and it was big enough to steady the trailer on the descent. No Iraqi incoming. She knew she would joke about how rattled she'd been, and Jared would give her a little squeeze around the shoulders, and Emily would say, "Mom! Even I know that isn't going to happen!"

She was going through the gate at the stables before nine. She could see a light in Marco's cottage, and then he appeared as she pulled up beside Sunlight's clean and empty stall. She got out of the truck and opened the front door of the trailer. Sunlight put his head out. His white-edged ears were pricked—home again. Marco said, "We turn pony out for tonight, okay?"

"*Sí,* Marco. Okay."

"Good trip?"

She nodded.

THERE WAS this woman who kept her horse at the stables, two stalls down from Pesky, who was the master of the Portola Valley Hounds. She was about Emily's height, and she always smiled at Emily and asked her how Pesky was; she did not say a word about when Emily might want to get on Pesky. She was way older than Mom and probably almost as old as Grandmother Andy. Anyway, Emily was in the stall with Pesky, brushing him with the soft brush (she had already curried him and brushed him with the dandy brush). She couldn't see the woman—Mrs. Herman, her name was—and so she didn't know who she was talking to, but she was telling a story. "We were out with the hounds, this must be twelve years ago now."

When I was a baby in Iowa, thought Emily.

"There were maybe twenty riders in the field—not many, because it was late in the season, and only the real diehards were still at it. We'd run the fox into the corner of what's now the Horse Park, and then chased it across Whiskey Hill Road. By that time, we two whippers-in and four of the field were still with the hounds, who were absolutely mad on the scent of a fox, which wasn't what was supposed to happen—we'd been drag hunting, and a gray fox happened to cross our path. The fox headed west, but doubled back, ran over Sand Hill Road, and what did it do but run into the Linear Accelerator Stanford has there!"

The woman Mrs. Herman was talking to screamed, "Oh, heavens, Denise!"

Mrs. Herman laughed and said, "Well, the hounds were after it, the whole pack in full cry, and they went right in, thank goodness, not in the end but just across—there's no door or anything, just a little barrier, and someone had to follow them. Since I was a whipper-in, it had to be me. I jumped in, ran across, jumped out. It took no time, but I was so embarrassed."

"How did you dare?" said the other woman.

"What was I going to do? It would've been a nightmare to lose the hounds, and you can't go around the Accelerator—it's two miles long. I had to make up my mind in about a second. Fortunately, Barkis is willin', always willin'."

Barkis was Mrs. Herman's chestnut hunter. He had a pretty zigzag blaze.

Emily knew where the Accelerator was—it was a white thing you could see from the road, and her dad always pointed it out, even though he had pointed it out a million times before. Her dad thought being a physicist was the most exciting job you could have, and he expected Emily to get 100s on all her math tests, including algebra. She had done it so far, all this year. It was not that hard.

"But that wasn't the last of it."

"Do tell!" The woman was laughing.

"The hounds chased that fox up into the hills over there, right into Jane Goodall's chimp compound. I don't even know if it's still there. We ran right past the building, and the apes all stood at the bars of their windows, screaming at us. I told my husband they were rooting for us, but maybe they were rooting for the fox. We had the kill right there, at the far end of the building." The two women laughed again.

Now Emily petted Pesky down the side of his near foreleg, then picked up his hoof and cleaned it out. She even leaned over and sniffed it—no thrush. She took good care of him. When she was finished grooming, she set her box outside the stall door, attached the lead rope to Pesky's halter, and led him out. The two women were gone. Barkis was looking over the door of his stall and nickered as she and Pesky walked by.

It wasn't a great day—a little chilly and windy—but Pesky had a thick coat, a forelock like a hat, and a mane like a fountain that sprang all around his arched neck. Emily was wearing a sweater, and now she pulled her leather riding gloves from her pockets and put them on. She walked down the aisle and turned left, toward the trail that ran along the edge of the property. It was starting to get green, but she knew that Pesky knew that she knew that he wasn't supposed to eat, so he didn't try, only followed in her footsteps, sometimes blowing out his nostrils and sometimes tossing his head. Once, he bumped her with his nose, and she said "No," and rattled the lead rope. They walked along. When they came to the long side of the main arena, she saw that Mary Alice Forman was having a lesson; Mary Alice was ten, two years younger than Emily, and she didn't have her own horse. She was the one who was always saying, "When are you going to ride him? He looks so nice!" But she didn't say it like a bully or like a grown-up; she said it like she was the kind of kid who always said whatever came into her mind.

There was a saddle. There was a bridle. Mom, however, did not press her, and clearly she had told Dad not to press her, either.

Mary Alice saw her, and shouted, "Hi! Hi, Emmy!"

Randi, who was teaching her, called out, "Watch where you're going, Mary Alice!"

"Oh!" said Mary Alice. "Yikes!"

But her horse, Peaches, wasn't doing anything bad.

Pesky flicked his ears. He was much better-looking than Peaches, not only nicely built, but that warm golden color that was supposedly Icelandic. Emily loved him, and was distantly grateful to Mom for giving him to her. At the end of the arena, she walked through the parking lot, and into a little grove of eucalyptus, where she let Pesky snuffle around for grass. He was an easy keeper, so he didn't get much hay, and was always hungry.

While Pesky was standing there, Emily stood next to him, facing him. She took her glove off, then started by his ears and smoothed her hand over his coat, as if she were brushing him, except that she could feel how smooth and silky he was. Emily found it soothing to do this, and sometimes, when she was in school, she took deep breaths and thought of it when the other kids were making her nervous. She had noticed this in her walks, too: If you looked at your feet, then you thought about falling over the edge of the road. If you looked at cars, you thought about them hitting you. But if you looked at the horizon, you kept going, and your breaths were bigger. All of these thoughts she kept to herself, because Mom pounced on them if she said anything about them. As soon as Mom took them up, they became flat and dumb. Emily didn't know why this was. Everyone else thought that she had the nicest mom.

Mrs. Herman walked by again and waved. The story she had told made her sound like so much fun that Emily waved back and smiled, and when she stopped, Emily walked Pesky over to her and said, "Would you give me riding lessons?"

Mrs. Herman was perfect. She asked no questions, made no faces. She just smiled and said, "Of course I will. You want to start now?"

And Emily said, "Yes."

JANET COULDN'T SAY that she'd forgotten to put in her diaphragm, only that she had been too lazy to put in her diaphragm, and it wasn't the first time—she and Jared made love so intermittently that the challenge of coming all the way to full consciousness and going into the bathroom, five steps away, was sometimes more than she could handle. But she'd gotten away with it so often that the possibility of actually needing birth control had sort of slipped her mind. It had taken her two missed periods and some bouts of morning nausea even to come up with the idea that she might be pregnant. Then she'd given herself a test, told Jared, told Emily, gone to the doctor, started on the vitamins, told her mother and Debbie, even bought two roomier pairs of jeans, but still the whole thing seemed abstract, something more talked about than experienced. Her body took it in stride, Jared stopped asking her how she felt, and Emily seemed to forget about it entirely. Janet continued to ride—her balance wasn't at all affected. She was riding four days per week and planning another trip to southern California in ten days.

One night, she was lying in bed, chatting with Jared about an odd thing Michael had told him: He had a friend who was a currency trader in Chicago. He'd stayed up late a couple of nights before, and, like all currency traders, he'd been unable to resist checking the rates. In a very odd way, he saw, the Deutschmark was crashing, as if someone somewhere with lots and lots of Deutschmarks were panicking and flooding the market. Of course, no one could tell where they were coming from, and then, twelve hours later, one of Gorbachev's most important advisers left the party and predicted a coup d'état. The question, Jared said, was who would be dumping Deutschmarks and why, and they agreed that maybe it was Gorbachev himself, or some other representatives of the Soviet government, thinking that refugees would be flooding west, and so overwhelming Germany. The first thought Janet had was just an image—refugees in black and white, as if on World War II–era film, flooding across a white line; then she had that moment of automatic panic that she always had when she thought of the Soviet Union. All she said was "I thought they didn't trade in capitalist markets," and they both chuckled slightly. She rearranged herself—it was getting harder to find a comfortable position, though she'd only gained ten pounds. Jared went to the bathroom and stayed in there, flossing. In the quiet, she felt a fluttering. She knew instantly what it was—the quickening—as if the intervening thirteen years since it happened the last time had simply dropped away, and she thought, "Hello, little guy."

As soon as she moved, the fluttering went away, but she stacked her pillows, sat up against them, and waited. There was a long stillness, and then it came again, a deep internal prickling, the sparking of nerves that were normally inert. She rolled over on her side; it stopped. She returned to her back; after a moment, it started again, then stilled. Jared came back and got into bed.

She didn't think much of it until the next morning, when she was walking through the living room in the silence of her empty house, and then she was flooded with a sense of pleasure and joy. Various images of the interior being started coming into her mind—a round face with a dimple and raised eyebrows, a tiny, fleshy behind, bent knees, an image of a diver doing a flip, tucked, hands holding his knees. The sensations in her belly were like little communications to her brain, each distinct but related to the others. When the interior being (she hated the word "fetus") was still, the images stopped.

The house was so quiet that it seemed to form another layer around her; she herself was the emerging person, going here and there, picking up this and that, contained and protected the way she contained and protected the interior being, and, more than anything, she wanted the house to remain silent so that she would not be distracted from that fluttering, those sensations. Finally, after about an hour of pretending that her life was the same as it always had been, she lay down on the couch. It was of course quiet. The side streets of Palo Alto were guaranteed by law to be quiet. The cottony roughness of the couch cushions felt pleasant against her back and the backs of her legs. She closed her eyes, took a deep breath, and waited.

He was a good boy, and an active boy—he started pinging her within a minute or two. She envisioned it: punching on the right, then kicking on the left, and then a tiny brush of the hand on the right. After that he was quiet; then he started in again, oh so softly. No one talked about this, these greetings from within, these most intimate communications from the child-to-be. Probably, she thought, she should resist. She should think of the fetus as an it, she should stop imagining it, she should make her joy conditional. She should imagine, instead, what could go wrong—she would be forty-one by the time of the birth. Given the precedents, even if he was healthy, he would most likely view her as skeptically as she viewed her parents, as Emily viewed her. But in two hours, he had captured the fortress and made it his, and Janet did not see how she could undo that.

MRS. HERMAN DIDN'T STAND in the middle of the arena shouting orders, like the rest of the riding instructors did. Her trick was to keep walking and keep talking, and interspersed with her stories was a patter of suggestions—"If you keep your thumbs up, you see, the reins run much more smoothly from little Pesky's mouth, and it's much nicer for him. That's fine, now just let him walk along behind me while I check some things." And so it was that Emily was in the saddle, with her heels down and her shoulders back, and her hips swinging along, with Mrs. Herman in front of her, wandering around the arena, and then: "You keep going that way. I'm going to stop here and check this jump standard, rotten to the core. You know, when I got married, way back in the Middle Ages, the maid of honor fixed it up with the minister to run the drag right down the aisle of the church. There you go, just walk along the railing there to the end, turn, and if he trots back to me, that's fine—grab mane if you have to."

And she did trot! She did not grab mane. Her posting was good!

"Now just go around me here, in a small circle, to the left, that's right. Well, there were four bridesmaids, and me, and we all went very solemnly down the aisle, and I wondered why there was such a long pause, with the minister not saying a thing, and then there was this sound, and here came the hounds right down the center aisle, running to beat the band! Giving voice, loud as you please! Very good, now turn and go to the right. Give him a little pop with your legs, just a pop-pop, right along with his steps, so he moves out. Very good."

Pesky stretched his neck and put his head down. Emily could feel his back end curling and stepping a little more.

"Let the rein out. That's his reward. Peter spun around and stared. I was just laughing. Then the side entrance of the church opened; Sally had stationed a whipper-in there, and the hounds ran out the door. Everyone was roaring with excitement, and I must say it did make the local paper. Now just pop him a couple of times with your right leg so that he will bend inward and make a larger circle—there you go. You are only signaling him, not punishing him. Pesky knows that."

Pesky was walking fast now; his head and neck were moving from side to side and his ears were half pricked, which, Emily knew, meant that he was paying attention to her, not to the two riders who were passing the gate. Walking, walking, and in the next stride, he rose into the trot, and his trot itself lifted her out of the saddle. She posted again, this time more smoothly. It didn't feel fast or scary, but easy, and just what someone riding a horse would like to do, even Emily.

Mrs. Herman kept talking. "At the reception, they all told me that they'd planned to use a fox! Can you imagine? But foxes are elusive— they never did catch one. Now, that *is* a good trot. Just loop outward to the rail, and then turn toward me. Very good!"

What was really strange was how different the landscape looked when she was on top of Pesky rather than walking beside him. It looked brighter and broader. Mrs. Herman would say, "Right over there we had a lovely gallop last winter, that's a beautiful spot," or, "You can't see it from here, but behind that stand of oaks, there's a trail that's perfect in the summer, very shady. Next summer, we'll go out there. Barkis likes a good long walk, two hours at least." Emily believed that in a year they would do all sorts of things, because Mrs. Herman knew just how to do them.

....

JANET HAD ALWAYS sneered at Stanford Hospital as the only hospital in the world with its own upscale shopping mall, but there she was, standing in Handbags at Saks, actually thinking of her mother telling her that Saks was fine if you had to go there, but if you needed to really spend money, she preferred Bergdorf's. It was a week before her due date, and that morning she'd gotten on the scale and wondered if she was going to hit thirty pounds, which some expert or other had recently declared to be the optimum weight gain. It had been an uneventful pregnancy; the day before, Jared had stoked her vanity by saying that, from the back, you couldn't even tell she was pregnant.

The waters didn't splash, she didn't make a scene, and she was wearing jeans, which soaked up the mess without showing it. She turned on her heel, walked right out the door, and said to the guard, "I'm in labor"; one of the mall managers got her car and drove her the five minutes to the hospital. One moment she was standing at the entrance, and the next she was flat on her back on a gurney, and the contractions were two minutes apart, and the public-address system was calling for her doctor, Dr. McLarey. They rushed her down the hallway. She heard the doctor and the nurse who were with her say that all the delivery rooms were full, they were going to have to use a recovery room; then Dr. McLarey was told to go to Room Something Something Something. No one asked her how she felt, but she felt fine; a contraction was a contraction, after all, and better to have them come over you all at once than to build and build.

Dr. McLarey, who was five years younger than she was, was sweating when he appeared, tying on his mask, and, apart from looking at her, she supposed to make sure that she was Janet Nelson, he focused his attention on the very spot that she, of all of them, could not see. All she could see was that he held out his hands, and the next thing she knew, he was standing up and Jonah was in his arms, Jonah Timothy Nelson, eight pounds, eight ounces, labor exactly forty-six minutes by the watch she still had on her wrist, every pain overwhelmed by a sense of speed and urgency. The doctor laughed and said to the nurse, "Talk about sliders!"

The nurse took him away, wrapped him up, and brought him back. Dr. McLarey petted her on the arm and ran off—he had another delivery. Now the nurse brought the baby to her, saying, "Here he is, Mama. His AP score was eight at one minute and nine at five. These quick ones, when there's no anesthetic, they are bright from the first." She removed Jonah's little blue hat. "Thank the Lord his head is pointy. Came out like a fish."

But he looked perfect to Janet; he looked handsome and debonair, his head slightly tilted and his chin lifted.

She hoisted herself up—truly, she felt fine—and held out her arms possessively. The nurse handed him over, then said, "Take a good whiff. That's how you know you're his mother. I'll just leave you alone before the onslaught." The nurse sashayed out, pulling the door closed behind herself.

Maybe Janet remembered the first time she saw Emily, but maybe not—she'd been drugged or panicked or tired from a long and painful overnight labor. She did remember that Emily had been a tight little bundle, self-contained, or self-sufficient, from the beginning. But now, when she sat up in the pale, brilliant California room where they'd sequestered her and brought Jonah to her, he relaxed. What it felt like was that something that had been cold was warming and softening. The effect of this on Janet was enormous, as if she suddenly sensed love coming at her, into her. How random this was! How dependent on the chance circumstances of labor! No story that anyone had ever told her, not her mother's stories about being put to sleep in 1950 and 1953, not her grandmother's dimly remembered tales of parturition on the farm (always terrifying), not even Debbie's earnest parsing of Carlie's and Kevvie's moment-by-moment progress, had mentioned this little thing, what the child did in your arms, next to your body. And yet, perhaps, that was the magic bean that dictated the anatomy of the beanstalk. At any rate, Janet couldn't remember ever in her life looking into anyone's face with the pleasure she now felt looking into Jonah's. She cradled him in her left arm, removed his little hat once again, and laid her right palm gently on his warm forehead.

And the nurse returned and said, "Want to try nursing? He does seem a sweetheart! Have you nursed before? Let's see if we can get some colostrum into this boy. Mmm. Delicious? Ready, babe?"

1992

～

Richie would not have said that he had many political opinions, but once the Dems put him in the race for Congressman Scheuer's seat, his mouth opened, and opinions came out. They were, he discovered, quite similar to the congressman's own opinions, and not that much different from Ivy's. In fact, they were pretty much standard opinions for someone living in Brooklyn (fortunately, his and Ivy's co-op was just inside the line separating his district from the next one over), but he realized as he enunciated them that he actually felt them—his voice warmed to them, shaped them, emphasized them. When he spoke, images came into his mind of Ivy and Leo and their neighborhood, and how they fit into the larger picture (or, indeed, sometimes how the larger picture fit into them), and he waxed profound. It was true, though, that he didn't want anyone in his family—certainly not Michael, but not Ivy or his mom, either—to come to rallies. He was convinced that if he saw them in the audience he would return to the shapeless being he had been before Leo was born, the same being he was only now emerging from.

He was thirty-nine, he was tall, he was friendly from all those years of showing properties, he had a good smile. He was called "Rick." He was "the son of war hero and self-made defense industry innovator Frank Langdon," and in this day and age Michael wasn't as much of a liability as he might have been—their relationship appealed to some of Richie's voters in the Manhattan portions of the district. Richie had connections to the Italian community and through Ivy and her parents to the Jewish community. Once he started purveying these advantages, he was rather amazed at how it had all come together without his realizing it. And then there was Loretta, an avid supporter of Bush. She was a little prominent around certain parts of the city now, though still registered to vote in California; she was so eccentric that Richie knew that, if anyone brought her name up, all he had to do was smile and very slightly roll his eyes and he would get the I-have-crazy-relatives-too vote, hands down. The political landscape seemed to be changing—to be smoothing out almost everywhere. And Richie had more energy now than he had ever had before. It was in this that he knew that he really was related to that kid Charlie Wickett, who occasionally stopped by campaign headquarters on his daily run between Fort Tryon Park and Sag Harbor, or something as insanely breathtaking. Richie liked Charlie, and threatened to put him to work distributing leaflets. Charlie said that he was only allowed to distribute leaflets about the greenhouse effect, but Richie didn't pay any attention to that—he just liked to see him. And, of course, he knew Charlie's looks, fitness, and good-natured out-to-lunch quality would appeal to the youth vote.

Ivy was almost proud of him; she let him know this by telling him that her parents had decided that he was a "late bloomer." They, of course, assumed that the blossom had a pinkish tinge (they continued to pay for his subscriptions to *The Nation* and *Mother Jones* and to refer to Herbert Marcuse and Raymond Williams), but Richie thought maybe those days were gone. Both sides had so sullied their reputations that what he had—a kind of get-it-done-and-shake-hands-across-the-aisle sort of openness—was the wave of the future. His Republican opponent was an obvious sacrifice, fifty-four, with the forgettable name of Kevin Moore; he had run against Congressman Scheuer twice, losing by twenty points and then twenty-four points. The Republicans had pretty much already conceded.

By early February, Richie hadn't actually answered when people (people from the *Times,* the *Post,* the *Village Voice,* the Key Food weekly circular) asked him what he thought of the presidential race—Wilder, Kerrey, Clinton, Tsongas, Harkin, Brown—Virginia, Nebraska, Arkansas, Iowa, California, with a tragicomic touch of Massachusetts in Tsongas. He said nothing. They all had their advantages; the main thing was to pick the one who best combined intelligence, decisiveness, compassion, and the will to win. When Gennifer Flowers had appeared on the scene, he'd kept a straight face and said, "We should wait and see what's really going on." When everyone started talking about Clinton's dodging the draft, Richie told his own story, about showing up to enlist in Boston, ending up on a bus full of antiwar activists, and having to wait and try to enlist again, but by then the war was over. This was a story that even Ivy had never heard—how Debbie had found him wandering around Boston, wondering what to do. He was so stupid that he'd thought he would sign up, they'd take him, and he wouldn't have to come up with bus fare home, so he spent his last dollar on, not anything manly like a pack of smokes, but an ice-cream cone. Ivy thought it was cute and funny, so Richie learned how to tell it in a way that promoted an image of self-effacing patriotism combined with subsequent moral and practical growth.

Richie watched all the presidential candidates—not to see what they thought, but more to observe how they presented themselves. From Clinton, he took sheer brazen forward motion; from Harkin, the habit of smiling just before saying something; from Brown, an air of contained impatience at the bullshit presented by the other side; from Wilder, a trick of dropping into seriousness just at the right moment—the joking is over, let me lead you into a discussion of the issues. From all of them he took a willingness to speak to any size crowd. At the end of February, he was asked to a breakfast group at Lefferts Historic House. His audience numbered three persons, including the one who had arranged the breakfast; she apologized profusely for forgetting to put it in the paper. Richie spoke earnestly and at length, as if he had a full house. The only truly awkward part was the question-and-answer period—dead silence. But he kept smiling.

People in his neighborhood began recognizing him. As the winter progressed into spring, they went from staring at him just a moment too long to saying, "Are you that guy, Rick Langdon? I saw your picture somewhere," to "You know, I heard what you said, and here's where you're wrong." It was both an advantage and a disadvantage that Leo's absolute favorite thing to do was to go for a walk in the park; on Saturdays and Sundays, when Allie, their nanny, was off,

Richie would carry him across Prospect Park West to the entrance at the end of Ninth Street, and as soon as they neared the Lafayette Memorial, Leo would start bouncing in Richie's arms, and then hit the ground running. The disadvantage was that everyone in the park recognized him, and most people had something to say. The advantage was that Leo had to be followed, because he wouldn't stand still or allow himself to be held, and almost all of Richie's interlocutors were left behind, while at the same time, Richie hoped, noting that the candidate was a responsible and involved father. He knew he could not let Leo (1) throw a tantrum, (2) appear to be in danger, or (3) eat dangerous (carrots) or suspect (Popsicles) foods. All in all, it was better to let the darling child go, staying right with him. In March, there was even a little squib on Page Six—"Eighteen-Month-Old Beats Candidate Dad by a Length," with a very cute picture of Leo running and laughing, Richie right behind him, also laughing. Richie had expected the fund-raising and the meetings with constituents to be arduous, and the campaign to be time-consuming, but in fact the people funding his campaign were satisfied by his relationship to and near-identification with Congressman Scheuer, whom everybody liked.

Michael called this "the machine at work," but Richie had never enjoyed anything so much in his life.

ANDY DIDN'T KNOW anyone as open and free with her opinions as Loretta. Just now, sitting across from her in the BG Restaurant on the seventh floor at Bergdorf's, Loretta had remarked that, as much as she loved Ivy, she knew in her heart that Ivy was more loyal to Israel than to the United States. When Andy responded that never, ever had she heard Ivy or her entirely nonreligious parents say anything of the sort, Loretta shrugged, took a sip of her oolong tea and a bite of her scone (it was four in the afternoon, and they had spent the whole day shopping), and said, "Well, wait till push comes to shove. It's inside all of them." But the other side of this sort of statement was the reason they were there. Loretta had called her up two weeks before (apparently after having her hair done) and said, "Andy, I look like hell, and I need you." For two weeks now, Loretta had been mining her for the two types of ore everyone knew Andy could produce—fashion advice and AA advice, one for herself and the other for Michael.

Frank had said, "So which will be the more difficult task?" but Andy didn't think like that—they asked, you answered, Fate unfolded.

Loretta was too short for the loose, boyish pastel suits they were featuring, but at least huge shoulder pads were out now. She looked reasonably good in shaped, not-quite-clingy dresses. She'd tried on the green sleeveless, which brought out her eyes; the black capped-sleeve; and a nice violet item with something unusual, an asymmetric hemline. She had good ankles and feet—they'd spent a fair amount of time in the shoe department. The nicest thing she'd bought was for parties: an elaborately embroidered, rather stiff, square-necked gold sheath with a smallish waist that stopped just above knee-length, expensive and flattering.

The most salient fact was that Binky would be in first grade in the fall; no doubt, over the last six years, many opportunities to conceive a fourth child had occurred and not been utilized, and so Loretta (thirty-eight?) must have accepted that that phase was over. And, of course, Michael had changed in the last year. In the same relentless way he had formerly pursued his selfish desires for sensation (speed, money, oblivion, independence), he now pursued the amazing new goal of family happiness. Andy and Frank were invited to their place on Madison and Eighty-fourth (two floors, four bedrooms) every other Sunday for Sunday supper—not a fake event. Loretta served (and cooked herself) prime rib, roast chicken, braised leeks, potatoes au gratin. Michael sat at the head of the table, Loretta stood at the foot of the table (she did the carving), and both of them pestered the life out of Chance, Tia, and Binky. Chance paid no attention, Tia enjoyed answering questions, and Binky was passively resistant. It was evident to Andy, and, she thought, to Loretta, that Michael was making up fatherhood out of whole cloth.

Now Loretta looked at the little pyramid of treats sitting on their table. Andy had eaten a single shortbread cookie and a strawberry dipped in dark chocolate. Loretta said, "What do you think of Weight Watchers?"

"Nothing," said Andy.

"I want him to desire me."

"Did he ever desire you?"

Loretta gave her tea a thoughtful stir, and said, "Not in particular."

"What were the girls like that he desired?"

"Unfortunately, all types."

"What did he marry in you?"

Loretta put her teacup down, gazed into Andy's face, and tapped her spoon on the plate. At last, she said, "I'm thinking he married a known quantity. I'm thinking he didn't have the patience to figure the other girls out, so he, well, he went for the easy option. I think he liked that I was definite and didn't take any bullshit." She stopped tapping. "And no one else was the only child of a hundred thousand acres."

Andy admired her ruthlessness; maybe it was the ranching background. She nodded, then said, "Well, my guess is that your looks belong to you, then—you can get in shape if you want to, and why not? It's very soothing to do it, especially when the kids are in school. As far as Michael is concerned, I think you should be specific about your requirements."

"You mean, like, sex?"

"I mean that, whenever he's indecisive, you decide. That could work for sex."

Loretta licked her lips. She said, "Yes, that could." She pushed away her plate and shifted in her chair. The waiter eased over with a smile and took away the pyramid of treats. Now, Andy knew, would come what Loretta would consider the twisting of the knife. Loretta licked her lips again and said, "Was he really a bad child? I don't mean disobedient, I mean not nice."

But for Andy, no knife could be twisted that she herself had not already twisted many times. She said, "To be honest, Loretta, only Richie knows the answer to that question."

"Richie seems so slick, especially now. I get the feeling he would read all my unconscious facial expressions and tell me exactly what I wanted to hear. At least Michael's brutally honest."

Andy decided that Michael and Loretta must have had an argument in the last twenty-four hours. She said, "And you like that."

Loretta nodded, but said, "I don't *like* it. I appreciate its benefits."

Now Andy regarded her daughter-in-law for a long moment. She had never seen her with a bruise or a black eye, and in all the tattling he had done, Richie had never reported that Michael hit a girl (though there was a suspicious incident from that period when they were both at Cornell, where Michael ended up in the infirmary with a slash on his arm or leg, after which Richie fled Ithaca and ended up at Rutgers; Andy had been so happy to have him around that she had, mistakenly perhaps, overlooked the details). She hazarded only, "Michael has always had a bit of a temper." Then, "And he's a foot taller than you."

"I'm quicker," said Loretta, and Andy saw that, though this might be a possibility that she herself was only thinking of now, Loretta had reckoned with it for a long time—her matter-of-fact tone told Andy that she had strategies in place. She said, hesitantly, "I don't know that you can rely on that."

Then Loretta said the reassuring thing—"I haven't had to so far"—and Andy found herself taking a deep breath. Had she really gone for so long without asking herself what Michael was capable of? But maybe that was what mothers were supposed to do. The conversation couldn't go on after that; they both put their handbags on the table, and Andy said, "Shall we?" and Loretta said, "I really like what we've chosen. You're parked in that garage on Fifty-eighth Street, aren't you?"

"Yes, but you don't have to walk me over there. It's only a block." And then, she had to admit, she fled.

THE POLLS LOOKED GOOD: Kevin Moore still had a problem with name recognition. Richie suspected that the problem was the "Kevin." Once you thought "Kevin," whatever came next fell away, whereas "Richard" was like "Mister"—it pointed at whatever followed. And "Rick" hardly existed at all. Even so, in the weeks before the convention at Madison Square Garden, the smart commentators predicted disaster for the Democrats. Clinton and Gore were marginally okay (in fact, whenever Clinton started talking, his poll numbers went up word by word, only to drop after he fell silent) but Hillary was a worry. Operation Rescue threatened to make a fuss about abortion; the Women's Action Coalition threatened to make a bigger fuss about choice.

When Richie looked around the convention hall the first night, though, he knew everything would be fine. It was filled, not with regular, cynical, bored functionaries, but with women, blacks, Hispanics, people in wheelchairs and with canes—all sorts of people who never thought they would see the day they could cast their vote and nominate the next president. The enthusiasm told Richie (and Congressman Scheuer told him, too) that almost everyone in the Garden, shouting, screaming, laughing, waving posters, was experiencing him- or herself, at last and maybe for the first time, as a power broker. Congressman Scheuer said that it was a fine way to go out and a fine way to come in. And he clapped Richie on the shoulder as if he were dubbing him with a sword.

As a delegate, Richie's job was to applaud, cheer, give information, and be a helpful public servant. He handed out a few "We Love Cuomo" signs so the New York delegation could cheer Cuomo's nominating speech. He stood respectfully during the movie about the governor, whistled and shouted when the governor came onto the podium, made sure to stand up straight when the TV cameras turned toward him. And then he actually listened to the speech and was affected by it—"Nearly a whole generation surrendered in despair. . . . They are *our* children." Richie could not help thinking of Leo. "This is more than a recession! Our economy has been weakened fundamentally by twelve years of conservative Republican supply-side policies." Of course, Richie could not fail to hear, in a corner of his brain, Michael laughing about outsourcing jobs, and Loretta saying, in her self-righteous way, "They don't have any *right* to those jobs!" and then Ivy saying, "She doesn't have any *right* to that ranch," but only to him, in bed, after Michael and Loretta had gone home. "In no time at all, we have gone from the greatest seller nation, the greatest lender nation, the greatest creditor nation, to today, the world's largest buyer, the world's largest borrower, the world's largest debtor nation. *That* is Republican supply-side."

Richie had met the governor several times, and, like everyone, found him attractive, but now he felt the man's words engraving themselves into his brain—words that he would use in his own campaign against Kevin. "This time we cannot afford to fail to deliver the message . . . The ship is headed toward the rocks!" And then he made a joke about the invisible hand of the market that everyone cheered, and Richie learned from him the whole time. "Prayer is always a good idea!" Only Richie laughed at that, since he had never prayed in his life. Richie had to admire the man's flurry of great lines—"Bush said, 'We have the will, but not the wallet!'" and he followed that with a reminder of the savings-and-loan bailout—"All of a sudden, the heavens opened and out of the blue, billions of dollars appeared, not for children, not for jobs, not for drug treatment or the ill or for health care, but hundreds of millions of dollars to bail out failed savings and loans." Richie stopped gaping and glanced around. The cameras were on Cuomo, not him, but he did not want to look stupid, though in fact he felt stupid: he had agreed to run for Congress, and just now he realized that he was not prepared, in spite of all of his years of working for the congressman and watching him decide this and decide that, vote on this, vote on that, give this quote and that quote. He felt a trembling in the back of his neck, because he was not a deep thinker, an A student, a well-trained military man, or even a lawyer. He was in the right place at the right time with the right look and the right vocal timbre and the right connections. The congressman had often said, over the years, that Richie had a "knack for this stuff," and maybe he did, because more often than not he could talk someone into something, but just at this moment, when he was watching the governor roll to a climax, he felt like he knew less and less, right down to nothing. The governor finished his speech to rousing applause; Richie yelled, clapped, whistled. A young woman from the office grabbed his hand, and the congressman gave him the thumbs-up. He was being taken upon the flood into the Congress, too young, too green, too stupid, but of course he would not stop it.

JANET KNEW, rationally, that if she'd had *Solve Your Child's Sleep Problems* when Emily was a baby, Emily would be a different person, but even so, and even though she'd read the book three times and nearly memorized it, putting the method into practice scared her. It seemed like a test, but not, say, a math test—rather, a driving test, dangerous and demanding. But Jared, who was hard to annoy, was almost annoyed because Jonah, nine months old, was still waking up to nurse at 2:00 a.m. and 5:00 a.m., and lately he was brighter—more interested in people and toys, and crawling all over the place—so it was harder to put him down at night. The whole time he was nursing before bed, his eyes would roll toward whatever sound he heard, whatever else might be happening. He was a curious boy, active. Jared said getting him to sleep through the night was now or never, and Janet didn't disagree with him. But.

The moment she knew they were committed was when, after she nursed him on the couch (instead of his bedroom), she sat him up and kissed him a few times (instead of easing him, sleeping, into his crib), then took him over to Jared, who was watching TV, and to Emily, who was reading *The Chronicle of the Horse,* for a good-night kiss. They were kind and supportive, as if Jonah were heading out into the wilderness with a secret message that he had to deliver to rebel forces all by himself. Then she carried him upstairs and into his room, laid him down, kissed him good night, covered him, and walked out without thinking about whether he might grab the top railing of the crib and launch himself, or whether she should have solved his sleep problems months ago.

The crying started after about a minute, first whimpers of disbelief, then shouts and wails. At three minutes, she went in, gave him a kiss, noted that he was still lying down, and walked out. After another five minutes, she did this again. The technique prescribed that she should then wait ten minutes, but she could only manage eight. She went in. Jonah stared up at her, his mouth open in horror, the whimpers ululating into shouts. He held out his arms. Janet spoke much more firmly and cheerily than she felt. "Good night, sweetie! Time to go to sleep." She patted his forehead, let her hand linger there; he was a beautiful child, with large, bright eyes, thick hair, and full lips. Then she turned and walked out, closing the door. Three minutes after that, the crying stopped abruptly, and she tiptoed down the stairs, exhausted. Jared's show was still on, Emily was still reading *The Chronicle.* Twenty minutes seemed like two hours.

He did wake up around two—two-thirteen. She went into his room and did what she was supposed to do. Then, outside his door, she was so tired that she slumped against the wall. Three minutes, five minutes. Two minutes after her second, supposedly reassuring visit, he went quiet, and she did not peek in to see whether he had put his head between the bars of his crib (not possible—the bars were two and a half inches apart). She went back to bed, lay awake for a while, noticed that Jared had not moved, and did, indeed, fall asleep. Jonah was up at his usual time, just after six. She entered his room with a feeling of such profound guilt that she felt thrilled, but also astonished, when he greeted her with his usual big smile and waving arms, and when she picked him up his arms went around her neck. Jared and Emily said nothing about the whole ordeal at breakfast. Jared said he would be late for supper, and Emily reminded her that she had promised to take her to the stables that afternoon—she had to ride both Pesky and Sunlight, especially if Janet planned to go out Saturday, like she'd said. Yes, she did. "Well, then," said Emily, in a Denise Herman sort of voice, "are you going to come over and clean your tack? You haven't cleaned it in two weeks, and it's a little yucky," which made Janet get up, go into the bathroom off the kitchen, and laugh silently into the mirror. When she came back out, Emily was setting some bits of scrambled egg on the tray of Jonah's highchair, and he was touching them with the tip of his finger. Jared was saying, "Honey, give him a bit of the watermelon."

That night, Night Number Two, it took him twenty-four despair-filled minutes to fall asleep, but when he woke up at two-thirty-four, he only cried out once; she stood outside his door for five minutes, and he didn't make another sound. On Night Number Three, he fell asleep in fourteen minutes; on Night Number Four, in five; and on Night Number Five, he took a deep breath when she kissed him and patted him, and was, as far as she could tell, sleeping by the time she left the room. And he didn't wake up until seven-thirty.

The only semi-sad aspect was that she had no one to impart this newfound wisdom to—none of her friends had babies, she didn't know any younger women well enough to give them unsolicited advice, and Jared and Emily thought that it was all a matter of course. So she kept it quiet, another pleasurable secret between herself and Jonah, another reason never to get a babysitter and to put off the nanny question for six months. She didn't actually want to be away from him, so why bother?

RICHIE HAD the lease on his little campaign office on Sixth Avenue near Ninth Street until the end of the year, which gave him plenty of time to get it cleaned up. The best thing about it (it was only fourteen feet wide and thirty feet deep, and so had been cheap) was that it was across the street from Colson's, where he always went for coffee. It was there that Charlie and the girlfriend ambushed him at 9:00 a.m. the day after the election. They let him get his coffee and pay for it, along with a rugelach and an apricot tart, so that his hands were full and his cup was hot, and he couldn't get away. And they stood between him and the door, too. Richie was tired of the campaign and ready for a break, but he said, "Okay, let's sit down," and Charlie pulled out the seat they had been keeping for him. Richie wondered if they'd followed him from Park Slope.

Richie had won, 53.4 percent to 46.1 percent, leaving out the handful who'd voted for the socialists and the three voters who voted for the Conservative Party. It was a margin that would have deeply shamed Congressman Scheuer. Richie himself didn't know if this was a good omen or a bad one, a sign of the times or something personal. He told himself that he was in, all that mattered.

Riley was talking. Charlie was smiling. Richie was putting on his paying-attention face. Riley said, "Sir, as far as I am concerned, and the people I work with, this is the most important issue of our age. I'm not kidding."

"She's not kidding," said Charlie.

Richie said, "Explain it to me again, in a way that I can understand."

She was good. She did not take a single impatient breath; she did not, even fleetingly, get a "you idiot" look on her face. She did what he would have done with an angry Perot supporter—she smiled and said, "Okay, Clinton was elected, just barely, and now is really our only chance. I mean, let's put it this way—"

Charlie interrupted, "Pornographers have control of the White House now, and militant homosexuals run the armed forces."

Richie actually glanced around to see if anyone was looking at them. Loretta had said almost that very thing a week or so ago, except that she, of course, meant it.

"And," said Riley, "we can close the ozone hole because that was an atheist plot, and now we've won." She had a big smile. That was her pretty part. She got serious immediately, and leaned toward him. "But the greenhouse effect is harder to deal with. We atheists and our trained-seal scientists can't do it alone, and God doesn't seem to care, so I want a job."

"What would your job be?" said Richie.

"Congressmen have staff," said Charlie. "People who get on TV and say, 'The congressman has no comment at this time.'"

"I do need someone like that. What's your name? Riley? Let's hear you."

Riley cleared her throat, then said, "The congressman has no comment at this time about whether six prostitutes did, indeed, jump from the third-story windows of the West Wing, but he would like to point out that all of the prostitutes signed the United Nations Framework Convention on Climate Change while they were visiting with the president, and are completely in agreement with the aims of the protocol, namely, to commit themselves to a reduction of carbon dioxide, methane, sulfur hexafluoride, and, their own personal favorite, nitrous oxide, or laughing gas." Her smile was perfectly flat and fake, just the way the networks liked it. She went on: "And, of course, hydrofluorocarbons and perfluorocarbons. We understand that, before the jump, three of the prostitutes were preparing a statement to this effect. We greatly regret what appears to be a heartbreaking tragedy, and we would like to remind the audience that everyone must pull together to reduce greenhouse-gas emissions by our agreed-upon five-point-two percent. Thank you, and, once again, the congressman regrets being called away on pressing business just now. I have no further comment." Her smile broadened.

Richie said, "Perfect."

Charlie said, "I've been coaching her."

Riley said, "I can also answer hate mail, death threats, and accusations that you bear the mark of the devil on your forehead, which is why you always wear a baseball cap."

"Do you have practice answering those sorts of letters?"

"We don't answer them, but I think they should be answered."

Charlie offered, helpfully, "She still has to write her dissertation, but she's finished with her coursework."

"What is the subject of your dissertation?"

"Methods of motivating governing elites to understand and address climate issues."

"So—I am your experimental subject?"

"You're the only one either of us has met."

Charlie said, "We drove through Iowa during the drought four years ago, but I was too shy to stop and see Joe or even Minnie. I really liked Minnie."

Riley turned glum, then said, "I am so sorry I missed that. But I did two papers on the Yellowstone fires."

"How old are you?" said Richie.

"Twenty-six," said Riley.

"Do you want to be part of an experiment?"

"Sure," said Riley.

"My sister-in-law would be one of those people writing you hate mail. You should meet her and try out your techniques on her."

"Michael's wife," said Charlie.

Richie nodded.

Charlie said, "I got that vibe off her. The my-dad-has-twenty-thousand-head-of-cattle-and-we-eat-ribs-for-breakfast-lunch-and-dinner-and-you-will-remove-them-from-my-cold-dead-hands sort of vibe."

Richie looked at the clock behind the baked-goods display. It was almost eleven, and he had done nothing yet this morning. Ivy was not sanguine about the presidential election. She thought the victory was enough to shrink the population of right-wing bacteria, but not enough to kill them all, so the stronger ones would reproduce and return, more "virulent" than ever (though she did think that eventually she would win over Michael, who was basically well meaning, and Loretta, who had to be more sharply defined than Michael just to maintain his interest and respect). Richie said, "What are you doing this morning, Riley?"

"Following you around."

Richie said, "I will pay you each one dollar over the minimum wage, which is four twenty-five per hour, to help me clean up my campaign headquarters, starting right now; one hour every day for lunch; no benefits until I get to Washington. But you can come for dinner Friday night and meet Ivy and Leo."

"Five fifty," said Charlie.

Richie pulled some change out of his pocket and threw it on the table, then said, "You got it."

1993

ANDY AND DEBBIE ARRANGED that Frank would invite Arthur to Englewood Cliffs after the inauguration. He would come for a week and at least be a little distracted. No one north of the Tappan Zee Bridge had seen the sun in twenty-six days; Debbie could tell Arthur was sinking. Debbie's husband, Hugh, was sinking, too. Hugh tried not to complain, but he thought, if the four of them could just get away to Stowe for a long weekend (away from Arthur, that was), then everyone would be fortified and ready to take on the ninth anniversary of Lillian's death. Hugh's unspoken opinion was that people die—his grandmother had died; his aunt had died; his grandfather had died. In his family, this was accepted as natural. He had spent nine years treating Lillian's death as a larger event than he felt it was. Andy said, "I understand completely."

Because Arthur might not answer the phone, and even if he did he would decline the invitation, Frank proposed that they drive up to Hamilton (Hugh was tenured at Colgate now) and kidnap him. They would take the kid, Charlie, with them. Andy asked Richie, who asked Riley, who asked Charlie, who said yes. Riley was in Washington, helping Richie organize his congressional office. But Arthur was happy to see them and not at all reluctant to accompany them to New Jersey.

He kept up conversation for maybe half an hour, then dozed off with his head against the car window, snoring for a while; then he seemed to suck air and gag, which was alarming. And even though the Mercedes was hot, Arthur shivered periodically as Frank drove.

Once they got back to Englewood Cliffs and Arthur had gone to bed, Andy, Frank, and Charlie huddled around the table in the kitchen. "He at least needs a warmer coat," said Charlie. "I can find him something."

"He must weigh a hundred and twenty-five pounds," said Andy. "And he's so hunched over. I can't believe he's our age." She turned to Charlie. "I'll be seventy-three in the summer, and Frank turned seventy-three on the first of January, but Arthur looks ninety. His father was still walking several miles a day the last year of his life. Was he eighty-something when he died?" Andy had bought tickets to *Jelly's Last Jam* and planned to take Arthur to simple things, like Central Park to watch the skaters at Wollman Rink, brunch at a deli, maybe to the Guggenheim for half an hour; but, judging by the way he had changed even since the fall, she wasn't so sure now.

Frank said, "He's tougher than we think," and it was true that Arthur had endured things that none of the rest of them had had to endure, but even if Frank was discounting his own good health by 50 percent, Andy thought he was overestimating what Arthur had become.

Andy said, "Maybe I should take him to a doctor."

But could kidnapping accomplish that, too?

When they were settling into bed, Frank said, "You know, it's okay with Arthur if he dies. I don't think he ever tried it after that one time, but he told me he thought about it. And thought about it."

Andy said, "You have to be brave and resolute to do it."

Frank tightened his arms around her and kissed her.

In the morning, Arthur was already up when Andy entered the kitchen. Charlie had toasted him an English muffin and made both of them some hard-boiled eggs and coffee. Arthur was sitting up straight and cracking the shell of his egg. Charlie was saying, "You can get used to your indoor temperature being sixty-two if you've weather-stripped the windows to take care of the drafts. Warm socks and a sweater work for me. We're lucky to have heat at all—we have friends who've never turned on the furnace. Even Riley dreads going to their place."

Arthur gazed at him with a fond smile and said, "Some indigenous peoples are built to retain heat. Thick around the center, thin at the periphery. But you don't look like one of them."

"I have the luxury of a six-thousand-calorie diet."

Andy wrapped her robe a little more tightly around herself and said, "Everybody sleep well?"

Charlie said, "I did get up to open a couple of windows, but I set a rolled-up towel against the threshold of the door so no cold air would leak into the house."

"Comfortable bed," said Arthur.

Andy offered them some Familia, which she liked with a little yogurt every morning, but they shook their heads.

It went like that all day: Charlie and Arthur sitting here and there, chatting, while Andy eavesdropped. Charlie was a good listener, and so was Arthur. Arthur didn't talk only about Tim, but he did tell Charlie about the time that Tim went with his friends the Sloan brothers when they sneaked out one night in their father's work truck. They were driving along a country road at about 1:30 in the morning. Two other boys were in the back, and the truck went off the edge and rolled into a field. The boys in the back were thrown clear, and everyone was fine. They went to the Sloans' place, and took the truck out behind the garage, found hammers in the workshop, and hammered out the dents. The dad, according to the older Sloan boy, didn't notice a thing.

Charlie told about how, when he was seven, he walked out of the house and took the bus to the pool without telling anyone. His mom had figured out where he was headed by the fact that his trunks and towel were gone. Instead of punishing him, she got him a bus pass and made sure that the driver for that route knew his name.

Arthur told about his boarding school—Andy hadn't known that Arthur went to boarding school. His favorite history teacher was a fellow from Belfast, who spoke with a liquid Irish accent. Instead of talking about whatever was in the textbook (though he did test them on that), he would give them poems to memorize—"The Charge of the Light Brigade," "Dulce et Decorum Est," "O Captain! My Captain!," "Sailing to Byzantium," "The Wind That Shakes the Barley." And Arthur said he could remember them still, all the verses, word for word; sometimes when he couldn't sleep he recited them to himself. When he then, at Charlie's urging, said a few lines from "The Wind That Shakes the Barley"—"And on my breast in blood she died / While soft winds shook the barley"—Andy's eyes filled with tears, and she went out the back door.

When she returned, they were laughing. Charlie was talking about how he would not be allowed to dive until he could show the coach that he had read his ten pages of *The Bridge of San Luis Rey,* or whatever the book was. He was required to read them even if the book happened to slide off the diving board and into the deep end.

Then Arthur told a story Steve Sloan had told him after Tim died, about how they would ride their bicycles to the local lovers' lane, crawl along the drainage pipe to the manhole, and set off firecrackers under the lovers' cars.

They lulled her. She gave them sandwiches and drinks in the living room. Charlie went out for a run in the mid-afternoon, but came back after an hour ("Only six miles, but I can make it up," he said). Arthur appeared to take a nap. It was Frank who noticed when he got home before supper that when Arthur stood up from his chair to go to the bathroom, he stumbled to one side, caught himself, and then stood there as if he was too dizzy to go any farther, and it was Frank who suspected what they discovered at the emergency room—he was having a little stroke, or what the ER doctor called "a transient ischemic attack" from a blood clot in his left carotid artery, and would need to stay in the hospital for at least a few days.

FRANK WAS NOT SURPRISED that the few days of Arthur's stay at the hospital turned into something much more lengthy and dramatic. He was not lulled by day one, when Arthur seemed back to normal, sitting up in his bed, chatting with the nurses and the orderlies as if he'd known them for years, telling Charlie about how their house in McLean had so many doors and gates that it took him half an hour every night to make sure everything was locked up. He went along with Arthur's refusal to call Debbie, but not because he thought Arthur was going to be all right. When Frank arrived on the morning of day two to find Arthur dressed, and busily, but quietly, getting his things together, he didn't help him. He said he had to find the men's room, then went to the nurses' station and asked if Mr. Manning had been discharged. The nurse, very slowly, Frank thought, went through Arthur's chart, and said, "No, sir. Mr. Manning is scheduled first thing tomorrow morning for a carotid endarterectomy."

"What is that?"

"Apparently, Mr. Manning has about a seventy-five- or eighty-percent atherosclerotic plaque blockage where the left carotid artery forks. The right artery is not clear, but the blockage is only about thirty-five to forty percent, which is not critical at this point. Dr. Marcus will open the left artery and clear out the plaque. It's a delicate operation, but not terribly—"

"Does Mr. Manning know what the doctor's plan is?"

"They had a consultation about an hour ago, sir."

He told her that Arthur was ready to leave.

Considering how thin he was, Frank discovered that Arthur was pretty strong. It was Frank who had to grab his elbow as he rushed the door, and retain his hold while Arthur tried to twist out of his grasp. The nurse kept exclaiming, "Mr. Manning! Mr. Manning! Please, sit down!"

Finally, Frank simply embraced him and held him until he went quiet. He could see the two of them in the bathroom mirror—himself half a bald head taller than Arthur now, Arthur's white hair fluffing upward, his own bulky blue-shirted arm across Arthur's narrow back. The nurse—her name was Ernestine—said, soothingly, "There's nothing to be afraid of, Mr. Manning. Dr. Marcus is a wonderful surgeon, he's done this a thousand times." Arthur said nothing. When the nurse went out to get him "a little something," Frank leaned over him and spoke in a low voice. He said, "I know you're not afraid."

Arthur shook his head. "That's not it," he said. "Why bother?"

"Because something could happen to you that would be a major pain in the ass for everyone else."

Arthur sat down on the bed. Frank positioned himself between Arthur and the door, but Arthur didn't make a move.

That night, in bed, Frank said to Andy, "When Arthur and Lillian ran off, it was Joe who drove to the soda fountain to pick Lillian up when she said she was getting off that night, at eight. When was that, '45? I was still in Germany, anyway. The fellow who ran the drugstore was dumbfounded: he hadn't seen her all day, she wasn't assigned to come into work, he said. He went with Joe around behind the drug-store and looked in the weeds, down by the river, for her body! Joe was afraid to go home. But by the time he got there, my mom had gone into Lillian's room, noticed the bed wasn't made, and found the note. Oh, she was beside herself, she didn't know whether it was from fear or rage. Then, two days later, I got another letter saying that Lillian had written home to say she was married. Postmarked Kanka-kee. They were on their way to Washington, D.C., she was as happy as she could be, goodbye!"

"Your parents never seemed to hold it against her."

"They were all set to see Arthur with horns and a forked tail—stolen the darling! But she wrote about how his first wife had died in childbirth, and the baby, too, and my mom couldn't resist that, and then Arthur sent her a Sunbeam toaster and a hand mixer. Lil-lian was so good at detailing everything about him that my mom came around by Thanksgiving—what was that, six weeks by then. I'm sure a baby blanket was half knitted by Christmas, whether or not Lillian had told them she was expecting."

"He was born to deceive," said Andy.

"No," said Frank, "he was a genius at keeping secrets, but he could not tell a lie."

After that, they lay quietly until Andy kissed him good night—two, three, four kisses, each softer and more searching than the last one, each one saying, We are old we are old, the end is nigh, yet each one so exactly like those kisses he remembered from when they were first married and living in Floral Park that he felt disori-ented. Certainly, one of the punishments of old age was experienc-ing this decline, but with Arthur, Frank thought it was worse than that. He remembered Arthur more clearly from those early days than he remembered almost anything, because Arthur had been a pecu-liar phenomenon, almost sinister in his ability to be that affectionate, fun-seeking, all-American dad when he was near Lillian and the kids, and that ruthless, suspicious schemer when he was grooming Frank for some intelligence-gathering project that Frank only half under-stood but was always flattered by, always game for. If domesticity was quicksand for a real man (and who in the fifties had not thought so?), then, to Frank, Arthur had held out the occasional lifeline, his only remuneration the satisfaction of being useful, feeling a frisson of risk. Frank was two inches taller than Arthur and must have out-weighed him even then by twenty-five pounds, but they both knew that Arthur was the more unpredictable, the more dangerous, or that was how Frank had felt at the time.

Had he liked Arthur? Felt real affection for him? Maybe, at first, only fascination, then dependence, then, now, yes, love. But Frank knew he wasn't good at love. Andy was training him in their old age. That she was right this minute sleeping next to him was one sign that she was having an effect; that he had looked at the pictures of Jonah with pleasure when they came in the mail earlier in the week was another. He had appreciated Janet—there was one close-up of her face right beside Jonah's, both of them grinning, that he had thought attractive, even affecting. Frank hadn't expected to change at this age. Andy turned in his direction and put her hand on his shoulder. He thought again of Arthur as he was now, practically dead. The surgery would be over by the time Frank woke up. If he happened to fall asleep. But then he did.

THE NEXT DAY, when Frank went with Andy to the hospital, they consulted first with Dr. Marcus, who said that he thought the proce-dure had gone well, a tiny bit more complicated than he'd expected, but almost every surgery was; he'd learned to live with that. He felt sure that they'd find Arthur in good condition in a day or two. Andy said, "What are the possible complications?"

"Well, we do look for signs that the wound is not closing properly. Should there be any hemorrhaging, that of course is very dangerous, given the location of the surgery."

As he said this, Frank could feel the blood pounding in his own carotid artery, the right one. He didn't even have to touch it.

"And there is another possibility that perhaps Mr. Manning could be vulnerable to, given his slenderness, and that is any sort of hema-toma that might cause a compression of the trachea. But the staff here is very attentive, and I'm sure everything will progress without a hitch."

It was as if the doctor had laid out the scenario of the next few days. There was a hemorrhage, and it did happen late at night, and Arthur did lose a lot of blood—he was asleep, and the night nurse discovered it only when she touched what might be a shadow on the pillowcase and the sheet and felt moisture. At that point, she turned on the light and saw that Arthur's shoulder and hair were red, too. Back into surgery. The next morning, Debbie arrived, beside herself with the suspicion, Frank thought, that every doctor in New Jersey was a quack and every nurse an idiot, and there were no words for Frank and Andy that expressed Debbie's fury at having all of this kept from her.

It was Arthur who realized, four days after the second surgery, that he was breathless, that he was, in fact, starting to pass out, that he only had time to put his fingers to his neck and realize that it was swollen and hot. He then aimed his hand in the general direction of the emergency button. The hematoma required a third surgery, and the doctor let slip to Frank that maybe 6 percent of patients who underwent the carotid endarterectomy did not survive, and then, of course, if there was that much plaque in the carotid artery, how much was there elsewhere? But that was another question that could be addressed later.

And so Arthur was in the hospital for two weeks, and when he was discharged, he and Debbie stayed with Frank and Andy for two more weeks (Debbie called Hugh about the children three times a day). When they left, it was well past the anniversary of Lillian's death, something that, if anyone noticed, they did not mention, and, Frank thought, maybe that was a good thing.

Andy and Frank slept for three days to get over the stress of the visit. Then Andy noticed that Frank's revelations (or reminiscences, Frank would call them) continued at a relaxed but steady pace. Frank, she thought, would not have admitted that Arthur's medical problems had confronted him with mortality. But it was not death that came over him, it was life, his life, and, for whatever reason, he could not resist talking about it. There was that first train trip to Chicago—'36. Maybe the passengers had been in danger of freezing to death, but what Frank most clearly remembered was seeing his first black person, the bartender. Andy had had a similar experience when her parents took the children to Minneapolis; she was six. A black woman was walking down Hennepin in the swirling snow. Her mother jerked her arm and told her to stop staring. Were their parents racist? Andy and Frank agreed, how were they to know? Race was one of the things no one had ever talked about, at least in Denby, at least in Decorah.

Andy wondered if maybe this summer they should go back to Europe for the third time, and see something more out of the way—Crete, Tenerife, Corsica. Frank mentioned that he had been to Corsica, and before he said another word, Andy felt a tunnel-like space opening in her brain. He had told her about North Africa, and Sicily, about Anzio and Monte Cassino. When their friends talked about Normandy, he talked about landing at Saint-Tropez (he was teased for that). She had listened silently to arguments about Eisenhower and Devers, as if any of these former corporals, privates, and sergeants now shooting off their mouths had valid opinions. But in Corsica, there was peace, there was beauty, there was leisure. And, yes, there was a girl, and when Frank's voice deepened as he talked about her, how she had called him "Errol Flynn," Andy knew that whatever had happened there was a cherished and much-remembered experience, unmentioned until now. She said, "You fell asleep? That was all?"

"Maybe that was what I needed at the time. She massaged my feet. She had all of my money in her hand, and she only took some of it."

He did not say that he and the girl had had intercourse, but Andy understood that they had, which reminded her of that last fall semester in college; when Frank was telling her—Hildy, as she was then called—that he loved her, he was doing something with her friend Eunice that could not be called rape, because it was mutually sought, but was hateful and violent. She knew that Frank thought that she knew nothing about that, and it was on the tip of her tongue to repay him for Corsica by telling him that Eunice had died in 1989 from complications of emphysema—after being on a ventilator for three years. But she didn't say anything, and then she woke up in the night; she remembered standing in the entrance of the Memorial Union, just beneath the wall of engraved names of Iowa State heroes of the First World War, blubbering about the German invasion of Norway, and Frank leaning toward her with such kindness and strength. The other students were passing and staring, and Frank hid her face against his shoulder so she wouldn't see them, and they wouldn't see her, a loving thing to do. Yes, he had run away to the war weeks afterward, but she had forgiven that long ago. Maybe, she thought, it had taken Frank these many years to know that love and sex could intersect.

One night, when they were laughing at the idea that there could be a street anywhere, even in Chicago, called "Wacker," Andy said, "You know, that day, I saw you. I followed you for ten minutes. I was scared to get near you. You looked so old and hardened. My plan was, if you recognized me, I would say, 'Hi, I'm Hildy, do you remember me?' But I thought you might not recognize me, so I thought, if I introduced myself as Andy, we could start from the beginning. I would say that I'd gone to Iowa and my last name was Peterson."

"I didn't recognize you," said Frank.

"No, you didn't right at first, I saw it in your face, so I started in on my plan, but then you did, so I made up that story about changing my name. The next day, I had to tell everyone at the office and write my parents. I was Hildy until that moment."

Andy knew that it would seem unbelievable to her children, especially Janet and Loretta and Ivy, that she and Frank had not shared these memories before, and it was not only, she saw now, that ever since she'd known him she, and perhaps he, had been afraid of what might be said—it was also that they had no model. One night she said to him, "Do you remember your parents talking about themselves to each other?"

"My father fell in the well out by the barn and didn't tell Mama for ten years or something like that. When Cousin Berta went to the insane asylum, no one said a word about it. She was at home one day and not there the next day. I think Joe asked where she was, and Mama said, 'She had to go up to Independence.' I think I thought she had moved somewhere to be on her own."

Andy said, "One time, my mother was really upset with my father for having the apple trees in the backyard cut down without telling her. She went out and drove the car around town for two hours rather than speak to him about it."

"But," said Frank, "what would they tell each other? My parents were from the same town—different churches, but they had lived the same lives. What would they bring to a conversation? Nothing exotic, you can be sure."

"My parents and their relatives talked in code. Someone would nod and say, 'Ah, you know what happened to Inga!' And then everyone else would nod, and Sven or I would ask, 'Mama, what happened to Inga?' and, more often than not, she would say, 'You don't want to know.' It wasn't until we were much older—high school, really—that we began to put all the parts together."

"Or they would talk German," said Frank. " *'Ja!'* and then blah blah blah, so fast that we could only pick out a word here and there. I would ask Eloise, and she would tell me, but I got to wondering after a while if she wasn't making things up just to frighten me."

"I was very fond of your aunt Eloise," said Andy.

"I went through a period where I agreed with Eloise's analysis," said Frank. Andy thought he was joking, but then he said, "I mean, I was fifteen. I was very impressed by Julius. He was a communist. He had that accent that said, 'I know things you will never even think of.' It's so ghostly now."

"What?" said Andy.

"Soviet immortality."

Their conversations made Andy think of things she hadn't thought of in years—her time in Kansas City, for example. Compared with Iowa, Kansas City was a strange world. The Halls where she worked was in the most elegant place she'd ever been at that point, a made-up town for shopping, a Fifth Avenue on the prairie (when she got to the real Fifth Avenue, she wasn't very impressed, because the Country Club Plaza had spoiled her). Her boss at Halls had seemed imposing, too, all of thirty-one, possessed of his own apartment just north of the plaza, on the third floor! He was a sharp dresser, talked about jazz, and implied that he was close personal friends with Count Basie and Charlie Parker. What was his name? She thought for a morning, and over her tomato soup remembered—Martin Sock or Scott. She had been shy, not really carrying a torch for Frank, more like frozen up. She read a lot; that was where she learned all those stories that she'd told her various psychiatrists in the early years of their marriage, tales from a book of saga translations, and *Giants in the Earth, The Emigrants, Kristin Lavransdatter,* anything cruel and resonant in her mind with the Decorah/Albert Lea axis. But Martin took her out—sometimes to a movie, once to a club, once to dinner—and one of those times, not the last one, he took her to his apartment, into the bedroom, where he started fondling her. Fondling was not easy, given her armor of girdle and hosiery and bra and petticoat, not to mention the tight belt around her waist and the long zipper down her side and the hooks and their eyes. But he had been patient, and pretty soon she was half dressed on the bed with him, him still in his trousers and socks and neatly pressed shirt, and somehow he had his knee between her legs and he was pressing her and rubbing her, and at the same time kissing her, and something happened, there seemed to be an explosion where his leg was that seemed to burn through her body, making her shake and tremble and stiffen and cry out so that he smothered her face against his side. And then they were both so embarrassed that she jumped off the bed and put her clothes back on as best she could. She didn't know what had happened to her, and he wasn't saying. After she got back together with Frank, in preparation for their marriage, she found a book in a used-book store in Chicago by a woman named Ida Craddock, called *Right Marital Living*. She'd been amazed to discover that what had happened to her was fairly routine. She knew that if she told this to Frank, while lying softly in his arms in the dark in their very own bed in the house they had owned now for thirty-three years, he would be amused and affectionate and see it as an exchange for his tale of Corsica, but she couldn't do it. She did wonder what had happened to Martin Sock. He would be almost eighty now.

GREECE WAS a place that people their age, Andy thought, could never understand why they had waited so long to get to. Certainly, standing on the uneven paving in front of the Parthenon, looking outward to the city beyond, Andy felt herself to have finally arrived at the apex of something, but not something so crass as civilization. Frank was good—he had been reading all summer. He supplied her with all sorts of information and helped her not to stumble, but he didn't care if she asked questions (she didn't), and he didn't imply that if she'd paid more attention in school she would know who Socrates and Plato were. At Mycenae (but they pronounced it "Mikinna"), he stood with her at the gate into the city, the Lion Gate, where, after gazing at the carving of the two headless lions standing on their hind legs, facing a column, they marveled for quite a long time at the grooves in the paving, where there had been a rectangular stone in the portal, as wide as the space between the wheels of a chariot, to help the charioteers orient their vehicles so that they could get safely through the gate. These three-thousand-year-old ruts were the ghosts of uncountable momentary thoughts on the part of uncountable lost charioteers. As they walked up the hill from there, Frank told her a little about the Trojan War, the Achaeans (the Myceneans) and their friends and enemies. They followed a narrowing passageway and peered into one of the beehive tombs. The orange color of the local soil made the landscape seem especially abandoned. Mikinna, Andy thought, was much more haunting than the Acropolis, not white but brownish gold, as if the light of 1600 B.C. were cooler and duskier than that of 500 B.C. Olympia she found flat, busy, and boring, as if the labor of the gods had been, not great doings, but gossip, bookkeeping, and shipments here and there of olive oil and flax. Andy strolled along, looking at the ruins and the sky, taking in the fragrance of the vegetation. Although it was impossible to stay in Greece forever, she had the feeling that you could remain, lifetime after lifetime, floating here and there very quietly, and with plenty of company. She'd never felt this way about New Jersey or Iowa.

It was the assistant cook on the *Flyboy,* the yacht where they stayed for three nights, who said that, after they looked at Knossos and Agia Triada, they should not miss Delphi. It was out of the way, and Frank had planned to skip it, but since Andy had expressed no desires at all so far, he was eager to do whatever she so much as mentioned.

Almost October now. They got to Itea late in the afternoon, nearly dark, and decided to take a room in a regular hotel there, rather than continue up to Delphi. They ate in the dining room, spanakopita and roast lamb. Frank did an unusual thing—he took a glass of ouzo, and ordered Andy one, too. They sipped quietly, and she enjoyed the sharp anise flavor, but not, as it turned out, the tingle of the alcohol. Their two little glasses, half full, sat side by side on the table, and Frank said, "I miss the kids."

He said this naturally, as if he had said it before, but he never had, at least to her. Andy almost said, "What kids?" but then she said, "Do you mean 'miss,' or 'missed'?"

Frank looked at her, and then at the two little glasses. He said, "What's the difference?"

There was a long silence, not uncongenial. If there was anything Andy knew, it was not to push something. Finally, Frank said, "I know that was a nightmare with Arthur, but I enjoyed getting to know—"

"Charlie."

"He's a little like Richie."

No, thought Andy.

"Like Richie might have been," he added.

Without us, thought Andy.

"Without Michael," said Frank.

In the morning, they found their car and driver. The day was blustery and the sky gray. The landscape was steeper and more intimidating than they had seen before, and it put Andy in a dark mood—not sour, not irritable, but strangely Nordic (and that thought made her laugh). There were switchbacks and precipices, and it took half an hour to get to the town, which, at least today, did not seem like a sunny Mediterranean Greek town, even though the buildings were pleasantly white with tile roofs. Once at the shrine, they got out, left the driver, and started walking.

The Temple was built on a slope facing down a valley that ran between steep, dark, upthrusting mountains. A brochure they'd gotten said that the Greeks believed this was the navel of the world, and Andy could understand that. She did have the sense that everything else she had ever seen was peripheral to this spot, these ruins, this view. Here, the brochure said, the Earth goddess, Gaia, lived. As so often happens, a self-confident newcomer, a muscular, aspiring young man, made his way straight to this spot, and he killed the son of the goddess, possibly out of revenge, possibly just to demonstrate that a new world had come to pass. His name was Apollo, but it could have been anything, and once he had done the deed, he laid claim to the most central and the most intimidating location, the one most difficult to get to, the one with the greatest view. He then installed an old woman, not so different from Andy herself. The woman sat on her three-legged stool, inhaled the gases, and said her piece, and her words were taken as prophecy. For her efforts, she got to remain in this spot, to be cared for, to forget all the rest of the world. She also, Andy thought, came to perceive herself, every day, as smaller and smaller, a black hole at the center of the universe, a dot in time where time stood still.

They walked around the theater and the stadium and looked through the museum. She touched blocks of stone and rough standing columns with her finger and appreciated that the Greeks allowed weeds and wildflowers to grow in every crevice, to give life to every vista. She stood quietly and felt the breeze, took off her sweater and let the particular Delphic sunlight brighten her arms. She thought of everyone in order—her father and mother and Sven ("Hyperboreans," according to Frank's book), then Frank, Joe, Lillian, Henry, Claire, Janet, Richie, Michael, Jared, Ivy, Loretta, Emily and Jonah, Leo, Chance, Tia, and Binky. She laid each thought of them upon the stones of the spot where the oracle was said to have been. She knew that the oracle had not prophesied only good fortune: many supplicants had been told of doom and despair, and as she breathed each name, Andy accepted that. But she suspected that the seer, in speaking, had always prophesied something meaningful—something that struck those who sought her, that stayed with them, that gave them, if not hope, then corporeality, the extra intensity of watching their own feet stepping away from the oracle, their own eyes gazing across the stadium, their own hands reaching up to push back their hair, which was tangling in the wind. Death might be worth that. Frank came up behind her and put his arm around her waist.

1994

THE FIRST TIME Ivy and Loretta had stopped speaking was the year before, when Ivy, Richie, and Leo were at Michael and Loretta's place. The food was on their plates, Ivy was helping Leo with his fork, Chance was kicking Richie under the table (thinking, Richie knew, that he was kicking Tia), and Loretta said, with just a twitch of the eyebrows in Richie's direction, "Can you believe that they kept the planes circling over LAX so that Bill Clinton could have a Beverly Hills haircut?" She tossed her head back and laughed what Richie considered a fake laugh, and Michael said, "He is ruthless. He'll do anything."

Ivy said, "No, I don't believe it," and there was nothing in her voice—she was preoccupied with Leo for the moment.

What she didn't know was that Loretta had already taken Richie aside about "the health-care mess" in the kitchen, when all he was doing was having a look at the pork tenderloin she was making, and informed him that she considered his work on health care to be a bona-fide un-American activity. In his best I-am-your-congressman-and-am-happy-to-listen-to-your-views, he had said, "Why is that, Loretta?"

"If I want to move to Europe and wait in line to have my heart attack attended to, I will, but right now, right here, I want actual good health care."

"Well, you can afford it," said Richie.

"And why is that?" said Loretta.

And Richie did not say, Because your great-grandfather showed up in the right place and the right time and bought good land, well-located land, cheap from the Mexicans, who, by the way, had to vacate. He said, "I don't know." Just so he might hear what she had to say.

"Because Michael is an innovator and a thinker. He's made his way by being smart and ahead of the game. Who realized that stocks were finished and bonds were the way to go? Michael. Who now has his own trading operation when no one had the balls to try it before? Michael."

Richie had known that Michael was casting about for something riskier to do, but he hadn't known the result. He filed away this bit of information, but he said, "So everyone else should suffer and die?"

"Don't be so aggressive," said Loretta, stirring the polenta. "It's not becoming."

And Richie backed down, the way Congressman Scheuer advised him to do, saying, "Now, this is how you do it: you listen, you nod, you maintain your focus, and you recognize that many of your colleagues are crazy or dumb. You are the tortoise, you are the bulldog. You keep holding on and you will win, but don't go at them. That way, you kill yourself in the end." Of course, Congressman Scheuer had also advised him to get himself onto the committee that was working on health care, a "can't lose" way to start his political career, and he had said that campaigns were wild and sometimes vicious but that after the election everyone accepted that those who won, won, and they got down to business. It had taken Richie two months to realize that those were the old days, the old days of 1990, and those days were already gone.

And so they started eating, and then Ivy said, "That item of bullshit was made up by Bill Kristol and parroted by the L.A. *Times,* same as Travelgate, same as the idea that Hillary is simultaneously a controlling superhuman bitch and an incompetent hag," and it was her tone, mocking and self-confident, that propelled Loretta from her chair into her bedroom, while Tia said, "What's wrong with Mom?" and Ivy said, "What's going on?"

Michael said, "She hates the Clintons. We were at a party last week and someone said she thought they were a breath of fresh air in Washington at last, and Loretta threw a bowl of chips in the woman's face."

After that, no invitations or phone calls for two weeks; then the two women had lunch and agreed not to talk politics.

The second time they stopped speaking came in the summer, around the death of Vince Foster, a decent guy who had come with the Clintons from Arkansas and had not been able to handle politics in Washington—and how could he? Richie thought. Loretta went straight from the discovery of the body to convicting the Clintons of murder in less than a day, and in fact told Ivy that her mother, in California, had proof that hired goons from New York City had done it, people so experienced in getting rid of potential truth-tellers that they had murdered hundreds of law-abiding Republicans over the years. Ivy laughed so hard that Loretta hung up on her, and that silence lasted a month.

Richie found the death of Vince Foster, whatever the circumstances, uniquely eerie because he had been driving through McLean the evening before the body was discovered. He had gone out of his way to drive past Uncle Arthur and Aunt Lillian's old place, noticed that it was repainted and updated, and then started thinking about what Uncle Arthur might know about various things, and then he started wondering about his dad and Uncle Arthur, what sort of friends they had always been, and what did they know about one another that they would never reveal. The whole idea made him feel a little dizzy, so he pulled to the side of the road for a few minutes, admittedly not *at* Fort Marcy Park, where the body was found the next day, but near there—he would not have been an eyewitness to anything—but when the discovery of the body appeared in the papers, he found himself confusing the two mysteries and deciding that, no matter what, he would never live in McLean.

When Richie brought this up with his mom, she had said, "Your uncle Arthur is a tragic figure, but your father is not," in her usual distracted voice. Was that Andy's way of not taking sides? He knew that she considered him a tattletale, always had as long as he could remember, but he considered himself a genuinely confused person. The same thing was true in Congress—he was genuinely confused. It was not like the old days in Brooklyn, talking to this person and that person about the congressman and his associates and enemies; in New York, everyone had been blunt about their motives. In Washington, he had discovered, you never knew. There was one senator, and a famous one, who kept on his staff a certain chatty young woman who was from a certain state. Whenever the senator needed help from the equally famous but very different senator from that other state, he would send the young woman to "gossip him down," which meant that she would get him in a good mood by talking about all of their mutual acquaintances, and not leave until she got a promise that he would help her boss on something or other. The entire building, all the buildings, the Capitol and the office buildings, buzzed with hidden agendas, and it took years to learn all the languages that were spoken. Some congressmen hated to be interrupted, for example—they saw it as a sign of disrespect. Others expected to be interrupted—if you didn't interrupt, you weren't paying attention (Congressman Scheuer had been like this). For just these reasons, Riley Calhoun was not a good staffer. She would argue vehemently about the greenhouse effect even with those who agreed with her—no one was ever as worried about the greenhouse effect as they should be (though now Riley said he was to call it "global warming"). Was insistence a Wisconsin trait? But Riley was a dynamite researcher, so Richie more or less paid her a legislative assistant's salary to keep quiet and keep investigating. He also got himself on the Energy and Commerce Committee, and for that he had to thank her, since his real first choice had been Foreign Affairs, and if he were on that committee, he would have to have an opinion about Bosnia and Serbia right now. He was glad that he didn't have to take responsibility for anything other than funding solar initiatives and counteracting the greenhouse effect.

His office had been running smoothly for almost a year. His "spokesmodel," as she called herself, or "communications director," named Geneva Nicoletti, was from Greenwich Village but dressed like she was from Cleveland, always wore a belt that showed off her narrow waist, and never stopped smiling. Richie liked both Riley and Geneva. They were in their twenties and seemed to accept the strange idea that he knew what he was talking about. Two people that he suspected knew that he did not know what he was talking about were Marion, his chief of staff, who had worked for Congressman Scheuer, and Lucille, his scheduler, who had been the congressman's scheduler.

She was black. She owned a house in D.C., and liked working for congressmen, though she'd been disappointed to move from Rayburn, where the congressman had his office ("I am the congressman!" thought Richie, every time Lucille referred to Congressman Scheuer as "the congressman") to Cannon, much tighter quarters. Richie expected Lucille to take immediate advantage of the next congressional heart attack if that congressman happened to have an office in Rayburn. Italian, black, Native American, Hispanic (Marion's assistant's parents were from Cuba)—Richie privately thought of his staff as a Rainbow Coalition that legitimized his election every single day.

He had also found that he didn't mind staying in Washington during the week and coming home on weekends. His apartment in Washington was a one-bedroom in the basement of a townhouse, with a futon, a TV, and a toaster oven, within biking distance of the Capitol building, and not only did he enjoy biking, but he wore a helmet and encouraged photographers from newspapers to take pictures of him standing beside his trusty Dahon. He was not, at forty-one, the youngest congressman, but he didn't mind looking like he was. The apartment was bracingly basic, and the more basic it stayed, the more he didn't have to share it with anyone or invite anyone over.

Another reason he didn't mind staying in Washington and going back and forth on the train was that Ivy was ready to try for another, which was fine in theory, but Leo was ill-tempered, fast, strong, and dictatorial. Ivy said it was the Terrible Twos just lingering a little, even though a book she herself had edited about child-rearing techniques said that three (he was three years, seven months, now) was supposed to be an oasis of calm between two and four. Leo was how Richie remembered Michael being when they were children, and when the thought occurred to him that maybe Michael had, indeed, tried the pregnancy experiment some night when he was in Washington and Loretta was in California, it was so debilitating that he had to force it out of his mind. Leo was better with Allie than he was with either of his parents—she had a way of standing quietly when Leo was misbehaving, as if he had turned her to stone and he had to become good to give her life again. Richie had tried this himself, but Leo's nervous system shot bolts of lightning into his own, and any quietness he managed felt and looked fake. As for running in the park, Leo still liked to do that—but he was better with Charlie, who sometimes came and walked with them (or circled them, running), than he was with Richie.

The reason Ivy and Loretta were not speaking for the third time in just over a year had nothing to do with the Clintons or the Serbs. The last time they had traveled to Eighty-fourth Street for dinner (and, yes, Ivy was already in a bad mood), Binky, who was sitting beside Leo in the highchair, held out her hand for the Barbie (her Barbie) that Leo had brought to the table. Binky said, "Please, Leo? Barbie doesn't eat with us." Leo had seemed to be giving her the Barbie, and so she had grasped it, but Leo had not been giving her the Barbie—when he pulled his hand away, it seemed to him that Binky was grabbing it, and he shouted "No!" at the top of his lungs, and then began pounding on the tray of his highchair and screaming "No! No! No!," his face turning red and his whole body contorted with rage.

It was Chance who calmed him down, by getting out of his seat and jumping around, making faces. The chicken stew was delicious, and it seemed as though everyone was going to forget about it, but then Loretta handed Ivy a child-raising book that promoted beating the child until he finally submitted to the proper authority for his own good, and as soon as Ivy saw what book it was, it was Ivy who said "Never again." Never again dinner at Michael and Loretta's, or even on the Upper East Side, never again Christmas. (She was Jewish! Didn't they realize that this Christmas crap was offensive to her? She didn't even know what day Christmas was!) She had afforded Loretta the benefit of the doubt for fifteen years now, and if she ever heard the words "Ronald Reagan" again, she would not be responsible for her actions. All in all, the chaos in Washington wasn't as difficult as the chaos in Brooklyn—the moratorium on even mentioning Loretta's name was only nine days old at this point, but since Ivy had been the one to make the first move the previous two times, Richie did not think this was going to end quickly.

FRANK ACTED ON impulse more often now that he had no career to focus on, but even Andy didn't see how he could resist this opportunity. Their trip to Greece had been such a success that it had given him a renewed taste for flying. He'd sat in the copilot's seat between Athens and Crete and between Olympia and Athens, and decided that, yes, the best view was always up front. He didn't want to buy another plane—the thought was so bittersweet and seductive that he made himself contemplate it as long as it took to recoil from it once again—expense, inconvenience—but he did contemplate it every few days.

And then Jim Upjohn, who, even though he never left the cranberry farm in South Jersey, seemed completely up-to-the-minute about everything, called and said a cousin of his, Jack Upjohn, maybe forty, who had an old twin-engine four-seater, was heading for the West Coast, where he lived, which was why Frank had never met him, but he was making several stops. Frank needed to get out, said Jim—he should go along for at least part of the way. One of the stops was Pittsburgh, one Chicago, one Ames, one Denver. Andy could go on ahead to Palo Alto, and Frank could join her. He was eager to see Janet and Jonah, and Emily and Jared, too, for that matter—Andy didn't need to laugh behind her hand at him, he was willing to admit that mistakes had been made, should be unmade. Frank would join her; they would stay for a week at the Stanford Inn and fly back together.

In Pittsburgh, he whiled away his time at the Carnegie Museum of Art, beguiled that you could find such enjoyment in a place you had never thought of before. In Chicago, he stayed with Henry and Claire—or mostly Henry, since after breakfast Claire went to her boyfriend's place for the weekend. Frank and Henry walked along the lake; Henry seemed a little lonely, and talked primarily about some Welsh guy he was resurrecting, only a little about how Frank seemed relaxed, happy, not quite himself. Jack was delayed in his meeting, so they didn't get away until after dinner, but they were only going to Ames, which wasn't much more than an hour's flight even in an old twin-engine.

They left out of Midway. Spying on planes parked in the field or those he could see in the hangars helped Frank give up his fantasy—it was rather like trading in the Mercedes for a Bentley; why would you, but how could you not? In some places these days, if you showed up in a Mercedes, they made you park in the servants' lot.

After they put their headsets on and took off, Jack started talking about how being in the Midwest reminded him of a side trip he'd made with his wife to a place called "The House on the Rock," in southern

Wisconsin. Before he bought the plane, they had been driving from Madison to Minneapolis, where she was from, and decided to go past Taliesin, the place Wright had built near where his uncles lived, and where he had grown up. No getting into Taliesin, but then there was this parking lot full of cars, and a sign that said "The House on the Rock," so they stopped. Craziest house you ever saw—perched on a two-hundred-foot-tall monolith, built in the supposedly Japanese style, and so full of junk and crap . . .

They were now out of Chicago, and this was the part Frank loved about a light plane: you flew fairly low. The earth rolled and bobbled beneath you; that you could see everything so clearly and yet pass over it so smoothly was a great gift to the senses. They were coming up on the river now, marking that line between Illinois and Iowa that Frank knew so well from every map he had ever seen but always found strange when he flew over it, as if a map had been given reality. The Mississippi was clear and attractive around here, almost blue. And then, past the greenery of the riverbanks and onward across the fields of corn—yes, he would talk to Jesse about the corn harvest and the bean harvest, but the rains were pretty good this year, not like the flooding the year before. Frank had sent Jesse a check for fifty grand in February; did Joe know about it? Frank was a realist about the farm: some years it paid for itself and some years it didn't, and that was not Jesse's fault, but Joe might be uncomfortable. . . .

The storm cell appeared off to the northwest, as they were passing Cedar Rapids, at first an isolated fuzziness in the dusk—there were even stars to the west and southwest. It seemed unaccompanied by any associated cells, but they couldn't really see—even Frank, whose eyes were if anything sharper now than they had been, couldn't make out the edges or the shape of the cell. Jack said, "There could be more behind it; it's hot here, and the line of storms usually runs northwest to southeast, especially across the plains." He radioed Cedar Rapids. The tower there said they didn't have much on the radar. They flew on, Jack changing course a little to the south.

When the cell hit, the plane jumped like a cat, up and to the side, and Jack leaned back, his hands tight on the yoke, which was quivering. He pressed down on the right rudder pedal to correct the yaw, which had been caused by the sudden turbulence. Night had come. Frank said, "How far are we from Ames?"

"About sixty miles is my guess."

They would be over Tama, then. Forty miles southeast of the farm, where, he imagined, Jesse was glancing out the window, counting the seconds between flashes of lightning and the subsequent booms of thunder. He noticed that it was too dark to see much, and suddenly water was flowing horizontally over the windshield. He said, "I don't remember there being a control tower or anything like that in Ames. You want to head to Des Moines?"

"That could be worse. Maybe this is just an isolated cell."

Frank nodded. He wasn't worried: he was so used to being in an airplane after all these years that he was still perfectly comfortable. He said, "The first time Jim ever took me up, he said he loved planes because a house was like a tomb and a plane was like a passing thought." That wasn't exactly what he'd said. Frank elaborated, "In a plane you could vanish."

"That sounds like him. My grandfather is fourteen years younger than him. All the brothers would do this when his name came up at parties"—he spun his finger around his ear—"but they loved him."

"He's a charming man," said Frank. "You look a little like him when he was your age."

"That's a compliment."

Turbulence buffeted the plane again, a harder smack this time, and the nose dipped. Jack leaned way back, gripping the yoke, and then turned it to counteract the roll. Above the whine of the engine, Frank could hear the thunder, the claps getting closer together. Outside the window, lightning strikes had devolved into a steady flare. He wanted to say some idle thing about the strangeness of the weather, something that would reassure both Jack and himself, but the noise was too loud now. The plane rocked again. In the glaring light, Jack began to look worried, then laughed. He had hundreds of hours of flight experience, but, Frank thought, glancing at his profile, maybe not this exact experience.

The next thing that happened was that lights on the ground appeared in the windshield and then disappeared again as Jack corrected the pitch of the plane.

"There it is," said Jack, his voice steady.

Below and in front of them, the Ames airport, such as it was, stretched wetly to the northwest, dark, narrow, and short, a few trees to either side, but no tower, only two parallel rows of dim runway lights, nothing welcoming. Now the plane was rocking and rolling, or, as Janet might say about a horse, bucking.

Jack radioed the tower in Des Moines. Through crackling static, they said that the storm cell seemed to be right over Ames—where were they? Jack said, "Landing in Ames."

The voice said, "Good luck."

Frank kept his mouth shut and stared at the runway. He could sense Jack beside him, intent, holding tight to the yoke as the plane shifted and bobbed, as the approaching earth bounced and shivered. Frank shoved his feet forward and leaned back in his seat, as if he could counteract all of these forces with just his weight. They touched down, safe for a moment, but then the plane swerved and went skidding past the dark buildings out Frank's window, not seeming to slow down at all, reminding Frank that there were many ways to die in a plane crash, and nose-first was only one of them. But the turf at the end of the runway caught them, and the plane shuddered, halted. They sat quietly within the noise of the pounding rain for a long moment. Jack said only, "Oh, shit," as he cut the engines.

Frank said, "Jim will be proud when I tell him about this."

Frank could see that Jack's hand was trembling on the yoke. His own hand, which came up to wipe the moisture from his lips, was trembling, too. Jack took several deep breaths. Frank checked his watch. It was eight o'clock. They had left Chicago at six-fifty. Amazing how long those seventy minutes felt, thought Frank.

Then the storm seemed to let up, and it was true, there did not appear to be another behind it, or, at least, right behind it. Jack got out of his seat and unlatched the door. He said, "I told my contact that I would call him to pick us up. He can put you up, too. They live right in town."

"Did I mention that I went to college here?"

"Really?" Jack was struggling into his raincoat.

After near-death, practicalities.

Really, thought Frank. They were only a mile or so from where, at seventeen, he'd pitched his tent beside the Skunk River.

Jack said, "Be right back. We've got to figure out a way to get the plane off the runway—but we may be stuck in the mud." He disappeared. Frank stared out the window, watching as Jack, hunched over, ran toward the building where there probably was a pay phone. Then he decided to have a look around: the cabin was tight, and he needed to stand up straight and stretch his shoulders and hips. He had been tense. Yes, he was willing to admit that.

When he got to the bottom of the steps, he couldn't see much—it was still raining fairly steadily. The fields to the south and west were not quite flat, and sloped away to a dark mass—probably trees and bushes along a creek. Frank walked toward the edge of the runway to take a piss, thinking how utterly familiar the landscape was to him, not only how it looked, but also the scent of the rain and the dirt and the summer vegetation. He unzipped his fly.

IN PALO ALTO, Andy was in the kitchen when the phone rang, squatting before the open refrigerator. She was supposed to be getting some blueberries for Jonah, but, really, they were just staring into the lighted space, and Jonah was telling her the names of things he liked: "Duce, mik, buberries." He was a mild-mannered, systematic child. Andy pointed to the catsup and said, "Catsup?" Jonah had eaten a dab of catsup on his turkey burger that day for lunch. The phone screeched twice, and Andy went on the alert—she hadn't heard Janet's phone so clearly before. Then there was silence, and then she heard Janet say, "Oh my God in heaven! Oh!" Andy stood up, picked up Jonah, carefully closed the refrigerator door, and went into the dining room. She knew it was Frank. She had agreed to the plane idea, but she hadn't been happy about it—old plane, long trip, unknown pilot. It didn't help that she had watched *Sweet Dreams* the night before on TV, and thought of Frank the moment that plane hit the cliff. She said, "There's been a crash."

Janet whipped around and held out her arms for Jonah. This moment, when she handed Jonah over, was the last moment of her normal life, so Andy did it slowly, carefully, kissing Jonah on the cheek, as if she were kissing him goodbye. Had she kissed Frank goodbye? Or had she run to her gate at Newark, late as usual, just turning and waving? She couldn't remember.

Janet said, "Mom, he was struck by lightning."

Andy's first reaction was a quick, rueful laugh, just at the rightness of it. Janet turned away, and Andy felt the rest of her life entering her body, along her nerve endings. So many times she had thought Frank could die—in the war, in his plane, in his restless perambulations here and there—and then he hadn't, and now he had. She got dizzy; she placed the palms of both her hands against the wall and closed her eyes.

Andy agreed that they would have the funeral in Denby, that Frank would be buried next to his uncle Rolf, down the line from his mother and father, even though this meant that she would then be without him. Frank had never said whether he wanted to be cremated or interred, or where. When other people their age started talking about their burial plans (ashes tossed into the Atlantic, composted, marble slab, whatever), Frank always said nothing. Maybe, she thought, he really did think of himself as immortal, or maybe he just didn't care.

Andy flew into Des Moines, then rented a car. She drove straight to the funeral home, walked in, and had an immediate argument with the funeral-home director about whether, that very minute, she would be allowed to see the body. The director said that it was not a good idea, that she would be too strongly affected. He was about forty-five, smooth, and good-looking. Andy said, "I am not leaving until you show me the body."

He shook his head a little, but turned and walked toward the back of the room; she followed him through a door. Frank was lying on a triangular, tilted table, his head lower than his feet. He was naked, with a sheet over everything except his face. The funeral director stopped, expecting Andy to stop, too—wasn't this enough for her? But, no, it wasn't. She walked over and put her hand on Frank's forehead. It was icy cold. She pushed away the sheet. He was not disemboweled or anything, if she had been expecting that. He looked like a wax effigy of himself, except that a fan of red lines proliferated, a slender tree, from his hairline above his right cheek, down the side of his face and his neck, then along his shoulder, and down his abdomen. Andy knew that most people survived lightning strikes, sometimes more than one, but the red vine seemed to encompass his entire body, to claim him for another world. The Upjohn boy, whom she hadn't met before, said that he had heard the clap of thunder, seen the lightning, but not realized that anything had happened until he climbed back into the plane and saw that Frank was gone. He'd been looking out the windshield, and by the light of another flash, he saw Frank stretched out on the grass beyond the pavement of the runway. Why Frank had gone there, no one knew—there was nothing there but dirt. Andy ran her hand down the chilled corpse, head to toe, sensed with her fingers the fact that Frank was dead. She leaned over and kissed him. She thought, this is what a girl who grows up expecting Ragnarök, madness, freezing deaths on the prairie, who is not at all surprised by the Rwandan genocide, might consider a happy ending.

1995

〜⁓

WHEN JANET brought in the mail, she saw that there was a letter from a law firm in New York, and she knew that there was something in it about her father's estate. Her mother had been very vague about her father's death and all the surrounding questions; Janet found out more in his *New York Times* obituary than she did over the phone. She had, in fact, bought the *Times* that day, cut out the obituary, and put it in a drawer. Before opening the letter from the lawyer, she read it again:

FRANCIS LANGDON, PIONEERING DEFENSE CONTRACTOR,
DIES AT 74

Francis Howard Langdon, who was known among the group of secretive defense contractors who came of age during World War II for his willingness to explore ideas that some among his colleagues considered more in the realm of science fiction than of usable weaponry, died Tuesday in Ames, Iowa, where he had flown with a friend. Local officials say that he was struck by lightning while standing at the edge of the airfield.

Francis Langdon was a veteran of World War II, where he served in the European Theater as a sniper, a rare thing in those days. He fought in the North African Campaign in 1943, the Sicilian Campaign, and at the Battle of Anzio. He was a great admirer of General Jacob "Jake" Devers, Commander of the North African Theater of Operations, who, he sometimes said, "gave me my first experience of St.-Tropez." After the war, Mr. Langdon, who was born in Iowa to an English-German farm family and was bilingual, spent time in Ohio translating captured German technical documents for the U.S. government, then worked for Courtyard Oil. But his great love was for unorthodox weaponry, and he spent many years trying to develop a weapon known as the supercavitating underwater missile, to be used against submarines. It had a concave nose, shaped to create a vacuum in the water just in front of the missile, allowing the missile to speed up rather than slow down. Forward Weaponry, from which he retired in 1986, was located in Secaucus, New Jersey.

Francis Langdon was married to Hildegarde Andrea Bergstrom Langdon, who was for many years a prominent figure on the Manhattan social scene, known for her elegant style and her ethereal beauty.

U.S. Congressman Richard Langdon, Democrat, of Brooklyn's 9th district, is the son of Mr. and Mrs. Langdon. Francis Langdon is also survived by another son, Michael Langdon, a Wall Street entrepreneur known for innovations in computer trading, and by a daughter, Janet Langdon Nelson, of Palo Alto, California. Francis Langdon's funeral was held in Denby, Iowa, where he grew up, and where he was interred.

Janet hadn't known that her mother's given name was "Hildegarde," much less these generalities about her father's career. When she showed the obituary to Jared, his eye fell immediately upon the underwater missile, which he said might have worked, might still work, but they would never know—probably it had been mothballed when the Soviet Union collapsed; it was fascinating. He gave her a hug. And of course the lightning strike was amazing, but, try as she might to generate some sort of grief for her father, she could not. He had been imposing, absent, frightening, threatening, every day of her childhood. There was no evidence in her memory that he had ever liked her, or that he was capable of love (though he seemed to have grown fond of her mother in the last couple of years). Nor did she, given her political views, admire his life work. But probably, she thought now that she'd read all those books about child care and the infant mind, he had simply never bothered to bond with her; she was forty-four and she didn't care.

The envelope in her hand would be the payoff, her compensation for getting Frank as her father rather than, say, Uncle Arthur, whom she had adored when she was a child, or Papa Rudy, Jared's dad, who was kind and told truly funny jokes. She slipped her fingernail under the flap and ripped the envelope open. Judging by everything Janet knew about her parents, her legacy could be sizable—she and Jared had already skirted the issue of paying off their house, or maybe looking for something on Kauai, or starting a trust fund for Emily and Jonah. She skimmed the letter, turned to the next page. Her father's will, it turned out, had been a simple one—the house to Mom, the farmland in Denby to Cousin Jesse, a hundred thousand dollars each, more or less, after taxes and fees, to Janet, Richie, and Michael. Janet turned the letter over in confusion. A hundred thousand dollars? Even Jared, from Minnesota, would be surprised that this constituted Frank's fortune. And nothing for her mom? What was she going to live on? She laid the letter on her desk, put the obituary back in the drawer, and looked at her watch. It was almost three, time to pick up Emily and take her to her dance class, which she was now taking twice a week to build her abdominal strength so that she could better sit the trot. Fiona considered this a good idea and wished she'd thought of the same thing years ago. The next step, said Fiona, was "a more competitive horse" (that was twenty-five or thirty thousand dollars right there), but Emily herself wasn't saying that yet—she loved Pesky and she loved Sunlight, and she thought a successful equestrian career was about friendship.

Janet rummaged around on the kitchen counter for her car keys and went into Jonah's room. Jonah was sitting cross-legged on the floor, doing his sixty-piece fish puzzle, which he preferred to the dinosaur puzzle. He didn't look up. He picked up a piece, touched it gently to his lower lip, positioned it, tapped it with his fingertip, and picked up another one. There was no mystery to the puzzle any longer, just some sort of pleasure that Janet didn't quite understand. He also liked to lay out playing cards, plain old playing cards, in patterns. Jared remembered doing the same thing. She said, "Ready, Jonie-boy? Time to go in the car and pick up Emmy."

He sighed, stood up. Although she had raised him perfectly and he was always cooperative, he was a strange boy. It was as though every solved set of parental difficulties revealed a whole landscape of unimagined difficulties beyond, a set of syndromes or conditions that could be active or could be incipient, or might not even exist. It was easier, Janet thought, just to think that they were bad or good, obedient or disobedient. She gave Jonah a hug when she lifted him into his car seat, and all the way to Emily's school she could not help glancing in the rearview mirror at red lights, just so that she could wonder why he was so quiet.

RICHIE KNEW what was in the letter before the letter arrived, because Michael had called him in a rage to tell him that the hoped-for millions were not going to materialize—they had probably been left to that little shit, Jesse.

"What did the letter say?" said Richie.

"A hundred fucking grand," said Michael.

"What do you care?"

Richie expected him to say something about losses—there had been a rash of losses in the big banks, including Michael's bank, articles in the *WSJ,* the *FT,* and the *Times,* and discussions in the Financial Services Committee—but Michael said, "It's the principle of the thing. Loretta is spitting mad."

Richie set the phone down on his desk and laughed for a second. When he picked it back up, Michael was still talking, hadn't even realized that he had lost Richie's absolute attention. "Her folks spent a pile refurbing the kitchen at the ranch, and they had to install ground-fault-indicator receptacles, and when they got into the walls to fix some of the wiring, they saw that rats had eaten the insulation every fucking where, it was all just bare wires waiting to burn the place down. . . ." Richie put the phone down again, and picked it up again as Michael was saying, "Five hundred grand, and she said she would cover it because she . . ." He put the phone down again, then disconnected.

When he called Michael back after looking in the mail (nothing at that point), he said, "Sorry. Don't know what happened. Anyway, Dad didn't have all the money. Mom did."

Michael said, "What?"

"Dad had his salary and his pension. That's all he ever had. Mom is worth, like, four million, maybe more."

"Because?" said Michael.

"Because she got an inheritance after the war sometime, from a dead relative who hated everyone in his family, and he said that his money would be kept in a trust until everyone then alive died, including the babies. I don't know how much she got, maybe ten grand or something like that. She did the investing. Well, Dad advised her. But I think when he bought out Uncle Henry's and Aunt Claire's shares of the farm, in '76, that was the last time he had lots of money to invest. I think so. How should I really know? I'm telling you what Mom told me three or four years ago." Then, "So—a hundred grand?"

He and Ivy could get themselves a bigger co-op, still in the district, but maybe facing the park. A hundred grand was a nice sum. And Ivy would appreciate it. Ivy hadn't been terribly appreciative lately—brusque and busy. She was an executive vice-president now, and constant reading and editing had been replaced, she said, by constant meetings about other people's books. She was getting a good paycheck, and there was no one in publishing who didn't want to succeed, but authors were, in their idiosyncratic (she put it politely but affectionately) way, more fun than colleagues, and especially more fun than publishers, who worried all the time. Was she in line to become a publisher? If so, was that good? Was that bad? And if so, more important, how could she refuse? When she started talking like this, she would stare at Leo, Richie saw, wondering if she could betray him by leaving him an only child. About this, Richie, himself out of town from Monday morning to Friday evening, said nothing. The geography of their success seemed to be stretching the threads that connected them to spiderweb thinness. Almost always, while he was eating his crab bisque in the bar at the Hay-Adams, he thought of Ivy reaching for a stuffed mushroom at a fund-raiser at the Met or in Astor Hall at the New York Public Library, and Leo in Brooklyn, eating macaroni and cheese with Allie, and he wondered, how could you be related if you didn't relate? He comforted himself with the idea of Michael and Loretta and their many kids, screaming at each other on the Upper East Side, but the idea wasn't all that comforting. Ivy, who still said she would never go there, thought that they were officially crazy and that they were driving their kids officially crazy, and that it was a good thing that Loretta sent Chance and Binky and Tia to California every summer vacation and every Christmas vacation to hone their cattle-roping skills.

And then people would come by, because they saw his bike outside the door of the hotel, which meant he was inside, and they chatted with him, and he chatted with them—yes, the Republicans had taken over both houses of Congress, but Richie had beaten Kevin Moore's successor candidate by eight percentage points. Fewer Democrats in Congress meant that those who were left had more gravity; Richie was no longer a hydrogen atom, more like an oxygen atom, someone to be sought out and won over. A life alongside Michael had given him a trustworthy quality—he looked like a guy who had survived many beatings. Anyway, he would sit and smile and chat. A colleague or two would wander in, offer, ask, confer, complain, shake heads, nod, pat him on the shoulder, smile again, and he would feel the pleasure of forgetting, just for the moment, Ivy and Leo.

JESSE MISSED Uncle Frank, and not because of the money, at least not this year. And he loved Uncle Frank, and not because of the bequest. Jesse had decided years before not to worry about who owned the farm. Chances were, in farm country, that the guy who farmed the farm did not own it, might never own it—the bank owned it in all but name. It might be that Jesse "owned" the farm now, but he thought of it as something he and his dad shared. Jesse missed Uncle Frank because Uncle Frank had been the most informative person Jesse had ever met, and Jesse loved information. When Aunt Minnie got the fax of Uncle Frank's *New York Times* obituary right after the funeral in the summer, everyone had read it, everyone had said, "Oh, I didn't know . . ." But Jesse did know, and he had a stack of letters to prove it. In that stack was the one about the supercavitating *torpedo*, not "missile." Uncle Frank had come very close to not renewing its funding—it was expensive and going nowhere. But, as he had said in the letter, you could not decide what, in the end, might win a war, so you had to hedge your bets and put money into everything. The Russians in World War II had been a never-ending, apparently invulnerable stream, each one dying only to be replaced by two more. It might be that everyone back in the States saw victory as inevitable, a sure bet, and that if, in England, they were not so sure, they remained quiet about their doubts, but Uncle Frank had always seen it as a close thing—atom bomb versus V-2 rocket, Russian army versus German technology, Mountbatten sacrificing a battalion at Dieppe in order to see whether Normandy might work better. Why had the Germans focused their defenses on Calais rather than Dunkirk? That was a mystery Uncle Frank had always thought significant, but that no one talked about. How many other letters did Jesse have? A hundred? All of them were handwritten, all of them informative, all of them friendly. When he wrote Uncle Frank that he was going to marry Jennifer Guthrie, he got the whole story of the mousetrap by return mail—how those bullies at school made life a living hell not only for Uncle Frank, who was six, but even for Jennifer's grandpa Donald, who'd been nine—once, they'd ambushed him on the way home and stolen his shoes, then thrown them in a ditch filled with rainwater. He'd had to wear them anyway, since in those days you ordered shoes by catalogue and only got one pair per year. And it wasn't a mouse-trap, it was a rat trap; Uncle Frank had noticed the blood both on Bobby Dugan's fingers and on his lips, because he'd put his fingers in his mouth. Always bullies, those Dugans. "My first and possibly greatest achievement," he'd written.

Jesse had seen Uncle Frank maybe a dozen times over the years, and they never talked much. And he had listened to the gossip about Uncle Frank, especially since the funeral—a naughty boy and a harum-scarum kid; Aunt Andy was crazy; and what about those twins? He knew that his own dad had forgiven Uncle Frank over and over, but those letters sat in a tin box in the glass-front cabinet beside the fireplace in the house, and they said something that Jesse would never deny—that Uncle Frank was the smartest guy he'd ever known. He said nothing to his dad about it, and nothing to his mom, who regretted that Uncle Frank hadn't been saved before he died, but maybe there was hope for Aunt Andy. As for Minnie, he caught her crying in the barn a week after the funeral, her face all puffy, and she'd said, "Oh, heavens me, I thought I'd cried all the tears I was ever going to cry over Frank Langdon, and here I am!"

Jesse sat next to her and then put his arm around her, and she leaned against him and sobbed again (this was something he hadn't told anyone). He said, "I always wanted to be like him."

"I can't imagine in what way," said Minnie, maybe to herself, but he couldn't explain without showing her the letters, and he couldn't show her the letters without worrying that talk would begin about them and then someone would want to read them, and then they wouldn't be his any longer.

Jesse sometimes drove past the graveyard; it was small, around to the side of the abandoned church, all grassed over. Most of the graves were old and the inscriptions on the headstones were flaking away—even Grandma Rosanna's was hardly legible anymore. Uncle Frank's looked almost mirrorlike in its brilliance by comparison (Jesse had overseen the installation). What flowers there were, were artificial, lying here and there. But Jesse appreciated that, too, that Uncle Frank had come back to them, that in death he wasn't too good for them, that his uncle was, in some way, his possession now, rather than Richie's or Michael's. All of this he kept to himself as he tested the moisture in the soil and the moisture in the seed, as he planned his rotation, as he went to the bank and the seed company, when they went to church, when he ate a pancake or two with the guys in the Denby Café, listening to his dad and Russ Pinckard recall that fertilizer salesman coming through town—was that right after the war?—and before anyone said a word about it, the salesman jumped out ahead of them and went on about how sorry the company was that that ship carrying ammonium nitrate, the very thing he wanted them to put on their fields, had blown up in the harbor—where was that, Houston? Some hundred people were killed, and the ocean literally boiled. How could anyone be surprised by a fertilizer bomb? said his dad. It was an accident waiting to happen. No accident, said some of the others.

There was something about the letters organized by date in the box that gave him faith, not in Jesus, of course—that was a separate thing—but in thinking, organizing, staying rational, finding out. The world was full of terror and insanity, as this bombing in Oklahoma showed, but didn't those letters he had prove that sense could be made of the senseless, that the cause and effect of things would eventually be found? That was Uncle Frank's real legacy, not six hundred thousand dollars' worth of farmland.

TO LOOK AT Carl Leroy, you could not tell he was fifty-nine, nor, thought Claire cattily, could you tell that he had been married to Ruth, once her best friend, then her worst enemy, after that an item of her past that she never thought of. Now that Carl was her boyfriend, she thought of Ruth fairly often, because Ruth wrote Carl letters demanding that he insist that their twenty-year-old daughter, Angie, call her or write her or visit her. Angie went to Beloit, which was a hundred miles from where Carl lived in Winnetka, but Ruth seemed to imagine that it was down the street, and that Angie's relative distance from Winnetka compared with her distance from Des Moines was a calculated slap in the face, a choice of the parent who had left her over the parent who had raised her. Carl had moved from Des Moines to Winnetka when Angie was six, about a year after Ruth and he separated and divorced—fourteen years ago. The result was that Claire and Carl seemed, even to themselves, to have just met, just gotten to know one another, just fallen in love. Those younger selves they vaguely remembered might have been anyone.

Angie was admitted to Beloit (not St. Olaf, not Grinnell, not Carleton, and so, therefore, she had gone to Beloit). It seemed simple to Carl, and simple to Claire, and simple to Angie, but it was not simple to Ruth. Even though Angie was a junior, and therefore had been attending Beloit for two years, the first letter of the semester had already arrived, informing Carl that Angie had been in school for four weeks, and Ruth had heard nothing from her. Carl wrote back, "Dear Ruth, Hope you are well. Neither have I. I'm sure she is busy, Yours truly, Carl."

There were several things Angie knew: she knew she was adopted; she knew she was mixed-race; she knew she was an only child; she knew she had a talent for languages and spoke French, Italian, and Spanish. There were several things Angie did not know: she did not know who her birth parents were, or where they were from; she did not know Russian (yet); and she did not know that her mother and her father's girlfriend had ever been friends, or even that Claire had once lived in Des Moines. Claire only said that mothers were very hard for daughters to understand; one of the nice things about sons was that they didn't even try. Even though Claire and Carl weren't married, she operated on the stepmother principle, which was that an intelligent stepmother never takes the bait, never criticizes, and, if there is something that the stepchild really really wants but her parents won't give her, then the stepmother gives it to her. Claire did not think Angie liked her, but she was always polite, which was enough.

But they *had* seen Angie, only because they had taken a rare weekend off from Claire's party business and gone to Lake Geneva. Sitting on the dock of the house they borrowed, eating breakfast, they saw a pontoon boat go by, eight kids laughing and yelling, and Angie among them. Claire's orange, which she was peeling, dropped right out of her hand into the water and sank. Carl hardly reacted, which was one of Carl's charms. He just moved his folding beach chair closer to the end of the dock and kept watching the boat. It circled around the lake, disappeared from sight, reappeared, finally docked at a house about a quarter-mile down the shore. Carl took note of which house it was (A-frame, main entrance flanked by two tall cedar trees), then got in his truck and drove down there. When he came back, Angie was with him, and so was the boyfriend, named Tyler. Tyler was seven inches taller than Angie and seemed to know her quite well. It was Saturday. Claire suggested they come for French toast, bacon, and scrambled eggs the next morning—all the kids should come. Tyler's eyes lit up—nothing like a good meal—and Angie didn't say no.

It did turn out that the parents were in Europe and didn't know the house was being put to use by the son, who they thought was safely ensconced in Beloit. Boys did outnumber the girls five to three, but the host boy, Tony, was twenty-three and had been driving the boat since he was sixteen. Liquor had abounded, but at 10:00 a.m. Sunday, everyone was awake, pink-cheeked, and hungry, no evidence of violent hangovers. Claire was in her element, serving these kids as if they were guests at one of her parties. (And a nice living it was—"Leave It to Claire!" said her flyers and ads in the *Trib*. "You should enjoy your own party, not be a slave to it! Contact Claire's Party Central for information! References supplied!") She served thirty slices of French toast and a pound and a half of bacon and ate a few bites herself—

probably the reason she was now doing parties was that there were many more things she wanted to cook and taste than she and Carl could eat on their own. Three of the boys followed Carl out behind the house to look at his antique Ford pick-up, a '47(!), painted grass green with a blue roof. Tony was glad when Carl offered to help him get the boat into the boathouse, hoisted out of the water, and winterized. Neither Claire nor Carl asked what Tony had planned to do if Carl hadn't shown up. Everyone, it seemed, was lucky, and Angie had bestowed a reluctant kiss upon Claire's cheek when they parted. Carl still said little, but all the way back to Winnetka, he was in a wonderful mood. Carl's wonderful moods were not all that different from his terrible moods—he was an even-tempered sort of fellow, the kind of guy who could open the basement door and see six feet of dirty water and not be daunted. She loved him. Yes, Ruth had found him stolid (she remembered that), and Henry said, "When's the last time he read a book?" and he could sit through supper on the farm without saying a word, not out of shyness but because he didn't have a word to say. Claire had never met anyone else like him. She thought he was the rarest of rare birds, and reached across the console to touch his cheek.

MINNIE AND LOIS'S ARGUMENT had started in the kitchen, but, with her usual determination, Lois had eased Minnie out the back door by pretending that she *had* to get some fennel from the garden, and now they were under the old lilac trees. The argument was not about any of their real differences, such as religion (Minnie had declared herself an "Indifferentist," and Lois had said, "That's not something you say in front of the children"), or travel (Lois had asked her in all seriousness why in the world she wanted to go to Athens—it was dirty and full of feral cats), or even about making a piecrust with shortening rather than lard (not possible, said Lois).

No one other than the two of them would have known they were having an argument. Lois continued to dig up the fennel bulbs and also to smile. Minnie was nodding at her sister, as if she agreed with her—that was an old habit. Lois said, "But you have to let them know early that they are on the wrong path. It's cruel not to."

"I don't think she is on the wrong path. She's just curious."

What Felicity had asked, at the supper table, was, what was that thing Perky had in his underwear? She had asked this in her usual matter-of-fact tone, and instead of someone saying, calmly, "It's called a penis" (and here was yet another reason why farmers should be raising animals, Minnie thought: much easier to talk about penises belonging to horses and cattle), Grandma Lois had gasped, Papa Jesse had barked a laugh, and Mama Jen had said, "Shhh. I'll tell you later." Is this the nineties, thought Minnie, or the thirties? With her customary seriousness, Felicity said, "Why?"

Minnie pushed. "Is curiosity the wrong path?" Then, "Really?"

"About some things, yes."

"Oh, for heaven's sake," exclaimed Minnie. "You can't possibly mean that."

"She's my only granddaughter. I want what is best for her." She stood up and stared at Minnie, her hands suddenly on her hips. "For everyone. For you, too."

"I know what is best for me."

"No," said Lois, but only in her facial expression, "you don't."

Minnie said nothing about Pastor Campbell or the Rapture or the Harvest Home Light of Day Church—she never did, though she was often tempted. She said, "She is almost seven years old. We knew what male sex organs were by the time we were three or four, and what they were used for, too. I remember watching Pa's ram mount one of the ewes, and Mama saying—"

"You think that was good? Nothing was sacred then. It was all dirt, everywhere. Makes me shudder to think about it—oh, tetanus; oh, mad-cow disease; oh, swine flu."

"Oh, walking into the street and getting hit by a car!" said Minnie. "How does this relate to Felicity wondering about the difference between herself and her brother?"

"She is exactly the sort of person who eventually goes too far."

"Like everyone else we know, Lois. If they're lucky." Like you, thought Minnie, but again kept it to herself.

Lois pursed her lips, and Minnie leaned toward her, put her hand on her sister's shoulder, and kissed her on the cheek. Lois would not be convinced, since she could not be convinced of anything, but Minnie thought that she would drop the subject long enough to find that book they had censored at the Usherton Library, *A Kid's First Book*

About Sex, ages five and up. She might have to go to Des Moines to get it, but, Minnie thought, she was glad to be reminded of it. It was perfect for Felicity.

RICHIE HADN'T MET the broker before, but their Realtor was taken ill, so, at the last minute, the broker agreed to show them the listing. The property was on Prospect Park West—the whole building, four floors including a basement apartment they might rent out. It was three and a half blocks from where they lived already, four blocks from the boundary between his district and the next one. It had come on the market Thursday, and the broker expected it to sell before Tuesday. They had given Leo his breakfast, thrown on their winter coats, and run most of the way in the sleet, but that was good, because it got Leo a little tired, tired enough so that Richie or Ivy could, between them, jiggle him into silence for the half hour it took to look over the place.

The broker was, like all brokers, full of smiles and information, and very glad to meet Congressman Langdon in person—sometime they would have to talk! He opened doors with a flourish, invited them to peek into closets, knew the names of all the varieties of wood that made up the woodwork in this incredibly woody house. With its bay windows and its original parquet floors and its many moldings, the place was the opposite of Richie's mom's house in Jersey; living here would throw him back fifty years, immerse him in every single thing that Frank Lloyd Wright had detested. That was a point in its favor, Richie thought. Two and a half baths, not counting the basement apartment; a doctor's office on one side, a couple on the other side with a child a year or so older than Leo. No one had to tell Richie it was perfect; they hadn't seen any other place in four months of house hunting that they hadn't had to talk themselves into. Until now. Until, standing in the kitchen wondering if she could replace the twenty-year-old Maytag gas range with a Wolf, Ivy put her hands over her face and said something that sounded suspiciously like "I can't do it."

Leo was pulling on one of the cabinet doors. He had a speculative look. He let it go, and it slammed.

Richie stepped toward Ivy, gently removed her hands, kept holding them, and said, "You can't do what?" Behind her, he could see the shadow of the real-estate broker on the herringbone floor of the hallway.

Leo opened the door again, squatted, peered into the cabinet.

Ivy looked up at him, her dark hair, now flecked with gray, bouncing, the tendons of her throat quivering. "I can't go on with this."

"We don't have to buy a house. This is a big undertaking. We'd have to replace the—"

This time, Leo gave the cabinet door a little push—bang! Leo laughed.

"I've been having an—"

With smooth congressional tact, Richie put his hand on her shoulder and turned her toward a dark back room—a family room, it looked like—but she said it out loud anyway: "—affair with—"

Richie propelled her a little harder, and she stumbled over the threshold. He glanced back, not quite sure what to do with Leo, but Leo seemed reasonably well occupied. He had moved on to the lazy-Susan corner cabinet. Richie called back to him, "Don't catch your finger."

The family room was carpeted and had drapes, and thus darkened and muffled what Ivy had to say: the affair was with a lawyer, he was in his fifties, he and his wife had been divorced for seven years, his two kids were in college, he had given up on love and sex, and now he'd met Ivy.

"How long?" said Richie.

"A year," said Ivy. "I don't dislike you." Then, "But I knew when you started talking about a new place that it was only a matter of time. I'm sorry I left it this long."

"Where does he live?"

"The house is in New Rochelle, but he stays mostly in his place on Riverside Drive and Seventy-ninth."

Richie tried to imagine Ivy in New Rochelle. A guy he knew lived in a brick Georgian palace up there with a grand foyer, circular staircase, formal garden, portico, elaborate crown moldings. He didn't think Ivy's parents would even enter such a place. Then he said, "Bob Newton?"

"Do you know him?" said Ivy.

Richie blew out some air.

"He never said he knew you."

Bob Newton was a slender, dark guy with a predatory look, beak and all. He was worth millions, certainly did not subscribe to *The Nation*. Richie wondered what Ivy's parents would say. Richie leaned backward so that he could see Leo, who had moved on to the refrigerator. He was standing with the freezer door open, staring into the interior.

Ivy said, "He's an avid reader. He's read all of Trollope. He belongs to some club." Then, a little embarrassed, she said, "Can we talk about this later?"

"Of course," said Richie, and that was that. They thanked the broker, who was as smooth and friendly as he had been an hour before, as if he had heard nothing. They said goodbye, and helped Leo down the outside steps, agreeing as they did so that maybe that house had too many steps for an active six-year-old. On either side of Leo, each holding a hand, they walked to the corner of Eighth and turned left. Ivy said, "The sleet seems to have stopped completely."

Richie said, "It's not really that cold." He glanced at her from time to time. It was true that a woman who would carry on with Bob Newton for a year couldn't possibly be interested in him. They were like worlds that did not, could not overlap, could only intersect at the point where Bob was giving him some campaign financing.

By the time the item appeared on Page Six, "Congressman's Marital Ship on the Rocks," Richie didn't even care anymore—better, at least in New York, to nod, shrug, say, "It happens. The most important thing is Leo." A congressman didn't have to defend the institution of marriage; that was entirely up to the president.

1996

◡◠

THE ONLY DIFFERENCE Henry could perceive between his former self and his present self was that he could not stand the cold anymore. A week after his sixty-third birthday last October—perfectly aware that Frank had been struck by lightning, had been seventy-four, had been unique in many ways—Henry had gone to his doctor and asked for a full workup. He was not one of those old men who dressed carefully in the morning in classic styles, who shaved twice a day, who got hundred-dollar haircuts to make the best of the bald pate, and then, when passing a plate-glass window, noticed that the hems of his trousers were above his ankle bones. When Henry passed a plate-glass window, he recognized his perennial self, trim, clean, coordinated, up-to-date. The doctor had told him, after two days of tests, that appearances were not deceiving. His blood pressure was 110/62, his lungs were clear and his heartbeat was regular, his reflexes were normal, his PSA was between 3 and 4, and his prostate was lump-free. He had good circulation in his toes. His LDL was 115, his HDL 62, his triglycerides 145. His blood type was O negative. His height was 6' ½" and his weight 158. But winter bore down upon him like an arctic blast. When his students were showing up for class in sweaters, he was wearing a down coat; when they donned ski jackets, scarves, and mittens, Henry wore all of the above, plus long underwear and thermal socks from Lands' End. His boots were insulated, and he had the heat in his place up to seventy-eight—Claire and Carl couldn't stand to come over, and didn't dare invite him to their place.

The most unfortunate result was that he completely lost interest in everything he had ever loved. He could not teach his Old English students *The Wanderer,* much less *The Seafarer. Beowulf* made him shake in his boots—not because Grendel was a monster, but because the mead hall was freezing and Wealhþeow was wearing a dress. Norse literature was out of the question—he didn't want to read the usual passages of Grettisaga, not because Grettir cut off several heads, but because he threw off his clothes and swam out into the winter ocean. Even the *Song of Roland* was difficult, because Roncevaux Pass was at three thousand feet, windswept and barren. He didn't mind *Orlando Furioso,* because Ariosto did not successfully imagine snow and cold, but they wouldn't be getting to that until spring. He was almost finished with his book of essays about Gerald of Wales, but he set it aside, not wanting to imagine St. David's, thrusting like a thumb into the North Atlantic. Toulouse was not warm enough, Béziers was not warm enough, Rome was not warm enough.

And he was too much of a tightwad to make last-minute reservations for St. Thomas, too much of a snob to go to Miami, too unimaginative to go to Maui, where, it turned out, Miles, the guy who had the office next to his, went for two weeks, even though his specialty was the Victorian novel. He told Henry that they went to Hawaii every year. Why go to London? They could do that in the summer. How stupid was I, thought Henry, that I have spent every vacation of my entire life doing homework?

And, he discovered, you could lie in your bed under flannel sheets and two down comforters, in pajamas with socks, your hands under the small of your back, a pillow over your face, and still feel the chill creeping over and around your shoulders and neck and the arches of your feet, across your belly, into your nostrils. You could decide very rationally that you were crazy, that the cold was something you were emanating rather than experiencing, you could sit up and take your own temperature and read that it was 98.8 and still shiver. Better to be one of those manic women who threw off all their clothes and ran naked into the street—at least those women were expanding rather than shrinking. To be freezing yourself to death was embarrassing by contrast.

However, it was not as though Henry didn't know Freud had existed, or Jung, or Adler, or Beck. He had read Freud's case studies of the Wolfman and Little Hans, though he didn't have them on his shelves. He had read *The Undiscovered Self* and *Man and His Symbols,* but had tossed them, thinking that Jung's take on literature was imprecise. There was, in fact, no book on his shelves that could help him; he had read too much, and grown too self-confident. And so he bundled up, went to the college bookstore, and bought a book about freezing to death, then read it under the covers, by flashlight. How did you revive someone whose body temperature had dropped below eighty-five degrees? Dry clothing, gradual warmth (he was sorry to discover that the old technique Frank had told him about—putting the chilled one in a sleeping bag with a warm naked person—could not work, because the chilled person would sweat and get colder). What you must not do under any circumstances was put the chilled person in a hot bath, which could cause sudden dilation of the circulatory system and probably a heart attack. And so Henry crept to his bathroom as across frozen tundra, turned on the hot water, waited until the tub was three-fourths full, shrugged off his layers of clothes, and slipped in, something he hadn't done in years, since he preferred to shower. Possibly he felt a distinct contrast between his core temperature (cold) and his peripheral temperature (hot), but possibly he was simply remembering the time his colleague Marie, who taught structural linguistics, told him about taking a long walk and getting so cold that she had this very feeling. His problem was that he remembered everything, wasn't it? That his mind was a library of images and interpretations, none of which helped him get over his lifelong solitude. Or perhaps his problem was that when Marie had told him this story—a little excited and scared—he had been less than sympathetic. He had stood still for a moment, said, "How peculiar," and continued into his office, closing the door—in her face? He had been preoccupied with something. In faculty meetings, he eavesdropped (with a superior look on his face?), but did not contribute. When Harold, the chairman (Irish Renaissance, specialty J. M. Synge) called the meeting to order, Henry would give his report on budgeting, faculty salaries, potential new hires, take questions, then sit back and ignore the rest of the meeting. For years he had taken an interest in students—quite an interest, in fact, though nothing sleazy, he told himself—but then Ralph Markson (Keats, Shelley) was fired for sleeping with two young women and raising their grades; the policy that forbade this was not new, but, the department came to realize, it had to be enforced. Henry retreated immediately—stopped closing the door when students came for conferences, stopped even looking directly at his male students when they spoke in class. He had always called them "Miss So-and-So" and "Mr. So-and-So," but now avoided even learning their given names. He was invited to the departmental Christmas party and the departmental Labor Day party, but he knew, and everyone else knew, that he didn't care for children, so he was left quietly in some corner or other, self-satisfied and neat.

Claire had moved out the year before. Frank had died. Joe was ill now with something undefined but debilitating. Lillian was long gone. Arthur—well, Arthur was alive, but, to hear Andy tell it, he was more or less mummified in the chill of Hamilton; better not to think of that. Henry slid down in the bathtub and turned the hot water on again with his toe. He was about to be the oldest something-or-other in his family, in his department, in his tiny world; he had nothing to offer and no experience with offering.

CLAIRE HAD LEARNED not to worry about Henry, but after New Year's, she did start, though not enough to overcome her fear of pestering him. Before Christmas, she'd asked him to dinner on the 23rd and to brunch on the 26th—she had parties to put on over the real holidays. There was no response to her messages; maybe he had gone to Europe after all. She called the college and asked when the new semester would begin: the 22nd. On the 17th, she was standing in the front hall of Carl's house, talking to Charlie. Charlie was telling her about his very strange and amusing wedding to Riley, so when the phone rang she didn't pick it up. Henry's voice came on the answering machine; she stopped laughing, lifted her finger, and listened: "I need to talk to you, is all." She didn't grab it in time, and when she called right back, he didn't answer.

They got into Charlie's car and drove over there. Claire knocked five times, not her usual three, saying to Charlie, "My automatic response is not only to take no for an answer, but to assume that no is the answer."

"Why is that?"

"Oh Lord, Henry sets the world record for self-contained, not to mention judgmental. When I lived here, it was pretty clear that he could hear, not only a pin drop, but a towel, a Kleenex, a Snickers wrapper. I'm not the neatest person in the world—"

The door did open, and Henry, wearing a knitted hat, peeked out. Claire was about to justify coming over without being invited, but Charlie opened the storm door, then the front door, and said, "Uncle Henry!" And then he enclosed Mr. Perfect in an enthusiastic hug. Henry staggered backward, so Claire took advantage. Charlie was already talking: "I was hoping I would see you! I left Denby about five, then I got to Claire's about ten. We were just standing there talking, and the phone rang—"

"How's Joe?"

"Oh, Jesse and Jen are so nice. And Guthrie made me watch him go up and down the living-room stairs on his hands. He is good! He makes a very careful left turn on the landing, and then does a sort of handspring—"

"I mean my brother Joe."

"Oh!" said Charlie. "I didn't see him. I guess he isn't feeling—"

"Come in here." Henry led them into the living room, a warm, friendly space that Claire had liked very much; of course, she had shifted the chairs, pushed the desk back against the wall, and bought three red pillows. The furniture had now returned to its former arrangement, and the pillows were gone. Henry sat on the couch, looking offended, but Charlie seemed not to notice and sat beside him. Claire said, "Did you call me? I mean, you called me. Everything okay? I called back."

Henry didn't say anything.

Charlie, with the smooth ill-manners of a born extrovert, said, "Do you mind if I finish what I was saying to Claire about my wedding?"

"You got married?" said Henry.

"Well, finally! Oh, by the way, I did tell Congressman Langdon that I was going to try and see everyone, and he said to say hi. Anyway, so . . . you remember when the Republicans shut down the government in November? Riley worked from home, but when they did it again on December 15, I said that if she wasn't going to be paid then I was supporting her, and so I was drawing the line—she couldn't work. Well, we sat around for two days. I think she read this new novel, what is it called, *Primary Colors,* for about a day and a half, because Ivy got her an advance copy, and she made a pecan pie, but then she was totally bored, so I said we were going to get married. By this time it was almost Christmas, but she said that the government would start up on the twenty-sixth. So we made a bet—if things resumed on the twenty-sixth, we would not get married; but if they didn't, I could take her somewhere and we would get married. So, on the twenty-sixth, I took her to a farm in Virginia where they have ecologically integrated the system. I mean, the cows go into the harvested oat field and clean up the stalks, then poop, and after that they let the hogs in there to clean up the cow poop—"

"Dung," said Henry.

"And then they bring in the turkeys, and after that the chicken coop on wheels, and they open the door, and the chickens pick up any bits that are left; the eggs are completely organic and fertile; and all the animals together have pounded the nutrients into the soil by walking around—"

"Where do you stay?" said Claire.

"Well, they have a bed-and-breakfast, where they serve only products they've grown and produced; the place is entirely self-supporting. If you want a bath, you throw wood into the boiler that heats the water, and there's some kind of filter in the chimney. . . ."

He went on. Henry glanced despairingly at Claire.

"After we got married, Riley said she needed a break, so I drove to St. Louis for a visit, and I thought I'd loop north to pass the time. Here's the great thing: when we moved to New York, I sold my Tercel, and then, when we moved to Washington, I found the exact same car, even the same color, but with fewer miles on it, at a dealer in Baltimore." He looked at his watch. "Two guys are going back with me. I pick 'em up at six. We should be back to D.C. by tomorrow morning. I've been averaging forty-two miles per gallon, and the price of gas has been around a dollar twenty-five, so each of us will pay about eight bucks for the trip." He grinned. He was a nice young man, but Claire could see how his wife might need a break.

From deep within himself, Henry summoned a mote of curiosity (Claire knew she was being catty to think this). He said, "How is Richie doing?"

Charlie crossed his ankle over his knee and got comfortable. He said, "You know, Riley and I talk about this all the time. He can say anything. He can say that Hillary is sexy, and no one goes bananas, not even Hillary. There's something about the way that he gazes at you, as if he's really listening, and you have this feeling that he cares about you, and you also have this feeling that he might punch you in the nose. In D.C., that works. It works with Vito Lopez—you know who he is? He sort of runs the Brooklyn machine. He gives the congressman no shit at all."

Then Charlie said, "You look like you could use some lunch. I could use some lunch." He glanced at Claire. Claire shook her head. "I have to take all the table linen from the weekend parties back to the rental place and talk to some people."

But Claire was curious to see how Charlie would pull this off. He said, "What's around here? Did I tell you about my marathon? It was in October. I got into that state you get into, you know, where you are a mindless machine of pain and transcendence, and then I crossed the finish line and fell down and passed out, and that was that. Never again. But I still run about five miles a day. A meatball sub? What is Chicago famous for?"

"Hot dogs," said Henry, inertly.

Claire sat up. She said, "You could go to the Superdawg drive-in on North Milwaukee. You can drop me at the 'L' station near there."

"I eat hot dogs," said Charlie.

After that, she saw how good he was. He did everything as if it were automatic, not pausing for a moment to gauge, or possibly even sense, whether Henry wanted to do it. He had Henry in his coat, with his scarf and gloves, out onto the sidewalk, into the passenger seat of the Tercel, burbling the whole time about hot dogs he had known, split, grilled, with onion rings, with French fries, mustard from Boulogne, not Dijon—he was a great lover of mustard. Henry looked stricken, but he did look—out the window, down the street, at passersby. Pretty soon, he was sitting up straighter and responding: No, he hadn't eaten sausage in Milwaukee; perhaps he should have; actually, he'd never been to Milwaukee. Claire and Carl had invited him to Lake Geneva, but in fact he'd only been to Wisconsin once. No, he wasn't much of a local traveler. Preferred France and Italy; maybe that was a mistake. Just before they pulled up to where she was going to get the train, he said, "I am getting hungry. Oh, Claire. I'll call you later," and then off they drove. She could see Henry's head turned toward Charlie, his mouth moving. She thought of the hot dog they would have, juicy, thick, poppyseed bun. Carl liked those; Claire preferred the deep-fried battered vegetables, rather tempura-like in a Chicago way.

When she called the next day, Henry was almost talkative. It was a shame about that boy. Thirty years old and utterly without direction; one failed athletic attempt after another—swimming and diving in high school, then skiing and mountain climbing, now running, but that was over. He had very much admired the sweater Henry was wearing, a cable-knit cashmere; Henry had simply handed it over. Undiagnosed dyslexic, maybe. Did Claire remember the Cheek cousins? Had 160 acres up by Gladbrook? None of them could read; there was a dunce cap at the school there with "Cheek" written on the inside of the brim.

Claire had never heard this.

Anyway, school started after the weekend. Henry had given Charlie a couple of books—not hard ones, fellow named Hinton, for kids, really, but he made Charlie promise to write him a short letter every fifty pages. Charlie swore he hadn't read a book in ten years, since he barely graduated from college.

Claire saw that Henry was out to change that.

EVERY YEAR, Jesse pondered the glyphosate conundrum, usually while lying in bed after Jen fell asleep. It was fortunate that the windows of their room looked south, away from the farm. Otherwise, he would be standing there, staring at the fields. This way, he just lay quietly beside her, trying to push thoughts about glyphosate out of his mind while coordinating his breathing with hers. The thing was, you could have the well water tested for calcium and magnesium salts. Supposedly, the hardness of the water did not change much year to year; supposedly, it had to do with the rock layers that the water seeped through. He had had the water tested, and discovered that the water from his dad's well was harder than the water from either the well by the old farm or his own well. The evidence was there—his folks went through a hot-water heater in seven years because of calcium and magnesium buildup in the tank. His had lasted ten years already. If the water was hard, you added ammonium sulfate to the glyphosate—Jesse usually added eight pounds, or maybe nine, though if your water was hard enough you could add up to seventeen pounds. When the mix was right, the emerging weeds drank it up and died. Sometimes the velvetleaf was harder to get rid of, but it did a great job on the foxtail. He turned over, opened his eyes. The moonlight made the pattern of the wallpaper look like a fence, though Jesse knew it was really flowers. He closed his eyes.

His dad was skeptical about all these chemicals (and they were pretty expensive, too), but what was the alternative? Repeated cultivating, sending the soil in clouds east to Illinois? Hoeing? His dad had plenty of stories about the kids hoeing the fields in the thirties, or maybe it was their own parents doing that in the 1890s. When Jesse imagined Uncle Frank with a hoe, Uncle Frank was wearing his army uniform from the war and aiming the hoe at deer in the distance. Perky hoeing? Guthrie hoeing? Felicity, maybe—even at seven, she was determined to outdo her eleven- and twelve-year-old brothers. And then he couldn't help stilling his body and listening for any sound that might indicate that a certain seven-year-old was up in the night; sometimes she woke up and read, though she was forbidden to go downstairs. No sounds.

Jesse was as precise as any farmer he knew. He sprayed between nine and ten in the morning, when all the leaves of all the weeds were stretching out, taking in the day's sunlight. Before he sprayed, he kept a record of morning temperatures for a week, and he noted the dew (enough dew and the glyphosate just slid off the leaves, nothing taken in). He thought that if he sprayed as precisely as possible, he would use less glyphosate and still get the same results. All of this was a constant topic of discussion at the Denby Café. A few farmers thought a light dew made the glyphosate more effective—"opened the pores," they said. "Hell, no, sun does that," said the others. Jesse didn't say much, but every year he wondered if he should be more precise, or less. More than one farmer at the Denby Café scoffed at all the complicated stuff and "just added some, don't know how much. What seems to work." One of his letters from Uncle Frank had a line about his friend the cranberry farmer dipping rags in glyphosate and then dragging them in the water behind a boat. His mom said her mother had been as casual with her baking: "Oh, some butter. A nice piece about the size of your thumb." Jesse didn't understand how anyone could farm this way, as if you could look at the ground and figure out whether it was time to plant, as if you could look off to the west and figure out what the weather was going to be. Once, his dad had said that all those years at college must have driven out his instincts, and his mom had said, "Hush!," so his dad had never said that again (and Jesse never complained about his dad; all those years at college had proved to him that he had the kindest and most easygoing dad of all). But you couldn't farm with instincts if you were aiming at 150 bushels of corn to the acre and 45 bushels of beans.

Or you could. There was something attractive about taking it day by day, following your instincts, hoping for the best, maybe worrying, but not parsing out every little detail night after night. Yes, the crop might fail, but God would provide, as his mom said, giving him a little kiss on the cheek, or Uncle Frank would provide (not anymore), or the bank would provide (for a price), or Monsanto would provide (as the local rep kept telling him).

That was what brought the subject of the beans into his brain every night.

His mom subscribed to a cooking magazine, and she was the one who showed him the tomato article a few years back: why tomatoes from Florida were so tasteless. Here it was—her fingernail tapped on the spot where the author went into the tomato field in Florida and ate a tomato. It was delicious! But as soon as you picked those tomatoes and put them into a chilled truck and sent them north, the flavor rose off of them like a vapor. Just the way she'd always said: You don't put a tomato in the refrigerator! Everyone knows that! And so they added a gene to tomatoes that slowed ripening—they could ripen on the truck or at the grocery store. Still tasted terrible, and, for that matter, against God's will, said his mom.

Jesse sat up very quietly, looked at the clock, moved softly toward the bathroom, turned out Felicity's bedside light on the way (Felicity was sound asleep, some Care Bear or other tight against her), lifted the toilet lid, took a pee, lowered the toilet lid, went back to bed. Jen was now on her stomach, her head turned toward the door. He bent down. Her eyes were closed; her breathing was steady.

Sometimes your glyphosate went ahead and killed your beans. You had to measure your poison accurately, and sometimes you didn't, or the margin of danger overlapped the margin of safety. Now you could buy beans from Monsanto that resisted Monsanto's own herbicide, and the margin of safety was expanded—the beans wouldn't die, but maybe the bank account would, since every improvement costs money. The rep said he would give him a deal. His dad said that there were no deals. His mom said that all deals were with the devil. Jen said that Felicity needed braces: one of her canines was coming in through the gum and had to be extracted, the other as well, and then two years of braces, uppers and lowers. Jesse closed his eyes.

ANDY KNEW that her new house looked like a servants' quarters to Loretta and to Janet, a piece of Iowa that had lost its way, somehow transported to Far Hills, New Jersey, but she liked it. It was, maybe, the first house she'd ever lived in that truly suited her. Why it was in Far Hills was a funny story. All during the Republican primaries, she'd paid little attention to Bob Dole, no attention to Pat Buchanan, but intermittent attention to Steve Forbes. It had taken her two months to realize that he was Malcolm Forbes's son; she kept looking at him and thinking he reminded her of someone. That day, which was a Sunday, she got into the car and drove to Far Hills—not far, though she had never bothered to drive there in her whole life before. The house, on Spring Street, was the third one she saw with a "For Sale" sign, modest in every way. For the first few years, she could have her bedroom in the attic, then on the ground floor, in the back. It was in a pleasant neighborhood and made for an old lady. She did not want to move into Manhattan (Loretta thought the right thing would be for Andy to live with them, but she didn't actually want her, Andy felt). She bought the house, called the movers the next day, paid with a check when it closed a week later, moved in six days after she saw it. The house in Englewood Cliffs sold for six times the price of the house in Far Hills, and Uncle Jens received a nice sum, which he put into Jared's computer-animation business. He also contributed the maximum allowed amount to Richie's campaign, the third one, and for this reason, perhaps, she opened the door one afternoon in October to find her son, the congressman himself, standing on the porch, his hands in his pockets, gazing around.

He said, "What are you doing?"

"I'm making a grilled ham-and-cheese sandwich for an early supper, then I'm going to read the latest issue of *The New Yorker,* then I'm going to bed."

"Your front door is unlocked."

"You tried it?"

"Of course I did."

"Were you going to just walk in?"

"Only after I looked in the window and made sure it was yours."

"What if I was out?"

"Then I would see what was in the refrigerator."

She gave him a grilled ham-and-cheese sandwich, too—Emmentaler cheese, Black Forest ham—and a crunchy bowl of romaine lettuce with some olive oil from Spain and some balsamic vinegar from Italy. They sat across from each other at her very modest kitchen table in her very modest chairs; none of the Englewood Cliffs furniture had fit in here, so she'd sold it (some for very good prices), and bought all new.

She did not ask him about the campaign.

She did not ask him about Leo.

She did not ask him whether he was seeing anyone.

She did not ask him about Michael.

She was curious to see which of these perennial topics would come up first.

She said, "How's your sandwich?"

"Crispy."

"I like that. That's one of my favorite words."

He said, "Mom. Why are you so strange?"

Andy laughed out loud.

"No, I'm not kidding. You are the ghost that the child reaches toward, who disappears the very instant he touches her."

Andy had thought that was Frank.

She ate the last bite of her sandwich and wiped her lips. She wanted, above all, to give a serious answer. She said, "I'm not strange to myself, but I realize that I contrast with others fairly sharply."

Now Richie laughed.

She went on, "How old were you, do you think, the first time you thought you might die?"

"I don't remember. But when I hit Michael on the head with that hammer that time, I thought he might die. I guess we were seven or eight. Nedra brought him back to life with a stick of butter."

"Well, I was four. My cousin Helga told me. She was seven. They had come over from Prairie du Chien, and she told me about a boy in her class at school who drowned in the river. She swore she saw him go under the ice and not come up. His name was Lonnie. I remember it so clearly. I was terribly stupid, and so she had to explain every little bit to me over and over, and so it got wedged in my mind. When I asked my mom about it, about death, she said, 'Oh, for heaven's sake! *Jeg kommer ikke til å snakke om det, det er en solrik dag!*'"

"What did that mean?"

"Something like 'I'm not talking about that on such a beautiful day!' We never did talk about it. But I thought about it. It was like all the details Helga told me made deep paths in my brain, and everything else that happened, or that anyone said, confirmed it and etched it deeper."

Richie said, "I never thought I might die, but I often thought Michael might die."

"Did you hate him?" Andy decided at the last second not to put this question in the present tense.

"What happens if I say yes?" said Richie.

"There are a lot of different theories about that."

"Mom!"

"Well, there are. But we're here alone. You are forty-three, I'm seventy-six, and you can say whatever you want."

"Because you'll forget it."

"Chances are."

But he ate his salad instead of saying it, which Andy thought was unfortunate. The past tense was for declaring that something was over, and Richie hadn't noticed that. She said, "How's Leo?"

"He got into Allen-Stevenson."

"Where's that?"

"It's near where Ivy's living now. All boys. 'An Allen-Stevenson Boy is a *Scholar* and a *Gentleman*.' He's a handful, so it's good they have twelve years to work on him. Lots of music. Ivy thinks he likes music."

"How's the campaign going?"

"I seem to be up by three points. I think the Republicans over-played their hand. They think so, too."

"Are you seeing anyone?"

"Not that I can remember."

"How's Michael?"

"I think he found religion."

"How so?"

"There was a monsignor when I went to dinner the other night. Monsignor Kelly. He seemed very comfortable around Michael, and he was good with the kids. I'm guessing a baptism is in the works."

Then they were both quiet.

After he left, she sat in her attic bedroom, with all the books she had yet to read, looking out the window. The brouhaha of Frank's death had settled down, and she had come to understand her own reaction, that sense of fatality and almost relief. She had not cried, had thought that maybe he would have been disappointed in her if she had cried. Sometimes, when she was alone, she talked to him: Was he happy to have gone in such a sudden and dramatic way? Was this better than Arthur's decline, or his own father's youthful heart attack (only fifty-eight—old then, young now)? More than anyone she knew, he had simply skipped old age—had he understood that? Her only regret was that the children had not forgiven him, although, she thought, he had forgiven them, but every time she broached this topic, they looked away, made a joke, didn't believe her. Well, the lesson of almost sixty years with someone was that no one but you remembered that darling boy, the stranger walking toward you down Lincoln Way. You were standing on the corner, at Welch, and out of the morning sunshine (Lincoln Way ran due east, due west) emerged this lithe, tall figure, his gaze hooded but avid, taking in every build-ing, every other student, every tree, and you, too. And so you turned and followed him back to Hayward, and stood beside him on that corner, and when he cocked his head to look you up and down, waiting ever so long to smile but finally doing it, it did not mean that you were beautiful, it meant that you had a chance, just a chance, to see this being again, to find out what was in there, and it didn't matter what you found out, in the end, because no one on earth would ever flash through you and light you up like he did.

1997

〜

A CROSS THE TABLE from Richie, Chance sat still, looking at his plate. Next to Chance, Bea (whom Richie still called Binky) was unabashedly rolling her eyes. Tia had already asked to be excused, been granted permission, and then bestowed a smile upon everyone, including Richie, including Monsignor Kelly, including Binky (though there was the usual touch of contempt in the smile she bestowed on Binky). The topic under discussion was where Chance would be going to boarding school. He had applied to only two and gotten into both, one to please his dad, the Stevenson School, in Pebble Beach, California, about a hundred yards from the site of Michael and Loretta's famous wedding, and one to please his mom and the monsignor, Woodside Priory School, about a hundred yards from Janet's house (okay, from where she kept the three horses, wherever that was). Dangers abounded. Chance did not want to go to boarding school, but the alternative was Regis, a Jesuit academy uptown, not, perhaps, far enough for Chance, who appeared restive. Like Richie and Michael, like their dad, Chance was tall and looked maybe two years older than he was (and, Richie thought, acted two years younger than he was). Whatever Perroni was in there made itself felt on the back of a horse or in the cab of a truck: Loretta reported, with some pride, that over Christmas Chance had gotten his grandfather to teach him to drive; it had taken a day, and then he had driven all over the ranch the rest of the vacation. Woodside Priory was all boys, the Pebble Beach school coed. When Michael called Richie to warn him that the monsignor would be there, he'd said, "The whole meal is going to be about the fact that Chance was caught in the hall making out with Patty Malone; he had his tongue in her mouth. So the monsignor is pushing the boys' school to give him some focus." When Loretta called a day later to make sure he was coming, she said, "I need your input. I know military school was good for Michael. But he's got his heart set on Stevenson. Twenty thousand a year! I mean, Michael can afford that, but I'm afraid they'll just baby him."

Now Richie said, "I think military school retarded our development."

Monsignor Kelly gave him a kindly look and said, "About education there are only theories, never actual experiments. You have to go with your instincts."

"My instinct is that military school made me aggressive and angry."

"And look where you are now," said the monsignor, still endlessly benign. "I'm sure you need real toughness in the political climate we have."

"More like the capacity to ignore almost everything," said Richie, but he made sure it sounded like a joke.

Michael said, "Military school felt safe to me."

"The guns were not loaded," said Richie. Then, "Well, they were loaded with blanks. That did make it easier."

"It was orderly," said Michael. "Nothing wrong with orderly."

"Orderly is a beginning," said the monsignor.

Richie said, "Which one has more athletic facilities?"

Chance now looked at him. He said, "Stevenson."

Richie said, "Swimming saved my sanity. If I hadn't learned to swim, I wouldn't have met my best friend, Greg, and I would have had to listen to your dad tease me about how I ran like a girl, every day of my life."

"I don't believe that," said Loretta. "Michael wouldn't do that."

There was a silence. Binky was staring at Michael, Loretta was shaking her head, the monsignor was looking like he'd seen plenty of boys over the years. Michael said, "I did say that, I admit."

"Boys will be boys," said Loretta.

Michael looked at Chance and said, "Chance, I've said a lot of things that I regret. Better not to say them, since you can't apologize for all of them."

Richie noticed that Michael didn't apologize, even now, for that old insult.

"Sin," said the monsignor, "is always with us." And he looked right at Richie, as if Richie were the embodiment of that idea.

Loretta said, "Boys learn differently from girls. They need more structure and they need to learn how to get along with one another. For heaven's sake! When they're ready for girls, the girls will get along with *them*. And the weather is much better in Portola Valley, sunnier and not as damp. No one loves Pebble Beach as much as I do, but it is worth your sanity to drive out there half the time. My mom said it's a wonder all those rich people rattling around in those huge houses don't kill themselves whenever they get the chance."

"I've never been to California," said the monsignor. "No further west than St. Louis, actually."

"Well," said Loretta, "you can come along when I take him. My dad will be happy to meet you, and I'm sure he'll get you on a horse inside of a day."

The monsignor lit up like the Irishman he was.

Afterward, when Richie went over the evening in his mind, he could not figure out when the decision was made for Woodside over Stevenson. Nor could he figure out why he was there, unless it was he who was meant to articulate, and therefore define, whatever Loretta would decide against. It was pretty clear to him, though, that Loretta now had Michael surrounded. She had decorated their place entirely to her own taste—blanched colors, abstract paintings on the walls that evoked seascapes, an antique carved oak sideboard that looked like an altar, until you realized that the objects grouped among the lit candles on top of it were just plates, saucers, and cups, though ornate. She had Michael pinned between herself and the monsignor, who ran a charitable foundation that she contributed tens of thousands to every year. She took Michael to Mass on Sunday; she had him driving a Lexus LS. Richie wondered how long it could possibly last.

CHARLIE THOUGHT of his uncle Henry not as a father figure (he had one of those) but as a teacher figure (something he had never really had). Uncle Henry didn't mind answering questions; in fact, the more questions the better. Charlie was reading a book Uncle Henry had assigned—*A Tale of Two Cities*. Some teacher or other had assigned this book many times over the years, but Charlie had only read the Classic Comics edition. As a result, and because he made himself read for forty-five minutes every day—sometimes fifteen pages, sometimes twenty—he was following the story, learning about the French Revolution (which he had heard people talk about), and enjoying the very strange Evrémonde brothers. Riley did not see Uncle Henry as a teacher figure (she'd made good use of many of those), she saw him as the embodiment of the Medieval Warm Period. Had he read the Saga of the Greenlanders? Yes. Did he really think there had been birch trees in Greenland? Yes. Had he read the Saga of Eric the Red? Yes. Where did he think they got to when they came to the Western Hemisphere? Uncle Henry gave her his copy of *Land Under the Pole Star,* which Charlie read, too, since it was about a Norwegian man and his wife who went from Norway to Iceland to Greenland to Newfoundland in a rowboat, just to prove you could do it, so, yes, Eric the Red had indeed contemplated settling Newfoundland around the year 1000, until the native population drove him off. She quizzed him: How historically based were the Sagas? Grapes in Maine? Or was it Martha's Vineyard, maybe? The Medieval Warm Period was an unfortunate conundrum that Riley did not like, because people who knew about the Medieval Warm Period were more likely to challenge the concept of man-made global warming, but she did her usual thing. She looked more deeply into the arguments, and discovered ways to understand the Medieval Warm Period—less volcanic activity, more sunlight, strengthened tropical currents. At first, Charlie was afraid that Riley would offend Uncle Henry, but she invigorated him.

Unlike her parents and his parents, Uncle Henry never asked when they were going to have a baby. Every few weeks (more frequently in the winter), he would come to D.C., put himself up at the Capitol Skyline Hotel, and do some work in the Library of Congress. On the Saturdays of these weekends, Charlie, and sometimes Riley, would meet him at the Smithsonian or the National Gallery, and they would go to various shows. He took Charlie to the Folger Library, and introduced him to Shakespeare and his contemporaries. He took him to Constitution Hall and the Art Museum of the Americas. Charlie asked a lot of questions, and if Henry couldn't answer them, he bought a book, which he read quickly and Charlie read slowly. Henry didn't seem at all surprised by this overwhelming plenitude of objects to look at or ideas to think about, but Charlie was. It seemed to him that he had spent thirty years circling neighborhoods and buildings without even wondering what was inside. And each building was a Fabergé egg, pleasant on the outside, a treasure trove within. Henry said, "Books are like that, too."

So Charlie read books on the train. He would get on at his station, read and ride to Dupont Circle, then get out and run three miles to the store where he sold hiking boots, kayaking gear, climbing gear. Henry was good for Riley, too, though not because he made her spend a couple of hours every so often walking around in the presence of art and artifacts. And he didn't mind her talking about global warming—he was born in 1932, and his first memories were of the winter of '35–'36, when the downstairs windows were blanked by snow, and his brothers, who would have been thirteen and fifteen, would jump out the upstairs windows (and Frank out of the attic window) and slide down the snow mounded against the house. Then Frank disappeared, and that snow-enshrouded season turned into a terribly dusty, hot summer, when, his mother later told him, he lay in his crib covered with hives, sweating and miserable. It was so hot that she had to spread wrung-out wet cloths over him—he sort of remembered that, too, though not as clearly as the snow. In '56, another drought year—oh, '56! And his stories wandered away from the weather to how he fell in love with his cousin Rosa, unrequited of course, and how the big scandal in the family was the reappearance of Minnie's father, a ne'er-do-well drunk who had disappeared years before. Walked into the house while Lois was away and Joe was out cultivating one of the fields, and fell down the basement stairs and died. Henry said, "Frank would whisper in your ear that Lois pushed him, but that was Frank. Yes, it was a drought year, but scandals overwhelmed the weather for me." Charlie felt his unknown past vibrating. He said, "Our family seems to have a lot of those," and even as Henry was smiling and shaking his head, Riley burst out,

"My grandfather proposed to my great-aunt, and then, behind her back, he married her younger sister, who was my grandmother. And she lived with them for the rest of her life."

After he went back to Chicago that time, Henry sent Charlie a nicely bound notebook and a pen.

"LISTEN TO WHAT Warren told me," said Emily. Janet was stirring the penne so that it wouldn't stick. Emily had become a vegetarian, so they were having a mushroom sauce with it, and Jared had told her that, although he would miss Emily once she was off to Mount Holyoke with Pattycake, her jumper, he would not be sorry to go back to guilt-free meat eating. Jonah was doing something noisy in his bedroom—maybe jumping on his bed, which Janet would allow for a minute or two. Warren was the farrier at the barn. Emily liked to encourage him to tell sixty years' worth of stories while he shod the horses.

"I'm listening," said Janet.

"Did you ever meet Melvin Case? He was one of Mrs. Herman's whippers-in."

"No," said Janet. She stirred the penne again.

"Warren said that he lives in a railroad-style house. I guess that's long? Anyway, he heard the phone ringing in the middle of the night, so he got out of bed and staggered to the living room to answer it. When he staggered back to bed, a eucalyptus tree had split in two, and half of it had fallen on the house, right through to the bed; the whole end of the house had collapsed."

Janet's spoon jumped in the water. She sensed what was coming— didn't you always?

"So listen to this. It was a friend of his who had had a dream that Mel had died, and the dream was so vivid that he had to get up and call him, just to make sure he was all right. He said that he was fine. The guy apologized for getting him out of bed. Warren said that, the next day, Mel called his friend and told him always to call him if he had any bad feeling about him." Then, "Do you believe that? I wish I had that kind of friend."

Janet thought, yes, I believe it, but she said, "I'm more than a little skeptical."

"I think it's creepy."

"It's definitely creepy."

When she woke up in the middle of the night, it was to thoughts about that phone call. Had it happened? Their farrier had plenty of stories, and Janet had listened to her share. Mostly she did believe him—peacocks in his trees; a woman mounting her horse, the horse slipping, landing on her, killing her; a trainer forcing his horse against its will (and Warren's advice) into a stream, the horse and man going under, the trainer's cowboy hat popping out of the water like a bubble (the horse saved the man). What Janet wondered about was the fact that this story didn't scare her, that it didn't trigger any personal reaction, either about eucalyptus trees or about psychic friends. It pinpointed her realization that she wasn't afraid anymore—something, since she had kept her fears so secret for so long, that no one else would notice.

She knew, lying there, that it had been her father's death that erased her fears. That, and giving away her inheritance to Fiona's favorite charity, the Thoroughbred Retirement Foundation; Jared's favorite, the Big Sur Land Trust; Emily's favorite, the Jane Goodall Institute; Jonah's favorite (after some coaching), PBS; and her own favorite, Save the Children. With each check she wrote, she could detect a snort in the empyrean, her father deploring this waste of his hard-earned cash (or maybe that snort was in her own mind). Her mother had said, "How good of you," but it wasn't goodness, it was a series of assassinations, and they had worked.

She and Jared had plenty of money, anyway. Their house had doubled in value, and Jared's stock in his company was at an all-time high. Spending twenty-five thousand a year to send Emily (not to mention Pattycake) to Mount Holyoke seemed prudent, not profligate. People were coming to Jared all the time, asking him to join their start-up—computer animation for every purpose! Once, he was tempted, but when he went into the meeting, he jokingly grabbed the elaborate identifying plaque beside the door of the offices, and it came off in his hands. He took this as a sign and didn't join them. The entrepreneurs were all twenty-two, anyway. They made him nervous.

But Janet did not think her fears had seeped away because of prosperity or age. Poverty and decrepitude were not what she'd always feared, it was Mutually Assured Destruction. Even after she did avoid

Pastor Jones's version of apocalypse, she worried that she'd only put it off (thinking about it now, she suspected that the knowledge that Lucas, too, had avoided it was what finally eased those fears). The marvel was not that she had dreaded the end of the world; it was that so few others seemed to. When she asked Jared if he remembered the Cold War "duck and cover," the Cuban Missile Crisis, he shrugged—yes, but no, not really. What she saw now was that she had known all her life that if destruction came her father would not care enough to save her. Now he was gone, and she was safe.

JESSE WAS SITTING with his dad, who was propped up but slumping slightly to the right. Jesse hesitated to interfere, because his father seemed to resent the number of times that his mother asked him: Are you okay? Do you need anything? You want me to sit you up a little? You want to get up and sit for a while in the chair by the window? No, no, the answer was always no. He'd be gasping for air as he said it, and then his mother would purse her lips and say, "Well, okay, then. But don't forget to ask." Jesse knew that asking was not the same as not forgetting to ask. Farmers hated to ask *for* things, but they didn't mind asking *about* things. Just now his dad said, "You scrape off the paint on the platform of that combine?"

Jesse had bought a new combine a week before, and harvest would begin in a few days. The cornstalks were tall, the ears huge. The kernels were down to about 28 percent moisture now, and the weather was clear and hot for the next couple of days. Jesse liked 26 percent—fewer lost ears. Once, he'd harvested a single field at 28 percent, but a lot of the kernels had been damaged by the equipment. Jesse said, "I did. It's not at all slippery now."

"Don't forget to turn off the machine if the intake gets clogged." Joe's voice, once friendly and melodic, had become scratchy.

Jesse wanted to say, "I never do," but he said, "I won't."

"And don't try to get any twine out of there. Goes in faster than you can react. Don't care who you are."

"I know."

"Who was that, Abel M—"

"I know, Dad. I always turn it off."

"Make sure Guthrie and Perky stay away from the intake areas."

"I will."

"This thing got all the shields in place?"

"It does."

"That rain we had, you be careful driving that thing through wet spots."

"I walked the first two fields. The ground is good."

"Even over above the crick there?"

"Even there."

"Did you check the spacing on the"—he coughed—"cornhead stripper bars and the belts for wear?"

Jesse did not remind his dad that it was a new machine, that he'd known it was a new machine three minutes before; he said, "Yes." Harvest made everyone nervous, even Pastor Campbell. How many stubborn men in a hurry does it take to harvest thirty million acres in a month and a half?

Joe said, "Harvest used to be fun. I loved the oat harvest. Now, some of the horses weren't suited to it—they might take off, run through the fence line—but Jake and Elsa, they were patient. Grandpa Wilmer knew how to breed a horse. Percherons. Good horses, you ask me. We went all around to everyone's farm and helped each other, and I've never eaten like that since." It took Joe a long time to say this. But Jesse was patient, and when Joe was done he said, "Mom would be sorry to hear that."

"Oh, I don't mean that the food was good. Sometimes it was and sometimes it wasn't. But the conversation was good. Not so much complaining as these days. More like, well, we made it another year, thank the Lord."

"Thank the Lord," said Jesse.

Now there was a long silence. Joe's oxygen tank was across the room, but he hated to use it. He called his condition "farmer's lung," as if that was a joke, but Jesse knew it was emphysema, caused by all kinds of dust (but do you really wear a mask when you are cultivating or plowing or closed up in the barn, maintaining equipment over the winter? To do so seemed both silly and frightening). When had the illness come on? If his dad had caught it early, what would he have done, moved to town? Gone to work in his mom's shop? Now Jesse cleared his own throat, and then he wondered if he would start panicking every time he got a cold.

Suddenly Joe said, "She's going to rope me into a big funeral and put up a headstone twice as tall and twice as wide as Frank's."

Jesse shifted in his chair. His dad hadn't mentioned his funeral before.

"You make sure I get cremated. Pastor Campbell be damned."

"I'll tell her—"

"Yes, you do that. I put it in a letter and I put it in my will, but she's going to ignore that, sure as rain. You know, when my dad died, I sat with him out under the Osage hedge there, and I knew in my heart that when I was going to die—and I thought that would be forever and a day in the future, or maybe never, you know how it is—I would make sure that I got buried under the Osage tree. I hated that old graveyard where they put Uncle Rolf and everyone. But here I go. Can't do a thing about it." He coughed again.

"I don't think she'll let me bury you under the Osage hedge," said Jesse, "but I will sprinkle some ashes there. I will do that. I promise."

His dad nodded.

It was funny how they talked about this, so matter-of-fact, Jesse thought. No tears were coming to his eyes, though he loved and respected his father. Nor did his dad pity himself. Death was death. If you went to church every Sunday, which they did, you had to accept that death was a release—they certainly told you that over and over, a harvest to be prepared for and then performed.

His dad said, "Don't you let those boys ride along unless they've got a seat to sit on."

Jesse said, "I won't, Dad."

"And don't you let Pastor Campbell say that I've been gathered into the arms of the Lord. I nearly walked out when he said that about your uncle Frank. Frank would have punched him in the nose for that. You know, when my Opa first came here, if an old man died in the winter, well, they just put him in the cellar for a few months, until the ground thawed. That wasn't a bad idea."

The door opened. His mom said, "Hi, sweetie. You two have a nice afternoon?"

Jesse said, "We did."

His mom said, "I roasted some extra Brussels sprouts and sprinkled them with olive oil and Parmesan. I made up a container for you to take home."

"Thanks, Mom. Those are always good." Jesse's hand was resting on his dad's hand, on top of the sheet, and now he looked down. So similar in shape—not beautiful or graceful, but strong and built for work. His dad's hand felt dry, hard, cool, ready to fix something or plant something, as if it didn't know that the system was shutting down. It was the hand of a kind man, a hand that had gently squeezed his shoulder or patted him on the back countless times. How did you deserve such a dad? he thought. But he said nothing, looked away. There would be some point when he would express all of this, but it frightened him now—bad luck, asking for trouble. He gave his father's hand a squeeze and said, "I guess I'd better check the weather."

"Could be good," said Joe.

BEFORE SHE WENT to Kyoto for the Convention on Climate Change, Riley moaned incessantly about the carbon footprint of her flight, how could she justify it, why couldn't they have the conference in . . . (but she couldn't come up with a sustainable spot). After she got back (and Richie had paid for the trip, out of pocket, not in his official capacity), she showed no gratitude at all—simply came into his office at all hours of the day and continued arguing with him about the new treaty, about emissions, about money for wind and solar. As far as Richie was concerned, Al getting Bill to sign the treaty was a major victory. The strategy now should be to back off, let Clinton regain his footing and his cool, and move forward from there. But no promise was sufficient for Riley, or for the World Wildlife Fund, or for any other environmental group. He said to her, "Look. The Senate is not going to ratify it. And they would like to tar and feather him for signing it. Can't you shut up for once?" What he did not say was that there was something else brewing, something that Riley might not care about in any way, but that the Republicans would certainly take advantage of.

Richie was not terribly fond of his scheduler, Lucille, but she had been working as a congressional staffer since the Johnson administration, and she was an accomplished eavesdropper—in the bathroom, in the lunchroom, in the gym, in the hallways, you name it, she had heard things everywhere. One of her strategies, she had told Richie, was to do a crossword puzzle on the can, her body movements stilled. He would not believe, she said, who was sleeping with whom, and where. Across the congressional office desk was the least of it. And now she had heard another thing, and if they got through Christmas without an explosion, they'd be lucky.

There was a girl, Lucille said. In her twenties, plain-looking, dumpy sort of girl. She had worked for Clinton in the White House. Lucille sniffed. Girls worked in the White House generation upon generation. Richie found this difficult to believe. Hadn't girls in the nineteenth century been required to stay at home? Well, since the Kennedy administration, said Lucille. Someday, they would talk about that. What the girl had done, well, the girl had given in—either to temptation or to the president, what was the difference, said Lucille. But here was the kicker: she had decided to start talking about it. She talked and talked and talked about it. Other people talked about it, too—that was how Lucille heard the news, sitting on the can in the Capitol, quiet as a mouse, doing her puzzle. When the talkers walked along the row of stalls, looking for feet, hers were tucked in the shadows. But they would have talked anyway—everyone loved to talk. Washington ran on gossip. Here was the other thing.

"What?" said Richie.

The woman this girl talked to just happened to make hours and hours of recordings. Lucille was not a fan of Bill Clinton, but her findings were that whatever he did was the norm on Capitol Hill. And the girl was twenty-four, not nineteen.

The next person Richie heard something from was Michael, who had heard it from Loretta, who had overheard it having lunch in the Oyster Bar at Grand Central. Someone at *Time* or *Newsweek* was already on it. "Everybody knows," said Michael.

"About what, that a Democrat has balls?"

"Everyone but you," said Michael.

"Mom wouldn't like to hear you say that," said Richie. "Nor would the monsignor."

"I say nothing about Monsignor Kelly's balls."

"At least, not as long as he's controlling the checkbook, right, Mike?" said Richie.

He saw that Riley had walked into his office yet again. He hung up without saying goodbye, and barked, "Where is Kenisha?" Kenisha was his press secretary.

She ignored him. "Okay, here are your notes for your speech about energy alternatives. I fixed them a little bit, since today is cold, so that they de-emphasize conservation and ramp up innovation and being ahead of the curve and all that. Just remember, natural gas is a stopgap; don't talk about it too much. And I know nobody likes the doomsday stuff, but Kenisha was in the Chamber a few minutes ago, and she says there's hardly anybody there, but we'll get it into the record, anyway."

She set the speech down on his desk, went to the coat rack, and got his coat, which she held out for him while continuing to talk. "And I have this friend. She just came to town last week."

"What is her policy specialty?"

"She doesn't want a job."

He thrust his arms into the sleeves.

She handed him his gloves. "She's willing to go out with you. I told her all about you."

"She hasn't seen me in the paper?"

"She has. That's why I had to talk her into it."

"Is she older than twenty-four?"

"She is thirty. She has a degree in engineering. She doesn't say much."

"I would like that," said Richie.

"That's what Charlie thought." She put his speech in his briefcase, put his briefcase in his hand.

"What's her name?"

"After the speech. I don't want you distracted."

Kenisha was waiting in the hall, with her coat already on. It was very important that a congressman never go to the Capitol by himself, as if he had no hangers-on, and Kenisha was good about seeming to talk without talking. Richie looked at his watch. It was after two. Kenisha was right: when he went to the Speaker's Stand to give his speech, there were four congressmen in the Chamber, and one of them was sleeping.

1998

⁓

ARTHUR THOUGHT he might have been to Florida before. The air, the humidity, the light, and the smell had a strange familiarity, but, logically, he would have gone to Miami, or maybe Key West, not to an island off the coast near Fort Myers. Even so, the shelly beach felt to the soles of his feet like words barely remembered, clinging to the tip of his tongue. There was a busy solitude enveloping his almost-memories of Florida: He would not have been alone, but Lillian and the children would not have been with him. He would have been there on business, maybe having told Lillian that he was going to New York or was staying in Washington for a couple of nights. I left my heart in McLean, Virginia, he thought—that was the most benign view of why he remembered nothing.

Debbie was supporting his arm. She thought he needed the vitamin D, his bones needed it, she thought. It was very peculiar that there was no one left who would remember whether he had been in Florida, and maybe no records of his trip, either—of whom he had talked to or what he had discovered. He would have communicated it in person, not in writing. He would have traveled under an assumed name, possibly by plane, possibly, in those days, by train, though that was unlikely. As they walked, his ankles got hot; the sunlight was an alluring contrast to frozen and snowed-in Hamilton, but it was brutal. Arthur pulled the brim of his hat down, and remembered suddenly how he always used to do that, how he had wanted to shadow his face but also to look rakish, the way his father had looked in a Panama. He had been a vain man. Lillian had egged him on in that, as in everything else.

They were not staying in a hotel. Debbie and Hugh had rented a house on stilts beside a golf course—if you were sitting in the living room or the dining room, you could sometimes hear a window break and a golf ball rattle onto the sill. Debbie had been instructed by the owner to run out to the course when this happened and hand the golfer an invoice for the amount that the window would cost to repair. Getting up and down the flight of stairs to the living quarters had to be managed carefully, but Arthur didn't mind. He wanted to please, and also not to seem reluctant or weak.

In the center of the golf course, across from the screened porch of the house, was a water hazard—with alligators. You could see them most of the time, at least their noses, sometimes their heads. Twice they had lumbered out onto the fairway. The golfers buzzed around them in their carts, hardly slowing down. Maybe that added to Arthur's sense that Florida was a menacing place. There were four bedrooms—Dean and Linda were to arrive for the weekend and stay until midweek. Carlie hadn't come—she was working for a boutique furniture manufacturer in North Carolina; she'd been on the job for three months. Kevin had gone to Stowe, snowboarding with some friends.

There wasn't much to do besides walk the beach, grocery-shop, or sit on the porch and look outward. Hugh did play golf one afternoon; Arthur watched him go by with three strangers. None of them broke a window.

Debbie took him to the beach, and once for a walk around the neighborhood. She grilled fresh fish with lemon and herbs. Hugh talked about tropical wood—teak, mahogany, Brazilian cherry, bocote, and about how, in the fall, he had invested some money in a tree farm in Costa Rica where they grew all sorts of rare (and fragrant, said Hugh) woods. He now "owned" the trees, and he would own them for as long as he wanted to. He could visit them, which always seemed appealing in Hamilton. As his first project, he was planning a coffee table, from some honey-brown striped hardwood that Arthur had never heard of. He showed his drawings each evening, the details refined from day to day. As Hugh got older and more skilled, their house overflowed with his pieces, which he sometimes gave away but refused to sell, because he didn't know how to price them. He had been to a crafts show, and the prices had been all over the place—no help. He was a tight-lipped fellow, equipped with hundreds of hand planes and chisels. Neither of the children seemed to have inherited his talents.

On the fourth morning, Arthur had gently refused to go for a beach walk. Debbie didn't force him. She made sure that he had a cool glass of water on the table beside his chair, then went with Hugh across the bridge to Fort Myers to look in galleries. The funny thing about the island, Debbie thought, was that the headquarters of the grocery store was outside of Minneapolis—the west side of Florida was the southern Midwest, whereas the east side was the southern Northeast.

The car drove away, and the house fell silent. As Arthur sat on the deck, staring out over the golf course, due south, across the lower bulge of the island, two hundred miles to Havana, he could not remember every failed operation he had tried to tweak or fix or reinterpret, but he did remember sending Frank to Iran to make sure that that crook, what was his name, did not steal the funds, either for himself or his buddies. How the funds were then put to use, Arthur had no control over, but Frank was game and cheap: all Arthur had to do was put him on the plane as a sign unto the embezzlers that they were being watched. What had the fellow taken—ten grand? That would be fifty or sixty grand these days. At the time, Arthur had thought you might not be able to control stupidity, but maybe you could control dishonesty. He had since learned otherwise. Arthur had stopped using Frank after Iran, not because he wasn't very good, but because he was good at stealth, not secrecy. Once the secrets began to proliferate, Arthur didn't dare outsource anymore—he had to be sure of loyalties. Loyalties grew first out of patriotism, then out of fear; Stalin knew that, Nixon knew that. Frank did not know that. Arthur also remembered looking into Frank's army records as soon as he met him. There had been lots of commendations, some rather excited remarks: "Squad escaped intact!" "Langdon seems to always bring them back. Recommend?" But even so he'd only risen to corporal; about that there was one remark, from '43, "Keep this soldier in the field." Had that been an insult or a compliment? But there was also a red flag—after the travesty at Sidi Bou Zid, and everyone knew it was a travesty, from top to bottom, Frank's disappearance called into question his loyalties. That he had managed to save himself and also to take out a tiny German outpost made no difference—he was gone for days. Where was he? Once you leave, even when you return, you are only partially forgiven. Better to be mowed down, since you can always be replaced. Arthur remembered reading it all more than once when he recommended Frank for the translation job in Dayton. And he remembered pausing before he wrote the word "trustworthy." Even though he had not doubted that Frank was trustworthy—by then he'd known him for months—he could not commit himself without wondering if he would somehow get in trouble for recommending someone who was too smart to be fooled every single time.

It took Arthur all afternoon to think these thoughts—his mind worked so slowly now. And other fragments cropped up among them, fragments that seemed connected, although the connections were only foggily apparent to Arthur: What about Bill Casey? When was it that he had been slated to testify about Iran and North and the Contras? At the last moment, he was diagnosed with a brain tumor, and the operation left him unable to talk. But, thought Arthur, why so secretive about such a small thing? Secrets, thought Arthur, were the real problem. Due south two hundred miles from this porch was Havana—not as far as Manhattan was from D.C. Here we have lived with Castro now for thirty-nine years. That was the bargain Khrushchev had offered—live with him or die—and, indeed, living with him hadn't been that hard. Living with secrets was what was hard.

And it wasn't just because secrets led to lies and lies led to chaos; it was because secrets led to the assumption, on the part of those not in on the secrets, that there were many more secrets than there really were. Arthur had already retired when Casey was diagnosed and operated on, rendered unable to talk, but he had been instantly suspicious of the strange convenience of it all. Logical connections abounded between dangerous secrets and convenient secrets. Does the president have a mistress back in Texas? Who cares? But it has to stay a secret. Have we infiltrated the high command of our most lethal enemy? Maybe—that's a secret, too. Has our operation gone wrong and resulted in tragic losses? It's a secret. All secrets had a way of connecting to one another and evening out—the mistress becomes connected to the infiltration, which becomes connected to the failed mission, and a secret has turned into a theory, which then turns into a cause, blowback, fallout. All of this leads to more secrets, since admitting a single thing requires admission of other things, and the plan, or the agency, or the government unravels.

Once upon a time, Arthur had loved secrets. He loved breaking codes in the early days, seeing a narrative unfold, peering through a pinhole and viewing the scene in sharp relief. During that war, everyone knew the consequences, and, anyway, the secrets were rather few, while the crimes were very many. But after the war, the crimes were secret, and the secrets, quite often, were crimes. The thing was, Arthur realized at some point, being secret made them seem like crimes. And keeping secrets made one feel like a criminal. These days, he didn't remember too many specifics, but he did remember that feeling, of telling himself that the necessary had to outweigh the good, that orders had been given, that someone, surely, was in control of the larger picture (though often that person was Frank Wisner, who Arthur thought was crazy, but maybe it was Arthur who was crazy—that had been his thinking).

Sitting in the hot Florida air, Arthur felt his temperature rise just contemplating these memories, anger and fear and shame. Eventually, the secret became the most important thing, didn't it, more important than the crime, after all, more important than the damage and the failures and the tragedies. The secret sucked every one of those things up into itself—danger, danger, danger. Arthur leaned back suddenly, threw his hand out, and toppled his glass of water, which rolled across the deck. Then he fell out of his chair.

When he came to, lying in a patch of burning sunlight, he thought, I don't want these to be the last things in my mind when I die. Am I dying? He was panting. He did not know. He did not know anything, and for the moment, that was a blessing.

AFTER JOE'S FUNERAL—on her way back to Chicago without Henry, who was staying for another three days, then flying to D.C.—Claire drove around assessing the decline of Denby. Frank's death had been such a shock that, although events seemed to move very slowly at the time, afterward it seemed as though he had been whisked over from Ames and shoveled into the ground. Claire hadn't noticed Denby then, only the faces of her relatives, blanched in the summer sun and eager to get the whole thing over with. But maybe because Lois had done such a good job preparing them, keeping everyone posted, calling them if they couldn't come for a visit (Claire had come for Christmas and Valentine's Day, pretending that she was just celebrating, though Joe wasn't fooled, of course), Joe's death seemed to rise like a tide and then recede, a matter-of-fact part of life to be understood and incorporated.

The grain elevator was still there, and the building that had been Crest's, now a funeral home. The only "market" in town was a Kum & Go. The little motel had become a restaurant for a while, maybe in the seventies? The drugstore was gone, too—no soda fountain in years. At this time of day, the Denby Café looked dark and abandoned; they served breakfast until lunchtime, and locked up at two. Lois's little antiques store was still in business; Claire peered in the window beside the "Closed for the weekend—please come back!" sign. Several couches, a table and chairs, two side tables, some dishes stacked on one of the side tables—all chintzy. The heavy, dark, ornate, beautifully made pieces that Lois had extracted from the dying farms of the seventies and eighties had been sold away. She had said at the wake that maybe she would close the business and move somewhere—or write a cookbook (twice she had overseen the Christmas cookbooks Pastor Campbell had issued for fund-raising purposes; Claire had both of those, and sometimes she gave recipes from them to her party caterers). Claire wondered if Pastor Campbell knew that Billy Sunday was born just south of Ames, if he knew who Billy Sunday was. Her mom had always spoken fondly of Billy Sunday, but he'd died before Claire came along.

Minnie had stared at Lois when she talked about moving to Milwaukee but not living with Annie. Minnie did live with Jesse and Jen—she had a pension, and she was useful. She had said to Claire that seventy-nine wasn't that old if you kept active. Lois would be sixty-eight, Claire thought. She herself was fifty-nine, and her business was booming. She could ask Lois to come to Chicago. She looked across the town square at the vast Worship Center and dropped that idea. But it all brought to mind another thing that Minnie had said—

when your parents died young, you had no idea what your own old age would look like.

The square was still green, and there were a few families making use of it, two of them Hispanic. The parents probably worked at the meatpacking plant out on Route 330, near where the hog confinement facilities were. Judging by the town, the people who worked there didn't have enough money to buy anything. However, the daffodil bed in the center of the square was yellow and thriving—someone was caring for the bulbs. The Worship Center was at the opposite corner of the square from Lois's shop—what Claire remembered as the Methodist church where her Langdon relatives had gone, now unrecognizably enormous and showy—buildings had been torn down on either side so that Pastor Campbell could add day care, parking, and offices. The Worship Center was the biggest business now. Denby itself could not possibly be supporting the Harvest Home Light of Day Church in such style, but Claire had not asked Lois where the congregants were coming from. And the Harvest Home Light of Day Church had no graveyard—no room for the dead, she thought meanly. St. Albans was gone, but the graveyard where everyone was buried remained neatly fenced, maintained by the county. Claire wondered where the Hispanic families went to services. She and Carl didn't go to church.

Carl hadn't come with her, at her request. She didn't quite know why, since he'd been willing to come, but maybe this was the reason, some time alone on a spring day, getting used to the fact that funerals started proliferating when you got older, if you were lucky. She kept walking, looping down Rain Street (why had they named it that?), where the houses were sturdy and all the front porches had rockers. It was one of life's treats, wasn't it, paying a visit to your past, swinging like a ball on a string away from the person you loved, always knowing that the string must pull you back, and you would be oh so glad to get there.

IT TURNED OUT that Charlie and Riley were good matchmakers, because Richie fell for Nadie Cantwell (born Nadya Chertsev in Leningrad, in 1967, moved to London at the age of two, when her parents defected, then to Boston at the age of seven). What Nadie wanted in a man was someone busy, thoughtful, good-looking, and willing to joke around. Whether anything would come of it, Richie didn't know. Nothing could come of it until the election was over, because Nadie was just a little suspect to the Republicans; her liberation from the Soviet Union was balanced by her very outspoken skepticism of all Republican positions on Ayn Rand, abortion, religion, extramarital sex, homosexuality, and communism (which Nadie and her parents felt had its good points and its bad points, just like capitalism). Although he had been seeing Nadie for almost a year, Richie had not told Loretta about her, or introduced them. That had to wait until after the election, too.

It was known to his constituents that his wife had left him for a billionaire from New Rochelle. He was still seen, sometimes, playing with his adorable son in Prospect Park, taking that very active but charming boy to the little zoo or to concerts at the Bandshell. They were darling together. Vito Lopez agreed that they were darling together. Vito Lopez had met the billionaire more than once, here and there. The billionaire had recoiled from Vito, or so Vito said (though maybe what he meant was that the billionaire was not terribly enthusiastic about bear hugs from Vito). Anyway, Richie had Vito's support. And Richie had $376,983 in his election coffers, compared with the seventy-six thousand or so that his self-employed electronics-store owner Republican opponent, who was fed up with Washington and hoped to throw out all the bums, had. Several of his New York colleagues in the House were running unopposed; Richie wasn't so lucky, and Michael occasionally told him that he was the one who was financing Rex Carr (could that really have been the name bestowed by his rival's parents?) just to keep Richie on his toes.

Once a week, since he was running a fairly lackadaisical campaign, Richie, Nadie, Charlie, and Riley had dinner somewhere, tonight at Bistro Italiano—Richie paying, of course, and Nadie, Charlie, and Riley telling him what to do and how to do it. The *primi piatti* had just been delivered. Nadie removed her hand from his under the table, reached her fork for a piece of grilled artichoke, and said, "Believe me, it would have never gotten as far as it did if she hadn't been egging her on."

"That is so true," said Riley. Riley was having the grilled pepper bruschetta.

"She" was Linda Tripp. "Her" was Monica Lewinsky. Richie did not love talking about the scandal every single moment of every day, but the tapes had, indeed, been so fascinating that even Riley had stopped talking about global warming for a while to talk about them. What was clearest to the women was that Linda did not like Monica much, that she would listen to her, play with her, sympathize with her, prod her. It was Linda, said Riley and Lucille, who worked up the Christmas phone-sex tape that everyone found so shocking (well, no, thought Richie, not shocking). "She was using her," said Nadie. "Just like junior high. Remember that? Some ninth-grader would come up to you and tell you how great your hair looked, and where did you get those loafers, and, by the way, didn't you carpool with So-and-So? And so you would be drawn into this plot to humiliate So-and-So—had she really given Billy Johnson a blow job behind the science building? Ugh. Been there, done that." Nadie shook her head hard, as if shaking spiderwebs out of her hair. Richie thought she was the most worldly female he'd ever met. She was fourteen years younger than he was, and for the first time he understood why men did this, fell for these much younger women—it was just another expression of that social ineptitude they were cursed with. In ninth grade, best go for an eleventh-grader; in college, a girl your own age knew what to do; but once you got her bundled away into a marriage, then both of you lost your touch. Witness Ivy putting her eggs in the billionaire basket.

Nadie was much more suspicious of the sources of the scandal than even Riley. Whereas Richie and Charlie assumed that Clinton was a horny guy whose brain was sometimes overwhelmed by his dick, and who was now paying the price for his obliviousness, Nadie had listened to her parents. She said, "You look at what they are doing to him. It is right out of the KGB—he can have no privacy. What if Hillary did know all about it, about everything over the years, and said, 'That's the way he is, I can live with it'? They would say: Not her business, our business. We are the police. You live like we do and do what we say, or we will ruin you."

"What is the KGB?" said Charlie. Richie wondered if he meant this metaphorically, or if he really didn't know what the KGB was.

Nadie said, "Kristol. Podhoretz. Wolfowitz. Once a commie, always a commie."

"My dad's aunt was a commie," said Richie. "Aunt Eloise. Everyone loved her."

"All of my relatives were commies," said Nadie. "The thing they want most is to be sure that you are thinking the right thoughts. Even if they change their minds, or *when* they change their minds about what the right thoughts are, they still have to make sure that you think them. There may have been hippies in America who thought sex and communism went together, but in the U.S.S.R., this was not so." She smiled merrily, and Richie laughed, but she went on: "They feel it is their right to know everything about you, to hide microphones and make tapes and invade your privacy, because not doing everything according to the party line contaminates and infects society." She sniffed.

"That's like people who are against solar initiatives," said Riley. "They see funding for solar and go bananas. They have arguments, but the bananas comes first." She sighed. Once the scandal blew up, Richie had pretty much stopped talking about solar and wind. Here was how it went: Gore liked solar and wind; Gore was contaminated by Clinton; Clinton was contaminated by Lewinsky; therefore, no talk about solar and wind. It appeared to Richie as though the KGB was winning.

However, they did finish the *primi piatti* and move on, with good appetites, to the pasta—in Richie's case, *paglia e fieno*.

He said, "Here's something. You know, my sister-in-law is a conservative bellwether. I don't know if they are training her or she is training them, but now her thing is abortion. She talks about abortion all the time. Did she once have an abortion? Is she suddenly afraid that her teen-age daughters might get pregnant? Is this monsignor that she always has to dinner firing her up? If my brother didn't father several abortions, I would be amazed, since, if he wanted it, last-minute birth control was up to the girl, but he doesn't say a word. She starts going off about abortion and he sits there, eating his food."

Riley said, "I think reproduction is a crime."

Nadie set down her fork and sighed.

Richie looked at Charlie, who continued to eat his ravioli. He remembered Charlie the first time he met him—what was he then, twenty? Gaily accepting Michael's arm-wrestling challenges, gaily thumping him. Charlie was certainly an example of exceptional breeding—strong, healthy, good-looking, resilient, canny if not smart—combined with intelligent nurture that Charlie was grateful for—he always spoke well of his parents and visited them even when he didn't have to. Surely, if you were his spouse, you would want to breed him. Charlie seemed fine with Riley's childless plans. Richie said to Riley, "So you guys are going to screw us on the Social Security thing?"

Riley said, "Yes. You get busy and make a world that my kids can live in, I'll give you a kid."

Richie knew she meant it.

Richie had spent his legacy on a down payment for a condo within biking distance of his office, and he was glad he had. With lots of light and some spare, appealing furniture, it made a place that Nadie enjoyed, rather like an inexpensive but newly renovated hotel where she could take a break from her own place, which was crammed with her computer, drawings, and papers. She worked from home, hiring herself out to small construction firms that were building groups of houses or apartment buildings. She organized materials, sets of plans, crews of workers; the driveways in Fairfax would be completed by Thursday, and then the crews would head for Arlington. The companies she worked for could throw up a house that conformed to building codes in a couple of months. She had gone around to construction sites and talked to the builders until two or three had hired her. When others saw what she could do, they hired her, too. Some weeks, she drove as far as Philadelphia.

Lying in bed next to her (it was not that late; they'd come home straight from the restaurant, since he had to leave on the 6:00 a.m. train to New York to get to three campaign events the next day), he said, "Could you come along and just spy on my brother? I could set you up somewhere with a telescope."

"I have a job," said Nadie.

She seemed restless, so Richie put his leg over hers and moved her toward him. She was tense for a moment, then relaxed and kissed him. He said, "It wouldn't be a job, it would be a charitable act."

"To whom? When you describe him, Michael sounds like an asshole. Do you want me to declare that he is an asshole, or that he isn't?"

"I want analysis. I want to know why he does what he does."

"What you really want to know is why you care."

"Why do I care?" said Richie. Maybe this was a way to get her to stay.

"I'm not staying," she said, answering his real question. But then, when she saw that he looked disappointed, she said, "I'll go to *What Dreams May Come* with you Saturday night, though."

Richie was not a fan of Robin Williams, but he said, "Okay." She eased herself out of the bed and got dressed. He walked her to the door. Her generation did not like to be accompanied home, he had discovered.

1999

&

THE NEW MAN, Pastor Diehl, had a way of letting his gaze pass over Lois's face without recognition. It happened every single time he stood in the doorway of the church, sending the believers away after the Sunday-morning or the Wednesday-evening services. At first, Lois said nothing to Minnie about this particular insult; she was, after all, Pastor Campbell's most industrious and helpful congregant, had been for years now. But she vocally dismissed Pastor Diehl's views about Clinton, liberals, homosexuals. There were ways in which Lois and Henry were two of a kind—careful, stylish, persnickety about details. She was not going to stand for any sass about homosexuals from a flashy kid who grew up in Missouri, and not even St. Louis or Kansas City, but Bucyrus! Where in the world was that?

First Lois talked to Cecilie Campbell about what she saw as a mutiny. She came home afterward—home to the big house, not to her own house—and made herself a pot of tea, then said to Minnie, who was reading, "That girl doesn't know left from right!" Pastor Campbell's wife was forty-two, Minnie thought, but said nothing. Lois said, "She's glad Pastor Diehl has taken over the ten o'clock service as well as the Wednesday-night service, not to mention the youth crusade! She says Ralph is relieved! He's so exhausted running the place that—"

"Administration is exhausting," said Minnie—a neutral comment, she would have thought.

"Then a young man should do it!"

"Why let him control the money?" said Minnie. That shut Lois up.

She then had a talk with Pastor Campbell himself. He said that he felt out of touch with the latest "fashions," and Lois told him that salvation was not a fashion, but of course it was—Minnie saw that all the time. He was sorry Lois felt that way, but the fact was that he had never considered his sermons much good, so he was happy enough to step back.

After that, Lois stewed for a few days. She went to Diehl, cornered him in the youth center, where he was putting up posters, and accused him of taking over. At first he advised her not to worry: there was no one he respected more than Ralph, and he had a perfect love of Cecilie, who was the ideal wife that he himself hoped for, a quiet, humble, but wise helpmeet, and the children . . .

She wasn't going to stand for it. Lois walked out. He was a hypocrite! All he wanted was to run the place, and he was using politics to make people afraid, to consolidate his power, to ease out one of the best men of God Lois had ever known, a man who was inherently humble and kind but brilliant—

"These things aren't really your business," said Pastor Diehl.

After that, Lois didn't feel comfortable going to the church at all, so she sat around her house, baking this, baking that, mastering cannoli at last. Minnie had seen it before: someone dies, and what had appeared to be peace and contentment explodes in frustration. Finally, on Lincoln's Birthday, which Minnie noted because it was a holiday, Lois showed up at breakfast in her eight-year-old pickup truck and went down into the cellar. The mazelike brick house she and Joe had lived in now for fourteen years had a small cellar, but for real storage, she used this place. Minnie hadn't realized how much was down there.

Lois brought up boxes of beans, lentils, peas, rice, quinoa, wheat berries. Cases of stewed tomatoes, her own canned vegetables, her own dried apple slices, pear wedges, cranberries. Bags of flour, wheat and rye. Bags of sugar, of course. Frozen cuts of pork and steaks; condensed milk. Dried pasta. Oils of various kinds. She was patient and strong. She was pleasant to Minnie and didn't ask her to help, but she did prop the door open. The day before had been warm, but today it was in the twenties again, so Minnie went up to her room, closed the door, and put on two sweaters. Sometimes she looked out the window. Loading the truck bed took two hours. Finally, Minnie saw her slam the tailgate, stand for a moment to regard her work, then turn toward the house. Minnie went down and met her at the door. Lois said, "Well, time to say goodbye."

"Where are you—"

"I'll stay with Annie for a few weeks."

"You're taking all of this to Milwaukee?"

"Heavens, no. I'm dropping it at the church. That Diehl may be telling them that the world is going to end on New Year's, but I don't believe it. Not anymore. Never did, really."

"What about your house?"

"Oh, I'm all moved out of there."

"What about Jesse and Jen and the kids?"

"I'll visit," said Lois.

Minnie said, "I mean, why are you giving all the food to the church and not to the kids?"

"They get the house." She said, "Jen is good. She can take over."

"Take over what?"

"Keeping up the garden. Making sure that you all don't eat poison, I guess. I've had enough. Joe isn't here anymore. Without him to care for, I feel overwhelmed with rage every time I look at the corn and beans or pass that Kum & Go. My heart sinks. It's like I fell asleep forty years ago and woke up in hell. I don't want to have to drive forty miles to Ames to go to Wheatsfield. The other night, in the middle of the night, I thought, 'I am out of place. Just out of place. Diehl is right.' " Minnie didn't dare say that she would miss her—she had that Lois sense of certainty still. Minnie was sorry to see her go, but she dared not object.

ALTHOUGH PART OF Michael's shtick (and as the representative of a district in Brooklyn, Richie could use that word with ease) had always been snickering at Richie's "job," he didn't say a word about impeaching Clinton, didn't say a word about NAFTA, didn't say a word about Bosnia. But when Phil Gramm and Jim Leach came up with their bill to loosen the banking regulations, Michael had plenty to say, all of it erudite and pleased. He started calling Richie on his home phone and his office phone after the Senate passed their version in May.

Richie didn't consider himself any sort of expert on banking, and so was going to vote along party lines—that's how the Senate had voted. Dingell, his colleague on the Energy and Commerce Committee, to whom Riley gave a B because he was from Detroit ("Gas-guzzler central," as Riley said), was completely opposed to changing the laws, and gave Richie an earful every time he saw him in the Capitol building. Dingell always said, "Take it from me, Langdon, those banks are going to expand until they don't know what in the world they are doing, and then they are going to come to us, hat in hand. How many staff do you have?"

"Ten, these days," said Richie.

"And you let them do mostly what they want, right?"

Richie didn't say anything.

"Well, who doesn't? There's only so many hours in the day. But your staff aren't gambling for a living, are they? Doubling down, then doubling down again. Statistically, I'm telling you, sixteen percent of these investment boys are going to be doubling down, and sixteen percent of those are going to go bust on their biggest bets. No CEO or CFO who's got his own life to live, now that he's made it, is going to know a thing about it." Of course, he had a point—he had been in the Congress for as long as Richie had been alive.

Michael said that the financial system would be much more efficient, both for investors and for savers, and that the banks would be safer, because when the economy was up the investors would carry the vig, and when the economy was down the savers would. This sounded reasonable to Richie, if not to Lucille, who didn't have a real argument apart from "disaster in the making" and "inherent greed," but, considering that most of Lucille's insights came to her on the can, Richie had reservations about that, too.

Even apart from the Michael factor, Richie had come to like Jim Leach (R-IA), who reminded him of his cousin Jesse a little, if only in the way he talked. Leach understood derivatives, and he had broken ranks and voted against Gingrich and for abortion rights. Gramm made him about as suspicious as Leach allayed his fears. And, said Michael, the president was for it.

"Who told you that?" said Richie. "His new best friend, Loretta?"

"I don't consult Loretta about money, and she doesn't consult me about morals."

Appropriate division of labor, thought Richie.

"Listen, little bro," said Michael—and, yes, Richie was a half-inch shorter and ten pounds lighter, though, as always, four minutes older—"it's all a mess already. You've got Citicorp eating up Travelers even as we speak. The waitress has dropped the tray, everything has spilled and is running together in a mess. You can't back it up, you have to go forward with it."

"You are making the case that they broke the law against merging investments and savings, and now we change the law to avoid having to punish them?"

"No, I'm making the case that there's a reason the law was broken—that the world is more complex now, and the law has to reflect that. Let's say that in Montana there's no one on the roads, so there's no speed limit. Then let's say that twenty years goes by, and now there are trucks and cars and school buses and motorcycles on the road, but there's still no speed limit. Your job would be to recognize that times have changed, and to institute a speed limit."

"Would you abide by it?"

"If I was driving my Toyota and didn't know any better, yes."

Richie smiled, and it was true that there was some irreverence, some self-conscious humor, in everything that Michael said. "I make no promises."

"It's a vote! Just vote! Who is going to hold it against you? Some fucking deli owner on Flatbush?"

"I'll talk to you later," said Richie. He hung up. Michael did not know when to stop. That was his perennial flaw.

Nadie and Michael, and, more important, Loretta, had now broken bread together. Michael was impressed by her youth, and Loretta thought she had a lot on the ball for someone her age. That was all they thought about her, as far as Richie understood. His mom liked her—she had driven up from what Michael called "the hut" in Far Hills and taken, first Richie and Nadie, then just Nadie, out to lunch. They talked about architecture, and Andy said that Nadie had "a worldly manner," and had read *Oblomov*. Nadie was the only person Andy had ever met besides herself who had read *Oblomov,* one of her favorite novels. Sometime after Nadie and Loretta met, Loretta told Nadie that appearances were deceiving—in spite of the hut and the old clothes, Andy was worth over ten million dollars these days, and she did all her own investing. Nadie's own parents believed that all investments should be portable and kept at home, but Nadie was making good money, and since she saw how houses were built, she didn't want to buy one. So all of that was going well, and, in fact, Leo didn't seem to mind Nadie, either; but one result was that Nadie told Richie more than once that he was obsessed with Michael, everyone thought so, it was his problem. As the vote on the Gramm-Leach-Bliley Bill approached, he could not ask Nadie's opinion, because that would cause him to talk about Michael, and thereby reinforce her idea of his obsession, and she would extrapolate from that to general obsessiveness on his part, and she would be even less inclined to make up her mind to marry him, which he ardently desired and she may have been inching toward, but not very quickly.

In the end, it was because Michael went too far—called him from Biarritz twice in one day, when Richie was pissed that his air conditioner was on the fritz and Washington boiling. He stewed in his seat for an hour, trying to make up his mind, then decided that he needed psychiatric help of some sort, then voted in favor, then saw that 137 other Dems had voted in favor, apparently without the onset of any personal trauma at all. Representatives stood up, stretched, walked around, yawned. Business as usual, torment confined to Congressman Richard Langdon of New York's 9th district.

HENRY'S BOOK of essays on Gerald of Wales, which had been published by the University of Wisconsin Press, had elicited one review in an obscure English journal. Books that Oxford and Cambridge published these days were larger and more ambitious consolidations of material that crossed disciplinary lines. And no one was much interested in historical linguistics; some authorities didn't adhere at all to the idea that there had been a Proto-Indo-European culture of the sort that his mentor, Professor McGalliard, had taught him about. Probably there had been a culture and a language, but who was to say that it had spawned in a logical way? Maybe it had simply fragmented and re-formed randomly?

Henry's new project, therefore, was to read everything that had been written since he'd more or less lost interest, and to add to that archeology, anthropology, paleobiology. It was a huge project, and he expected to die before he finished it. A very invigorating thought. Who was that scholar, in Germany somewhere, who had spent her life putting together a Gothic-Germanic-Nordic dictionary, and when she died her filing cabinets were discovered to be filled with empty brandy bottles? But scholarship was different now, with conferences and computers and cheap travel, no longer lonely and cold. Especially, no longer cold. He was not looking forward to going back to Chicago, back into his cave of books. Maybe Lois, who was living at his place while he lingered in D.C., would sell them—she was practical like that. Minnie and Claire burbled on about Lois "abandoning the farm, her whole life," but Lois herself didn't seem to feel it as a crisis. Henry admired her.

Every week, he saw Charlie and Riley, and sometimes, he saw Richie and the new girlfriend. He had them all convinced that he was very, very busy. He made it a practice to refer to people that he met in the library, what they said, what they were like, when, really, he was only overhearing something or other from time to time. The person in the library that he talked to was one of the security guards, an African American man who lived in Alexandria, whose hobby was the Civil War, or, as he called it, the War Between the States. Twice he took Henry to visit battlefields, Spotsylvania and Manassas. Henry could tell that the man—Forrest La France was his name—felt sorry for him. But Henry didn't feel sorry for himself. Every single day when he put on a pair of lightweight khakis and a pima-cotton shirt with the sleeves rolled twice, every day when he put on his straw hat, every day when he took a clean handkerchief out of his drawer and knew that he would be using it to pat the sweat off his brow, he was happy, because he was not in Chicago, it was not winter, the wind off the lake was not laden with snow.

He had accepted that if you were a bookish person the events in your life took place in your head. Once upon a time for Henry, those events had been dramatic; as the years went by, his skin prickling when Heathcliff ran out of the house calling "Cathy!" had given way to a gasp when Mr. Carker the Manager was hit by a train, and then to a quiet thrill when Beowulf found himself in Grendel's mother's cave. He had learned early on not to look up from the book and say, "Listen to this." In graduate school, his pleasure in the dramatic gave way to something more abstract—yes, there had been the pleasures of words and their roots. Not only was "foot" connected to "fetlock" and "pedal," but it was also connected to "impeccable" and "appoggiatura." Not only was Artemis the sister of Apollo and the virgin goddess of the hunt, she was also Britomartis on Crete, an archaic mother goddess, no relation to Apollo at all. There were books that Henry remembered so clearly that he could still picture the pages he had read and the places where he had read them. One of these was *The Hero with a Thousand Faces*. Henry was in Berkeley and he dared to say to his cousin Rosa, "Who is Joseph Campbell?" She handed him the book, and he read it in a day, sitting on her mother, Eloise's, porch in the sunshine. Gods and goddesses had eventually paled in comparison with wheat, rice, and corn, thanks to *Les Structures du quotidien*—that would have been on the beach beside Lake Michigan, sitting under an umbrella with Philip (he kept looking at Philip, the way you did when someone fascinated you), grinding his heels into the sand nearby. All of these books were carefully sorted and shelved in his apartment, and though he had loved them, perhaps they had held him back—they had been so lordly in their tone, so sure of themselves, so hardbacked and dense. Lost in the library, Henry had forgotten that the very men who wrote these books were out and about—some of Eloise's friends of friends remembered Campbell himself on the beach, yakking it up about crabs and sea urchins with Ed Ricketts. The two men would have been half the age that Henry was now.

His problem was Chicago, not books, but he was retired, wasn't he? Didn't have to go back to Chicago at all. If your life remained in your mind, complex and busy, full of what you had read as well as what you had done and whom you had met, you could carry it into the future, and it would all, somehow, flow together. That was his hope, and his superstition, and he planned to stay in D.C. as long as he could.

RILEY SAID THAT deciding to hike the Appalachian Trail was not something that you did by waking up in the middle of the night the day before Halloween, and, as always, Charlie had nodded and agreed with her. Nevertheless, when he got to work at the outdoor outfitters Monday morning, he went straight to the book-and-guide department and pulled out a guide. By lunch, he saw that he could start down in Georgia, where the weather was still pleasant, and just keep walking until it got too cold to go on. He had the equipment, even the orange vest (obviously, there would be plenty of people hunting, since it would be November), and he could get the trail provisions at a discount. His manager would give him the time off—their busy time was the spring and summer, and Charlie hadn't taken any vacation in two years.

By his afternoon break, he was walking around the shoes-and-boots department, wondering if he needed a new pair: you never wanted to break in your boots on the trail, but his were getting pretty worn. Supposedly, you would start out hiking eight miles a day, but Charlie thought he could do twelve or more. After work, he ran to Dupont Circle double-quick, got an earlier train than usual, and could not keep his mind on his book, which was *The Hound of the Baskervilles*. Henry made him alternate, man's book, woman's book; the last one he'd read was *Northanger Abbey*. Riley had him reading books, too—next to his bed was *A Sand County Almanac*. Riley was powering through *Guns, Germs, and Steel,* marveling from time to time that those Menominee ancestors (but really "Mamaceqtaw") had managed to survive at all, and Charlie glanced at her surreptitiously while suppressing the yawns that came from his own reading material. More than once, he lost his place and started over, only dimly recognizing passages he'd read minutes before. He had two books on his side of the bed. Her side was close to the window, and her "currently reading" set ran in a line along the sill, blocking out the morning light almost as well as the shades they hadn't bothered to buy yet.

He got home. He helped make dinner very pleasantly, broccoli soup, veggie omelet. He chopped the vegetables and warmed the day-old whole-wheat baguette. She set the table.

Charlie said, "I talked to Fred. He doesn't need me after Thursday, so I think I will—"

"Oh, for God's sake."

Charlie looked at the wall above Riley's head and assembled his arguments.

"Hey, babe. I need a break, and it's not that expensive. Say I'm out there for a month, which is not likely; at the most that's three hundred dollars—well, three fifty. I've got all the equipment I need. That old sleeping bag from Aspen that's good down to ten below, we haven't used that in years. Perfectly good tent, too." He tried to sound conversational. "I looked at the boots, but I couldn't justify getting a new pair at this point. Maybe in the spring or summer—"

"You will be gone for a month?"

"Three weeks, then? I thought a month would be the absolute outside."

"What if I have to go away for a few days? How will you know?"

Charlie knew she was talking about Thanksgiving, which, as a semi-official Menominee, she would not celebrate, but she didn't mind spending the day with friends. He said, "The house will be empty and the oven will be off."

"Oh God."

But she didn't raise her voice. She sounded more or less resigned. Charlie pressed on.

"You know that too long in the city makes me jittery, you know that. When we lived in New York, I went upstate every couple of weeks." He smoothed his voice. "You went, too."

"I cannot take a month off to walk the Appalachian Trail."

"Eventually, you will have to take time off."

"The congressman takes enough time off for both of us."

This could be a sticking point: Charlie knew that Riley knew that Charlie knew that he liked Richard Langdon better than Riley did. "Hard-hitting" was not the word for Congressman Langdon, but every Congress needed some congeniality, that was Charlie's view of politics.

"Ivy is pretty strict about sharing the child-care duties, at least when Richie is back in Brooklyn."

"I don't disagree with her," said Riley. But she did. It would have helped if Leo had been a charming, sunny fifth-grader with a smile for everyone, but he was not. He had been known to lie facedown on the office floor and refuse to move, so that everyone had to step over him. Of course, that had last happened when he was six; he was now ten.

Charlie reorganized himself. "I know you—"

"You should go." She set down her soup spoon.

"Well, I do think—" But he felt himself backtracking.

"No," she said, "don't think. It's me that hasn't been thinking. You have to move. You have to walk. You have to— Well, shit. Look at you. All day long you equip people for adventures, and your biggest adventure is running a loop around Dupont Circle."

Charlie said, "You aren't seeing someone, are you?"

Finally, Riley laughed a big, hearty laugh, and said, "I am only seeing the light, sweetie pie. I am looking up from my keyboard and recognizing . . ." She paused, gazed at him. "I am recognizing that you are, indeed, the most patient male I've ever met." Her toe began to rub his ankle, and he had no need of his third and fourth arguments.

The Tercel, he thought, was happy to be out. Fifteen years old, a hundred thousand miles, and why replace it? said Riley. It still got forty-two miles to the gallon. She had her eye on something called a "Prius," already available in Japan, and supposedly ready to go on sale in the United States, though every time she drove into a Toyota dealership in the Tercel, they said they had no idea when the Prius would be available, and had she ever considered a Corolla? No, she had not.

The Tercel was also perfect for this trip, since it was too old to get stolen. Charlie left D.C. at 5:00 a.m. on Friday, and was in the Chattahoochee National Forest by three; it was bleak, gray, and cold. The trees were nearly leafless, but the trail was hard enough, only muddy here and there. He locked the car with two hours left until sundown, and set off.

Charlie didn't care much about day and night. His eyesight was good, he had been outdoors in all weathers, and as long as it wasn't pouring rain he was comfortable enough. He started walking, and almost immediately it came over him, that energy. Inhale. Step. Step. Exhale. Inhale. His boots felt good, the way they conformed to his feet and embraced them. His socks felt comfortably warm, friendly. His old wool pants, hard to find anymore, were warm even when wet. His hat was pushed back on his head. Inhale. Exhale. Ponder the Cherokee—Riley had read him a few things before he left. But his thoughts kept drifting to Jordan Del Piero, with whom he had smoked some weed in high school (in the bedroom; yes, Mom), who now had three kids and was working for an important law firm in Clayton. And could he believe that Rianna Gray—that little thing, she looked twelve when she was seventeen—had published a novel? His mom had seen Moira Lutz at Kroger's—in the baby-food aisle. She had two kids, and was married to someone important at Monsanto. His mom always said these things in a gossipy, idle tone, as if she didn't care, but she did, and he knew what she told them: Oh, Charlie, he's a late bloomer, I guess. Or: Oh, Charlie, he lets poor Riley do all the work.

To his right, just for fifty feet, the hill fell away in the twilight. With the onset of night, the forest gave up its scents, but Charlie was too far south to recognize what they were. Inhale. Exhale. At parties, Riley did hug him and say, "Oh, this is just Charlie. He works at Hudson's." Some of the men then chatted with him, but none of the women, not in Washington. He lengthened his stride. His skin looked like he'd spent years outside without sunblock, but the only way he seemed to be aging was that his hairline was receding. Was it strange that he had given so little thought to the future, that he was so engrossed in the next few steps that he had forgotten about the cliff at the end of the path? It felt good to walk, though. Good, possibly, to be dismissed and given up on. He lengthened his stride again, and thought, Being given up on is the nature of freedom, isn't it? And then thought that maybe this was the first real thought of the rest of his life.

2000

JANET WAS on the verge of deciding that the whole thing wasn't her business after all when the last call came in, from Loretta in Antigua. Janet looked at her watch; it was ten in Palo Alto, so it might be two in Antigua, time for lunch. Loretta said, "Did they call you and tell you they found him?"

"Yes, he's at the ranch. He sneaked in in the night, and your mom found him in one of the guest rooms after the school called her."

"I can't believe the school let him escape."

"I don't think the grounds are fenced or anything; I mean, I've only driven past it, but it's not high-security."

"Shit."

"How long are you in Antigua?"

"We just got here two days ago, so two weeks. Magnus has a sailing yacht. This afternoon, we're headed for Montserrat."

Janet looked at the mirror on her closet door and made a face like a dog growling.

"—can you please go get him and take him back? I would be so grateful. I don't dare ask my mom to do it—she shouldn't be driving at all, she says her shoulders hurt too much. Dad only drives on the ranch."

Janet heard herself say, "I can do that. It's—what?—an hour and a half. Jonah has art class after school today, so I don't have to pick him up until four. That's six hours from now." After all, she had never been to the ranch.

"I love you," said Loretta. "Michael thinks—" But then the connection failed, and Janet never heard this piece of very interesting information.

When she got there, Chance was on a horse in the arena beside the barn, practicing spins and slides. Janet had never seen him on a horse. She recognized at once that this was his real self, not the neatly trimmed and well-clothed boy she saw at restaurants or when she'd picked him up at SFO a couple of times. His heels were down, his body was limber, his shoulders were loose, and his cowboy hat (Janet would have put him in a riding helmet) was dirty and well used—it fit him perfectly. What was he, sixteen or seventeen? Janet couldn't remember. Then she looked again, and saw that there were several Angus calves milling in a pen attached to the arena, and that Chance had his riata looped over the horn of his saddle. She walked toward the calves, and one of them put his nose through the fence and mooed. That was when Chance saw her.

He cantered over, slid to an easy halt. He said, "Aunt Janet. You came to get me."

"I did," said Janet.

"Mom sent you."

"She did," said Janet. "What's your horse's name?" Janet reached through the fence and tickled the chestnut on the cheek.

Chance said, "Bogey. Grandma named him. He has a sister named Bacall." When Janet grinned, he asked, "How's Emily doing with Pattycake?"

"I don't know who hates the New England weather more, Emily or Pattycake. They should have gone to Pomona."

"Grandma says I can stay here. The season is about to begin. I'm going to practice for the spring, and then go on the circuit."

"What circuit?"

"Roping."

"What about school?"

"I hate school."

Janet knew that if this were Jonah talking she would be hitting the roof, but that was Loretta's job.

"Is your grandmother in on this?"

"Gran thinks I have talent and should use it while I can. Bogey is thirteen, we've trained him perfectly, he's peaking, and so am I." He sounded very reasonable. He patted the horse and said, "Reining horses take a long time to grow up. Grandpop told me that when he gave him to me, when I was in first grade."

Janet said, "Don't you graduate this year? Just graduate, then do it."

"Nope."

Janet climbed onto the lowest railing of the fence and leaned over it, grabbing Bogey's rein. She said, "Chance. It's four months. Graduate."

"Mom already sent my college applications in. Georgetown, St. Louis U., Fordham. Not Notre Dame, because it's not Jesuit."

"What does your dad say?"

"Do you mean Michael or Father?"

Janet barked a laugh, but Chance wasn't joking. She said, "Michael, I guess."

"He says, fuck you."

To whom? thought Janet. But she said, "Okay, even so, I think we can work this out. Just come with me—"

Bogey started backing up, fast, tucking his chin, flopping his ears, right out of her grasp. Then he spun, and a moment later, Chance and Bogey were galloping across the arena, then through the open gate at the far end. Janet stood up, shadowed her eyes, saw them disappear around the barn, and then reappear moments later, galloping up a trail that crossed a hillside behind the house. They were going fast.

Janet drove to the house. Loretta's mom was standing in the doorway, a little hunched, perhaps waiting for her. She said, "He's a very stubborn boy," as she stepped back to let Janet in. It was now twelve-forty-five.

Janet said, "I wonder where in the world he gets that."

"I say nothing," said Gail Perroni. Janet had liked her every time they met—three or four times now.

Of course there was food. Gail led her into the kitchen, where two places were set. She said, "I thought you might be hungry. Pop is out with Teo—that's the foreman—checking the fence line at the far end of the ranch; heavens, that's miles and hours away. And a good thing. I'm going to have to break him in easy to having Chance here."

Janet said, "I thought he was crazy about Chance."

"Oh, he is, but he's going to be just like Lori about this. I've spent her whole life trying not to be outnumbered by the two of them."

She ladled out what looked like tortilla soup, then offered Janet crisp tortilla strips, slices of avocado, and chopped tomatoes for garnish. She said, "I'm having iced tea, but we have some Cokes somewhere."

"Iced tea is fine," said Janet as she pulled out her chair. The soup looked so good that the trip became worth it.

Gail looked at her bowl with pleasure, then began eating. She seemed very relaxed. Once Janet had eaten some, and taken a few sips of her tea, Gail said, "I guess you'll have to leave by two, in case you hit traffic."

Janet said, "I guess Chance won't be going with me."

"Oh, I doubt he'll be back by then. Bogey can be out all day. He's as fit as they come."

They continued to eat.

Gail touched her napkin to her lips—very gently, since she was wearing lipstick, a fuchsia-orange, and plenty of rouge, too. Janet said, "Loretta is very upset."

"She'll be fine. A fait accompli is about the only thing that has ever worked with that girl."

To the best of Janet's knowledge, Loretta was not yet forty-five. Gail looked older than her own mom, but that could be years of sun. Gail tipped her soup bowl and spooned out the last bite, then helped herself to another slice of avocado. Then she sighed, and smiled. She said, "Well, I feel a lot better now. So—I knew this was coming."

"Did he say something over Christmas?"

"I knew this was coming sixteen years ago, when Dalla— Remember her? She was the nanny?—she would say to me, 'Ma'am, do you think that boy can hear? I call him and I call him, and he just walks away.' So we did a test. He was stacking blocks, and we sneaked up behind him—you know, to clap or something? Well, he heard us coming, no problem. Nope, he hears you fine, but only when you are saying what he's interested in. It isn't going to do him one bit of harm to take time off from that prison in Portola Valley. I don't know why she sent him out here. I told her not to, but she would do it her way. If he goes out on the circuit for a year, he'll learn that that's a hard life.

A friend of ours had a boy who was determined to be a rodeo clown. He did that for exactly a year and screamed to come home, and Jane, that was his mom, she said, 'Nope, you do it till you've learned all about it.' It's dangerous. He lasted a good four years." She stood up and picked up her bowl, then Janet's. "Now he's a vet. Even vet school is a breeze compared to being a rodeo clown."

"Who tells Loretta?"

"Don't you have caller ID?"

"On my phone?"

Gail nodded. "Then you don't need to answer, do you?"

"Will she ever speak to me again?"

"Oh, she'll come back from the Caribbean, and then she'll come out here fit to be tied, and then that boy'll show her what he can do on that horse, and it's a sight, I'm telling you. And he'll kiss her and hug her and pooch out his lips and say, 'C'mom, Ma, please?' And she'll stomp around the house for an hour and maybe go call that priest, whatever his name is, but she'll come around."

Janet said, "Is she going to be mad at you?"

Gail looked relaxed in a cat-that-ate-the-canary sort of way. "I'm used to that, believe me."

Then Janet said, "Can I call you when I need parenting advice?"

Now Gail squeezed her across the shoulders. Then she nodded and said, "Almost two now. Takes twenty minutes just to get out to the road."

As she got into her car, Janet decided that this was, indeed, a Perroni matter, not a Langdon matter. Of course, a part of her thought Loretta was getting what she deserved, but another part of her applied this lesson to Jonah—when and if Jonah were to put his foot down, would Janet then be getting what was coming to her for encouraging, or not discouraging, Chance? Janet had never told any of her Palo Alto friends about her period with the Peoples Temple; they thought she and Jared were fresh out of the East, Minnesota, Iowa, vaguely New Jersey. Nor did she often go into the city, as different as it was now from the chaos it had been in those days. No one she knew now could imagine what San Francisco was like in the 1970s, and she didn't know anyone now that she had been close to in the Temple. She hadn't heard from Marla, who was teaching theater at Wellesley and doing occasional plays in Boston and the Berkshires, in seven years. She doubted she would recognize anyone else besides Lucas—ah, Lucas (was he the love of her life?)—who was putting on weight and had safely moved on from youthful good-looking nice young African American man roles to more substantive and weathered father roles, mostly on the TV, though she had seen him twice in movies. And that was a good thing.

When she arrived at the school twelve minutes past her usual time, Jonah wasn't the last child waiting—only the second to last. She apologized to the teacher. Jonah was sitting quietly on the wall that ran along the drive, kicking his heels against the bricks. When he saw her, he sighed and jumped to the ground. He dragged his backpack to the car, picking it up only when the teacher said, "Come on, Jonah, you can carry that."

Janet opened his door, and Jonah got into his car seat. He was small, and she still had nightmares about him slithering under the belts of his very expensive Britax and rolling up like a millipede beneath the passenger's seat. He was, she had to admit, much like Emily had been at his age, reserved and suspicious. She suspected that those who discussed this behind her back agreed that he got it from her.

Two days later, she was brave enough to answer the phone even though she could tell the number was international. It was Loretta. But she wasn't angry. She thanked Janet for "doing her best" and said her parents' "united front" with Chance against her and Michael was like the Great Wall of China. Loretta knew better than to argue at her age.

AFTER BILL BRADLEY dropped out of the presidential race in March, Riley stopped speaking to Richie. Riley's support for Bradley had rather surprised Richie, since Gore said a lot more about global warming. But Riley's mother had mentioned to Riley that when she was working in a factory of some sort in 1968, the minimum wage had been $1.60, and her mother had, in fact, been paid $1.75. Now the minimum wage was $5.15, but Riley calculated that, according to inflation, it should be $8.00. That $2.85 per hour times however many minimum-wage workers there were in the United States was the exact price of the Clinton administration's failures of character and policy, and Riley thought Gore was a fraud, though with a small "f," not with a capital "F," like those sleazy Clintons (nor did she believe a thing the Republicans said about their activities in Arkansas). Nadie (whom Richie still saw once in a while, although she said that her relationship with him had convinced her that she was a lesbian, and he should take that as a compliment) said that they were living in a fool's paradise if they thought that (a) Bradley had a chance and (b) Bradley was a real liberal, but Riley was nothing if not stubborn. Her attitude had hardened toward everyone except, Richie thought, Charlie. Charlie had had a revelation in the fall, on the Appalachian Trail, and was now getting ready to apply to nursing school after taking a few courses that he'd missed in college. He wanted to be a nurse and an EMT trauma specialist—one of those guys who fly to people who find themselves on narrow cliffs overlooking precipitous valleys and must be rescued by someone swinging from a rope underneath a helicopter. Riley was very enthusiastic—she said school would keep him occupied for at least three years. The nursing school wasn't far from their apartment.

Ivy, too, found herself single again. The first thing that happened, around New Year's, was that Ivy uncovered the fact that the billionaire was sleeping with a twenty-three-year-old M.B.A. student at NYU. When she confronted him, he asked her to marry him, and for about a week she considered this option, but then, at a party at the manse in New Rochelle, a woman she had met through him said, "Oh, heavens, Ivy, don't you know Bob's philosophy of the bedroom? 'A wife, a mistress, and a bit on the side.'" According to Ivy, who came to Washington with Leo and spent the weekend on Richie's couch, Bob had confessed that wifely duties were rather more arduous, and possibly less rewarding, than mistress duties, but he still considered marrying him to be a promotion, and so she let things go along, apparently congenially, until Valentine's Day, when she sent him a breakup valentine. For Richie, as for many divorced men with no talent for being single, the fantasy of reuniting with Ivy persisted, but in fact that would mean weekends together with Leo. Leo was much easier one to one. Ivy said that it was her experience that the marriages that lasted forever were in fact the worst ones. Richie knew she meant Michael and Loretta, and he wasn't about to disagree with her—the screaming matches about Chance (with the monsignor refereeing from the sidelines) were as loud as he'd ever heard. They did not argue about whether or not Chance was going to spend the next year or so trailering Bogey and Bacall from rodeo to rodeo all over the West (and maybe up to Calgary)—he was. Rather, they argued about who was to blame, either because of a failure of parenting styles or because of dysfunctional genes. Tia and Binky seemed to get the message, though: they got all A's and did what they were told.

As for Richie's reelection campaign, his seat was safe—his opponent this time was a thirty-year-old possibly being trained to do such basic operations as read, add, subtract, and sign checks. The boy's main qualifications as a candidate were an aggressive posture and a readiness to say, "I would like to see what Congressman Langdon has actually done for the businessmen of the ninth district!" The national Democratic Party was on track to raise more money than the Republicans, and more money than they had ever raised before since the fall of Rome. It seemed to Richie that all he had to do to get funds was smile and say thank you; his coffers were at $560,000, including what he hadn't spent the last time. Nadie found this worrisome, as did her girlfriend who ran a fitness gym in Arlington that was full of Republican women in leotards ("She has claw marks all over her body," said Nadie). But Richie felt good—he felt that he, too, had survived, just like Clinton and Gore. What he said about Clinton on the campaign trail was that he admired the man. Watching him get through his presidency was like watching someone strolling along on the other side of a nice green hedge. He was smiling, he was chatting on his mobile phone, he was enjoying the landscape, and he seemed to know where he was going and what he was doing. And then there was a break in the hedge, and you saw that vicious dogs were attached to both of his ankles by their teeth, growling, biting, being dragged across the grass, refusing to let go. Riley was right in her way, but Richie thought he was also right, and the donations pouring into Democratic coffers seemed to demonstrate that the voters thought that anyone would be better than the Republicans.

JESSE HAD DECIDED, with some input from Jen and her brothers, that it was better to raise GMO crops than not to do so, and the logic was simple: There was only so much land, and the world population was rising faster and faster. A farmer's primary moral obligation was to avoid famine and soil loss, and, at least for now, GMO corn and beans were doing that. You had to be careful, you had to be precise, but Jesse was. His dad might have been a saint (every time he'd said this, his dad shook his head), but when he started farming in the 1930s (*and* grew his own hybrid seed, according to an old story), things were much different. The GMO corn Jesse planted was Roundup-resistant, like his beans. He could and did make the ecological case.

It must have been mid-August, and hot, when Jesse was driving on the other side of Denby, past the Gorman place on Quarry Road, and saw three heads in the cornfield, just visible above the very green and very tall rows. He didn't think anything of it; no one else mentioned it at the café. But after Labor Day, it came out that Bill Gorman had gotten some legal papers in the mail accusing him of stealing Monsanto property, and Jesse thought of those heads, in feed caps, looking down, pausing once or twice. He realized that those men had been taking samples of Bill's plants—maybe leaves, maybe kernels—and then they must have tested the genetic material. At first, according to Russ Pinckard, Bill treated this as a joke—he really did think some prankster had forged some papers in order to tease him for not using Roundup Ready seed, which was expensive and picky. Then he had put off addressing it; there was too much else to do around the farm, around any farm, especially at harvest, to waste your time looking for a lawyer and dealing with something that was obviously crap.

Except that he then got a bill, or something of the sort, saying that he owed Monsanto money for stealing their property. Rumors abounded concerning the amount of money—$1,500, $15,000, $34,500. No one, least of all Bill, could take this seriously, and then he went to a lawyer in Usherton with the papers, and the lawyer had never heard of such a thing. However, a lawyer in Des Moines had heard of such a thing. When Bill pointed out (in a rather loud voice) that he did not use Monsanto seed and never had, it was suggested that pollen from the neighboring farm, which belonged to a big operation based in Omaha, must have drifted into his field—a kind of wave of Monsanto-related corn pushing into a larger population of unrelated corn indicated that possibly wind drift "accounted" for the "theft"; however, Monsanto asked permission to test the rest of the field, and to test the crop already harvested, before it was taken to the grain elevator.

But, of course, much of the harvest had already been taken to the grain elevator.

If that was the case, said the Monsanto lawyer, then they would present an estimate of what was owed according to how large the field was, how close the neighboring field was, and the weather patterns over the summer, and they would expect that estimate to be paid out of Bill Gorman's sales to the grain elevator.

Jesse was not the only one who considered this eye-blinkingly crazy.

Bill's lawyer presented the Monsanto lawyer with five years of seed-purchasing paperwork—genetically modified corn had only been on the market since '97, so five years seemed like plenty. No Monsanto seed had ever been purchased at any point. The lawyer made the case that Bill was not responsible for wind-borne pollen. The Monsanto lawyer made the case that Bill had benefited from property that Monsanto owned, and that he was, in effect, selling stolen goods. The law stated that even if someone sold stolen goods unknowingly, once they found out, they had to compensate the rightful owner of the goods. The very fact that Bill had gotten quite a good harvest—165 bushels an acre—indicated that he had, knowingly or unknowingly, benefited. His yield was closer to that of farmers who had planted Monsanto seed than it was to that of farmers who had not.

Jesse had gotten an average of 169 bushels per acre.

Of course, then everyone remembered hearing of this before— somewhere in Ohio, somewhere in Illinois. Finally, one day, at the café, Jesse himself piped up and said, "Well, I did use Monsanto seed, and I did choose to pay more for it, so maybe they have a point," and without Jesse's meaning for it to happen, lots of farmers stopped speaking to one another, and all their disagreements were entirely about the principle of the thing.

Garst was in trouble, too, because some of its feed corn that included a pesticide against corn borers turned up in taco shells at a Taco Bell somewhere. Minnie said that her dad had always liked Garst—the company had started over in Coon Rapids, though it was now based down in Slater, and had been the first one anybody knew of that really pushed hybrid seed. Jesse had paused over the Garst seed, called StarLink, in the spring. It was different from the Monsanto, not resistant to herbicides but resistant to corn borers and caterpillars, really, which could destroy your field, eating not only the ears but the stalks. He had studied corn borers, which originated in Europe, in ag school. They were indeed a pest. But he had decided in the spring that they weren't enough of a problem around Usherton—more down around Burlington and over into Illinois and Indiana. In addition to that, you had to plant a field of nonresistant corn the next field over, as a refuge for the corn borers. Whether you could do this or not depended on how the fields were configured and where your neighbors were. Jen wouldn't have liked him to plant the Garst—she was nervous the way his mom had been about contaminants in the kids' food—but Jesse saw it as a dilemma that was possibly not soluble. Every time the chemical companies said that they had conquered a problem, the moths, or the weeds, regrouped and attacked from another angle. Jen's dad said that maybe everyone should give a thought to rabies, or trichinosis, or cow pox, or bovine tuberculosis. Those were the diseases his parents and grandparents talked about, not some allergy to some pesticide that was hardly there in the first place.

But old man Guthrie didn't say anything in the Denby Café, and Jesse stayed away. He figured that the ruckus would die down once the lawyers worked things out for Bill Gorman—chances were, he was only being made an example of, and people would be more careful in the future. By February, everyone would be looking at their bank accounts, not their fields, to decide what to plant and which seed company to stay friends with. Every farmer Jesse knew had principles, but you couldn't tell what they were by looking at their fields.

AFTER LOIS LEFT, Minnie got restless. Goodness, she was eighty-one now, but she still felt fine, so she went to a travel agent in Usherton and booked herself a trip to Paris. The woman kept saying in a loud voice, "And is this a gift, Mrs. Frederick?" until, finally, Minnie had to stand up, lean over the desk, and use her most principally manner, "No, Vivien Carroll, it is not a gift. *I* am going to Paris." The only hotel she could afford was south of the Eiffel Tower, near the Bir-Hakeim Métro stop. The trip was to last for ten days; she would walk off her restlessness, she would explore parts of Paris she had never visited and parts that she had enjoyed before, she would learn to negotiate the Paris Métro at last. For two weeks before her trip, she walked around the farm (the weather was beautiful), repeating French phrases—"*Je vous en prie*," "*De rien*," "*Où est la toilette, s'il vous plaît?*" Would it be better if she had some old man to go with? Some complainer with a cane? Some aged man-about-town who would always be talking about better times? She didn't think so.

But Paris turned out to be too much for her. The Métro was well meaning but complex, taxis were expensive, she couldn't figure out the bus system. She ended up walking around that neighborhood—Boulevard de Grenelle at the Quai Branly—for seven days, a few hours a day. The most cultural thing she did was to walk down the Quai de Grenelle and back up the Avenue Émile Zola, and it exhausted her. It was no help that women her age, small, wrinkled, dressed mostly in black, seemed to putter along on the sidewalks, never looking in shopwindows or at passersby. When she looked in shopwindows, she looked like those women, so she stopped looking in shopwindows.

She told Jesse and Jen that she had had a wonderful time, couldn't wait to go back, but she knew that this was her last trip, that somehow it had served as a punishment, though exactly for what she couldn't say, maybe for being so sure of herself all these years.

And yet she was restless. A week after she got back, she drove her old Mazda into Usherton and parked in the lot of the Peaceful Acres Nursing Home. She was wearing her best dress and carrying the handbag, yellow leather, that Claire had sent her at Easter, maybe as a joke. She made herself straight, strong, and determined, and went inside. The young woman at the desk gave her a kindly smile and also spoke rather loudly, forming her words carefully. Minnie said, "May I speak to the manager, please?" Then, "It's about employment. I would like to apply for a job." Why not? she thought. All hands on deck. She had just read in the *Register* that young people were deserting Iowa in droves.

The difficult part, it turned out, was telling Jen and Jesse that night at supper. She didn't tell them that she had told her new boss, Marian Crest, that she would do anything—cook, mop floors, push old people around in their wheelchairs, wash dishes—but since she

had a résumé that Marian (maybe about forty) was vaguely familiar with, Marian had hired her to maintain records; in an old folks'
home, records had to be maintained about every single thing. Her
first week or two would be spent filing. The unspoken plan, both she
and Marian knew, was that at some point in the future she would live
there, perhaps still performing her job.

Jen said, "What are they paying you?"

"Five fifteen an hour, eight hours a day, three days a week. It
might go up if I do a good job."

Felicity said, "Aunt Minnie, you aren't going to be here when I get
home from school!"

"Well," said Minnie, "three days a week, no. But if you get on the
junior high basketball team, I can pick you up on my way home."

"I'll never get on the basketball team," said Felicity.

Jen said, "If you worked on your layups the way I showed you . . ."
But Felicity stared her down. Felicity was almost twelve, ready to
consign all of her relatives to the outer darkness. Jen was the first
to go, but Minnie thought it wouldn't be long until she, too, was
beneath contempt.

The drive to work was harder than she thought it would be, more
full of unpleasant surprises. Like the car she hadn't seen when she
started the left turn, which suddenly appeared in her passenger-side
window, honking. Like the bike she did see, but came so close to anyway that the cyclist gave her the finger. Twice, when it was storming
at the end of her shift, Marian let her stay in one of the empty "suites"
for the night, and the suite had a distinct air of being her future home.
As for her job, well, there was nothing an old woman liked better
than setting things straight. She even, thanks to Felicity, managed to
upload all the records onto a couple of disks and bring them in after
a weekend. Marian gave her a harried raise, ten cents an hour; the
Peaceful Acres Nursing Home didn't have a lot of money to spare. It
was working out, Minnie thought, but it was working out the way
transitions did—organizing itself, smoothing itself, breaking you in
to a new, less desirable life, helping you forget what you cherished
about the old life. She told Jesse and Jen that everything was fine and
kept her other feelings to herself, as she always had.

ANDY THOUGHT that she understood her computer pretty well. Jared had brought it to her—it was an Apple—and he had overseen the installation of her dial-up connection. She enjoyed it. It worked most of the time. She found that she could look at pictures of lots of places that were quite beautiful, and she would never have to visit any of them. She rummaged around in magazines, printed out recipes, communicated with Janet and Richie and Loretta by e-mail, read newspapers and other "Web sites." But, most of all, every few days, she checked her brokerage account. There were certain mysteries, such as why the connection worked sometimes but not all the time, why pictures came up instantly or not at all, why she was sure she had typed in the proper password but it still didn't work. She had never encountered the mystery she encountered on November 6, the day before Election Day (Richie had told her to vote for Gore). According to her account information, the previous Friday, she had had $10,765,986.23. On Monday, she had nothing. The first thing she did was reboot the computer, and the second thing she did was call her broker. His line rang and rang, and no one, not even the secretary, picked it up. With some alarm, she then signed into her bank account. She remembered her password, though it took a moment. In her two savings accounts, she had $68,900.23. In her checking account, she had $14,465.87. So her financial obliteration wasn't global, as they might say on the Internet.

When she called Michael, he said, "Not you, too." Her broker, who was someone that Michael knew, though he didn't have any funds with that firm, was a man almost her own age. She and Frank had put the Uncle Jens fund (twenty-five hundred very impressive dollars) first with that real-estate criminal Rubino (he had been charming, in his way, but when she saw *The Godfather* she had wondered about his origins). After real-estate investments had rolled it over several times, Frank put it into the stock market with a fellow Jim Upjohn recommended, and then that firm was taken over by this man, who stayed on the job when it folded into a larger firm. What was it, 110 years since the death of Uncle Jens? Andy's mom had remembered vaguely that he'd left maybe seventy-five hundred dollars altogether. It was a very Norwegian thing to do to hold a grudge for sixty years after you died.

The youngish man who had been overseeing the funds for the

last four years had come highly recommended, and she had paid not much attention to him at all, since she had a pretty good track record on her own. But now, according to Michael, and then according to the head of the firm, who called all of his bigger clients, the forty-five-year-old had transferred almost a hundred million dollars to a mysterious account somewhere, and had himself left the country. His whereabouts remained mysterious for another four days, until he turned up in Venezuela.

At first, as Andy sat quietly at her kitchen table, stirring her mint tea and looking out the window at a group of crows arguing in the tree beside her little garage, the most shocking thing was the amount of money he had taken. Andy had thought she was rich—ten million dollars! Maybe because of that old TV show *The Millionaire,* which she watched when Janet was little, when they'd bought their first television and were living in that tiny place in Floral Park, she'd continued to think that a million bucks defined great wealth. A hundred million dollars! How could you spend that in Venezuela these days? When Andy had visited there with Frank, they had remarked upon how cheap even the most luxurious houses or views or gardens seemed to be.

Only gradually did she realize that she now had about eighty-three thousand dollars to her name, which had to last for some number of years. She was healthy and active, so the number of years might be considerable. She stirred her tea again, drank some more, watched two of the crows, who looked young, square off against one another, then fly away.

No mortgage payment. Not a lot for food—maybe fifty dollars a week? Heat could pose a problem, but her biggest fuel bill had been about three hundred dollars last year. She went down the list. Maybe she could go for three years or four? No new clothes, probably. She sat there. The tree was leafless, still; fog was vaporizing upward in small plumes. Andy took a deep breath and realized that she was happy now, happy that the disaster had finally arrived and had turned out to be nothing but money.

2001

THE FIRST THING Janet hated about Bush was not that he had stolen the election—that was bad, but he had had accomplices. He might even regard himself, she thought, as the ignorant beneficiary of the unknowable power of beings greater than himself (Cheney, Rumsfeld, brother Jeb, and Al Gore, who, not having won his home state, buckled). No, the first thing Janet really hated him for was his offhand comment that the Clinton boom had busted, and that we were now in a recession. He seemed to have no understanding that to a lot of people (namely, those who had invested in Jared's company) that sort of edict was a death knell—money was running to safety now (gold and, for God's sake, diamonds), and Jared was worried. It was Bush's final campaign statement, the ultimate repudiation of the Democrats, and a self-fulfilling prophecy. She told all her friends that he had been nonpresidential and irresponsible to say such a thing, but most of them pooh-poohed her.

The second thing she hated him for was that she was stopped on El Camino Real at the Sand Hill Road light, and the traffic light went from red to black. Everyone at all three of the lights stayed still for a long couple of minutes; then, realizing that the system had gone out, they began creeping across the intersection. Janet was heading for the barn, where she was going to take Sunlight on a little trail ride, maybe ponying Pesky, who could no longer be ridden though he liked to get out, but she turned into the mall and drove slowly around. The mall was dark, too, and people were coming from the stores in droves, yakking and exclaiming. Then a cop car showed up, and a policeman started directing traffic on El Camino Real. Thinking that some sort of war had begun (probably no one else thought this), she turned on the radio for news. But it was not a war, it was another chapter in the ongoing energy crisis, brought to you by Enron. The most enraging thing about the energy crisis, apart from the sneering on all Internet message boards about how California must deserve this for some unknown reason having merely to do with the fact that California thought it was so cool to have attempted to scale back energy usage, was that it was closely—and, Janet would have said, seminally—connected to Bush and his cronies, who were, with absolute impunity, rigging the system in order to overcharge for the electricity they were refusing to send when the lines were available, and then insisting upon sending when the lines were jammed.

Janet finally overcame her rage sufficiently to drive out Sand Hill Road, creeping with everyone else through the black traffic lights, and she controlled her rage long enough to groom both horses and give them a little outing, but on the way home, all she needed was a Bush-Cheney bumper sticker in order for her actually to see red (she had never seen red before; what happened was, a sort of blood cloud closed in from either side, and she began to tremble in her seat so that she had to pull over). It didn't help that the sticker was on a '98 white Chevy pickup that looked a lot like the one Chance drove, although she thought he was in Phoenix at a rodeo.

She looked at her watch; it was two-thirty-four. She pulled into Town and Country Village, sat quietly in the car as the rain began to drizzle down, and took 150 deep breaths, which nearly made her fall asleep, but did mean that, when she picked up Jonah half an hour later, she was fairly sane, and this lasted through dinner, through the evening, and all the way until Jared started snoring beside her in their lovely but now deeply indebted bedroom.

The next morning, she wrote a long complaining e-mail to her congressman—not Anna Eshoo, whom she had met and did like, and therefore could not badger, but her own personal congressman from Brooklyn, who always replied with a stock e-mail entitled "Congressman Langdon Responds to Your Concerns." This time, though, the return e-mail included a note from Riley, who said, "I know exactly what you mean! It is like a coup around here, and not just because everyone knows that SCOTUS scuttled the recount on VERRYYY questionable grounds. Everyone is scared! My friend Nadie Cantwell says that her parents say it's just like 1964 in the U.S.S.R., when Khrushchev was ousted and Brezhnev took over—the same sort of watch-your-step chill in the air." Then, below that, "BTW, an hour later—I guess your mom got all her money back. The congressman says you can call him about it when you get the chance, but the brokerage firm managed to get it somehow, and the bonus is that she gets back what it was worth when it was stolen, not what it's worth now, since the crash. Isn't that funny?"

Janet wrote back, "My mom is always lucky. How is Charlie?"

Riley wrote back: "Charlie busy! Somehow, talked his way into nursing school at Georgetown! He just started, midyear. He finished his EMT course, and took two courses at another school in the summer, and then he was sharing a cab with someone, and you know Charlie, as soon as he found out that that person was in admin for the nursing school, he started asking questions and getting excited, and pretty soon, that person wanted him, even had him come over for an interview, and wrote him a recommendation! The reading isn't easy, but it gives him more hope than his source of rage, which, now that he's been on several hikes in the Appalachians, turns out to be hilltop removal mining! (Congratulations, me, since I have been talking about this for years, but he had to see it to believe me.) Anyway, we are hunkering down here. Not happy, but hoping for the best."

On February 17, Bush bombed Iraq—Janet read all about it in *The New York Times*. This time, she wrote e-mails to Bush, Cheney, Richie, and Congressman Eshoo, as well as a letter to *The New York Times,* and various messages on various message boards under her alias, Sunshinelover. She spent all day doing this, and failed, it turned out, to cook supper. When Jared came in and the oven was as cold as the weather, she snapped, "Shit! I will just order a pizza, okay?" He hit the roof (finally, many of their friends might say). He set his laptop gently on the dining-room table, then dropped his briefcase, threw down his coat, and said, "I have had enough."

"Enough of what?" But she did not phrase this as a question.

"Enough of this over-the-top reaction at whatever Bush does, whatever the Republicans do, whatever doesn't go exactly your way in the world we live in."

Jonah appeared in the doorway, and disappeared. Janet's heart seemed to push toward him, but she said to Jared, "That's right, put your head in a damned hole and wait till someone shoves his dick right up your ass. It's the American way."

They had not agreed on the election. Jared had wondered whether Janet wanted Gore to wreck the government over the vote count, when the outcome of that would have been iffy at best.

Now Jared said, "There is something wrong with you. I don't know what it is." His voice was mild, enragingly forgiving. He went on. "Your attitude toward your father is, honestly, insane, especially considering that he's dead. And you extrapolate that attitude onto everything masculine."

"I do not." That was the only defense she could think of at the moment.

"I *liked* your dad. Frank was interesting and complex. I enjoyed talking to him and working with him. I thought he was generous in his way. He was a *man*. Your idea is that if a man makes any mistakes, no matter how old he is, he is never to be forgiven, his mistakes are never to be forgotten."

"What are your mistakes, then? I suppose I need to know." As soon as she said this, and in a frozen, spiteful voice, Janet realized that she should take it back, that she had confirmed her identity as a bitch, maybe permanently.

Jared said, "Fuck you. If I disagree with you, you argue with me until I can't stand it anymore, and if I agree with you, I get depressed. I'm going out for dinner. And I am taking Jonah with me."

Janet stared at her computer screen and sat still, all through the slamming of the front door, the turning on of Jared's car, and the backing around. Jonah hadn't made a noise or said a word, which meant, she thought, that he was either a very good child or that he was scared to death.

It was clear that she was supposed to ponder her sins while they were gone, so she did for a while, at least as long as it took her to eat the leftover tagliatelle and chicken sausage from the night before. Then she went back to the computer, did some more complaining (because she was right, after all), then felt exhaustion flood over her. She went to bed. At eight-thirty in the morning, she realized that Jared had slept in Emily's room. The only words they exchanged when she got up to find him sitting at the breakfast table were that she asked him where they went, he said they went to see *Little Nicky,* she said, "Is that appropriate for a nine-year-old?" and he said, "Yes," gritting his teeth. Then he said, "I'm going out. My sincere and honest suggestion is that you find an Al-Anon meeting somewhere." He finished his cup of coffee, got up, left. When Jonah came into the kitchen half an hour later, it was Janet who said, "Where did your dad go?"

Jonah said, "He said he was going to go skiing up at Dodge Ridge for a couple of days, and he'd be back Wednesday."

She should not have said, "I guess he doesn't give a shit about his company, then."

Jonah said, "I don't know," and went back to his room.

EMILY HELPED with the horse show—it was at Mount Holyoke—but she didn't ride, because Pattycake had come up with an abscess in his left front hoof. No one minded an abscess—as soon as you got your horse out of his stall and panicked because he was hopping lame and then felt the hoof wall, and realized that it was burning and the horse had a bounding digital pulse, the vet came, pulled the shoe, excavated the abscess, and packed it, and a day later the horse was soundish, and the hoof wall was cool. But even though it was not serious, it was a couple of weeks off, and that wasn't bad if spring break was coming, and your roommate and another friend were planning to drive to Florida just to escape the everlasting cold and snow. It was possible that if Emily had known what she was getting into, she might have gone to Sweet Briar for the weather, even though her mom had gone there. Mount Holyoke was more prestigious, and she liked Boston, but she was learning about trade-offs.

The three of them agreed, no Miami Beach and no Key West, but no other restrictions—none of them had been to Disney World, for example. Two days down and back, five days driving around in Miriam's mom's Civic, staying in cheap hotels. It was a daring vacation for three girls from South Hadley.

It was Miriam who suggested Ocala; her mom thought the horse farms were beautiful. You could make a St. Augustine–Daytona

Beach–Orlando–Ocala–Jacksonville loop and it was almost an American history lesson, and so they did, driving past the rodeo on the way into town. Miriam said, "Horses!" and Tory said, "I like horses!" and when they both looked at Emily, Emily said, "I know zip about rodeo."

It was before noon; the class was not an important one. The speaker system had a hum, but it was interesting to see how many guys there were, compared with a horse show. At a horse show, there were male trainers, but most of the riders were girls. Here, it was hard to recognize what few girls there were. The three of them bought Cokes and headed into the empty stands. Miriam and Tory put their elbows on the wooden railing and stared. At the far end, a gate opened, and a calf came running. A guy on a buckskin came right after him. Four fast strides, and his rope was twirling above his head, sailing toward the calf, but the calf spun and the loop missed.

Emily picked up a program that had fallen under the seat. In the class they were watching, the sixth horse was Bogey, #345, ridden by Chance Markham. Moments later, the gate opened (somehow the previous calf had been scuttled out of the arena), and here came a bright chestnut with a lean kid in an orange shirt. The calf moaned; the rope went out and settled itself over the calf's head. A split second later, the calf put his right foot into the loop, and the rope tightened around both the leg and the neck. The calf continued to baa in short bursts. The horse slid to a halt and stood, while the guy in the orange shirt, who was, indeed, her cousin Chance, eased his hand down the shivering rope until he got to the calf, at which point he tilted the animal onto its side, tied three of its legs together, then sprang up, raising his arms in the air. The timer read 7.3 seconds. Emily said, "You're not going to believe this, but that guy is my cousin."

Both Miriam and Tory looked at her, jaws dropped.

"I thought he was in California."

"How old is he?" said Miriam.

"Nineteen."

"He's cute," said Tory.

Time to go, thought Emily. Chance left the arena, and three other guys in boots and hats ran to the calf and untied it; it stood up mooing and headed out the other end of the arena to its buddies. They watched a few more, then some of the bronc riders, including one kid who was tossed on his face. Disney World seemed bland by comparison.

When she called her mom a day or so later about seeing Chance, Janet said, "I told you he was in Florida for a month. Then it's Texas. Loretta bought herself a nineteen-foot camper van to stalk him with. I'm surprised you didn't see it."

"He calls himself Chance Markham."

"That was some relative on her side who rode with the Texas Rangers."

"Did not," said Emily.

"Pony Express, then," said Janet.

The natural next question was "Dad there?" but Emily was afraid of the answer, so she said, "I'm sure Pattycake's abscess will be fine when I get back."

"Keep him sound."

"I do, Mom!"

"I wish he had more turnout."

"So does everyone!"

And their voices rose.

ONCE SHE STARTED looking into it, Janet found out that there were Anonymous organizations for just about everything. The easy thing was to go to all sorts of meetings as—she told herself—an observer, or a contemplator of George W. Bush, who she quickly decided was a dry drunk. A person with her history was not going to accept the existence of any power higher than the power of the group itself to induce conformity. That was fine. What was not fine was that she was exceptionally sensitive to bullshit. Having known Pastor Jones at the Peoples Temple, she now found herself gripping her hands together or writhing in her seat when the Al-Anon people used certain words—"wayward," "backslider," "healing," "God," "we," and, sometimes, "love." Certain tones of voice—kind, generous on the surface, but hostile underneath—also drove her from the room.

The meetings were held at a modern building that was also a yoga studio just past the light-rail station in San Carlos, not an area where she normally went. The yoga mats were rolled up and the shades drawn; overhead lights made the room dim and yellowish. The six tables pushed together for the group looked like old schoolroom tables, and the chairs didn't match, either, but Janet knew it was her task to cultivate gratitude, and so she did, for about ten minutes of each session, until the revelations began to get edgy. It did not help that most of the participants were younger than she was—sometimes half her age. One who was her age—nearly fifty-one now—had only just emerged from his room in the last two years. He had been hiding out since his father beat his mother to death before being put in Soledad Prison. The father had died in 1987. Another of the terrified ones said nothing except "That's not true" under his breath. He never said what was true. The majority of the participants were risk takers, though, not risk avoiders. One had started hang gliding in high school. He was now twenty-eight, and the sole survivor of his hang-gliding group of friends. He had broken both ankles in a ski accident on a closed slope in the winter of '99 and decided that maybe he was out of control in the most literal sense. Several had had three or more car accidents, one regularly drove his BMW 1000 motorcycle at over a hundred miles per hour. One woman had, like Janet, married someone she hardly knew. Janet admitted that she had once joined a cult, but didn't say which one, and implied that it was located on the East Coast. The problem was that the risk takers and the risk avoiders found each other deeply irritating, and each of the four meetings she dared to attend eventually devolved into arguments—after the fourth, she saw one of the risk avoiders pause outside the door of the building after the meeting and elbow one of the risk takers hard in the ribs. Janet ran for her car, avoiding risk, leaving the fracas to the more experienced members.

However, she rather liked Sex and Love Addicts Anonymous, because the participants' stories were adventurous and sometimes funny, and she didn't mind AA itself, though she could not speak honestly about her drinking habits, since she didn't drink. By comparison with the offspring of alcoholics, the alcoholics were good-natured, often helpful, and eventually it got somewhat easier to say that she was powerless over the Bush administration, that she had come to believe that some power greater than herself would have to restore the nation to sanity, that she had been a pain in the ass to most of her friends and relatives for a long time, that she could give up her shortcomings rather than give up her marriage, that she was willing to make amends not only to Jared and Jonah and Emily, but also to her mother and Richie, if not to Michael and Loretta, that she could get in the habit of admitting she was wrong when she actually was, and that a few minutes per hour of silent meditation were better than none at all.

Every time she picked up a newspaper, though, she saw Bush, Cheney, and Rumsfeld through the lens of AA, barreling out of control toward something she could not name, which they called redemption. The main thing she learned from AA was to shut up, even when Rove and Cheney admitted that they had stock in Enron, even when a government official confessed to being "a wholly owned subsidiary of the Department of Defense," even when Tommy Thompson decided to extend health care to "the unborn." She got through the summer, though they had to sell Pattycake for sixty thousand dollars (they would have gotten $150,000 the year before). She and Jared got through the summer, though he had to fire a quarter of his staff. She and Jonah got through the summer—although he didn't love his day camp, he made a friend there from two blocks away that he hadn't known before, because the friend went to public school. She and Emily got through the summer, because Emily admitted that she preferred Sunlight to Pattycake after all—Pattycake was good in the show ring, but acted as if he didn't know you from Adam when you arrived at the barn, and he could not go on the trail, which was what she wanted to do until she headed off to Idaho in August, to help Aunt Tina run her gallery.

CHARLIE CONSIDERED HIMSELF a brash, or bold, or even brave person. Certainly Riley often said that he was ready for anything, but it wasn't until his mom sat him down over the Fourth of July, when she and his dad came to Washington (for the first time!) to visit various buildings that they had heard about all their lives (and maybe also to see for themselves that no grandchildren existed or were forthcoming), and said that he needed to try to see his birth mother before it was "too late," that he seriously considered contacting Fiona McCorkle. And so he got up from the table where his mom was sipping her iced tea, went to the Rolodex, found the number, and dialed it. Riley, who was at the stove, stirring half-and-half into the broccoli bisque, glanced at him and gave him a little nod. Out of the corner of his eye, he saw his mom's eyebrows lift and then lower, and he heard his dad say, "What is he doing?"

"You dared him," said Riley, reaching for the salt shaker, and Charlie was willing to believe that this was true.

Charlie looked at his watch. It would be 10:00 a.m. in L.A. A voice said, "Over the Top Stables. This is Fiona." It was a self-possessed voice, a bit distracted, the voice of someone in the middle of something. Charlie said, "Hi, this is Charlie Wickett," in the exact same tone that people used when they called to ask you whom you were going to vote for. Fiona said, "Yes?" Then there was a pause, and she said, "Well, what do you know."

Charlie said, "Not much, to tell the truth," and Fiona laughed.

Charlie laughed, too. He glanced at his mom and then looked at the floor. With the Langdons and Arthur Manning, he had felt no competing loyalties, but now, unexpectedly, he did. He said, "I'm thirty-six. Oh, I guess you know that. Anyway, my mom says I should meet you."

Well, he had bungled that. He felt his face grow hot.

"I hear about you from time to time," said Fiona. "It sounds as though I would like you."

Charlie said, "Now you have your chance."

"Where are you?" said Fiona.

"We live in Washington, D.C. My wife works for Congressman Richard Langdon, of New York."

"What do you do?"

"Right now, I go to nursing school, but since I've gotten into a lot of trouble over the years, I decided that I'm going to specialize in rescues." Fiona laughed again.

His dad was patting his mom on the shoulder, and his mom was looking away, toward the windows. Riley stirred the soup again, turned off the burner. Charlie said, "I just wanted to make contact. I need to get off now." Awkward again.

Fiona said, "We come to Washington from time to time. There's a big horse show. We have a horse that might qualify."

"I'll give you my number."

"I have it. It's right here on the phone." Then, "Oh, here's my student. Sarah! Wait a second."

And then she said goodbye and hung up.

After his folks left, Charlie grilled Riley about whether she thought he had hurt his mom's feelings, and even brought the subject up one night when Uncle Henry took them to his favorite restaurant, Galileo. Uncle Henry said, "She's always encouraged you."

Riley said, "She *pushes* him. She was glad."

"She didn't look glad."

Uncle Henry said, "Sometimes when you first open the door to the attic, you aren't sure. But then you're happy to clean it out."

"Spoken like a hoarder," said Riley.

And Uncle Henry said, "You got me."

They all laughed and went on to a discussion of the casserole—celery root, onion, potatoes, wild rice, food originally from the Mediterranean Basin, Iran, Minnesota, and South America, according to Henry, and delicious according to all three of them. Riley said that the name "Menominee" meant "eaters of wild rice." It was not what the Menominee called themselves, but what the Ojibwe called them. Uncle Henry looked impressed.

At the beginning of August, Fiona called him when Riley was at work, taking advantage of what she called the Idiot Vacation. The apartment was quiet, and Fiona, as before, had a strangely pleasant voice. She said, "Is it Charlie? Charles?"

"Always been Charlie."

"Good. Anyway, as soon as the vet diagnosed the injury, I thought, well, he's out for the season, so I won't get to see Charlie."

"What is his injury?"

"Oh hell, he kicked the wall of his stall and fractured his coffin bone. What a dope. He'll be fine next year, though. He's only seven. You should come out here."

"I should."

"September would be good. I don't have to put you on a horse. We can go to the beach, or take a drive into one of the wilderness areas. We can go up to Desert Hot Springs. There are a lot of weird little places around L.A. Death Valley."

Charlie said, "I would like to come." And it was true.

Riley said she could not go with him. The new congressional term would have started, and she had to prove to the congressman that she was more essential to him even than Lucille. Sometimes she got the sense that he was getting tired of her, which wasn't surprising—she and Lucille were the only ones left of the original eight staffers. But now they would be moving into Rayburn. She didn't want to miss that, and she didn't think he would fire her as long as she was married to Charlie. But of course that wasn't the *only* reason she remained married to Charlie. She kissed him smack on the lips. He knew it wasn't the only reason, but they were an odd couple, he admitted that. He got himself a map of California, and imagined driving around—Pasadena, Indio, Twentynine Palms, Escondido ("Secret")—the place-names were evocative of darkness and sunshine all at once. He began to get a little excited.

RICHIE WASN'T SURPRISED that Riley was crying in the bathroom—she was crying everywhere, and she wasn't alone. His mom, of course, said, "I felt he shouldn't take that flight. I even picked up the phone to call you, but I couldn't do it. It is killing Arthur. Arthur will be dead by Christmas." And then he could hear her voice shake, and then she said, "Oh Lord," and hung up. Richie had done his share of crying, too, as had Uncle Henry, as had Charlie's parents in St. Louis, who called Riley every few days. Richie put his head in his hands. Ivy had seen the towers fall from her new place in Brooklyn Heights—or so she said—it was all jumbled in her mind. He knew scads of people who had looked up, or looked over their shoulders, or seen something, or heard something, or sensed the ground shake upon impact, or saw the plume of fire when the plane, Charlie's plane, hit, then plowed through the Pentagon. Michael and Loretta knew two men who had been in the second tower. Maybe one of them had jumped. Michael said that *he* would have jumped. Every thought about it was terrifying. Why would you jump? thought Richie, and then he stopped thinking.

However, Lucille said that Riley wasn't crying in the bathroom—or not *only* crying. She was also throwing up. Richie did not understand what this meant until Lucille said, "Well, Congressman, open your eyes. She's pregnant."

Richie said, "I don't think that's our business."

"If you say so," said Lucille.

"I say so," said Richie. What was their business? That was the question. Just after they heard about the Trade Center attack, it had been decided that everyone should evacuate—Richie was arriving at the Capitol building with his new press secretary, Alia, when they saw Hastert being whisked away, and knew that they should leave, too. Richie sent Alia home—she lived in College Park. Then he found Lucille in the office and told her that the Secret Service said everyone had to leave, walk south. Right then, it would have been, at that very moment (Richie pictured his feet, brown loafers, green socks, stepping across the pavement), Charlie's plane was arrowing into the Pentagon. That evening, Richie joined the others on the Capitol lawn, when everyone agreed to stand behind the president. Since then, though, their job had not been as clear. The perpetrators were dead, and there were all sorts of theories about who was behind them. Most of the Congress was eager to fund some sort of reprisal, or at least investigation. Although his district did not include Ground Zero, as they called it, it did include parts of Lower Manhattan, so he helped Jerry Nadler author a bill that would give grants to businesses around there, to keep them running.

But it was a nightmare, trying to figure out how to get to the neighborhood, who should go there (a day-care business?), what to do with the site. He was the only congressman he knew of who was related to a victim. He hadn't mentioned it to the papers, and so no one knew it—*how* he was related could be a problem. Only Cheney and Rumsfeld seemed not overwhelmed. They came, they talked, they promoted strict policies and aggressive laws, and though Richie didn't like them, he was foggy about why—he needed Riley, he discovered, and Nadie and even Ivy, to get him organized. But the only person he had was Michael, and Michael wanted to kill them, whoever they were, no matter what, no matter where, no matter how.

2002

Arthur wasn't dead by Christmas, but he was dead by New Year's Day. On the 3rd, Richie and Nadie took Riley and Uncle Henry to the service. The funeral was at a funeral home in McLean, easy to get to. As they drove past the neighborhood that Tim had roamed around, and then past Arthur and Lillian's old place, Riley stared out the window but didn't ask to stop or say anything; Charlie himself had no connection to this landscape. Uncle Henry, too, seemed small and quiet. But Richie remembered Tim vividly here— how grown up he'd seemed when Richie was just a kid. He and Michael hadn't been there when Tim did some of his more legendary things, like jumping off the roof of the house into the pool, but, merely sitting at the supper table or teasing Janet, he had had an air of danger that Charlie, with all of his good nature, had never had.

They were the first to arrive at the funeral home. The casket was sitting forlornly in "The Memorial Center," a large, dim, empty, greenish room. Tina arrived next, having taken a cab from Dulles. Richie introduced her to Riley and Nadie, and Tina gave Riley a heartfelt hug, then kissed her. Richie hadn't realized that they had had much of a relationship before Charlie died, but afterward, Riley mentioned that they exchanged letters or e-mails every month or so—she had sent them a beautiful carved panel after their wedding, medieval-looking and ornate, but the faces of the couple were the faces of Charlie and Riley as Adam and Eve; Charlie was laughing, and Riley was looking pensively at the apple in her hand. Then Dean and Linda showed up, after them Debbie, looking pinched and sad, Hugh, looking bland, Kevin and Carlie, looking like the twenty-somethings they were (unsure of themselves). Except for Tina, the Mannings stood together in a bunch, while Richie, Riley, Uncle Henry, and Nadie stood in a line, space between them. Janet's plane had been delayed for so long out of San Francisco that she had decided in the end not to come. After the chat about Arthur's end ("peaceful") had subsided into an uncomfortable silence, the director of the funeral home walked in and out a few times, asking if everyone was all right, and looking at his watch. Finally, Debbie stepped up to the casket, put her hands together, and said, "I asked my dad several times what he wanted for his service. He said, 'Small, secret, out of the way.' So—here we are."

Just at that moment, the door opened and Richie's mom slipped in. Debbie stopped speaking, looked at her, smiled. Andy, who was wearing a perfectly cut black wool coat with a tight waist and wide skirt that was probably as old as Richie was, glided down the aisle between the rows of empty chairs and took his hand. The service was indeed short, and maybe, in some sense, it was for Riley. There had been memorial services for the victims of all four 9/11 disasters, and the remains of many of the victims had been identified but not, so far, any of Charlie's. (Riley had spent a week in November trying to convince him that Charlie hadn't actually been on the plane, until Nadie finally said, "So he's using this as an excuse to leave you?" which shut her up about that.) Richie hoped that you could add up memorial services like interest on investments, until they finally produced a payoff—comfort, acceptance, hope, especially if you were pregnant and due in May. (It was Nadie who insisted that Riley confess—was she pregnant or not? Yes, she was, and although she had thought about it, she could not bring herself to have another abortion, even in spite of the nature of the world she saw everywhere. Nadie had put her hands on Riley's shoulders, looked her in the eye, and said, "Do you love me?" Riley nodded. Nadie said, "My mother lived in a much more horrifying world than you do, and abortion was routine there. I am a good reason not to have an abortion." She said it lightly, and Riley said, "We'll see about that in the future," but took what she said to heart. Nadie had reported this to Richie at the office Christmas party.)

Everyone said something. His mom was last. Her voice was soft and vaporous, almost like memory itself. Richie could see how, once upon a time, her voice had been taken to indicate that she was dumb or thoughtless, and even she said that she had been both, but now listening to her talk was like feeling a light breeze that made you wake up to something, maybe your own existence, for a moment. She said, "I always thought my dear friend Arthur's great tragedy was that he knew what love was better than anyone else in the world, and he could feel it wavering and swelling or dissipating and flowing away as no one else could. It was a terrible burden for him. It was as if he had an extra sense, the way dogs hear sounds that we can't. That's why he did what he did, that's why he loved Lillian as he did, that's why he put up with me and Frank, that's why Tim's death and Charlie's death tormented him so. If he took you in, then he saw something in you that was worth caring for, sort of like a vibration in your surface, and so he tried and tried, but we all slipped away from him, because that's what life is. So many times he would say to me, Andy, I give up, but he could never give up; something or someone would pull him back. I am eighty-one now, and so Arthur would be almost eighty-two, and the last time we saw each other"—here she looked at Debbie, who was crying, but she went on anyway—"he said, 'When do I break out of this joint?'—you know, the way he had of always making a joke—and I do believe I said, 'When you've given up on us, darling,' and we laughed." She laid one hand on the casket and then the other one. Then she said, "I know you are not supposed to say this at a funeral, but I'm nearly as old as he was, so I am going to be a crazy old lady and say, 'I am glad that he did.'" Now she looked at Debbie again, but Debbie was, in fact, nodding, just a bit, even if she didn't realize that she was nodding.

Well, she looked sixty, that's what Nadie and Riley agreed as they drove back to Washington after the interment. Graceful and unlined. Richie joked and said, "I'm not sure she has actually used her body much over the years. My dad might have had two hundred thousand miles on his, but Mom has been driven very little." Uncle Henry said, "It isn't that. It's the Norwegian bloodlines. Survival of the most efficient." Riley unconsciously put her hand on her belly. At the brunch,

Debbie and Tina had both made much of the fact that they were going to be great-aunts, and at such a miraculously young age; they couldn't wait to give Riley all sorts of unnecessary advice, how exciting, many kisses, much holding of hands, many reminders to stay in touch, until Riley had begun to reciprocate. When they were back in D.C. and had dropped her off at her place, he, Nadie, and Uncle Henry watched her for a few extra moments before waving one last time and driving away. Then Nadie said, "Maybe that did the trick. She seems more like her old self. Her old self can handle anything."

WHEN SHE PICKED UP her phone and Loretta's voice said, "I didn't know who else to call," Janet knew that this was literally true. There were things that no one Loretta was close to—her mother, the monsignor, either Tia or Binky—was allowed to know. But Loretta had to tell someone, so Janet was allowed to know these things. Janet did not understand why Loretta thought that she, Janet, could be trusted to keep a secret, but in fact she hadn't told any of the secrets. In her own mind, she threatened to tell them. If, for example, Loretta said one more word about how easy the "victory in Afghanistan" had been, and how "Al Qaeda has been routed" and "I expect to see Bin Laden's head on a pike any day now," she, Janet, would spill all the beans about Chance's girlfriend, who was the eighteen-year-old daughter of illegal immigrants, about how Loretta's dad was drinking and driving (if only around the ranch), and that he would put the two Australian shepherds and the German shorthair in the bed of the truck and then take off. When he started driving erratically, the dogs would jump out and head home. Twice her mother had had to go find him, and one of those times he had driven into a ditch and fallen asleep, leaning against the wheel, his door wide open.

Janet said, "Where are you? Are you around here?"

"No, we're home." Then, "Well, I'm home in New York. Michael is in Vermont at some hunting club."

"What is he hunting?" said Janet, meaning, deer, bear, elk.

Loretta said, "Democrats."

Janet felt her hackles rise.

"Listen," said Loretta. But she did not go on. Instead, she put the phone down and, apparently, went to close some door. Who would be home? thought Janet. It was the middle of the semester. Loretta picked up the phone. She said, "Has Emily ever had an abortion?"

Now it was Janet who closed the door, not because Emily had ever had an abortion (that she knew of) but because Jonah and Jared were watching the Super Bowl and shouting. To Loretta, she said, "No. I don't know. Not that I know of. I've never even met a boyfriend." As if that made a difference, but in fact Janet had always, she now realized, relied on Emily's pickiness to keep her out of trouble.

"Well, she's pregnant."

"Who?" said Janet. She licked her lips. This was like a test, indeed: If it was Tia, then that was a sign that plain, bookish girls could have a wild side. If it was Binky, then that was a sign that the apple had rejected the tree—Binky and Loretta were very close and looked a good deal alike. Loretta said, "Hanny—Alejandra, the girlfriend."

"Chance's girlfriend is pregnant?"

"I guess about eight or nine weeks."

"They told you?"

"She called me."

"Jesus Christ," said Janet. "But why would you think I know anything about this? I never had an abortion. The last person I knew who had an abortion was in college. Her parents sent her to Europe somewhere. Did you ever have an abortion?" Janet said this in a challenging way, knowing that Loretta would say, of course not, but Loretta said, "I didn't have to. I had a miscarriage."

"No shit," said Janet.

"It was before I met Michael, and he doesn't know about it." Another secret to keep: everyone had assumed Loretta was a virgin on her wedding night. In the ensuing silence, Janet thought of Fiona. It was a week or ten days now since she had at last brought up the subject of Charlie. Janet had been too out of the loop to know that Charlie had been heading to L.A. to meet Fiona when his plane crashed into the Pentagon, and then nervous about referring to it, but someone had to say something, didn't they? When she asked, "Didn't it just kill you?," though, it was she herself who started crying, not Fiona. Fiona said, "I was shocked, but, Janet, when he was born, I was out cold from the drugs, and they took him away. When the pregnancy started to show, they stuck me in a convent in Normandy— you know, around St. Louis somewhere. It was full of pregnant nuns. It wasn't torture—they didn't make me scrub the floors, like in Ireland—but they did make me go to Mass every day and say maybe a hundred thousand rosaries, and I was just waiting to get back to the horses. All I thought about was the five-year-old Thoroughbred I'd been jumping and how I could manage to gain as little weight as possible. I think I gained twelve pounds. I was eighteen when he was born, and I walked away without a thought. I have no kids. I know what people think that says about me, but . . ." Then she said, "I've seen one snapshot. To be honest, I can hardly even remember Tim. It was all horses, horses, horses." Then, at the same time that Janet said, "I loved Tim," Fiona said, "But there was no one like Tim, really." The last thing Fiona said about Charlie was "He sounded very good-natured." Loretta was talking again; Janet made herself listen.

"He can't marry her. He doesn't want to marry her. I don't think she wants to marry him, either. It was a mistake. Her parents are very traditional. She's eighteen. They think that's plenty old to get married. Her sister was married at seventeen, and there are a couple of adored grandchildren. I think Chance has been on the road for the last four weeks. She is terrified that her dad will find out. Or her mom. Someone."

Janet said, "Where are they?"

"The ranch."

"What do you want me to do?"

"I don't know." That was why she had called, Janet realized—she was the one who was supposed to come up with a plan.

Loretta said, "The hospital out there is out of the question."

"Have you told Michael?"

Loretta said, "No."

"Why not?"

"A, because he wouldn't think twice about it, and, B, because he would swear to keep it a secret and then get mad about something and start shooting his mouth off."

Everyone knew that everyone knew that women had abortions, had always had abortions. Possibly, rumor had had it, her great-aunt Eloise had had an abortion; possibly there had been abortions on the Bergstrom side, back in the ancient days of Queen Anne's lace—her mom had always implied that if something bad could happen it would have happened to the Bergstroms.

"That," said Loretta, "is what money is for."

And Janet did not wonder aloud what the monsignor would think. Finally, Janet said, "I'll ask around. I'll call you tomorrow."

Loretta said, "Nothing but the best, okay?"

"Of course," said Janet.

The next day, when she called her gynecologist and asked the question, the first thing he said was "What is her medical insurance?"

"No idea," said Janet, "but there is plenty of money."

Dr. Fox said, "I like a place in Oakland. Very professional but very supportive. Here's the number." That afternoon, she called Loretta. That evening, she got an e-mail from Loretta. The plan was that Hanny would tell her parents that she'd been invited to San Francisco by Chance's aunt, who understood that she wanted to go to a community college but hadn't decided which one. The aunt had invited her to stay for a week, and promised to take her to visit several colleges and to show her around. She would come on the bus, which she would pay for; Loretta thought this would arouse much less suspicion than if Janet went to pick her up.

She was small and young-looking, pointed chin, luxurious hair. All she carried was a rather large tooled handbag that Janet recognized as American West and a raincoat. As she came down the steps of the bus, she wiped her eyes with a Kleenex. Her makeup was smeared. Janet plastered a big smile on her face and strode up to her. "You must be Hanny? How was your trip? Are you cold? The weather hasn't been great. Sorry." Why did she apologize?

It didn't take her long to understand why she had apologized. Everything about this event felt to Janet like she was the one forcing the issue, the one requiring this "procedure." Every story was plausible. The story about school—when Jared asked what Hanny wanted to study, she said, "Vet tech. Or I could be an accountant. I'd like that." And who wouldn't, if getting off the Perronis' enormous Angelina Ranch and into the Bay Area was your choice? The story about Chance: "Oh, he's doing great. The horses are perfect. He loves it all, everything about it. Of course, he travels most of the year." The story about Loretta: "I can tell her anything. I think she's so wonderful and kind. She sent me this bag I have for Christmas, and it was exactly the one I saw when we went to the mall in Salinas. I couldn't believe it." The story about her family: Her dad had come to California as a child from Guadalajara, her mother with her family from Mexico City. They had met in L.A., and moved to the ranch because Chance's grandmother loved her grandmother's cooking. Her dad no longer worked at the ranch; he drove a truck for a waste-management company. She had a sister and two younger brothers. One of them, Alonzo, went with Chance to rodeos to help with the horses and the equipment. How much does he get paid? thought Janet, meanly.

Hanny went into her room after supper, after asking to borrow Janet's copy of *Vogue,* which was lying on the coffee table, after both Jared and Jonah watched her go, then looked at each other and shrugged. Later, Janet heard her crying and didn't do anything, but when she heard her crying again, just before bedtime, she knocked.

Hanny was sitting up against the headboard, in a pair of blue pajamas with a feather pattern. Janet sat on the edge of the bed. Hanny licked the tears off her lips. Janet said, "Would you tell me why you're crying?"

Hanny nodded. "I'm really scared."

Janet said, "Who knows?"

"Mrs. Langdon. I think my mom has an idea, but—"

"But?"

"Don't ask, don't tell."

She had washed her makeup off, and without it, she was prettier, but also younger-looking. Janet said, "Are you eighteen?"

Hanny didn't say anything for a moment, then shook her head just a little bit.

"Does Chance know how old you are?"

"He thinks I'm eighteen."

Janet had read about the parental-consent amendment in the papers, maybe five years before, and had been glad when the California Supreme Court struck it down, but now she wished she had some ally who actually knew this girl. She said, "Tell me the truth, Hanny. Do you want to do this?"

Hanny nodded, but she did pause before she nodded.

Now for the hard part—did she love Chance, what were her hopes?

Chance, she said, was a silly boy, not serious, an overgrown kid. When he wasn't working with the horses or the cattle, he drank and smoked weed and did some other things that Hanny wasn't sure of.

He was moody. Hanny didn't trust moody men. And she didn't trust handsome men. And she didn't trust Anglo men, either.

Why was she crying?

Because she was embarrassed, said Hanny. Humiliated. Because she was a girl who did all of her homework every day, and she was missing school. Because she was a girl who had always kept her half of her room much neater than her sister had, and now the same thing was happening to her that had happened to her sister. Because she was a girl with a rosary in the top drawer of her chest, and maybe she could never touch it again. Because she was afraid.

Janet reassured her that a vacuum extraction was a very safe procedure, especially at eight and a half weeks.

Hanny nodded.

Janet said nothing about what she always remembered as "the flutters"—that first sense she had had of Jonah's presence, of the love it had set off in her. She saw right then that those sensations didn't have to arouse love: they could as easily arouse fear and rage.

That night, Janet got up about twelve-thirty, put on her robe, and went out onto the patio, wishing she was a smoker or a drinker or could go to an AA or an SLAA meeting right now, this minute, and ask her fellow contemplators what to do. She hadn't brought this up at the last meeting because she had mistakenly assumed that, although she was involved, it wasn't her business. On the one hand, she thought as she stared at the thin sliver of moon that was visible through the branches of the largest oak tree, thank goodness Hanny's view of Chance coincided with Janet's own, and her griefs were appropriate for her age. On the other hand, she couldn't sleep, she couldn't think, she was beginning to obsess about whether she would be too tired to drive safely to Oakland. When she was finally freezing cold, she went inside and drank a shot of Jared's Limoncello, which seemed to mildly electrocute her as it froze its way past her tongue and down her throat. But it did, if not put her to sleep, at least put her into a trance. She lay quietly next to Jared.

Who was that? Janet thought the next day when she was walking around the block in Oakland, passing the time while Hanny had her "procedure." Some friend of hers whose husband had left her had booked a reservation to the most frightening and remote place she could think of—Port Arthur, Tasmania. It took her thirty-six hours to get there (from Philadelphia), by train, plane, and boat, and when she did, just as she was congratulating herself on being adventurous and exotic, an American couple walked by, from Pittsburgh. They had just arrived from New Delhi and Johannesburg, and would be returning to New York through Hong Kong. The man was wearing a Pitt T-shirt and the woman white sneakers. Janet's friend told her—oh, it was Eileen Grogan, now she lived in Montreal—that she had lost all sense of her own adventurousness instantly, and in fact felt oddly comforted. That was how Janet felt after checking Hanny into the clinic. Oh, she realized. She was not the first. Oh, she realized, it happened many times a day. Oh, she realized, life continues.

Hanny was cramping on the ride home, but she looked less pale and happier than she had getting off the bus. Janet decided to believe the evidence of her own eyes and accept that they had done the best thing.

It was Loretta who had no doubts. When Janet saw her over Easter (she and Michael came into the city and vacationed for two days at the Mark Hopkins), Loretta embraced her, kissed her, thanked her, gave her an antique platinum brooch that looked like a dragonfly and was encrusted with amethysts and tourmalines. A commemoration? Hush money? All Loretta said was "I love you. You are the greatest."

RICHIE'S TIME in office had begun after Cheney's was over, so he hadn't known him as a fellow congressman. When Bush was elected, with Cheney vice-president, even some of the Democrats thought they would be fine with him. He had a reputation of being able to listen, at least, and of not saying "Fuck you" to every Democrat every time. Michael liked Cheney because he was "uncompromising" and "had principles," which Richie considered a truer indicator than the faulty memories of his colleagues. However, he had not expected the onslaught of arm twisting that began after they came back from recess. And he hardly had Riley to help him. She came to work with the baby (Alexis Aurora Wickett), but she was ruthless: she would work on solar and wind and electric cars and some idea about harnessing the energy of the tides, but she had no opinions about anything else, not even whether Cheney should pony up documents to the General Accounting Office about conflict of interest among members of the late and unlamented Energy Task Force. "Enron, Enron, Enron," echoed in everyone's heads, but Cheney brushed it off until, with the help of Richie, Congressman Dingell, and Congressman Waxman, the head of the GAO finally sued Cheney for the materials.

But you would not have known that Richie had ever said "boo" to anyone from the White House, or so much as frowned in Cheney's direction, because, in preparation for the vote on the Iraq Resolution, the Capitol was swarming with them—Cheney, Rice, Rumsfeld, Powell, all the way down to Rod Paige, who was the secretary of education. They came to his office, they knocked on his door, they took him aside in the corridors, they sat down with him in the cafeteria. They talked to Lucille, Riley, Corrie, Leslie, Rudy, Ben, Sam, Jenny, everyone. His staffers pretended that he was inalterably opposed to giving President Bush the power to go to war, when, in fact, Richie had always planned to vote yes, in spite of what his constituents might desire. He did, in fact, expect to be thrown out of his seat on November 6, and to be showing up at Michael's office on November 7, hat in hand.

He had stayed with Ivy and Leo in Sag Harbor in August, and Ivy was furious with him. She was right about everything: there was no evidence connecting Saddam Hussein to 9/11; Saddam Hussein was contained; Saddam had no weapons of mass destruction; the Middle East was a powder keg and so fate should not be tempted; Afghanistan was the point; Osama bin Laden was the point. Richie's view was that the Resolution did not have to lead to war—it was meant to put the ball in Saddam's court, to challenge him to clean up his act. It was a *resolution,* not necessarily a declaration of war, even though some of his colleagues thought it was. Ivy said that Richie was deluding himself, and maybe he was, but he felt Charlie like a weight on his conscience that got heavier every day.

No remains had ever been found. He was one of six. Perhaps, Richie thought, he had taken a window seat in the front of the plane, and that was the reason—the remains had distributed themselves in an airplane shape diagonally from outside of the first-floor Defense Intelligence Agency through the Naval Intelligence Agency and into the office of the administrative assistant to the army. There was bunching, scattering, and empty space. The empty space appeared to be where the wings had been, but perhaps that was an illusion.

Charlie and the five other ghosts (as Richie thought of them) had been included in a memorial at Arlington a year after the attack. After attending the ceremony with all of his staff and Nadie and Alexis (aged four months, born May 11), Richie had felt less at peace rather than more. Since then, he'd found himself saying words like "united front," "strong response," "hit back," "gathering threat," and "wake up and smell the coffee." That he could agree with Cheney (and disagree with Jerry Nadler) in this, and yet go after Cheney about the Energy Task Force, made him feel schizophrenic and flexible, though not both at the same time.

It didn't help that Alexis, whom he saw every day, was emerging into that stage of infancy that was maybe the cutest and most appealing. She was smiling; she was staring at her fists; she was grasping rattles and fingers and growing out her mop of hair (brown, like Riley's); her gaze followed Richie as he walked away from her, saying, "Are you my dad? Are you my dad?" Nadie, too, was encouraging him to be more aggressive. And Lucille. And Ben and Sam. Enough had been had by all. If Saddam was allowed to do as he wanted, well, what about Iran? Those opposed to the Resolution brought up Iran all the time. Iran was our enemy. Iran was Saddam's enemy. Saddam had been our friend all through that war—there was a photo of Rumsfeld shaking Saddam's hand. But Cheney and his minions made the case that if Saddam had been our "ally" (and the word always had oral quotation marks around it), and he was out of control, then it was our job to rein him in, and, in the process, show Iran an example that they would do well to heed.

Richie knew that there was some fuzzy background there that both his uncle Arthur and his dad had been involved in. His mom was not clear in her own mind what it was, only that, when he and Michael were about six months old, his dad had disappeared for four days and come home looking sun-swept and haggard. (Well, "jet-lagged" was the real word, she said, but it looked like more than that. It looked as though his trip had taken him somewhere that even World War II hadn't taken him.) Only when the embassy had been attacked in '79 had he mentioned that he had once been to Iran, had helped to deliver cash to the . . . well, to someone. But she had noticed a change in their marriage that she dated from that summer: he was sharper, more ambitious, away more often. She'd thought at the time that he simply hated fatherhood, or her version of motherhood, but imagining that trip he'd taken gave her pause. She'd once mentioned it to Arthur, but he hadn't taken the bait, said nothing.

And so the Resolution was passed—the New York vote split down the middle. Jerry Nadler stared at him when he cast his vote, maybe in disbelief, maybe in contempt. The balls were in the air now, Richie thought, as he sat in his seat and gazed around the Chamber at all the yakking, at DeLay, Gephardt, Pelosi, Hastert, Armey. Yes, many balls were in the air of all different colors, and Richie didn't see anyone who could catch them.

2003

THE DUPLEX Henry shared with Riley and Alexis was in Northwest. It was an attractive, faintly Colonial brick cube with two
entrances and a pleasant lawn that looked out onto trees in three directions. It was about as unlike Chicago and northern Wisconsin as you
could get without palm trees, Henry and Riley agreed. Downstairs,
there was a living room, a largish kitchen, a dining room, a sunroom,
two bedrooms, and two baths. Upstairs, there was a bedroom, a bathroom, a room "formerly known as the kitchen," as Riley said, and
stacks and boxes and shelves of books. One of the last things that
Charlie had done before 9/11 was drive Henry's U-Haul full of books
from Evanston to Washington. Henry had bought the house, but had
planned to rent out part of it. After Charlie died, the plan changed.

Henry didn't see Riley and Alexis very often. His entrance went
to the garage and the driveway, her entrance out the front door to the
sidewalk; she and Alexis usually took the bus to Tenleytown Station,
then the Metro to work. He didn't hear her often, either; the insulation was so good between the two apartments that he would have
said that Alexis didn't cry at all.

Henry did cry, though, and surely Riley did. He liked Riley, he
liked Charlie's parents, who had visited twice, and he liked Alexis,
for a baby, but it was painful to discover how they receded in his
affections now that Charlie was gone. He had known that he liked,

or even loved Charlie in an avuncular way. Sometimes joked that, had he produced his ideal son, that boy would have been like Charlie, unlike himself, a throwback to the regular Langdon/Cheek/Vogel/ Augsberger stock. Charlie had said, "What about the mom?" but smiled as he said it, and Henry had to admit that he hadn't thought to imagine Fiona. Henry didn't think Riley liked him much, but living here was convenient, cheap, and pleasant for her. He could be relied upon to look after Alexis if Riley went out, and to talk to her, and even hold her (carefully, gingerly) if he had to.

When Claire had visited in December, she was astonished at the mess, and congratulated him: he was loosening up! But it wasn't that—the boxes of books were not unpacked, but they were neatly stacked and out of the way. It was that he was on to something new, and most of his days were spent at the Folger. What he was interested in was not Shakespeare, though he had started by looking at archaic origins for some of the plays, just out of curiosity. But then he saw, lying on a table in the reading room, a manuscript in Gaelic, and he realized that he had missed his calling. His calling was Ireland—the strange mix of Gaelic, Viking, Anglo-Saxon, and indigenous inhabitants that the English and the Icelanders and the Scots and the French only thought about when they had to. He felt Gerald of Wales inside himself, lifting his gaze and looking across the Irish Sea, toward Waterford.

Henry had always been amused at the Langdon/Vogel attitude toward the Irish—that they didn't exist. When his aunt Eloise moved to Chicago, his mother had muttered to his father that now she would undoubtedly marry an Irishman, and what would they think about that? When she married a Jew, his mother had breathed a sigh of relief. Jews, at least, were intelligent, not cunning. Henry realized that he had imbibed this prejudice when he studied Anglo-Saxon rather than the Celtic languages. The Celtic languages were far more interesting, and a much greater puzzle than the Germanic ones. And, yes, the Vikings had been all too familiar with Ireland—they had raided and marauded and enslaved; a study of Icelanders after the Second World War had shown that they were as Irish as the population of South Boston.

But his real pleasure was in the mystery of the Celtic languages— Irish, Breton, Scots Gaelic, Welsh, Manx, and Cornish. Gerald of

Wales would have been fluent in at least one. Celtic speakers may have lived at the periphery of Europe, but their language was closer to Italic than to German—the Irish word for wheel was *roth,* akin to the Latin *rota*—eventually to show up in modern English as "rotate," whereas the Old Norse *hvel* and the Old English *hweohl* had evolved into plain old "wheel." The Irish had split off the common Indo-European trunk half a millennium before the Germanic languages. Henry imagined those Celts—cunning, handsome, leading small but spirited horses, telling each other stories and myths that made no sense to anyone else, making their way to the edges of the Continent, then being driven farther west. The only things interfering with his plan to spend the summer in Wexford and Waterford were that he was seventy, and was thus rather nervous about driving on the left side of the road, and that George W. Bush, that craven pig, was about to start a war that could end anywhere. Henry and Richie had had a screaming argument about Richie's vote for the Iraq Resolution and his apparent support for the imminent invasion. Henry had, in fact, been more violent in his opposition than Riley was.

Henry would have said that he was gifted at taking the long view—he *enjoyed* taking the long view. Yes, the Roman Empire declined and collapsed, and you could put the turning point at any one of several places; Henry himself thought the conquest of the Germanic peoples by Julius Caesar had been a mistaken use of resources, both military and natural, and that Caesar's assassination was a testament to the instability the Gallic Wars had caused. The British Empire had collapsed much more quickly, and not that long before Henry's own birth, but he felt a good deal of equanimity about that in spite of his long history of Anglophilia. Libraries had a way of smoothing over the pain of convulsive change. But he was having difficulty taking the long view about intervention in the Middle East. His particular bête noire was Tony Blair.

Tony Blair was three months younger than Michael and Richie, and, given what Henry knew of those two, he had very little faith in the depth of Tony's analysis of the pertinent issues. According to Tony's biographer, he had been quite like Michael and Richie—always in trouble, a student whom his teachers "were glad to see the back of," someone whose main desire in life was to emulate Mick Jagger. At the press conference Blair held with Bush, a reporter had asked the question (noted only as "Q" in the *Times*), "Mr. President, Bob Woodward's account of the White House after Sept. 11 says that you ordered invasion plans for Iraq six days after Sept. 11. Isn't it the case that you have always intended war on Iraq, and that international diplomacy is a charade in this case?" Neither Blair nor Bush had addressed the question—all tough questions (including the question of whether there was any evidence of direct links between Saddam and Al Qaeda) were avoided. But Henry really understood what he was seeing only this morning, when the *Times* reported that Blair's most recent report in support of the war in Iraq, which Colin Powell had used to support invasion, had been cribbed from various magazines rather than resulting from independent research.

And so the boy who got through Yale because he was a legacy had as his biggest ally the boy who cheated on his papers and passed others' work off as his own. How many times had Henry seen that over the years? Was this why he took the invasion personally? Why it made him physically uncomfortable? Why, during his work in the Folger reading room, deciphering *Scéla Muicce Meicc Da Thó* word by word (and, slow as it was, enjoying it as a form of rejuvenation), he felt the White House over his left shoulder, reminding him how quickly empires fall apart, and how much, perhaps, that collapse hurt even those who tried to take a long view?

DURING THE FIRST IRAQ WAR, Jesse remembered his dad telling him a funny thing—that, after missile silos were installed near Omaha, in the fifties, he would be doing something in the field behind the big house, which ran east-west, and he would be okay going west, because he could keep his eye on the horizon, but he would be nervous going east, because he kept sensing a mushroom cloud behind him. He would tell himself not to glance around—to hold off until the end of the row—but more than once he could not resist and looked over his shoulder. And one time he nearly fell off the seat of the tractor: there was a cloud, which he at first saw as a mushroom, that turned out to be a tornado at that moment reaching down. Yes, he had jumped off the tractor and headed toward the house, but he had been more relieved than frightened, not a normal reaction to a funnel.

Jesse never thought that the Iraqis had nuclear weapons or biological weapons. Somehow, the very expanse of the world around him—flat, huge, time-consuming to cross—had dispossessed him of those fears. And anyway, if Saddam had them, Jesse had said to Jen, why didn't he use them when the Americans threatened invasion? He might have said, "You come any closer and my representative carrying a dirty bomb in his briefcase will emerge from his hiding place in London (or New York City), and take revenge." But Jesse did think that Saddam had been foolish. He should have put his hands above his head, metaphorically, and said, "I surrender." Then Bush and Blair would have had no excuse to invade with tanks and bombs and depleted uranium. Jesse was no pushover. He was skeptical about the war, he was skeptical about the peace, and he was skeptical about the skeptics.

But he was especially skeptical when he was sitting at the supper table, listening to Perky and Guthrie discuss whether to join the military.

Guthrie said, "The war is over. Bush said so. The rest is cleanup."

Perky said, "Not everyone gets sent there, anyway. There's other places to go."

"Like Afghanistan," said Jen. But that was the closest she would get to attempting to dissuade them. She still believed in the Socratic method of child rearing. For both boys, joining the military was an alternative to farming, and the one thing they agreed on was that any alternative to farming was better than farming. Felicity rolled her eyes, adjusted her pony tail, cut a piece off her pork chop, and ate it—chewing it ten times, the optimum for swallow-ability. She was fourteen and disdained her brothers' views, but welcomed them—she had told Jesse around Valentine's Day that he could leave the farm to her and she would be one of those women farmers like Alexandra Bergson in *O Pioneers!,* which she had read over Christmas for a school report. She had also said that if he, Jesse, died young (because men always died at younger ages than women, and farmers died younger than other men—it was statistics), she would make sure that her mother had everything she needed, including going to Phoenix for the winter, where she was more likely to find a nice retired man than she was around Denby. Jesse had ceased taking anything Felicity said personally, because she would say anything at all: it depended on what she was reading on the Internet and elsewhere. And she didn't have many social skills. (Where did that come from? All the Guthries had social skills.)

Guthrie did wolf his food down—his plate was clean, and he was still wiping a piece of bread over it as he talked. He could eat anything in any quantity and never gain a pound, unlike Jesse himself, or Jen, for that matter. Jen said, "You want the last chop? It's a little overdone."

Guthrie said, "Like a hundred and fifty soldiers have been killed the whole time. That's less than one-tenth of one percent."

Jesse smiled, not about the troops, but because Guthrie had done the math. Guthrie had graduated from high school, just barely, having played on every team with tremendous enthusiasm but not much strength or skill. There was no sport at Iowa or Iowa State anymore that was just fun, because every team was expected to win and to bring in funding. Jesse had heard that the football coach at one or the other of the two was earning a million dollars a year, but the farmers at the Denby Café tended to exaggerate these sorts of things, especially if they themselves were not raking in a million dollars a year—those who were didn't eat breakfast at the Denby Café. Perky hadn't graduated yet, but he was doing somewhat better than Guthrie had, with a B average in all subjects, about the same as Jesse at the same age. Guthrie didn't have Uncle Frank as an inspiration. College sounded boring to him, more classes, more reading, more papers that started with an introduction, continued with a main body, and then ended with a conclusion at the bottom of page two. He hadn't applied to ISU or UI. When Jen brought it up (only in her Socratic, you-might-consider-this way), he said that there were four community colleges within forty miles—he would decide later. At least every other day, the two boys talked about the military.

When the war started, Jesse had gone to his box of Uncle Frank's old letters and read a few about the Second World War. When he'd read them as a kid, they'd seemed weird and exciting: swimming beside a water moccasin in the Ozarks had seemed right out of the movies, not to mention the anecdotes about Anzio, the Rapido River, and Sicily. He didn't think that Uncle Frank had been nostalgic for the war; he was too unsentimental for that. But he had appreciated the way that his life developed out of the war—the German papers he had translated, that he understood the dangers of the world and how they must be confronted head-on. Why had Jesse grabbed his soil testers and mapped his own little world? Because, if you were going to make it as a farmer, you had to do it right, and Uncle Frank was all about doing it right. After supper, while Jen and Felicity watched a rerun of *Unsolved History* concerning the death of Princess Diana, Jesse reread a letter Frank had sent him about the farm. It had come not long after Frank gave him the acreage that he'd bought from Cousin Gary. He wrote, "Dear Jesse, Imagine my surprise when I looked into it and found out that I could have gotten this three hundred fifty acres at half price a few years ago. I'm not telling you what Gary charged me, but I will say that in '73, he would have charged me $750 per acre and been taking me to the cleaners. Anyway, the lesson for you, as a twenty-year-old owner of real property, is that land is only a commodity once in a while. Keep your eye on the price of gold, the price of land. Just telling you right now, land is about $1,600 per acre, gold is $144 per ounce. Get back to me in twenty years. Love, Uncle Frank."

Jesse went into the kitchen and got the morning paper out of the trash. Gold was $355 an ounce. Land, he knew, was about twenty-two hundred. He passed through the living room and said, "Felicity, can I use your computer for a moment?"

Felicity nodded, her eyes glued to the TV set.

The computer was turned on; in fact, it was never turned off. A fire hazard? He searched about for an inflation calculator. When he found it, he saw that both his land and his fictional gold had lost plenty of value since 1976. His land should be worth almost five thousand per acre, and gold should be worth almost $450 per ounce. He stared at the computer for a long minute, then went to a site he enjoyed about wild plants and herbs. He must have gotten his taste for roadside chamomile from his mom, he thought.

That night, just after Jen got into bed, she said, "Honey, I have to tell you this. David is selling the farm."

David was her brother. He had 640 acres up near Grundy Center, a whole section (worth, Jesse now knew, $1.4 million, or four thousand ounces of gold). Jesse frowned and said, "Why now?"

"Because the debt is driving him bananas. The buyers said they would take it and the equipment for the price of the debt, and he could keep the house and live in it and work the land for them. It's some corporation. They will pay him to work the land."

"So—he becomes a tenant farmer."

Jen sniffed, was quiet, then said, though not resentfully, "Who isn't, really?"

And, thinking of his own debt, Jesse said, "I don't know."

OVER THE YEARS, Richie had come to understand that the motto of the House of Representatives was "This, too, shall pass"—this campaign, this fund-raiser, this debate, this lecture from an irate voter, this two-year term, this bill, this item of paperwork that no one, least of all the congressman himself, had time to read. A year before, he had, indeed, truly thought his office-holding phase was also about to pass, but, alas, no. Enough of his constituents forgave him for his support of the Iraq Resolution so that he squeaked by. (And who was to say that Vito Lopez had not helped in that effort, just a bit? And, for that matter, Michael had, at last, contributed to his campaign, the largest legal amount.)

This latest "letter" that he had to read sat on his desk with a Post-it arrow and exclamation point from Riley. Richie tried not to understand what she was getting at. The letter was about funding for high-tech solutions to low-tech threats: Iraqis would leave bombs along the roadside in cans, plastic bottles, the carcasses of animals, old cushions. American soldiers would walk or drive by, and the bomb would go off. The army maintained that they had foreseen this tactic all along; however, they now needed "tethered blimps with cameras" (almost forty million bucks), jammers against remote controls (no price tag), and seventy million more bucks for "new solutions" (read: "desperate measures"). The desperate measures were due for immediate shipment (after New Year's, after Easter, maybe sometime next summer). Richie made no sarcastic comments in public. He only nodded and looked grave. Our soldiers were still dying, and Iraq had been conquered!

But Richie could not say that he had a solution, other than time travel. Sometimes, walking through the halls of the Capitol, he thought of *The Terminator* (who didn't?)—Arnold Schwarzenegger returns from the future and guns down the Hammer and everyone else who asked Richie day after day if he was "on board." Richie didn't ask for that. He would settle for *Galaxy Quest*—just a few extra seconds to have changed one thing. But, he thought, what would that thing be? The moment he said yes when Congressman Scheuer asked him if he wanted to run? The moment he said yes when Alex Rubino said he should go over and work for the congressman, just to keep an eye on the old man? The moment he said, "You know, I think it would be interesting," when Ivy made a face at the idea of his running?

It was worse because Michael showed him off now. He came to Washington at least twice a month and stayed at the Hay-Adams. Richie would go for breakfast or lunch, and they would eat so good-naturedly together, laughing at the same jokes, looking much the same (Richie had to make sure that he wore Michael's least favorite colors on those days, just to be certain that they were not dressed alike). Twins weren't supposed to look as much alike as they aged, but people would do double takes, even those who had known Richie for years. Richie always said, "I'm the left-hander," to smooth over the moment. Michael seemed jolly and harmless and incredibly rich—no one in Washington objected to that anymore. Yes, he had a watch collection, something Richie, with his Timex, could not fathom. Yes, he now drove a Ferrari, but he drove it sedately. Michael grabbed his hand and smacked him on the shoulder when they parted.

When he was in New York, Richie went to Loretta's dinners, which had transformed from family to society after Chance, Tia, and Binky made their escapes (the walls of their place were now plastered with pictures of Chance on his horses or astraddle the haunches of a terrified calf). The mix was financial, mostly—bankers, hedge-fund managers, stockbrokers, and their wives. They gave equally to both parties, were in general agreement that "strong measures" were necessary. (Even if that included leading a boy at Abu Ghraib around on a leash as if he were a dog? Rumors abounded in the halls of Congress, but it seemed that no one else had noticed the press coverage, and Richie was the last person who would say anything.) He was not the only politician, but he was the only one who looked exactly like the host, and whom the hostess came up to every time she thought of it and linked arms with. She made him feel like a beloved pet, and every time he voted with the administration, he felt himself inwardly licking her hand and asking for a treat. She took personal credit for "converting" him. Former Monsignor Kelly, who was now a bishop and head of a diocese in Minnesota, an outpost if ever there was one, was present in spirit, if not in person, she said, since she still sent a lot of money to his favorite charities, and also flew him in from Duluth whenever she could.

To go from the letter on his desk to dinner at Michael and Loretta's felt, to Richie, like swimming in molasses. He wasn't drowning fast enough; in fact, everyone told him he looked better than ever and seemed "to be coming into his own." Even Leo, now fourteen, was more respectful. Loretta had gotten him into Dalton; he enjoyed it, and Ivy was not complaining. Younger members of the House gazed at him respectfully, perhaps the very way he had once gazed at Congressman Scheuer.

THERE WAS a car parked in the driveway, which Henry didn't mind—he'd just awakened from a nap and wasn't going anywhere. It was cold and damp, and he was tired. He'd finished his translation of the *Táin Bó Cúailnge,* and was trying to decide whether there were any plausible connections between Cuchulainn's transformation into a monster and Grendel or his mother. Monsters were an interesting study. There were plenty of them in Indo-European literature, and he was inclined to think of them as being a remnant of the indigenous peoples that the Indo-Europeans had overcome on their journeys west. Henry yawned. A woman came out of the front door and headed to the car. She got in and drove away. Henry looked at his watch. It was five-thirty-four. Riley would be cooking (she was strict about giving Alexis wholesome food). Henry thought he might sneak downstairs and hang around for an invitation.

He opened his refrigerator and pulled out a nice blue cheese that he'd picked up, and, yes, there was an unopened box of water crackers in the pantry. Riley was a sucker for blue cheese, and Alexis did love crackers. Thus he bribed his way into Riley's kitchen.

Riley was putting an onion quiche into the oven, and Alexis was sitting in her usual spot, a small chair that hooked onto the table. She was patting her hands on her red placemat and saying, "Go go go go." She was eighteen months old, which meant that Charlie had been dead for two years and two months. Alexis was like a small clock to Henry, measuring the period of his loss. He and Riley never talked about this. He set the cheese on the table and opened the box of crackers. He said, "May Lexie have a cracker?" Alexis said, "Yes!" Riley laughed, and said, "She's good at giving herself permission to do whatever she wants."

"I've never seen her want anything you wouldn't want her to have."

"That's her genius," said Riley.

"Who was here?" Henry sat down in his usual spot, put his hands on his cheeks, pulled them out, and crossed his eyes. Alexis stuck out her tongue. They both laughed. It was possible that, before Alexis, Henry had never played with a child. It was rather fun.

Riley said, "Bunny Greenhouse."

Henry said, "Did you make that name up? It's perfect for a friend of yours. Animals and global warming, all at once."

"No, I didn't, and I only hope she becomes my friend. I'm wooing her, or maybe she's wooing me. She has the goods on Halliburton."

"Who's that?"

Riley spun around. She said, "Please go back upstairs and do your homework, Professor Langdon."

Instead, Henry unwrapped the blue cheese and set it on one of the plates that were stacked in the middle of the table, then lined some crackers up beside it. It was cold, but it was fragrant. That worked. Riley took a knife out of the drawer, cut herself a sliver, and laid it on a cracker. She ate it and said, "That's a nice one."

"It's a Stilton. I buy it in honor of the Mercians." But she didn't rise to the bait, so he held out his fingertip, with a tiny fragment of cheese on it. Alexis took it and put it in her mouth. Then she made a perplexed face that caused him to laugh.

"Bunny is in procurement for the Army Corps of Engineers. She knows what everyone is charging the taxpayers for gas in Iraq. Halliburton, which Cheney used to run, is charging two sixty-something per gallon. Everyone else, including the Kuwaitis, is charging around a dollar a gallon. The Halliburton contract was a no-bid contract—the DOD just rubber-stamped it because it had 'Cheney's Bank Account' scribbled across it. I think it's called extortion? Or maybe just fraud? Corruption? Like that. I want the congressman to do something about it."

Then they exchanged a look that said, Oh, right. We're talking about Richie here.

Henry said, "There's always hope."

Riley said, "I used to think that because I wanted to. Now I think it because I have to." She leaned over and kissed Alexis on the top of her head. Henry said, "Has Michael captured him?"

"You tell me. I think he's been obsessed with Michael since he was born. I wonder if that's always true of younger twins."

Henry said, "Richie is older. By something like four minutes."

"Well, I wish he'd remember that. Anyway, Bunny is moving with all deliberate speed. Her younger brother is Elvin Hayes."

"He was good," said Henry. "He had a great jump shot."

"She can handle herself."

Now she opened the oven door and peeped in. From where he was sitting, Henry could see the top of the quiche, brown and crinkly. He got suddenly hungry. He said, "I can set a table very nicely."

"Oh," said Riley, "you are so like Charlie at worming your way into my affections."

Henry said, "I'll take that as a compliment."

2004

J ANET WAS FEELING kind of empty and cold, the way you did in California when the air was damp, the sky was overcast, the holidays were over, and your beloved eleven-year-old had turned twelve and begun to disdain (well, maybe ignore) you, and even though you knew it was essential for his development into manhood that he do so, it still hurt. So, when the phone rang and it was Emily on the other end saying, "Mom! I'm in Pasadena! You have to come!" she called Jared and said she was going to meet Emily in L.A. that evening, spur of the moment, and would he pick up Jonah, and she would be back the next evening, or they could join them . . .

Jared was no fool. He knew that any invitation from Emily was a big deal, so he said, "Of course," and she got in the Audi, leaving Jared and Jonah the van, and left, though not without swinging by the barn and taking pictures of both Pesky and Sunlight for Fiona— she was sure that Emily must be staying with Fiona.

California did what it always did in January, get greener and sunnier and more eerie as she drove through the Central Valley and over the Tejon Pass. The Audi was sprightly and quick, and in no way drawn to precipices. It felt safe to be without a horse trailer.

But Emily was not at Fiona's. She was at a gallery a block over from Fair Oaks Avenue, where she, Tina, and the owner had just installed Tina's show, which was running from January 18 until March 12, three rooms of works, including the main hall. When Janet came in the door, Emily ran up to her, hugged her, kissed her, and said, "I am so glad you came! You represent the victims!"

Tina was behind her. She was thin, like her dad, Uncle Arthur, and her thick gray hair hung in a kind of waterfall down her back, but she looked not five years younger than Debbie, more like fifteen. She kissed Janet on the cheek and said, "Thanks for coming."

"You have to see," said Emily.

The main gallery was full of Tina-ish objects—etched glass, sticks bound together in the shapes of animals, musical instruments that looked playable but were made of papier-mâché. Emily hurried her past them to the last room, long, narrow, brightly lit. The installation was called *Autobiography*. Emily said, "No, start here. Right beside the door."

Right beside the door was Tina's birth certificate, "Christina Eloise Manning, January 19, 1953." To all of the letters, glitter had been carefully added, and tiny designs had been scattered all over the paper—stars, moon, sun. The art pieces ran away from it in a long row down one side of the room, across the far wall, and back up the other side. Janet began.

She had seen some of the childhood pictures—in fact, she was in one of them—but she remembered them as snapshots. These versions had been blown up and manipulated, painted on, pasted on, torn, layered. The sixth image, especially, did give her an uncanny feeling. It was a picture of Aunt Lillian and Uncle Arthur's house in McLean, Virginia, from the front and slightly below, as it might have appeared in a real-estate ad. Tina must have reprinted it hundreds of times and then cut apart the images—house, front door, windows, tree, mailbox, bits of lawn, shingles on the roof—then piled them on top of one another. How she did it, Janet could not figure out, but it had a 3D/memory effect, a place appearing in your mind, not as it really was, but as you wished it to be, in this case far more mysterious and alluring than a real house could be. The colors made it look both heavenly and unattainable. No one could have gotten into that house, either, because the door was locked—Tina had padlocked it. Janet shivered and moved on.

Across the shorter wall was a series called *Y Chromosome*. The title and all of the frames had been chrome-plated, and glinted in sunlight that came through a skylight in the roof. The series had seven pictures, each of them three feet by four feet. The first picture was of a man in an old-fashioned army uniform, glancing at the camera, not quite smiling but good-natured. Tina had manipulated his features, too, superimposing pencil marks that emphasized the lines of his cheekbones, his jaw, his forehead—Uncle Arthur's father. Uncle Arthur, Tim, and Charlie were interspersed with three other faces, which Tina somehow manipulated so that the real images seemed to mutate through the intermediate image into the next one. Janet remembered Tim's picture quite clearly: it was his senior photo from high school, his hair ragged and plentiful, daring for 1964. When Janet left the East Coast for California, she had made a special trip into Aunt Lillian's living room to kiss it goodbye, to kiss, as she thought, her entire past goodbye. Tina had done something to each of the images. Tim's she had aged somehow, maybe with pencil, too, but over that, charcoal? It was hard to tell. But he did not look eighteen—he looked fifty. Janet turned and smiled at Tina, who was not far away, watching her, and she realized that she had made Tim look like herself, aged fifty—but also like himself, aged eighteen. She looked again. It was eerie. Under the picture was the title, *Missed*. Janet nodded. The image that morphed into Charlie's was one of Tim's childhood pictures, in which he was wielding toy six guns; Janet remembered that every kid had done that. But the face had not Tim's characteristic intent look, but Charlie's cheerful grin. In the last picture, Charlie's face was superimposed on that of Uncle Arthur's father, and crusted with some sort of paste that made it almost 3D. The title was *Pentagon*, and there was a five-cornered shape in the lower right corner.

Along the third wall were twenty-one pictures, also three feet by four feet, but Janet had never seen any of them before. The underlying images were photographs that appeared to have been taken over the last ten or fifteen years, always from a distance. A striking one was of Charlie around the time he first showed up, running in Central Park. A lake glinted in one corner, and there were buildings above the tree line. The third picture was of Richie and Leo, standing on the steps of their old place in Brooklyn, framed by the white banisters. Leo was screaming, his mouth wide open, and Richie was looking quizzically downward. It was entitled *Nanny State*. There was one of Michael getting into a limo, actually surveying the neighborhood with a masters-of-the-universe air. The sunlight reflected in the roof of the limo had been enhanced so that it appeared to block out the surrounding landscape. Another was of Debbie and Uncle Arthur in a supermarket. They were wearing heavy winter coats. Debbie was looking at lettuce, and Uncle Arthur was hunched, but looking over his shoulder at images Tina had painted and pasted of toys from their childhoods—Tiny Tears, a teddy bear, a game of Clue. The aisle they were standing in was a yellow brick road. And then there was a picture of herself, outside of Jonah's school, with Mary Kircher and Eileen Chen. Their clothes had been painted in bright colors, and their faces, though recognizable, had extra lines—on Janet's face were worry lines. Behind them, the double doors to the school had swung open, and the kids were emerging—glittered, the way Tina's birth certificate had been.

Every third picture was of Uncle Arthur, and in each he looked uncomfortable and suspicious. One of the last pictures was of her mom, through a window of her house in Far Hills, the one everybody called "the Hut" now. The wall of the house was dark, and the window was yellow; through it, you could see the edge of the refrigerator and a magazine on the kitchen table. Of all the subjects, her mom, gaunt-cheeked, her eyebrows lifted, was the only one turned toward the camera. This made her look not as oblivious as the rest of them. The only thing Tina had done to enhance that image was to outline each of the boards of the exterior siding in gold. Janet looked at that one for a long minute, then went all the way down the line, feeling, she knew, what she was supposed to feel, that someone was watching her. The name of this group of images was *I-Thou*. When she came to the end, Emily jumped in front of her and grabbed her shoulders. She said, "Aren't they great? I so love them."

Janet kissed her, appreciating her appreciation, and said, "They are very powerful." She wondered what people outside the family would think; the images impressed her, but they also made her anxious.

They ate dinner at Celestino, and Janet could not help thinking that it was appropriate that Tina was having the risotto with squid ink, as black as any food Janet had ever laid eyes on. But she made herself act friendly and affectionate, because Emily, as she had with Mrs. Herman when she was learning to ride, seemed to have adopted Tina as a goddess. Janet had always viewed her as you did younger relatives—interesting in their way, but not important. Okay, she admitted it: her entire childhood had revolved around Tim. Yes, Tina was good-looking; yes, she was successful (but her success had taken place so far away); yes, she was adept—she had always been adept. But she had never said much, or made much eye contact, and she didn't talk about clothes or cooking or children, she talked about "media" and "blowtorches" and the thickness of glass. Finally, sipping her wine, Janet sat back and said, "Those are some amazing images. I mean, especially in the last row. Emily must have taken that one of me waiting for Jonah. What was he, about five?"

As she was realizing that this was impossible—Emily had been away at college when Jonah was five—Tina said, "Oh Lord! I hired a private detective. I employed her off and on for twelve years."

Janet felt her eyebrows lift.

"Those are just the most interesting images. I have boxes full of film."

"You had us tailed?"

"My dad would have been proud. He, for one, never had the first notion he was being spied on. I have a whole video of him in his apartment in Hamilton."

"Is that legal?"

"I have no idea. But the world is full of private detectives."

Emily laughed, then said, "There are pictures of me and Lila smoking weed in our dorm room."

"She climbed a tree for those."

Emily and Tina laughed together.

"Why in the world?" Janet lowered her voice.

Tina said, "Well, it didn't start out as art. It started out because, after Mom died, everyone just fell apart, and I didn't hear from anyone. I got lonely, but every time I called anyone, they said, 'Oh, we're fine. Don't worry. How's business?' That was all. I would call my dad, and he would pick up the phone and cough—remember how he did that?—and then not answer a single question. He made it seem like he was being interrogated. So, one night, I just thought of this, you know, a sort of payback. But then it got more and more inter-esting, and I was making plenty of money, so it mushroomed." She looked up. "Are you going to sue me?"

Emily said, "No! Of course she's not! It's such a great show. So great."

Janet said, "Jared and Jonah should come down and see this." The dinner proceeded smoothly for another twenty minutes (crème brûlée for Emily, who had come a long way from the picky eater she'd once been); then Emily and Tina called a cab for the ride to LAX, back to Idaho. Janet might have offered to take them, but they seemed so well organized, and she was suddenly so exhausted that she kissed them goodbye and let them go. Once upon a time, she would have stayed at the Ritz-Carlton, but she didn't do that sort of thing anymore. She checked into the Santa Anita Inn, where she stayed at the horse-man's rate—nice gardens, lots of noise. The horses were running, and although she probably would not hang around until post time, it was nice to have the opportunity. And it was easy to go from there past Fiona's. When she called Jared, she said she would be coming home the next day, but he should see the show before it was taken down and maybe buy something. They had a pleasant conversation.

The sheets and blankets were thin, and the room was cold. She lay quietly, thinking of the pictures—especially of how young Charlie looked running—hardly more than a teen-ager. It took her a while to realize that there were no images of her father, the famous Frank Langdon. Even Aunt Claire was present—through the window of a passing bus. Even Uncle Henry—also through a window, his finger in the air, expounding before a class. Even Joe, Jen, and Minnie, out-side the front of their house, picking up nuts of some kind under a very big tree. But no Frank. If Tina was having Charlie stalked when he was first in New York, then her father had had at least five years still to live. But Tina hadn't been interested in Frank Langdon. It was a revelation. Cars drove noisily into the parking lot, drunks got out and stumbled up the stairs. Janet burst into tears.

IN HIS WHOLE LIFE, Jesse had never experienced the perfect year, at least on the farm, in terms of plowing, planting, and harvesting, but everyone at the Denby Café, and even their wives, agreed that 2004 was the one. The sign in front of the Worship Center flashed over and over "REJOICE!" It was not only that Jesse expected to harvest at least 160 bushels an acre of corn and forty-two of beans, it was that the only astonishing thing about the weather had been no astonishing things—early planting, then sunshine, rain, some heat, some cold (no frost). Not everything else was great. They were constantly worried about Guthrie, who was about to be deployed to Iraq and pretty excited about it; his head was not only shaved, but tattooed in the back with an eagle. ("Mom," he wheedled when he came home, "when I get out, I'll just grow my hair over it." For a while, thought Jesse, but he didn't say anything. Tattoos were common, these days.) Better to think about the harvest than about Iraq.

Of course, there was that downside—he expected to get about $1.90 a bushel for the corn, if he was lucky, even though his inputs had been up—he'd had to use maybe 10 percent more herbicide because of the foxtail, which took a bite. And where would it be stored? As soon as you had a giant harvest, then you started wondering about moisture content, grain bins, who was going to buy. Fortunately, stocks were down from 2003—as low as they had been in years. As a result, Jesse was driving around, doing something he hadn't done for a long time, which was looking at cattle.

What was it that his dad had told his granddad he was going to raise when he was grown up? Not Herefords, not Angus—Red Poll, or Belted Galloways, something like that. As far as Jesse knew, the only people in Iowa who raised anything out of the way were kids getting their 4-H projects ready for the state fair. Jen's nephew David, who was now working as an insurance man in Kansas City, had raised a Blue Brahma once, beautiful but wild, perfect for a Guthrie. Jesse wasn't looking at anything exotic anywhere but on the Internet. In fact, he wasn't looking at anything long enough to pull out his checkbook—only long enough to pay some compliments and ponder using some of his own surplus feed corn instead of selling it off for less than two dollars a bushel. On the Internet, he did like to look at the cattle—White Park (beautiful pale hides, black noses, graceful horns), Highland (shaggy hair, deep-red color). But he also looked at houses in Malibu—there were lots of real-estate sites on the Internet.

Or hogs, but for hogs you had to build a confinement building. No one just let the hogs run around in a pen anymore. In fact, now that no one had hogs, everyone remembered that hogs were dangerous—big, fast, and opinionated—they would run you down and trample you. Stories about someone who got in trouble with the hogs back in the old days came up rather often in the Denby Café. Or hogs that had been allowed to run loose, go feral—not in Iowa—oh, yes, in Iowa, grew tusks and bristles, ate acorns, three hundred pounds, five hundred pounds, chased some farmer out of his barn and all the way to his house. When was that? Oh, back in the forties.

It was Felicity who e-mailed him (from her bedroom to his, a distance of about seventeen feet) a pdf of an article from *The New York Times*. According to the article, there *was* someone in charge of climate research, and he *was* forecasting bad weather to come, which Jesse did not intend to report to the farmers at the Denby Café, because if what they were having was the bad weather to come, they would say, "Bring it on!" And most of them were Republicans, so they could say that with pride. Jesse read it idly until the end. Many of his attitudes toward global warming had been shaped by a movie he'd seen with Perky and Felicity early in the summer, *The Day After Tomorrow.* They had been eating popcorn and gaping, just like everyone else in the audience, and thinking what if what if, and then, apparently, New York City froze solid in the space of about five minutes, and Jesse wasn't the only person in the audience who laughed out loud.

The end of the article referenced a study someone had done in Colorado, on the short-grass prairie, good cattle country (for those Belted Galloways, in fact, who liked to forage). Whoever had done the study mimicked the effect of doubling the amount of carbon dioxide in the atmosphere and then tested the grasses; the carbon dioxide elbowed out the nitrogen, and the resulting grasses (Russ Pinckard often said of carbon dioxide that more would be better for the plants, if not for the people) were less digestible and more fibrous. In the last paragraph, even worse—carbon dioxide was like fertilizer for invasive weeds. The article didn't say which, and Jesse hadn't yet found the study on the Internet, but he could imagine: foxtail, thistles, bindweed, velvetleaf, all the weeds that were his nemeses.

He e-mailed Felicity back: "What should we do?"

Then he sat looking out the window, into the foliage of the butternut tree. His mom, who was living in Minneapolis, where she had access not only to Whole Foods but also to Lunds, would be showing up one of these days to look at her crop. He would be glad to see her, and also to see that apple pie of hers. He had mail. He clicked on it. Felicity had written, "Wind Farm!" Well, he hadn't thought of that before.

RICHIE COULD TELL how completely the Republicans now trusted him by who they put up as his opponent for re-election, a kid just the same age he had been twelve years before, but shorter, and with a degree from Albany State. He spoke in a piping voice. Every sentence ended as a question. Richie wondered if his wealthy Republican parents were sponsoring his campaign as a way to get him to stop whining about going into government service and enter the family business. It was an old parental trick that Richie often used with Leo: You want to walk all the way over to Flatbush and back just to buy a candy bar you can get at the bodega around the corner? Fine, go ahead. You really want to go to the Putney School? Well, you put in the application, and when you get in, we'll talk about it. If your child was not so much daring as challenging, you had to call his bluff.

He had voted for the Iraq Resolution, the Patriot Act, the Homeland Security Act, and further appropriations for Homeland Security. He had voted for the Healthy Forests Restoration Act without consulting Riley, who was home with Alexis, who had the flu, and he had received a tongue-lashing, but he did think the act was not entirely bad. He had agreed with Al Gore about deploring Abu Ghraib, but had stopped short of calling for resignations. He had voted for Sarbanes-Oxley, but, then, so had everyone except Collins, Flake (notorious or legendary skinflint, take your pick), and Ron Paul, who, as someone said, wouldn't have regulated a sewer pipe running through his child's playroom. He had gotten himself quoted a few times when Maloney gave his report about global warming, but that report had been made during recess, during August—possibly, Richie thought, because Cheney was in the Rockies and Bush was at his ranch and everyone else in the world was water-skiing. The report, along with his remarks, had disappeared without a trace. After all of these votes, he had gotten a nice call from Loretta, who seemed to be acting as Michael's capo. Would he like to come with them to Cannes? They were going for just a couple of days of the film festival, then off to Dolceacqua and Apricale for some sightseeing? Fraser National Park? They were looking for a place. Michael loved trout fishing now—he was working much less, and learning to tie flies—he had a wonderful talent! When he saw Michael in New York or Washington, Michael was as nice as he had ever been, offering him actually good advice about Leo and about Ivy, who was dating a best-selling thriller author some ten years younger than she was (Michael's advice: read the books to see whether she was gossiping about him, but stay on her good side). Michael had given him Loretta's car, a perfectly good and not at all flashy Subaru wagon, green, leather uphol-stery, twenty-six thousand miles on the odometer, and twenty-three miles to the gallon. Not even Riley could disapprove, and she often borrowed it.

But now there was Bunny. Bunny Greenhouse. Riley was mod-erately intimidated by Bunny Greenhouse, as anyone would be. She reminded Richie of that old Johnny Cash song about the boy named Sue. Bunny was a predator, and she was after Halliburton. Riley expected Richie to join in the hunt. Richie had tried to use the Maloney report to explain to Riley about priorities—if he was going to hammer away at climate change, then he could not waste his ammunition on $2.63 gas. Anyway, according to Riley's logic, gas in Iraq should be five dollars a gallon, in order to incorporate the external costs of the invasion and the costs to the environment; it was the one-dollar-a-gallon gas that ought to be investigated. But Riley wasn't standing for that: this was so cut-and-dried, such a perfect example of corruption, that to bring down Halliburton and Cheney would be a step in every conceivable right direction. He did not say that if he talked about Ms. Greenhouse on the floor of the House and pressed the importance of her charges against KBR, Halliburton, and Cheney, Cheney himself might cross over from the Senate and tell him, "Go fuck yourself," as he had told Senator Leahy in June. Or that he might not be re-elected. Richie didn't know if he cared whether he would be re-elected. Let his opponent take over—why not? Judging by the nebbish's talking points, he truly believed that the market was free, he truly believed that Bush had had no warning about 9/11, he truly believed that there were terrorists named Mohammed in every alley in Brooklyn, he truly believed that his trust fund was God's gift, he truly believed that his co-op about six blocks farther toward

Grand Army Plaza was worth five million dollars. He had a weaselly little wife with buck teeth and two minuscule daughters who were schooled at home.

Bunnatine Greenhouse was not fixated on $2.63-per-gallon gas in Iraq. She had also noticed that the Corps of Engineers had all sorts of rules on the books that they did not follow. She had been hired by her boss, since retired (forced out?), to see that the rules were followed, and she had all sorts of degrees and was an outspoken presence at meetings. Her conviction was that "emergencies" don't last as long as companies seeking "emergency contracts" want them to. Probably she was going to be fired. Her bosses were already drumming up grounds for firing her, though Cheney had not told her personally to go fuck herself. The most Richie could do was make a speech defending her on the floor of the House and then have it go into the record. So much of being in Congress was putting stuff on the record.

He did it for Riley. He did it for Alexis. He could see that reporter from the *Times* in the gallery, but could also see him get up and walk out ten minutes into Richie's speech. So he wasn't going to get into the paper, either. At best, he was background. And this wasn't a local issue in Brooklyn, so no local rag would mention it. Just some thoughts tossed into the void. Even so, when he was finished, Dingell gave him a smile. Riley gave him a hug; then she hurried off to day care to grab Alexis, and Richie was alone.

It was late afternoon. He decided to go for a walk before finding the Subaru and driving home. His first thought was to head over to the Hay-Adams and sit at the bar, but then he couldn't take that anymore, either, so he wandered around to the south of the Capitol building. In spite of the various security installations, the evening was pleasant; the grass had that late-fall brilliance that contrasted with the fading of the trees. He passed the botanic garden and then walked west past the various buildings of the Smithsonian. This was a walk he sometimes made, and he also sometimes went into one museum or another. Now he saw a group of kids standing in a row in front of the *Ad Astra* spear at the entrance of the Air and Space Museum, being photographed by their teacher. Was his old military school the only school in America that didn't dare take the kids to Washington for a field trip? He paused to look at the kids. The Air and Space Museum was one of Leo's favorite outings.

The woman wasn't like anyone around D.C. or anyone in Brooklyn. She was wearing loose black pants and a black sweater. Her hair was long, and looked like she cut it herself, grabbing it in her fist and clipping the ends with shears. In spite of the dark colors, she was big—five ten for sure, and large in the bust and the derriere—okay, Richie thought, watching her pass him, the ass. She had a real ass, and shoulders. She turned to look at the Hirshhorn, and he simultaneously thought that she was pretty and that she had no makeup on, which was why she didn't strike you. He looked again, then dropped his gaze. But he sped up. How did you pick up someone not in a bar? Riley and Nadie were not there to advise him.

She kept walking—past the main building of the Smithsonian, toward the Washington Monument, which got taller and taller. Richie glanced surreptitiously down at his chest and swept what might have been a few crumbs off the gray cashmere blend of his overcoat. It was too warm for gloves and a hat, but he looked respectable, congressional. She was a good walker, long-strided and self-confident. He caught up to her at 14th Street and stood beside her as they waited to cross. Their shadows stretched before them. He glanced at her sideways, and smiled. She said, "Are you following me?"

Richie nodded.

She said, "Why?" But she didn't seem nervous in any way.

He said, "I want your vote," then held out his hand. "Richard Langdon, congressman, New York ninth district."

Without missing a beat, she held out her hand. She said, "Jessica Montana."

Richie said, "You're kidding, right?"

And now she did smile—the smile made her. She said, "No, I'm not. But it's been an inspiring name."

"Because?"

"My great love is women's semi-pro boxing. Do you know anything about that?"

"Nothing," said Richie. "I am in politics. Do you know anything about that?"

"Nothing," said Jessica.

"Then," said Richie, "let me take you to dinner. We are made for each other."

"I'm always hungry," said Jessica.

2005

〜

EMILY HAD BEEN a little surprised to be asked to be a bridesmaid for Chance and Delilah's wedding (Delilah Rankin, lawyer, two years older than Chance, Emily's own age, supposedly the daughter of a big Texas family), but when Tina pointed out to her that twelve bridesmaids was standard for a hundred-thousand-dollar wedding, Emily saw that she was being dressed and cast in a supporting role. Her only job was to smile and not catch the bouquet. Her aunt Loretta had prevailed on her maternal counterpart to have the wedding at Pebble Beach rather than in Dallas, which was fine with Emily, since she could go there with her mom, stay two nights, go home to Palo Alto (thank God, she thought, Jonah was too old to be cast as ring bearer). And so she stayed in the background most of the time, eating treats, reporting her observations to Tina by cell phone. One thing she hadn't told anyone, though (and everyone was in a flurry, because they were dressing the bride and the service was due to start in half an hour), was that, if they hadn't roped Delilah into her bridal corset, at least some people would have noticed the bulge, though maybe not Chance. Maybe Chance would be amazed to commence parenthood about a month after his twenty-third birthday.

She'd seen dresses that she knew were chosen by the bride to make sure that the bridesmaids looked appalling, but this dress even Tina approved—it was silvery, with an irregular hem and a slanted collar.

The shoes were silver, too, and so were the decorations. At least nine out of the twelve bridesmaids looked pretty good in the dress. What Delie saw in Chance, Emily could not imagine, unless it was pure sex. Since moving to Idaho, Emily had slept with plenty of cowboys, and eventually they all came to look alike—limber and dry, their cheekbones getting sharper and sharper, their eyes getting twinklier and twinklier. They all had stories about being rousted out of bed at four in the morning to go retrieve the calves in the freezing rain. Her favorite was one a very nice guy had told her: He was following a cow and her calf up the side of a mountain, he was bored, he tickled his horse with the tip of his quirt, the horse startled and jumped off the cliff. Fortunately, Ryman was quick—he went left when the horse went right and landed on his feet, looking down at the horse, who landed on a ledge. The horse assessed his situation, then scrambled up the mountainside on his own, a good thing. But Ryman was exactly why Emily would never marry someone like Chance.

Finally, the girls got Delie into her dress. Her mom handed her her bouquet; the wedding planner set her veil on her head and floated the netting over her face. Delie did look happy. It seemed as though she saw Chance as a real catch.

The wedding planner opened the door to the corridor. When they lined up, Emily found herself beside one of Delie's Texas cousins, who was fat and did not look like a cowboy. Tia was a maid of honor, and Binky was fourth in line, craning her neck to see everything while talking and talking, the way she always did.

Most of the family had flown in on a jet her uncle Michael had rented. They were sprinkled here and there like clover blossoms in a green field. You could recognize them even if you didn't know them, because they didn't have the hair—the men weren't wearing pompadours and the women weren't puffed up. Even Aunt Loretta was neatly trimmed. Mrs. Perroni was wearing a dress from the eighties—encrusted with beads—and Grandma Andy was wearing a dress from the Kennedy era. Emily had plenty of time to notice all of this as she walked down the aisle they had made in the ballroom (the Rankins were not Catholic, so there could not be a Catholic wedding). Emily and her partner reached the satin-draped platform and parted. When she took her place, Emily realized that the bridesmaids were arranged in order of height. All of this was *interesting;* Tina told her over and over that she would be much happier if she observed rather than judged, but they both knew how hard old habits were to break. And so, during the reception, she observed her uncle Michael and Chance. They did a lot of the same things: they danced with Delie, they danced with Aunt Loretta, they danced with Mrs. Rankin. They looked rather alike—more alike now, Emily thought, than Michael and Richie. She leaned over to Tia and said, "Don't you think your dad and Chance dance alike?"

Tia tossed her head, watched, then said, "Chancie dances like he's doing it with you. Dad dances like he's doing it *to* you."

Emily laughed out loud.

But, still, your eye was drawn to the older man, not the younger, wasn't it? She could see around the room: Her mom was looking at Uncle Michael. Two of Delie's aunts were looking at him, too. One of the bartenders was watching him. Emily shivered, just slightly, but she didn't know why. At the next table, she saw Tina scribbling on a napkin—a cloth napkin. She made up her mind that that objet d'art would not be left behind. The music stopped, then started again. Her uncle Michael went over and asked Grandma Andy to dance. Everyone fell silent, even the singer, but the music swelled, and her grandmother—what was she, eighty-five?—curved the line of her body, stepped out, and let her son spin her across the floor.

FELICITY WAS SITTING on her old purple rug. The sleeping porch looked out over the fields to the north. It was a sunny Sunday morning. Her dad and mom had gone to services, but she had said she had a sore throat so she wouldn't have to go. Some Sundays, she just could not take Pastor Diehl. His lips were too big or something. He looked like a cartoon to her, though her mom thought he was nice enough. There was also that thing about how he got out on the basketball court with the kids. His feet were really big. He looked disgusting. Her room had a door to the sleeping porch, and so did Perky's, and she was listening to Perky and Guthrie talk about something. They thought their conversation was private. They didn't realize that Felicity had opened their door just enough to hear.

Guthrie was on leave. His first deployment had ended, and now he was waiting for the second one. According to her dad, Great-Uncle

Frank had been in Europe for a whole war, but that wasn't the way it was anymore. Perky said, "That was the biggest battle."

Guthrie said, "You know what it was like? It was like attacking St. Louis. It's right on the river. It's about the same size, and St. Louis has a lot of churches. Well, Fallujah has a lot of mosques. And they were all full of weapons. Not much happened there during the invasion itself, so the insurgents had plenty of time to get ready."

Felicity's mom had told her that Guthrie would be different when he got home. No really bad things had happened to him, like getting shot or driving over a bomb (an "improvised explosive device"— Felicity mouthed the words), but every war was full of things that you didn't want to see unless you had to, and Guthrie had seen plenty of them. He came home more serious, more jumpy. But he did want to go back.

"I mean, we kicked them out once, but that didn't work. There was this old Baathist resort nearby. Kind of like that casino outside of St. Louis, in St. Charles. So they weren't going to let it go easy."

"What was the scariest thing?"

Felicity saw that she was fiddling with her hair, winding it around her finger over and over. She unwound it, put her hand in her lap. Guthrie didn't say anything for a moment. The dark-red oak floorboards of the porch were cool and smooth, and one of the windows rattled in the breeze. She imagined either Guthrie or Perky noticing the crack in the doorway and discovering her, but just then Guthrie said: "I don't know. It's scariest before you go in. It's scary to imagine the IEDs and the booby traps and the insurgents around every corner. Then you do go in, and something happens, and you're so jacked up you don't take it in at the time. You just keep going. I mean, this guy in my unit who was behind me got hit by a rocket. Just blew him up. We saw it, but no one said anything. There was nothing to say."

Felicity rested her palm on her forehead. She was suddenly feeling a little dizzy. She knew that there were women soldiers in Iraq, who wore camo and everything.

Guthrie said, "It's fucking hot. You're covered from top to toe and wearing boots and carrying, carrying like a hundred pounds of shit. If you're in a tank, it's boiling. A guy passes out, you just shake him and hydrate him, and he's got to get it together." Then he said, "I mean, there were almost twenty thousand troops. That seems like a lot, and it was way more than when they went in there the first time, a year ago, and fucking lost. But they learned their lesson. Forty thousand would have been better, in a way. Or bombing the place flat with NE—you know, novel explosives. Those are scary. The marines did some of that. That's what the IDF would do."

Felicity knew that the IDF was the Israelis. They had talked about it in school.

"What about the white phosphorus?"

"Who said anything about that?"

"I read about it."

"I'm not saying you can't use it. You got to use what you got to use."

Now there was a long pause, so long that Felicity had to extend her legs, very slowly, and she made a noise, because the rug shifted. Outside, in the top of the apple tree, two squirrels started running along a big branch, as if they were playing tag. Finally, Guthrie said, "Well, we saw some stuff. I'm not saying that our guys aimed it *at* anyone. Stuff goes up, stuff comes down. You flush them out and then shoot them. Maybe that's putting them out of their misery."

Perky said, "Yeah." Dully, agreeing.

Then Guthrie said, "The skin just gets burned off where the crap lands, then it keeps burning into the flesh as long as there is any of it. I mean, you fucking took chemistry."

Felicity stared at her pale, cold knees and shins, imagining this.

Suddenly the door opened, and Guthrie stepped onto the porch. She thought he was going to yell at her, but he didn't even notice her. He went over to one of the windows, opened it, lit a cigarette. Felicity pulled her knees up again and sat quietly. He was wearing briefs and a T-shirt, even though it was cold. She hadn't seen him in briefs for a long time—in their house, everyone was very modest. His legs were hairy, all the way down to his ankles. His tattoo was a little covered up, but she knew he would shave his head again when he was ready to be sent back. He was all muscle; that was another way he had changed. He stared out the window long enough to smoke the whole cigarette, then stab the butt into an ashtray that she hadn't seen on the windowsill. He turned around and saw her. "Hey, kiddo. What are you doing?"

She was brave. She said, "Eavesdropping."

He smiled his usual old smile and said, "Well, I guess someone has to." He came over and held out his hand to her. She took his and stood up. He said, "I hear you learned how to make popovers."

"Grandma taught me."

"Well, let's have some."

She said, "Have you killed anyone?"

He said, "No one I know."

"Do you care if I ask?"

"No. Because I think about it."

She got a little closer to him, and put her hand in his. He squeezed it. When they made the popovers, he separated the eggs.

IT TURNED OUT that Jessica Montana was really Jessica MacKenna, or would have been if her ancestors had not moved from County Cork to Butte, Montana, in the early twentieth century. This was what Henry found interesting about her. Otherwise, she seemed like a good match for Richie. Riley, however, found the name change highly suspicious. Jessica was sitting at the table, with her back to the kitchen door, saying to Henry that she herself had never been back to Inishannon, or anywhere in Ireland, though her sister, Aileen Montana, had rented a car and driven from Dublin to Galway to Limerick to Cork to Waterford and back to Dublin. Henry was saying, "I would love to do that," but even so he heard Riley snort. Richie turned his head in Riley's direction, but Jessica paid her no mind. Jessica seemed like the type who went blithely forward, eternally surprised but not daunted by impediments. There were Calhouns from Ireland, and plenty of Rileys, but when Henry prodded her, Riley said that her Riley grandmother was English and her Calhouns were Scottish. She said nothing about her Menominee side.

Henry knew he tended to go on at boring length about all sorts of origins, and it had taken Richie months to agree to this little supper, so he made himself shut up. Alexis, who was almost three, about as big as a minute, and had Riley's dark, penetrating eyes, said, "Do you like tofu?" in a serious voice, and looked at Jessica. Riley had been trying to get Alexis to eat tofu for a couple of weeks now, with no success. Alexis was a good talker and a good passive resister. One of her ploys was to solicit opinions on those things that her mother was trying to foist upon her.

Jessica said, "Not really. Grilled, maybe." She answered as if she were talking to an adult.

Riley came in, set the eggplant Parmesan on the table, and said, "So—you're a meat eater? How many times a week?"

"Every day, I suppose," said Jessica. "I don't really think about it. I have a big appetite."

She looked as though she did, thought Henry.

"We've been vegetarian for a long time. Alexis has never had meat."

Except for those bits of hot dog Henry had given her.

"But she doesn't like tofu, I'm sorry to say."

"Yuck," said Alexis, but with an alluring smile on her face.

"My grandfather was a butcher," said Jessica. "You can't imagine the offal that my father and his brothers ate. Kidneys were just the beginning." She helped herself to the eggplant, ate with pleasure. It took Riley about a minute to say, "What's the difference, really?"

Jessica let this go by.

After Richie and Jessica left and Alexis was put to bed, Henry helped with the dishes.

Riley said, "This can't last. She is the most oblivious woman I've ever met."

"Maybe she's just easygoing. I mean, what is she, forty? Never been married."

"Yes, she just does what she wants. Boxing. Bacon. She drives a diesel pickup. She voted for Dubya once, then Kerrey once. I'm not saying she's unprincipled, but—"

"Yes, dear, that's precisely what you are saying."

"She likes Michael."

"I like Michael."

"You have to like him! He's your nephew. I mean, she likes him voluntarily."

That seemed to be the crux of it. Henry wiped the last plate carefully and placed it in the cabinet. He said, "I know you have reasons to disapprove of Michael, but he's got a sense of humor. He's observant. He's well read. He does his thing, and he lets others do their thing."

"Fucking free market," said Riley. "I would love to have a look at his portfolio. I'm sure every investment is in something that gets government subsidies, all the time that he is saying the free market must decide what works and doesn't."

"Hypocrisy is not confined to the financial sector."

"I don't understand how he thinks," said Riley. "I just don't." Henry let it go at that.

Henry felt he did understand how Michael thought—he thought like a hunter, he thought like an invader, he thought like a predator. He sought high status, which in the modern world was measured by money, houses, cars, looks, rumored but unproven mistresses, and demeanor. A thousand years ago, he would have been wearing only the best furs, only the most brilliant neck chains; he would have spent his free time hunting wolves and bears. Two thousand years ago, he would have had slaves and concubines; five thousand years ago, he would have had multiple wives, many horses, and a nice circular dome for a house, with a neat fire in the middle of the stone flooring. What was to understand? The incomprehensible thing was that in the modern world his type seemed confined to certain regions—New York, Washington, L.A., London—but in retreat elsewhere—Berlin, Paris, Madrid, maybe Beijing. That he held no appeal for Riley was no surprise, either—all of her eggs were in the high-priestess basket. She adhered to a calling that molded her thinking, she had suffered a sacrifice, she had a three-year-old postulant, she hated profligacy of any kind. And she was in a battle for the soul of Richie. It was clear to Henry that Richie's soul was indeed embattled, and thus he clung to Riley as an antidote to Michael. But what would she gain were she to win him? Better, in Henry's view, to admit, not defeat, but that the prize was not what it appeared to be. Richie would never not fold, never not compromise. Henry had discovered Blockbuster, where he loved to wander as he had once wandered library stacks; recently, he'd come across a *Hamlet* he had missed, with Bill Murray as Polonius, set in New York City. He'd watched it in fascination and discovered that he did not want Hamlet to come to the point and avenge his father, he wanted him to cross the boundary from feuding society to a society of laws and bring his uncle to trial. In his whole life, Henry had never disagreed with Shakespeare, but now, old man that he was, he did. Michael had his place, but it was as a historical marker.

....

THE NEXT PERSON Richie took Jessica to meet was his mother. He didn't know which one made him more nervous. He was well aware that Jessica cared nothing for her appearance. When she was naked, she was wonderful to look at, at least to him; she was muscular and strong, but her muscles were smooth, did not ripple and bulge. When he embraced her, he could feel the warmth and spring of her body. And she was indulgent. In the eight months that they had been dating, she had never once criticized him or told him what to do—she didn't believe in it. Nor did she tell Leo what to do; when he challenged her, she said, "Suit yourself." When he found out she was a boxer, he'd insisted upon donning boxing gloves and going a couple of rounds. She had rope-a-doped him for maybe six minutes, then given him one in the jaw that knocked him down, though not out. He hadn't asked for a rematch, though she offered to take him along to the gym and get him a few lessons.

Richie knew his mother could fall short in many ways, from a vacant look on her face, to wearing something truly antique and strange, to offering them six pieces of romaine as their entire meal. However, he had not imagined that she would fail him by inviting Michael and Loretta and Chance and Delie and the baby—what was his name?—oh, Raymond, after Loretta's dad. Raymond Chandler Perroni Langdon, because there was also some old Hollywood connection between Raymond Chandler and Gail Perroni's father. He was now three months old. They called him "R.C."

The weather was pleasant, not so hot as it had been; everyone was in the tiny backyard. Richie had explained to Jessica that both Michael and his mom were veterans of AA, so Jessica received her virgin tonic water and lime wedge with her customary cordial good nature. One good thing was that Loretta had taken over food detail; she whispered to Richie that she'd brought along ribs, potato salad, carrot cake. ("There is exactly nothing in the refrigerator! I asked her what she lives on; she said there's a bakery somewhere that makes wonderful chocolate croissants!") Jessica observed where R.C. had been placed, and sat far away from him. That put her near to Chance, and Richie saw them start talking. Michael sat down beside him and said, "Hot."

"I'd like to think you are referring to the weather."

"No, you wouldn't."

"She's a lovely, harmless girl who could beat you to a pulp in about five minutes, so keep your opinions to yourself, okay?"

"Is she gainfully employed?"

"She's a bouncer at a gay bar." Out of the corner of his eye, Richie saw that Michael was impressed. He said, "I'm joking. She manages a fitness gym."

"Low on fertility, is my guess."

"I think she's opted out of the asshole-reproduction role. She has six brothers and a sister. She is the second oldest."

"You're sure she's a girl, right? I mean, you've had plenty of time to look by now. You can't judge by the exterior add-ons or even the fake vagina. It's really in the hips."

Richie knew that part of his problem for his entire life was that he couldn't come up with ripostes. Michael's barbs surprised him every time, and he was missing whatever part of your brain it was that batted back.

Michael went on, "I have this *Playboy* in my permanent collection from five years ago, the December issue. You could tell the one who started out as a guy—great hair, beautiful face, but hips like Chance's."

And why not say something mean about Chance the dope or his floozy wife, whose hair seemed to have been put on like a football helmet? But Jessica was chatting with Delie in a pleasant, animated way. Chance had gone around to the other side of the house. Richie felt his teeth grinding. He said, "Mom seems immortal."

"Gail Perroni is ten years younger than she is, and looks ten years older. Loretta says there's some group that does calorie restriction and they live to be a hundred. Maybe that's it."

"It isn't genetic. Uncle Sven died in his seventies."

"I think she's using an artificial preservative. Formaldehyde."

Richie said, "You have a sick imagination."

"I call it creative. If you refuse to think outside the box, then you get stuck in Brooklyn."

Richie made up his mind to ignore this. Michael was clearly bursting with pleasure at some market innovation he had recently come up with. It was true that he never told Richie any of his net-worth particulars, but Loretta didn't mind tossing around large numbers as if they were the price of pasta—"I think it was fifty million. Was it fifty million, Michael, or forty-five? Binky, have you put in your paperwork for the Year Abroad program, or haven't you? Please give me a straight answer." Or, "That place on East Seventieth I told you about—it went for twenty-four million! I nearly fell over. I can't imagine what our place is worth now."

Chance had returned, and what did he have with him but a lariat! Now he and Jessica walked toward the back of the yard, him swinging the rope in a leisurely way above his head. He and Jessica were still chatting away. He lassoed a lawn chair and pulled it toward him, took the rope off, set the chair upright. Then he performed some rope tricks that Richie had seen on TV from time to time—bringing the rope down around himself, then raising it up, enlarging the loop so that he could step through it, spinning the rope on one side of his body, then switching arms and spinning it on the other side. Michael said, "That's the hard one, but he's ambidextrous."

"Did he bring a calf along, too?"

"Only R.C."

Richie glanced over toward the rest of the group. R.C. was snuggled against his mom, a baby blanket over his head. Ivy had never been so modest. Once, when she was nursing on an airplane and the flight attendant said they had run out of food, Ivy snapped, "This is making me hungry, so I'll take what the captain is having."

The flight attendant brought the food. Richie had been the one who wanted to hide his head.

Now Chance coiled up the rope and handed it to Jessica. She was tentative at first, so that the rope caught and fell, but within a few minutes she was leaning over it, her arm up, getting it to go around. "Told you," said Michael. Very slowly and smoothly, but with evident strength, Jessica now began making the lariat twirl unevenly above her head, and then, quite smoothly, she tossed it toward the lawn chair. It hit the top of the curved back, slid downward. Chance and Jessica both laughed.

It was Loretta, with, perhaps, some input from Delie, who decided Chance was having too much fun. She got up, went in the house, and came out with plates, napkins, silverware, the food. When she called out, Jessica looked up, startled, as if she'd been enjoying herself quite a bit.

On the way home, Richie was in a bad mood for the first time since he'd met her, but Jessica seemed not to notice. She said, "Chance is a cute kid. He's practicing being able to do rope tricks and talk at the same time."

"That's been done before."

"Oh, really! Who did that?"

"Will Rogers."

"Who was that?"

Richie didn't answer, just said, "What does he want to talk about?"

"Well, the goal is, someone in the audience yells out a word, and he talks about it for a minute; then someone else yells out another word. We tried it."

"What word did you give him?"

" 'Campaign.' "

"What did he say?"

"He said that that was a region in France where they grow a Pinot Noir and a Chardonnay grape, and then he described the two kinds of fermentation."

"Did you correct him?"

"Yes."

"Then what did he say?"

"He sang a verse of that U2 song, 'Beautiful Day.' But then he lost control of the rope. He needs practice."

Richie was willing to admit that if Chance had been his son he would have liked him better.

JANET HAD ASKED AROUND, and so far, she hadn't found anyone else her age who was getting regular e-mails from his or her eighty-six-year-old mother. And concerning things that Janet knew next to nothing about. The one she opened (her mom's e-mail address was handyandy435@aol.com) read, "Janet, dear. How are you? Trees are very bright this year. You should come for a visit. It is a little frosty, though, so I brought in the pots of herbs, including the lavender. Mary Watkins (next door? Don't know if you met her) made me a batch of lavender ice cream. It is profoundly purple. Am almost afraid to eat it. Did you know that if you eat too many carrots, the whites of your eyes turn orange? BTW, what is a CDS? Your brother seems to be after my money. He wants to infest in something—oh, I mean invest, isn't that funny. I tried to get him, OVER the PHONE, to explain what he is talking about, but I couldn't tell if he had no idea or if he wasn't willing to tell me. I looked it up. The only thing I could find out was that sometime last month a lot of bankers had to meet and apologize to the head of the Federal Reserve about not keeping their records up-to-date. This seemed like a bad sign. So I said no. Oh, do you remember that woman Richie knew who was after Cheney? Here is an article about her (link). You should read it. She lives in Reston. I remember when Arthur and Lillian were look-ing for a place there. So they fired the woman. The man who fired her was careful to say that it was 'not in retaliation for any disclosures of alleged improprieties she may have made.' So that's how you know it was. Do you have a recipe for Aunt Lillian's angel food cake? I always thought that was delicious. Love." Janet looked up the recipe, which she hadn't made herself in twenty years. It called for ten egg whites. She found it in an online cookbook and sent it. She read the article her mother had linked to, about Bunny Greenhouse. She wondered why Michael wanted her mother's money, and then she wondered how much money her mother had; then she went over to the family-room wall and looked for the hundredth or thousandth time at the picture she'd bought from Tina's exhibition, of her mother sitting in the light, looking out the window, innocent, harmless, still beautiful. Or not.

2006

B EFORE GUTHRIE'S UNIT was redeployed to Iraq, his dad asked
him if he wanted to read some of Uncle Frank's letters about the
Second World War. How many times did his dad mention those letters, as if they were the Bible or something? Guthrie didn't want to
read them, but in the end, he couldn't resist. The paper was yellowed
and thin, and most of them made the war sound like an adventure, not
something Uncle Frank looked back on with fear or regret. He had
been in the North African and Italian campaigns, which might have
been a little like Iraq, and Guthrie thought the letter about watching
the German tanks roll over the Allied trenches and sort of grind the
men in those trenches into the ground was pretty interesting, mostly
because Uncle Frank said his commanding officers were such idiots.
Guthrie didn't think that way, at least about his own commanding
officers. The main thing he wondered about while reading the letters
was where the local population was. There didn't seem to be the sort
of insurgency in North Africa or even in Italy that there was in Iraq—
maybe the Allies had bombed them to kingdom come, but, whatever
had happened, Uncle Frank's letters were about armies going against
armies, not about subduing the population.

When Guthrie got back to Baghdad, he saw at once that things
were much worse than they'd been in '04. There had been talk about
this—it shouldn't have been a surprise—but the feeling itself was a

surprise. It was as if Fallujah was everywhere now. And the guys who had lived through the change were on edge, pissed off, and ready for a fight.

There were folks back in Denby who didn't know the difference between Shia Muslims and Sunni Muslims—there were maybe some guys in his unit who didn't know, or at least didn't care—but Guthrie did know the difference. The Sunnis thought that Muhammad's father-in-law should have taken over when Muhammad died, and the Shia thought that his son-in-law, who was also his cousin, should have taken over. He kept to himself the thought that farm families in Iowa would understand the bitterness of this antagonism over issues of inheritance perfectly well; you said it was about principles, but really it was about loyalties and property. Guthrie also knew that most of the Iraqis were Shia, and that they resented the Sunnis in the same way that Evangelicals—who were always talking about how God was their personal savior, who spoke to them on a regular basis—disdained old-style churches for being all about rules and not about being saved. His grandmother and his mom had had "discussions" about this, and rather warm ones, more than once. And there were the Kurds. As far as Guthrie could tell, they were like American Indians on reservations, trying not to offend either group. It was as if the Episcopalians had all the money and the power, and the Evangelicals were bound and determined to take that power for themselves, because they were the saved ones. So, when some Sunnis blew the dome off the big Shia mosque in Samarra a week or so after his return, he knew that there was going to be trouble. He remembered the mosque and the dome from when his unit had gone through there after the operation against the insurgents, before the Fallujah attack.

He wasn't a prophet—everyone in his unit knew there would be trouble. The only question, they decided when they were talking about it late that night, was: Bombs? Rockets? IEDs? And aimed at whom?

There was a guy from Wyoming, Harper, who was the smart one, Guthrie thought. He didn't whine about whether or not the Iraqis were grateful to the Americans for getting rid of Saddam Hussein, nor did anything surprise him. He was ready. He said, "Okay, you bring the cavalry in to steal more of my cattle, what's the difference between you and them? I don't give a shit that they are in uniform—

you bought them off anyway, because you've got the money and the politicians in Cheyenne." He shrugged.

It was the Iraqi army, not the coalition forces, who were supposed to suppress the reaction against the explosion of the mosque, but it turned out they just stood there, and so the Mahdi Army could go into Sunni houses, drag the only man inside out, shoot him if he was lucky. And then it turned out they were killing children and women, too. After that, they started taking their rocket launchers into the streets and firing on Sunni mosques. It was said that they killed some imams.

Guthrie was feeling as jittery as everyone else. He had spent the day in the mortuary, helping guard the bodies of the dead. People kept coming in looking for their relatives, mostly men, but some women, too, all wrapped up in their veils. They would come to the window and say they were looking for someone, the way you went to the window at the bank at home. Then they would be shown pictures of the faces of the corpses. Was it worse to see that face you knew, or worse not to? Guthrie didn't want to think about it. And he wasn't good at estimating stacks of bodies, but he did think there were more than the three hundred the U.S. military was saying had been killed.

It was tempting to repeat what his buddies said, that this was a fight Saddam had started and not their business. If the Shia and the Sunnis wanted to kill each other, they should go for it. The fewer Iraqis there were, the better for the coalition forces; it saved ammo, for one thing. But even when guys said it, they didn't say it like they were happy about it—they said it like they were pissed to be caught in this shithole that was supposed to be pacified by now and ready for the modern world.

Supposedly, it happened in March, but everyone was hearing about it now, at the end of June. Whenever there were rumors, Guthrie had discovered, most of them were true in some way, but not in the way you first imagined. What made it come out was the two American soldiers: they were abducted, killed, apparently tortured, then their bodies were dragged around, and there was said to be a video Guthrie had not seen that showed some insurgents kicking one of their heads down the road like a soccer ball. Of course, all the guys he knew were pissed, and then, when the first rumors about *why* the insurgents did it came out, everyone thought it was just an excuse. Why would you capture and kill two Americans who were not even the ones who had raped the girl and killed her family? Why wouldn't you go for the ones who had done the crime?

But what was the difference, maybe, if you were an Iraqi? Every one of the coalition troops was wearing the same camo, the same boots, the same caps. Everyone carried the same weapons, and everyone had been trained to treat the Iraqis the same way—from a distance. Partly that was self-defense: you don't express friendship to someone with a multitude of enemies; you try to stay neutral, so that at least, if you were killed, it was a neutral IED that did it, not some kid with a weapon staring at your very own face.

A day or so later, more about the rape and the killings came out. It was a squad who guarded a checkpoint just south of the city, a place no one wanted to be assigned to, it was so dangerous. Six guys kept staring at this girl who lived in a house nearby. They got drunk, and that was probably the least of it, and went over to the house and killed the parents and the sister first, then raped the girl, shot her in the head, and tried to burn up the evidence. They then blamed it on Sunni insurgents, but that unraveled. Another episode, said Harper, in the History of Stupid People, which, Guthrie had to agree, was a long and eventful history. Everyone involved had kept this under deep cover for a while, but of course it would come out— the Iraqis got to know all about it, and the longer it went unattended to by the coalition forces, the more certain it was that something bad would happen, and then it did. But that was the way it was this time, Guthrie thought. His first deployment, he had been scared, but the worst days were at the beginning, even including the Fallujah battle. This time, the vermin, and pardon him for saying that, were getting the upper hand, but he was speaking scientifically—bacteria always evolved immunity to antibiotics, broadleaf weeds always evolved past the Roundup, the insurgents always developed better methods of resistance. In the meantime, the army kept promising vehicles that might actually withstand a roadside bomb, but where were they? And though there were checkpoints everywhere, the violence was getting more frequent and more menacing; if you were manning a checkpoint, any person approaching, any child, any dog, not to mention any vehicle, made you nervous. Yes, maybe the Shiites hated the coalition forces the most—Muqtada al-Sadr tried to make sure of that—but no one, at this point, had a reason to befriend the coalition forces.

Guthrie asked Harper if his dad or his uncles had been in the army. No; one uncle had been a career naval officer, got in during Vietnam, got out after the Gulf War; he was against this war and had even rallied against it in Santa Cruz, California. He had said to Harper that if he had to join up, the navy was the place, but Harper decided he was too tall for the navy. This was his first deployment. Maybe that was the key—he hadn't expected it to be any easier. Guthrie watched him; he was good-humored, and things rolled off his back pretty quick. He was also uniquely observant, Guthrie realized. For some unknown reason, Harper could sense something odd in any scene; if he bumped into a shelf and something wobbled, he caught it without thinking about it, every time. Month by month, Guthrie had come to the conclusion that somewhere not far from Harper was the safest place to be. But in Baghdad, even that spot wasn't terribly safe.

One morning after the story about the murders came out, they were at their assigned checkpoint. They had been there since dawn. Dawn was cool enough, but now it was getting hot, and Guthrie, as always, was feeling sweaty and uncomfortable in his gear. A kid did approach, a little skinny kid in shorts and sandals. He came toward them with his hands away from his sides, his shirt flapping in the wind. Their checkpoint was not out in the open; there was a wall and some wrecks of apartment buildings not far away. The road to the checkpoint had been cleared, but it came down a small rise. The boy had a can in his hand—a Coke can. He was smiling, and he waved the can, then threw it. As it left his hand, someone, not anyone right around Guthrie, shot the can like a clay pigeon, and the boy jumped back. The very moment he jumped back, Guthrie expected the can to explode, but it didn't, it just fragmented from the hit—the aluminum sparkling in the sunlight. It was the boy who was killed, shot in the neck and the chest. He collapsed to the ground. None of the coalition soldiers went out to him. He lay there. His blood was dark on the dirt. After what seemed like a long time, two guys in Iraqi uniforms drove up to the body in an old jeep. Even they approached the body cautiously. But the corpse didn't blow up. They laid it in the back of the jeep and drove away. Guthrie, like everyone else in the squad, watched, said nothing. Then the corporal said, "I don't see why the insurgents shoot kids with Coke cans." And that was the explanation—another example of in-fighting. Guthrie knew better than to look around for any telltale grins, knew better than to ask, knew better than to wonder. It was the kid's own fault, wasn't it? Throwing that can.

EVERYONE TALKED ABOUT how Zarqawi was the mastermind behind some beheadings, plus lots of bombings and attacks. He was a Sunni from Jordan, Bin Laden's best friend, but after Zarqawi was killed, Guthrie noticed that all the coalition commanders seemed to be surprised that the insurgents got more and more violent. It was like they looked within and said, Gee, if I died, the war effort would grind to a halt. Why didn't that happen when Zarqawi died? Guthrie told Harper about another letter he'd read from his great-uncle Frank to his dad: Frank's company was somewhere in Italy, attacking a monastery or a castle on the pinnacle of a hill. The only plan of battle was to send platoon after platoon up the sides of the mountain, even though the hillside was barren of cover except bomb craters, and the German planes came in all day, every day. After they'd been up the mountain a couple of times, one of the guys in Frank's squad told the lieutenant he would kill him if he ordered them to attack again. And then he did, and they did kill him, though they pretended the Germans did it. When you came right down to it, why would troops keep fighting if they thought they could get away with not fighting? Pride, said Harper.

Revenge, said Guthrie. If Zarqawi was really Al Qaeda, and the insurgents were Al Qaeda, wouldn't a desire for revenge motivate them the way it would anybody else? But you didn't avenge generals, you avenged your buddies, and the more of your buddies that got it, then the more pissed off you became.

Bombs were everywhere. The worst bomb they'd heard about must have been a Zarqawi idea, a car bomb the year before. Some American soldiers were handing out candy to kids in a busy part of town, not far from a checkpoint. Then, out of nowhere, an old car like a Ford Explorer (that's what Guthrie imagined, anyway) barreled into the crowd and blew up—killing twenty or thirty kids and the soldiers. It was a Shia neighborhood—poor, too. Were they really

Al Qaeda? Or were they Sunni, enraged at how the Shia seemed to be taking over? Everyone had a theory, but the only solution was Harper's solution: pay attention. If there was an indentation in a road, or a figure on the horizon, Harper went on the alert. It wasn't like the movies—Iraqi bombs didn't know to go off on their own, so someone had to be watching, waiting to detonate. More than once, when they had been driving along, Harper had stopped: something about the setup, whatever it was he couldn't himself always explain, had bugged him. So he halted the vehicle, waited. When kids approached for candy or money, Harper put one of the kids, usually the most talkative one, in the vehicle with them, and drove carefully along to the checkpoint, where he let the kid go with some money or some food as payment. Once, when he was especially nervous, he made the kid sit on the hood of the vehicle as they drove. And it had to be a boy. Harper said that the Iraqis didn't value girls enough not to set the bomb off.

It was said that, for every coalition soldier killed, ninety to a hundred Iraqis were killed. Harper said that the War Between the States had lasted 1,488 days (that he would know this was the sort of guy Harper was); 620,000 people had died. That was 417 people per day. What was especially interesting, according to Harper (where did he get this stuff?), was that the population of Iraq was about twenty-five million, more or less. In 1860, the population of the United States was about thirty million. So were the Iraqis in a civil war yet? Only they would know, Guthrie thought, and they weren't saying.

Guthrie, unlike Minnie and his mom, had not opposed Operation Iraqi Freedom. The congressman, as he was called around the farm, had supported it, or at least not opposed it. Guthrie would not have said at the time that he knew enough to oppose it—when half your family voted Republican and half voted Democratic, then you had to believe that both parties were basically okay. After his first deployment, he would have said that he'd seen some bad things but that, all in all, it was not a war like previous wars that they'd studied in school. You could be, he had thought, against the Vietnam War and in favor of the Iraq War. But all the guys agreed that this war was going south, and there wasn't much the coalition forces seemed to be able to do about it. The Iraqis complained that the coalition was keeping the good weapons and good armor and good equipment to themselves—but why would you give weapons to people who might turn around and kill you? They could kill you because they hated you, they could kill you because you were in the way, they could kill you because they didn't know what they were doing, they could kill you because they didn't have anything better to do.

GUTHRIE DIDN'T LIKE IT when he and Harper got different assignments, especially if his assignment included driving the road between Baghdad and the airport, which was about as dangerous as any road in Iraq—maybe not a bomb (but maybe yes), but rocket fire, sniping, mortar attacks. He had worried about the insurgency when he was first redeployed, and all of his worries had been not nearly enough. The plane, who was in the plane? It was a cargo plane. It was coming in, and then started circling; Guthrie, hunkered down behind the security perimeter at the airport, could see it approach, turn, disappear into the cloud cover. But the pilot seemed determined to land. Then he did land, and everyone on the plane was hurried to a helicopter, and that took off without being shot down. Guthrie could see Condoleezza Rice get off the plane and into the helicopter; only a few other people went with her. Guthrie and his squad then accompanied the rest of them into Baghdad on the road—no explosions, insurgent recon wasn't always very good. Harper was assigned to get her from the helipad to the Green Zone; he carried a machine gun and stayed a few paces behind her. He heard her asking about Saddam Hussein, where was he, what was going on with the trial. Guthrie had forgotten that Saddam was still alive. Harper had also heard someone ask her about a book that had been published, but he didn't hear what it was. Apparently, it was uncomplimentary, because she had stopped walking, snorted, and gotten huffy about it; the guy behind her had almost knocked her down. She was a pain in the ass, said Harper— not because she wanted to be a pain in the ass, but because she was used to being listened to and respected, she was used to the lights not going out, she was used to standing a certain way, walking a certain way. Harper, who was as cool as a cat, came home freaked out after they put her back on the plane and chased her away. That no one had shot her or blown her up was just a matter of luck, he thought.

Harper stayed freaked out. When they went on patrols in eastern or western Baghdad, Harper was jumpier than everyone else. One night, Guthrie asked him about it. He said, "It's like we've gone over some edge, where there's just too much shit going on. You know what scares me most? It's not being killed, it's being blown up but not dying. Used to be, they got you or they didn't. Now they only get part of you. The medics rush in, and they do their shit, and they think they are doing you a favor, saving most of you, but are they? I think about that every time we go out on a fucking patrol."

Guthrie tried not to think about anything. Even when Kassen was shot in the neck and Peters had his leg blown off, Guthrie kept his thoughts muffled down, flat, stuffed away somewhere. He would deal with it later. He also stopped talking to Harper about stuff, because Harper was rattled, talking in his sleep. Guthrie thought maybe Harper had never confronted any situation before where he didn't know his way around. But he wasn't the only one. The guys who had had their deployments extended were worse. The army said it was only six weeks or a month, but everyone knew that, once you started down that road, there would be no end—you joined up, they said they would give you certain guarantees in exchange for the fact that you could get killed or worse, and then those guarantees turned out not to be guarantees at all, but just crap. He'd never thought he'd say this, but thank the Lord he didn't have a girlfriend back home, or, for fuck's sake, a wife. Those guys were the worst. They tried to keep in touch, or they didn't try to keep in touch; they tried to have something to live for, or they were restless with longing, or, the worst, they didn't give a shit anymore but they didn't dare say anything about it. And where were the hookers? According to Harper, World War II had been all about hookers, and in Vietnam the soldiers had access to hookers like no American had ever seen before, but no hookers in Iraq, at least that anyone Guthrie knew had discovered. Harper said that hookers were practically a soldier's right. No hookers, and the female soldiers expecting not to be hit on—it was an impossible situation.

One night, Guthrie and Harper talked about how you would run a war if you could do it right. The only thing they could come up with was a standing army of fourteen-year-olds who didn't know what death was, who would never be allowed back home, who would be conditioned and trained to kill or be killed, who would be bred to the game and then penned up (though treated well) after the war was over. Not an all-volunteer army, but an army of purebreds, like racehorses or hogs. It made them laugh while they were talking about it, but then Harper talked in his sleep again, and Guthrie didn't get any sleep at all.

EVERYONE WAS SUPERSTITIOUS about approaching the end of their deployment. Only an idiot talked about what he was going to do when he got home. Harper said that there was no objective reason to believe that you were in more danger in the last weeks or days or hours before they got you out of this hellhole, but, still, he did not say what he was going to do when he got home. Even so, things entered Guthrie's mind. When he heard about the Shiites' kidnapping of dozens of Sunnis from the Ministry of Higher Education, he got the image of the Memorial Union at Iowa State—he'd been there on a school trip senior year and was impressed by it. When the Sunnis then attacked the Health Ministry, he couldn't help imagining the big square white buildings of Usherton Hospital, where he'd gone once after a basketball game for an ankle X-ray. Baghdad was nothing at all like Usherton—maybe it was like Phoenix? But he didn't want to think that, either. Sadr City he did not mistake for anywhere he had ever been. There were palm trees, there was heat, there was chaos, there was dirt, there were donkey carts, there were holes blasted in walls and doors, there was beautiful Arabic writing in black and blue on white walls, there were lines of people waiting to go into a bank, there were women in full black burqas, men in long robes, and children running and jumping everywhere with hardly anything on, there were soldiers aiming their weapons around corners, standing beside women sitting on the pavement, holding babies. There was a terrible stink. There was the absolute flatness of the landscape, absolute flat blueness of the sky. There was an everlasting rolling blast of noise, and sometimes, or at least that one time, there was a series of huge explosions in the middle of the afternoon, when five car bombs went off one after another in a square that Guthrie had walked through the day before, and after that there were bodies and blood and rubble and mess. No one, no one could stop them, no matter who wanted to or how much they wanted to. The folks back in

Washington could say this or that, they could ask for more money in addition to the millions of dollars per day that they were spending, but it was all for naught, and everyone in Guthrie's unit knew that as well as they knew their own names.

A WEEK LEFT; go out on patrol, be glad it was cold and the streets were more or less empty. Six days; work the checkpoint, hope that no one would appear, scream at anyone who even twitched an eyebrow the wrong way. Five days; go out on patrol again. Go slow, watch out for doorways and corners, don't say anything about the future. Day four; go out on patrol again, this time in Karbala, not Sadr City. Don't look at the women—every billow in every burqa could be a bomb. Don't look at the fingers of your friend lighting his cigarette—they are trembling.

Remind yourself that the Americans had nothing to do with the execution of Saddam Hussein. He had been tried by his fellow Iraqis, found guilty of crimes against humanity, and now was going to be hanged. Most of the guys in Guthrie's unit had seen that picture of Saddam and Rumsfeld shaking hands in the eighties. But most of them didn't care—if you enlisted, even for practical reasons rather than patriotic reasons (or religious reasons; there were guys scattered about who had imagined in another lifetime that they were going to witness to the Iraqis and show them how to be saved, but nobody did that when they got their boots on the ground), then you did not pretend to understand the ins and outs of two guys shaking hands one day and attacking each other another day. But Harper knew something that Guthrie didn't know, that the Shiites in the government had chosen to hang Saddam on the worst possible day—some sort of holy day. Harper said, "It was like they hung the Pope on Christmas, or even Good Friday. It was like they handed their enemies a martyr." One of the other guys said that was pretty rich, Saddam Hussein as a martyr or a victim, and Harper just shrugged. He didn't care anymore what you thought or whether you agreed with him, he was just waiting, like they were all just waiting. What they all knew was that when Saddam was hanged, no matter how secret that might be, everyone would know instantly, and the Sunnis would go bananas, and Baghdad would have another one of those weeks—most casualties since the invasion.

One day to go. The afternoon of Saddam's hanging, the skies were cloudy and the weather was damp—it could get that way. You didn't know whether you wanted to be wearing all your gear or not. They were assigned to a checkpoint. The first car that came through seemed harmless: a family, a veiled wife, a husband who was friendly, three kids in the back seat. Behind them, close behind them, were three guys, maybe nineteen years old. They seemed jumpy and impatient; their old, dirty car bumped against the back of the family's car. Harper, Corning, and Randall made them reverse, get out and leave the doors open, then the three kids cocked their weapons, gave the guys the once-over, and sent them back the way they came. A farmer went through in a little truck with a couple of goats in the back. A man in Western clothes went through in a rather nice car, papers on the front seat. The jumpy guys did not return. The weather warmed up and the clouds dissipated. Off in the distance, they heard the boom of an explosion, saw a flare. It was too far away for them to hear the screams. Randall made a face, and said, "Happy New Year."

2007

THE PARKING GARAGE was not full at all. Claire found a roomy spot in a corner, got the kids out, and assembled them in two columns in front of her, Lauren with Dustin, Ned with Dash. She took Rhea's hand and Petey's hand, and said, "Think about what you want to buy. The slower you go, the more you get." What she was really curious about was what, when given the choice, each of them might pick.

Yes, being a grandmother was a wonderful thing. With her own mother as a model, she hadn't expected that. Frank had always said that Rosanna appraised her offspring with an eye to their market value. Though Claire hadn't actually believed him, she'd seen no evidence of the adoration she felt for her grandchildren. No faults in them, and she didn't take credit for it, either, since she found plenty of faults in Gray and Brad, and certain faults in Angie, Doug, Lisa, and Samantha. The children walked into the atrium and paused to stare at the fountain, then up at the ceiling. They kept going, though, and stepped carefully onto the escalator. They looked around, pushed their hoods back; their voices were low; they held the hands they were instructed to hold. In the eyes of her fellow customers, only admiration.

She had enjoyed working here before her party business took off, and agreed with irate customers that they could have retained "Marshall Field's"—not every department store in the United States had to be called "Macy's."

The toy floor was bigger than Claire remembered, and she felt a little intimidated, but upon arrival the kids all stopped and looked up at her. What next? She walked down one aisle and halfway down another, stopping in front of the Legos. She said, "Petey and Rhea and I will stay here. Look at the display at the end of the aisle. Dustin, what's that?"

"Elmo. They're all Elmo," said Dustin.

"Okay. We are right by Elmo. You guys stick together, and come back to me when you find something. Don't go away from the toys, and don't talk to anyone, okay?"

All at once, and involuntarily, she remembered an occasion at Younkers—when was this? The late eighties, anyway. A woman was trying on a coat, and she turned around to discover that her daughter was missing. She alerted Colleen—Colleen was the manager of Women's Wear back then. Colleen wasted not a second, and had the store doors locked. The woman estimated that it had been at the most two minutes since she lost sight of the four-year-old. Then everyone who worked there combed every corner and room and aisle of that Younkers, and they did find the child, one floor up, in Children's Clothing, curled in one of the dressing rooms. Claire remembered Colleen talking about it; the girl seemed okay, but she was not wearing the clothes she had worn into the store. It was creepy. Everyone knew that whoever had taken the child was still locked in the store, but there was no way to find him (or her). Claire stood on her tiptoes and watched the kids as best she could, but they were good. Petey rummaged among the Legos, and Rhea walked to both ends of the aisle, playing with the Elmos at one end and the Doodle Pros at the other. Lauren brought a leftover Holiday Barbie to Claire for safekeeping; she was dressed in elaborately embroidered, fur-edged black, with a thick braid falling over her shoulder. She looked as if she had come straight to Chicago from Salzburg, and was not quite what Claire would have picked. Samantha disapproved of Barbie, so Claire said, "Very lovely, sweetheart," and set it on the floor beside her. As the toys accumulated, she would take them to the counter.

It was useless, she said to her friends and to Carl, to remark about their own childhoods that when they were ten or eight or six they were heading over hill and dale with only a cracker and an apple, six miles to school and back. Why should children do that? thought Claire. Did it toughen them up, as her friends asserted, or simply prove to them that the world was a cruel place, and so ensure that they would prolong that cruelty when they themselves were grown? Even a young child could tell the difference between circumstances and intentions. Claire could see, when she was growing up during the war, that their house was old and uninsulated, and therefore she was cold, that there was no extra gasoline, and therefore it was a long walk to school, that all scrap, all cloth, all extra provisions went to the war effort, and therefore her mother reknit sweaters and patched clothes and had meatless Wednesdays and Mondays (though never Friday). But if a child lived in the midst of plenty and got none of it, then he would quickly learn to blame his parents for neglecting him or teaching him a lesson—take your pick. Paul had gloried in his success, and so showered Gray and Brad with more belongings than their friends had. They seemed fine, modest in their display of wealth; they had learned a lesson from watching Paul, and not the lesson he had meant to teach them. Dustin brought a video game and set it next to the Barbie. After sitting cross-legged with the Doodle Pro for a while, Rhea put it back on the shelf, then brought Claire a board game based on a labyrinth. She went back and found another one, by the same company, called "Castles of Burgundy," a game Claire thought quite seductive. Petey turned away from the Legos and chose a stuffed lion and an actual book, *Millions of Cats,* and Ned returned with a set of what looked like lethal weapons but turned out to be spinning tops. Claire did not like or approve of the case full of fake makeup that Lauren chose next, but maybe, she thought, it was better than a toy stove with toy pots and pans. Dustin found another video game, and Dash, who had more or less disappeared, suddenly turned up with a transparent gun that shot soap bubbles, a thousand-piece jigsaw puzzle with a rock-and-roll theme, and a magic set. All the kids seemed happy. They did not look half drugged by greed, they looked intent and interested. Claire felt pleasantly vindicated.

After only half an hour, the kids started acting bored, and Dash said, "Can we get something to eat?"

They took the toys to the cash register, and Claire was especially friendly to the rather brusque sales associate while she bagged the toys in six separate bags. Claire asked her to staple them shut (there was a stapler on the counter). The kids were agreeable even to losing access to their toys until they got home. They ate in the Marketplace. Lauren ate only gelato, Ned only French fries, Petey only the toppings off his slice of pizza. All in all, when they got home, Claire decided that she had been an ideal grandmother, and that all six of the kids would remember this day, at least for a while.

AROUND EASTER, Henry sent out a mass e-mail. It read,

Dear All,
     Happy Easter. I hope you are well, especially those I haven't talked to in a while (this means you, Claire—I miss you. I will try to call sometime soon). I am enjoying my life and my house in Washington, D.C. The weather is so strangely different from the weather in Chicago. I'm not sure I deserve it! Anyway, my work is going well, and I'm off to Ireland this summer for about two months—six weeks working with some materials at the University of Dublin, and two weeks in the west, driving around (with a friend! I would not attempt to drive in Ireland on my own).
     My real news is that I have asked to adopt (though it is more complicated legally, it amounts to the same thing) Alexis Wickett, Charlie's little girl, who is soon to turn five (May 11, to be exact). From "in loco parentis" to "legalis parens." Charlie's folks have agreed to this—I get along with them quite well when they come for their twice-yearly visits, and they agree with Riley and me that she needs some sort of safety net (will she be taking me to court for child-support someday? We shall see). Anyway, Alexis is very dear to me. I never thought I would become a father at 74, but it's a very medieval thing to do.
                                                                Love to you all,
                                                                Henry

Obviously, this was a good thing, but it prodded at a point of contention that Claire thought she'd put aside, her discomfort at the way everyone in the family seemed to go crazy when Charlie died. Claire had liked Charlie—he was a charming boy—and the circumstances of his death were horrifying, but, still, he was only peripherally their child, and he had become the family obsession. At least, that's how Claire saw it. Carl didn't agree, but when she pressed him, he did his Carl thing, smiled and shrugged, leaving her to understand that, however crazy she acted, he had learned to live with it.

Claire put on her coat and went for a walk around the block. The daffs were blooming and the tulips had thrust up beside them. It had been a strange winter—sinister warmth over Thanksgiving, then, two days later, ten inches of snow, an inch of freezing rain, plummeting temperatures. Carl, whose business had dropped off, was suddenly overwhelmed: he spent long days for two weeks at a house in Evanston where a huge tree limb had fallen through the roof of the solarium. Then, after the calm over Christmas and New Year's, more snow, more work. Claire had felt the same flutter in her customers—doubt because of strange happenings in the markets, followed by a surge of what Carl called "Spend-it-while-you-have-it" parties, Friday, Saturday, Sunday afternoon, Thursday, caviar, sterling silver, Cristal champagne, best orchestra you can find, is Elton John available. In her pockets, Claire crossed her fingers.

Why was the family not obsessed with Guthrie, who had returned from Iraq and was, Claire thought, just barely holding it together? Or with Perky, who had joined the marines over his mother's loud objections, as if to say, You think the army and Iraq is something, try the marines and Afghanistan! And no one said a word about Chance, who was on the road nine months out of the year, as if he didn't even have a wife and child. (And did he? Apparently, Delie had moved back to Texas.) Jonah, she had heard through the grapevine, had several "diagnoses," but she hadn't heard exactly what they were and was a little afraid to ask—Janet was Frank's real failure, because she mistrusted not only him but anyone connected to him. Emily seemed to be emulating Tina and hiding out in Idaho. Tia and Binky were supposedly going to school, Tia at Georgetown, Binky on a year abroad in Paris (a likely story, thought Claire).

Richie had ceased being in the news. When Claire looked him up in *The New York Times,* there was nothing, not even a wedding notice when he married the girl, what was her name, Jessica Montana. Michael was quoted in the *Times* once, not with the frequency of two or three years ago. His quote was typically slippery: "These innovative instruments are revolutionizing the landscape and bringing about an era of steady prosperity that really isn't like anything we've seen before. Risk should be spread around! It makes for a more stable world economy and a better balance between all parts of the market." But whether that slipperiness was his own or was just jargon belonging to his Wall Street world, Claire didn't know. A month ago, Carl had brought home a copy of the *Financial Times* he'd noticed in a trash can down by the Board of Trade; there was Michael's photograph, looking spiffy and sinister and just like Frank, with the caption "Michael Langdon, CEO of Chemosh Securities, in London for a meeting with Barclays Bank." She hadn't heard from Debbie in ages—Claire didn't know what Kevin and Carlie were doing. How your world was cast when you were young seemed not to matter at all as you aged. What was it like for the firstborn or the second? Claire could not imagine. But for the fifth and last, it was like walking onto a stage where the lights were up and the play was beginning the third act, gloriously permanent, soon to close, but always a lost world. No one would ever seem as handsome and dashing to her as Frank, as kind as Joe, as beautiful as Lillian, as smart as Henry, as reassuring as her father, as strict as her mother, and, maybe for entirely coincidental socioeconomic reasons, people these days didn't have those Greek choruses of relatives, freely offering their opinions about everything that happened. Maybe she had tried to reproduce it all, imagining in Dr. Paul the very man for the job, an aspiring playwright with a grandiose sense of himself, but she had failed in her production— hadn't she walked out just before the curtain went up?

Carl was a wonderful gardener; her mother would have told him what to do, loved him all the same, and given him all her best bulbs. Truly, she and Carl had made this harbor here, this Midwestern island of peace and prosperity, and Claire couldn't take much credit for it. Carl didn't live onstage, he lived in a workroom, putting the finish on this, sanding the edge off that. He was still the happiest man Claire had ever met, a saint of tremendous patience whose greatest pleasure, other than a good dinner and some friendly sex, was the neat fit between mortise and tenon.

PONIES HAD BEEN KNOWN to live to the age of forty, and though Janet didn't think Pesky would get there, he was almost thirty, turned out in a grassy refuge for elderly equines down near Big Sur—she visited him every couple of months with some apples and carrots. Jared didn't mind going along, because he liked to have dinner in Carmel. Sunlight had lasted a long time, too—the summer he was twenty-three, she had come to the barn to find him lying in his stall with his eyes open, quiet and stiff. No horses after that until now, two years later: in February, she had agreed to buy Jackie Milkens's retired event horse, fourteen, very experienced, mostly sound, good at dressage. Her name was Bluebird. Since no one at home seemed to require her maternal services and the house seemed to clean itself, Janet's enthusiasm for the equestrian life had resumed—she showed up at the barn every day, stayed for two or three hours, went on trail rides, and kept her tack clean and oiled. The barn was full of all sorts of people who engaged their horses in all sorts of disciplines, and everything was fine, until the man who had owned the place since the seventies decided he was done, and another group bought it. These were people from out of state—Arizona or somewhere, rich people who wanted an equestrian facility in a vineyard, or near a vineyard, or with its own vineyard. Janet tried to stay on their good side.

The dumbest thing they did was kick the stable workers off the property and tear down the little houses they had been living in since the property was built. This meant that Marco and his wife, Lucia; Chico and his wife, Anna; and Pablo (who was too young to have a wife, and went back and forth to Guadalajara, where he played piano in a band) had to find places to live in the most expensive rental market in America. Marco, who had been at the barn as long as Janet had kept a horse there, was now about forty-five, Janet thought. He had gotten a little set in his ways, and he was not happy when his hours were shifted so that, instead of working seven hours a day, six days a week, he had to work ten hours a day, four days a week; but he got used to that, and the grumbling subsided. Things were fine for about two months, and Janet could speak to the new owners politely when she saw them.

In May, on a beautiful day that had Janet singing under her breath, she was in Birdie's stall, putting the saddle on, and she heard Marco say, *"Sí, se acabó cerca de Los Banos."* When she led Birdie into the aisle, Marco was in the next stall over, cleaning it out. "Los Banos" had caught her ear, since that wasn't terribly far from the Angelina Ranch, so she said, "Marco! Do you have friends over in Los Banos?"

"*Sí, señora,* but, really, I have bought a house near there." He grinned.

She said, "You have! How wonderful!" She'd almost said "amazing," since she knew for a fact that Marco made minimum wage or no more than a dollar above that. She said, "It's so far away, though! Isn't it like a two-hour drive? Are you leaving here?"

Marco stood up, leaned on his fork, and said, "No, *señora.* My wife stays there. I go for three days, come back. I am staying with my cousin in Los Altos four days."

"What's your wife doing now?" When they lived on the stable grounds, Lucia had run a cleaning business: she went around to people's houses once or twice a week with an assistant. She called it "Mini-Maids."

"She is cleaning, like before. But over there now, so she can live in the house."

Janet had been through Los Banos, to the Perroni ranch, and a little bit around that neighborhood. She could not imagine that Lucia could prosper the way she could in Palo Alto, but she didn't say anything except "Well, congratulations. Drive safely."

"*Sí, señora. Gracias,*" said Marco. He went back to sifting shavings and tossing lumps of manure into his wheelbarrow. On the way over to the arena, leading Birdie, who walked along politely, she passed Marco's truck, a huge Ford pickup. That was pretty new, too—newer than Janet's 1998 Chevy. Nothing made sense anymore, but it was too beautiful a day to care.

FELICITY WAS LOOKING FORWARD to ISU, but she didn't think about it much. She could have started the year before, but she had decided to focus on her job at the vet clinic. Her mom said she was obsessed with that job, but Felicity would not have used the word "obsessed"—she was busy and happy, that was all. She cleaned cages, mopped floors, helped around the office, watered plants. Sometimes she pulled on latex gloves and helped Dr. Carlson by holding a cat or a dog. Most vets were women now, and she knew she could be one, but she hadn't decided. What her dad considered a bad thing had happened: Lou Carlson, Dr. Carlson's brother, had taken Felicity down to Des Moines, on a visit to the Great Ape place there. Her parents might have heard of the Great Ape place if they read *The Des Moines Register,* but they didn't. Though she had told them all about it, she saw that they were not convinced that primate research was her destiny. She felt some despair about whether they would ever learn a thing. In an effort to sway her father (or maybe teach him), she had given him his own copy of *Our Inner Ape,* a book that Pastor Diehl would have found sinful and ungodly.

To tell the truth, Felicity had indeed been surprised to discover that there was a sort of ape she had never heard of, called a "bonobo," a much more playful and less vicious ape species, in which the females were dominant and the males had sex all the time in preference to fighting. Felicity had read the book three times, though she still went to church with her parents. She passed the time there by imagining Pastor Diehl as an ape with a mask on—he was definitely from the chimp side, since he was prickly, aggressive, and loud. Felicity could easily imagine him patrolling the grounds of the Worship Center, Bible in hand, eager to wrestle nonbelievers to the pavement. He was already talking about the Iowa presidential straw-poll, which wasn't until September.

Over supper, she told everyone about the personalities of the dogs she was caring for. Did a dog hang back, waiting for her to take her hand away from the food dish before he approached it, or did he eat as soon as the food was given out? When presented with a rope toy, did a dog immediately pounce and want to play, or did the dog have to be encouraged? Did a dog show sexual behaviors even after being neutered? These would include mounting, humping, masturbating (her parents exchanged a glance but didn't say anything; Aunt Minnie smiled to herself). Felicity pushed her glasses up her nose and pressed on. Canute, her "boyfriend," wasn't much better, but he did ask her a question every so often. Canute had his own passions that Felicity respected—as he said, Canute Rose was his name, and brass instruments were his game. He was a year younger than Felicity, and played the trombone in the school orchestra. In the all-state orchestra, which had given a concert in the winter, he'd played the trumpet, because there were six chairs as opposed to four. Sometimes Canute and Felicity had conversations that she knew were weird, him making remarks about mouthpieces and her making remarks about bonobo grooming behaviors. He was a wonderful musician, and he was good-looking, too. His folks had a farm—754 acres west of town—but Canute had no interest in it. None of their friends gave a shit about farming; they cared less than Felicity did, and she was only distantly interested now. What she imagined was that she would have a small-animal vet clinic somewhere very fancy, like New York City, not far from the alleged palace where the cousins lived, and she would specialize in shih tzus and Cavalier King Charles spaniels while Canute would play in brass quartets and, maybe, the New York Philharmonic. They would not have a shih tzu—they would have several rescue dogs, and parade proudly around Central Park. Iowa State could prepare you for all of that.

JEN WAS IN a cleaning mood, so she had left six boxes of books on the front porch. Jesse could see them from his desk. The rule was that he had to go through them, and only those volumes he actually wanted could come back into the house; the rest would go to the Usherton Library. It was midsummer, and there wasn't much else to do; Jesse had proposed that they take a trip somewhere, only a week or two, but Jen said they didn't have the money. That was discussable—they could go to a lake somewhere not far away, like Bemidji, Minnesota, for almost nothing, but Jesse also knew that Jen wanted to be around if maybe, by some small chance, Guthrie or Perky might call. Jen and Jesse didn't talk about either Perky or Guthrie. Perky they didn't talk about because he was being trained in South Carolina to manage a bomb-sniffing dog, and there was nothing to be said about it. Guthrie they didn't talk about because he was in Georgia and they never heard from him. And, anyway, they had argued between themselves so many times about every facet of Guthrie's enlistment and Perky's enlistment that all they had to do was look at one another in order to know where they stood. The argument was not about whether the boys should have enlisted or what might have prevented them, it was about whether the wars should be there to lure them, to offer them a dangerous alternative to life on the farm. Yes, Jen had a cell phone, but Guthrie or Perky might only try one time, and the signal could be very bad in northern Minnesota.

Life on the farm this summer had been far from dangerous—only strange. The weather was cool, maybe too cool for a really good crop, but it was interesting. Their county and the one just to the west had had normal precipitation; the crops were growing nicely. But due north and due south it was very dry, while due east it was swampy. In Jesse's whole life he had never seen it so varied. Usually, a system came through, southwest to northeast, and on the edges of the system, storms struck or didn't. But this summer, it was too cool for really dangerous weather, perfect for really strange weather.

Jesse hoisted himself out of his desk chair (he had been paying bills), went out, and opened one of the boxes, then two more. He saw that most of the books were old ones that Uncle Henry had left behind.

Jesse had thought of going back into the commodities market: he'd had a little surplus in the winter, forty-seven thousand dollars. He hadn't done badly trading in the old days, when he thought he was so smart playing both ends. He had even rather enjoyed visiting the pit one time and listening to the shouting, but while he was turning over the idea, before he mentioned it to Jen, the Board of Trade decided to consolidate with the Mercantile Exchange, so they would be trading beans in one spot and euros in another, and who knew what else—Ebola-death futures?—somewhere else. However, as soon as he heard the two exchanges were merging, he gave up his nascent plan, and that was the moment he knew he was old, the moment that the feeling he'd had for such a long time of being sharp, knowledgeable, organized, ready for anything, the anointed heir of Frank Langdon, evaporated into the humidity.

Underneath the books, folded up, was a gift from Uncle Henry, a print of a painting by John Constable, an English artist. For a while, Jesse had cherished that print as he cherished his uncle Frank's letters—an object showing the affection Uncle Henry held for him (the inscription on the back said, "You will like this! To my favorite future farmer! Love, Henry").

Jesse carried it inside and spread it open. It was large, so he sat with it at his desk, in the morning light. It was a painting of a man with a scythe in his hand, standing at the edge of what looked like a field of wheat. A river, a green meadow, a cathedral, and some trees were in the background. He remembered that the picture had given him a sense of the Langdon and Cheek past—the past behind Great-Grandpa Wilmer, who had died in the early fifties, and Great-Grandma Elizabeth, whom he hardly remembered. The Cheeks were from Wessex, and the Langdons were from the north somewhere. This painting had been made in the southeast, of flatlands that would have been alien to the Cheeks and the Langdons. Now he looked at it rather sadly, as at an old girlfriend whom he had overestimated, who had grown careworn and dull. What struck him was the smallness of the field and the overwhelming weight of the heavy labor. If he had spent his life scything wheat and shocking oats and shoveling manure and hitching and unhitching draft horses, would he still be alive? He and Jen sometimes complained about the passing of youth. He was fifty and Jen was forty-nine, but they hadn't thought yet to complain about the onset of old age—his joints didn't ache, he had only just purchased his first pair of glasses, the fifteen pounds he had gained ten years before he had gotten rid of by walking around the farm more and driving less. Jen was the same age that her mother had been when she married Jesse, and looked ten years younger. Were they flattering themselves, or had they arrived at a golden age of agriculture without knowing it? The fields and rivers Constable depicted, Jesse now knew, were rife with cow pox and tuberculosis, rabies (he remembered his dad telling him that they didn't dare have a dog when he was a boy, because of the danger of introducing rabies) and brucellosis. In the cottage and cathedral, there were no moms and dads reading novels or watching the news or discussing fishing trips that they weren't going to take.

Jesse got up from his desk and went upstairs to go to the bathroom and find out what else Jen was throwing away, but also to go through Guthrie's old room, out to the back-porch windows to the north, to look over the bean field. A bean field wasn't as dramatic as a cornfield—just rows of leafy green, this year a little damp and yellow to the east of them, a little dry to the north and south, but perfect here. His field ran as far as he could see in both directions. It was clean, healthy, mostly weed-free; he wasn't having the problems with monster velvetleaf that some farmers were. He had always been precise, and precision seemed to be paying off, but, to be honest, he didn't know how long that would be true. His field contrasted pleasantly with the Constable print—as a reflex, he congratulated himself. But the longer he looked, the more the field looked as though something was about to happen, as if it were a blanket about to be sucked into the sky. He shook his head. There was no peace on the farm—that man carrying the scythe could have told John Constable that.

IF RICHIE HADN'T NOTED it already by himself, he would have been reminded by Loretta that when the money guys met to consider a crisis, they always met somewhere expensive and grandiose, like Aspen or Davos. Richie wondered if this made it easier for the losers among them (those worth less, say, than a hundred million) to throw themselves off a cliff? Loretta was sure to e-mail from wherever it was (this year, Jackson Hole), just to complain about how sleepy she was in the economic stratosphere, though enjoying herself anyway. And there was a crisis—everyone in the world except Michael seemed to acknowledge it. When Richie and Jessica went to their now intermittent Sunday supper two weeks later, there was no discussion of the housing bubble and its collapse, and Richie did not remark, glancing around the palatial ground floor, where they dined among the collection of California artists, that the place must be worth—what?—ten million now, rather than fifteen. He and Jessica did admire the painting of men panning for gold in 1849 that Loretta had picked up from a private collector in Los Angeles. She said, "I don't think people realize there was a series of these. The most famous one is in a museum in Boston, but I like this one better. It's more intimate." She had added a lot of paintings to her "collection" recently. Richie hadn't realized that it was a "collection"—here he had been thinking these dusty things were just reminders of the ranch.

Over their roast chicken (which Jessica seemed to be devouring, much to Loretta's pleasure), Richie kept his eye on Michael, but he could see nothing. Michael's cheeks weren't flushed, his eyes weren't rimmed in tears, he was not wringing his table napkin, his hair hadn't turned gray. Given the economic news, Richie was a little surprised, and, maybe at last, a little gratified to feel that his lifelong desire for Michael to suffer had dwindled away. It was the Jessica effect, surely—she was so indifferent to so many painful things that he seemed to be imbibing her indifference. Even in the spring, when Leo had been quoted in his school newspaper to the effect that his father could and should be replaced in Congress by someone with real convictions—his example was Rep. Walter Jones (R-NC), who in 2003 had come up with the name "Freedom Fries" but now opposed the Iraq War and wanted to publish redacted pages from the *9/11 Commission Report* pointing to the Saudis. Richie had laughed and asked Jones if he was looking for an intern, but only as a joke.

After dessert, Loretta got up from her place, carried the pie plate (maple-walnut, delicious in every way) into the kitchen, and invited Jessica to go with her into the front room. Jessica got up, dropped her napkin on the table, and glanced at him with a merry look. They walked out. After the door closed, Richie said, "Where are we? Windsor Castle?"

"Not yet," said Michael. He leaned back until his chair was teetering, and reached his long arm for the Cognac. No butler. He poured Richie an inch, himself nothing. One thing to be said for him—he made up his mind to do something or to stop something, and his mind was made up. The Cognac was in a spherical bottle set in a sort of blue crystal bed with a blue crystal stopper. Richie had never seen anything like it. He took the tiniest sip. Michael said, "What does it taste like?"

Richie considered, then said, "A little smoky. I wouldn't dare say sweet, but it's not a hundred percent removed from a chocolate latte. Are you tempted?"

"Only to take a whiff."

Richie handed him the glass. Michael took a whiff. He said, "That's the best part, really." He took another whiff and handed it back. Richie enjoyed his second sip more than his first; then he said, "Are we supposed to discuss Mom here, or national policy? Loretta must have a plan."

"Always," said Michael.

Then he dared. He said, "You okay?"

Michael knew exactly what he was talking about. He said, "The office could be better. I saw the writing on the wall in March, though, and stashed my own portfolio in concrete goods."

"Like concrete?"

"Not quite, but close. Zinc, cadmium, neodymium, sulfuric acid."

"What is neodymium?"

"It's a rare-earth. They use it in batteries. Priuses, that sort of thing."

Richie nodded, took another sip, consulted his inner sensor to see if Michael really did seem calm. He did. So Richie hazarded, "Everyone else is fucked, right?"

Michael said, "Maybe not. I'm not as bearish as some people are. But here's the real problem."

He stopped, stared at the Cognac bottle for a moment. Then he said, "As many are fucked as are not fucked. That means, as far as I can tell, that you guys can't really do anything, and you had better not do anything. Some have to live and some have to die, because almost as many are short as are long. There's too much fucking money."

"I never thought I'd hear those words out of your mouth."

"Well, let me say them again: there's too much fucking money. It's like a hurricane of money, or, no, better, a quantum field of money. It pops here and it pops there, and settles somewhere else, but the wrong signal will explode the whole thing, and all the money will disappear."

"But not the neodymium, right?"

"Maybe not. Maybe not."

"You don't seem as, I don't know, as worried as you could be."

"That's only because I don't quite know what to be worried about, so I'm taking a worry vacation. Do I worry about the Fed? Do I worry about Greenspan? Do I worry about the rising tide of stupidity?"

"You never have worried about that," said Richie.

"Something to fucking float onto the surface of," said Michael.

"Did Dad ever give you any advice?"

Now Michael looked right at him and grinned. He said, "He did, actually."

Richie felt a weird and unexpected stab of pain. His father had never given him any advice. "Do tell."

"He said to never forget that money is boring."

"So—the equation would be, too much money equals too much boredom, and that's the root of the problem?"

"I think he would say so, but he never told me which came first, the chicken or the egg."

"I would like to be bored," said Richie.

2008

~~~

FELICITY AND JESSICA, Richie discovered, were two of a kind. Jessica, like Felicity, had been a pudgy, earnest girl in glasses that were always slipping down her nose, and then boxing had given her purpose, strength, and contact lenses. Felicity had grown into a willowy young woman (though strict). Over Christmas, when Richie, Jessica, and Leo made their postmarital promenade to Chicago, Denby, and Montana to demonstrate their familyhood, Jessica did with Felicity what she did with everyone in Richie's family: she showed a sincere interest in Felicity's yakkety yak about the personalities of animals, and she went with her one day to the local animal shelter to look at cats. They also compared their biceps and their quadriceps, and Jessica gave Felicity tips about stretching before and after stall cleaning. Richie thought that Felicity didn't look like any of the Guthrie women or Aunt Claire, or the sainted Aunt Lillian— more like he himself might have looked as a girl. In the meantime, he and Leo went jogging with Guthrie. Richie huffed and puffed in the back while Guthrie and Leo pressed ahead, talking about Iraq and Afghanistan, too far away to ask him any questions about Robert Gates or Merrill Lynch—a good thing.

Felicity, now nineteen, was registered and planned to caucus on January 3 with the Denby–North Usherton Democrats, who numbered exactly eleven. Felicity grilled Richie: Had he ever met Hillary

Clinton? Yes, of course. Barack Obama? Yes, he had seen his keynote at the 2004 convention, and sometimes he saw him in the Capitol—they had a nodding acquaintance. John Edwards? Yes. Bill Richardson? Yes. Dennis Kucinich? Yes, Richie offered that he admired Kucinich (and he did, the way you admire someone who is the guy you dare not to be) but he might be a little too pure. Felicity stared at him. Richie shrugged. Jesse and Jen had never caucused. Richie had never caucused. It was a strange process.

He did not say what he truly thought of the candidates: apart from Kucinich, they all looked better than they were, according to Lucille's inside dope. Only Kucinich, who was short and not physically appealing, looked worse than he was, and so would never get anywhere. Lucille's view was that you could be an ugly Republican and wield enormous power, but that didn't work for Democrats. She wasn't sure why.

In the summer, after their minimal June wedding, Jessica had moved out of her place in Stanton Park and into his condo, bringing her bike, a newish couch, and a Therapedic mattress. She didn't even bring the book she was reading—she finished it the night before the move and gave it to a homeless man they passed on Constitution Avenue. To the Brooklyn co-op, she brought nothing but a Waterpik and some spare underwear. She had never been to Brooklyn before. She liked wandering around, and could end up anywhere, calling him on her cell and asking how to get back to "your place." When Loretta heard about the secret wedding, she insisted on giving a reception at the Langdon establishment on the Upper East Side. Jessica ignored the insistence for two weeks, then said, "Oh, shit! I forgot!," called Loretta, and said that, before anything like that could happen, she and Michael would have to come to Brooklyn for supper. That was the end of the reception idea. She did whatever she wanted in a completely disarming way, and Richie planned to get through the election year by having her walk in front of him into every gathering, a female bodyguard, a female spirit guard. He had never been so happy.

After the caucuses, Felicity wrote to say that her caucus had met for two hours and twelve minutes, and voted seven times. One person voted for Kucinich, four went for Vilsack, four for Hillary, and two for Obama. Edwards was considered suspiciously good-looking—

not a single vote. Felicity had voted for Hillary six times. She had made a case that, as the youngest person in the caucus, she needed a good role model for being a strong, intelligent, and well-educated woman. However, since the women in the caucus outnumbered the men seven to four, and all of them were at least twice as old as Felicity and one had been caucusing since Truman, they seemed to feel that Felicity was putting them down. One of the Obama supporters said that she had caucused in the eighties in Ames—did Felicity go to Iowa State?—and their precinct had been the only one in the whole state to go for Jesse Jackson. The four who went for Vilsack never shifted their votes, but when Felicity finally switched from Hillary to Obama, he got a majority and won. Jen told Jessica that Felicity was electrified by the whole process, and now viewed the congressman as her personal seat warmer for when she would go to Washington as the first female veterinarian/politician. Richie told Jessica that it couldn't come soon enough, and laughed when she kissed him and began unbuttoning his shirt—there was that relaxed and agreeable and passionate part, too.

RICHIE WANTED TO believe that the House of Representatives was less corrupt than the Senate, but he knew that this was not true, that, for all of U.S. history, the public had assumed that the House was a swamp of dirty money, nefarious influence, and continuous arm-twisting. Maybe only Jessica still had faith, but Richie could see that her faith was fading fast when they drove to the Hut for a weekend with his mom. She reached into the glove compartment, helped herself to a peppermint Altoid, and said, "Do you think seventy-five thousand dollars is a lot of money?"

Richie said, "No."

"Would you take seventy-five thousand from Exxon to stop working on solar?"

"Only if I didn't mind being shot by Riley. Well, not shot, since she doesn't believe in firearms, but decapitated with her Wüsthof six-inch cleaver."

"It just seems so small to me. Isn't Dodd rich? He's from Connecticut."

"I don't know if he's rich. He's been in Congress his entire adult life. His dad was a senator." He thought for a minute, then said, "He dresses pretty well."

She said, "My parents' mortgage is from Countrywide. They just refinanced last year."

Dodd had proposed a housing bailout, then admitted that he was best friends with Angelo Mozilo, the CEO of Countrywide. Richie didn't know if the surprise was in the scandal or in the fact that it was being seen as a scandal. Angelo Mozilo had never approached Richie, and Richie had been too lazy to refinance his mortgage on his own. Riley had asked him about it two weeks before—some other senator had gotten a good loan from Countrywide. Both Dodd and the other senator were Democrats, which was why Riley had gotten nervous: she was always worried that Richie might slip the leash and get in trouble.

Richie preferred to take Route 202, though it was somewhat slower than 95. Jessica was looking out the window. Sometimes, while they drove, she made fists, flexing her forearm muscles and her biceps meditatively, and she breathed in an even, deep, oxygen-enriched rhythm. She worked out three days a week these days—she had stopped doing even practice bouts, but she still trained. Other days, she watched movies on TCM while running the treadmill.

When they got to the Hut, his mom was on the porch, digging her forefinger into one of her pots of lavender. She was so enamored of it, and had so much of it, that its fragrance seemed to envelop the Hut. When he pulled up, she trotted down the steps like a fifteen-year-old and embraced Jessica as soon as she was out of the car. Richie kissed her on the cheek. It was nearly time for supper, but Richie and Jessica had made sure they were prepared for anything by eating ribs and fries for lunch and stashing the leftovers in a cooler in the back seat of the Subaru.

It was easy to imagine his mom lost in space as well as time—Spring Street was so quiet and so green and so architecturally archaic that he expected *The New York Times* sitting on the kitchen counter to be dated 1985, if not 1955. When his mother handed him his tonic water and lime, he sipped away the rumblings of Washington, D.C., in 2008, the anxieties of trying to get a black man with a Muslim name into the White House, the price of oil inching toward $140 per barrel (how much had Michael invested in oil?). He was in fact dozing off, listening to Jessica and his mom discuss underwire brassieres, when suddenly she said, "Say, do either of you know what a CDO is?"

And Jessica said, in her customary even tone, "Oh, that's a type of financial instrument. A bank bundles together a big pile of mortgages and sells them as a bond to investors. The investors get a larger or smaller rate of return, depending on the amount of risk in a particular bundle."

His mom said, "What if I am getting ten percent?"

"That's high-risk," said Richie.

"Oh," said his mom.

After that, they had dinner. She had made something of an effort—a large Cobb salad, neatly constructed. Richie didn't even have to exchange a glance with Jessica to know that they would take a nice walk down to the fairgrounds or over to Moorland Farm around nine, and stop at the cooler, where they would devour the rest of the ribs.

The windows were all open, and the air was humid and thick, but fragrant, of course, with the scent of lavender. Moths kept landing on the screens and fluttering away. His mom said, "Michael was here. Have you seen him lately?"

Richie said, "I thought they were in Chile, trout fishing."

"It's winter in Chile," said Jessica.

"Well, then, Scotland."

His mom poked for bits of hard-boiled egg in the salad. "I think Loretta is in Scotland. She's having some kind of spa retreat where they hike for a couple of hours, then get salt rubs and massages for the afternoon."

"Have you ever had a salt rub?" said Jessica.

"Oh, yes," said his mom. Richie tried not to imagine it. "It's invigorating. Richie's dad liked them, too." Richie closed his eyes.

His mom said, "Michael looked a little hollow around the eye sockets. I thought maybe it was just age, because I remember your dad looked a little the same way when he was your age. But you look fine. Something is worrying him."

"Something is worrying me."

"But, you see, you're used to it."

In a nutshell, thought Richie.

"Oh, heavens," she said to Jessica, "Frank nearly lost his mind when Janet joined that cult in California. We both did, really, but nothing surprised me in those days."

"What cult?" said Jessica, pleasantly.

"The one where they all killed themselves."

"Waco?" exclaimed Jessica.

"No. Before that."

Richie said, "The Peoples Temple. It's not clear that the Branch Davidians killed themselves." It was amazing to Richie that he hadn't thought of David Koresh or Janet Reno in years. When he was first elected to Congress, he had thought about them every hour of every day.

"There have been so many," said his mom, shaking her head. "You can't count them all, really."

Jessica glanced at him. He knew she was thinking, as an Irish person was welcome to think, of the Catholic Church. And he wondered, but didn't dare to ask, why nothing surprised his mom in those days. He had thought she was the paradigm of innocence.

He said, "Why do you bring this up, Mom? Has Binky or Tia or Chance joined a cult?"

"No, they're fine, according to Michael. He said he was just feeling lonely, and it didn't take him long to get here—once he crossed the GW, not much more than half an hour."

That was something like fifty miles.

Jessica's eyebrows lifted. Richie said, "Oh, that Ferrari, always getting out of hand."

"He wasn't driving the Ferrari," said his mom. "He was driving the Lexus. He said he sold the Ferrari."

"Then maybe he was feeling lonely," said Richie. He smiled at his own joke, but neither his mom nor Jessica did. Jessica's response when he said things about Michael did make him feel mean. He and Jessica had cleaned their plates, and Jessica was scraping the salad bowl with the serving spoon. His mom had selectively eaten her tomatoes, her hard-boiled egg, and her bacon, but only bits of her chicken and her avocado. He looked at her. She was five seven; she might weigh 120 pounds.

He said, "Why did you ask about CDOs?"

"I don't know. I asked him what he was working on, and he gave me so many letters of the alphabet that my head started to spin."

He said, "As long as I've known him, he's managed to get through the slamming door without catching his tail. When I talk to him, he seems upbeat." But he hadn't really talked to him in months.

"Isn't that the truth," said his mom. She got up, took their plates, returned with pineapple sorbet from her favorite shop in Bernardsville. By common agreement, it seemed, they stopped discussing Michael. The evening progressed with pleasant conversation about weather, flowers, Montana, clothes. At nine, his mom went to bed, and Richie and Jessica went out for their snack. They walked for forty-five minutes, all around the fields, in the humid grassy warmth.

RICHIE WAS at the kitchen table, drinking the last of his coffee, half listening for Jessica and reading a review of *The Dark Knight*. He was perhaps the only person in the world who had enjoyed that wreck of a movie, *Batman & Robin*—George Clooney as Batman. Even Leo had disdained it when Richie took him—what was that, ten years ago now? The city in the picture with the review did look like Chicago, rather than New York—there was something Michigan Avenue–y about the shot of Heath Ledger in the middle of the empty street. And then his Mac mail seemed to beep with extra insistence. He clicked on Riley's link (subject line—"!!!!!"), which was to Bloomberg.com. Merrill Lynch; Goldman Sachs; BlackRock. He scrolled down. Then there it was, toward the end, "Banks and brokers have taken more than $435 billion of writedowns and credit losses since the beginning of last year as mortgage-backed securities, CDOs, leveraged loans and other fixed-income assets lost value." Richie stared at this for a moment, then went to his Dashboard and tried to type out the number into the calculator, 435,000,000,000. The calculator wouldn't take it by three decimal points, but he remembered enough arithmetic to do the division anyway. That kind of debt was worth $145,000 for every man, woman, and child in America, though only $60 for every man, woman, and child in the entire world. He took a sip of his coffee, and comprehended that that was a lot of money in a way that he never had before. He understood instantly that there were only two things that that amount of money could do—it could go somewhere, into some sort of money Grand Canyon, say, or it could disappear. According to the Bloomberg article, this was the amount of money that had disappeared.

Since Richie wasn't on the Banking Committee, he had done what most congressmen did, which was to study up on his own subject and hope that the others were studying up on theirs. He did wonder why Michael had stopped hanging around, why Loretta had gone to California for the summer rather than to their new house in Burgundy. His one specific financial thought about Michael in the last week had been to wonder whether he could borrow some of the twenty-two thousand he would need to finance Leo's first year at Brown, since Ivy was complaining, too, about the book business. Part of the problem, he now realized, was "illions"—once you were counting in the "illions" your mind got hazy about the real amount. When was that article in the *Post*—Riley would have it filed in her forebrain—that declared that the Iraq War had cost three trillion? A perfect example of the "illion" problem. Richie had looked at the "three," lost interest in the "trillion." "Three" didn't seem like much. They should have printed it out—$3,000,000,000,000. He might have taken it seriously. And here he thought he was doing okay, a co-op in Brooklyn that was worth about a million, a condo in D.C. that was worth about $750,000, $158,000 in salary, and $376,000 in investments (Edward D. Jones, thank you—a name you never saw in the paper). Was Michael worth ten times what he was? Probably more like fifty or a hundred. But, looking at the Bloomberg article, he realized that everyone, really, was worth nothing—the numbers were a story people told about themselves, were told about themselves. He was fifty-four years old! How had he not realized this before? He shook his head and closed his laptop. He felt a little dizzy.

Jessica came into the room. She was wearing a pair of shorts she had bought for him—silk with a leopard-skin pattern—and a shirt buttoned with a single button. Her hair was flipped here and there; clearly, she hadn't looked in the mirror before going in search of her coffee. She was worthless, too, a momentary occasion in the history of the universe when matter happened to coalesce in a being as ephemeral as a smile or a turn of the head. Richie thought that there was nothing he could do to save her, and his eyes got wet. She said, "I woke myself up laughing. Isn't that funny? I have no idea what I was dreaming about, but the first thing I heard was this giggle. I wish it would happen every morning. I am in such a good mood!"

Richie grabbed her hand and pulled her down on his lap, then kissed her and said, "Do you remember that Foreigner song, 'I Want to Know What Love Is'? All the howling at the end, 'I want you to show me!'" She kissed him back, fully, richly, with fervor. She murmured, "Sort of," and closed her eyes. Richie remembered it as if it were on the radio right now, that desperation that had gobbled up his own and screamed it back at him. Jessica said, "I can't believe how you love me. I never met anyone like you." But Richie knew that he was the lucky one.

ANDY'S FIRST URGE when her money disappeared again was to look for a set of pearls she'd mislaid months before. She had checked everywhere when she realized they were missing—under the seat of the car, under the bed, behind the couch, in the canisters in the kitchen, in all of her suitcases and handbags. The Hut was clean and neat, but she tore it apart, remembering how nice those pearls were—not terribly valuable, plain and old-fashioned, but they could be reset in a more stylish way, interspersed with something semi-precious, like tourmaline. She didn't know why she wanted them; perhaps they had simply slipped off her neck at the movies or something, and, in her inattentive way, she hadn't noticed. But she was newly certain that they had to be somewhere. It took her most of the afternoon, but she didn't find them when she was thrashing around in every box, she found them when she was picking a coat up off the floor in front of the closet by the back door—and they slipped out of the pocket and landed with a rattle on the tiles, arranged in a graceful curve, as if in a store window. She bent down, picked them up, pulled them gently through her fingers, touched them to her cheek, carried them into her bedroom, and put them in her jewelry case.

Then she went back to cleaning up. First she gathered up everything she had thrown down, rearranged everything she had dug through, set back the cushions that she had tossed on the floor, lined up the shoes she had pulled out of the closets, straightened the rugs she had looked underneath, made the beds, unloaded the dishwasher, put the books back on the bookshelves, organized her cosmetics, threw out some shirts and pairs of jeans that were out of style. Only after all of that did she let herself wonder where that money had gotten to and whether it was a bigger deal, since it was a bigger sum. In 2000, when the absconding broker transferred his clients' money to Venezuela, she had been worth ten million. Since then, she had gone up to twenty-five, but recently she had settled temporarily at seventeen, or thereabouts. She'd been tempted to buy this investment and that investment, but for two years now, it had been rather like the old days, when she'd gotten over the first flush of having money—say, when the twins were three or four. She would leave them with Nedra and go into Manhattan and wander around Bergdorf's or Bendel's. Her eye would see something, her hand reach out. She would try it on and be told by the saleswoman that it looked wonderful, and indeed it did, but as the moments passed she would find it, whatever it was, more and more awful. She could have those two thoughts at the same time—it suited her, but it was awful—and she would shake her head and walk away. Once, a saleswoman ran after her and said, "Madam! Please! I always lie, but this really was made for you, it really was. The designer ought to give it to you!" She had thanked the woman, regretfully shaken her head. She couldn't buy it.

Thinking of this, she knew she would do nothing about the money. She knew it had gone to Michael somehow, though she didn't know how. She was eighty-eight, she had no desires, she had found her pearls. Some abyss, perhaps, gaped around her, but it looked like a vista up in the Catskills, hills receding, orderly and green, into the distance. She could not make herself afraid of it.

November 10, 2008

Dear Janet, Jared, Claire, Carl, Jesse, and Jen,

I understand that it has fallen to me to write a little history of the last two months, in order to explain what has happened. I admit that all of this was as much of a shock to me as it must have been to you, and for several weeks I did not know how to address, or, perhaps, want to address it, but Riley Calhoun, Charlie's widow, my housemate, and my fellow parent (and Richard's former aide), has impressed upon me the need for clarity. Whether we will be able to put any of this behind us, I sometimes wonder, but history says that we will.

Riley has assembled a timeline that I am using to relate all of this. She is a very dedicated and organized young woman. At any rate, let me get started.

It now appears certain, that on or about September 15, Michael did forge papers that transferred his mother's trading account to his own firm. For most of the end of September, no one understood this. When Andy's broker asked her if she had authorized the transfer, she said that she had, but the broker was, let's say, both suspicious and disappointed, and he called a friend of his in the Manhattan DA's office and asked him as a favor to look at the papers. It turned out that there were a few errors in the wording of the transfer, and that, when they had a forensic handwriting expert examine the signatures, there was reasonable uncertainty about Andy's signature. She continued to resist pressure to admit that she had not signed the papers, but in the end, they noticed, she could not say that she HAD signed the papers. I guess she kept saying, "The signature is fine. It looks fine."

When the realization hit that Michael's company had gone bust right at the end of September, the coincidence was just too great, and so the DA's office began investigating Michael. There was that picture in the *Post,* you will remember, of Michael in handcuffs, with the caption, "Is this the only financier who will pay the piper?" Of course, Michael only spent one night in jail, and maybe, if the picture had been in the *Times* rather than a more populist paper, it wouldn't have had such an impact. He was very well dressed in that picture, which I think turned out to be a disadvantage. I believe the immediate motive for the forgery was that Michael was, as they say, "short" on some investments, and that he was trying to maintain payments on them, so that if they crashed he would benefit and repay his mother's account. However, this did not work out. I do not know when his trial date is, and I don't think he does, either.

At any rate, the newspapers were now on to him in a way that they were not on to other traders that perhaps behaved even worse, and of course Michael always has a certain facial expression we are all familiar with, which I suppose is best described as "haughty," and it does no good to explain to the average person that he has always had that expression, Wall Street or not.

All of this was happening around the same time as the bailout, so there was a lot of chaos. Riley informs me that she did not allow Richard to vote for the bailout, either for the first bill or the second bill, but, as you know, neither his remarks concerning the unpopularity of the bailout (I guess Riley read that government purchase of toxic assets always has a deleterious effect on recovery, and stood next to him during both the votes) nor his vote had any effect (but see below).

You may have read the article in the *Times* about Richard. If not, I enclose a copy. I believe that this was a hit job, unwarranted by the true circumstances, but Riley says to me that, as soon as they saw it, Richard and the office staff started packing up to leave Washington. No one in Congress would sit with him at lunch, or even talk to him. The writing, as they say, was on the wall, written there by *The New York Times*. I have only spoken to Richard once since the election. He and Jessica are still in Washington, of course, because it takes a while to undo sixteen years of your career. Their condo is on the market. The housing market is pretty bad, but it may be that, once the new administration is inaugurated, the market will pick up.

There are many ironies here, but I will refrain from pointing them out, as even I understand that pedantry is sometimes out of place.

I look forward to seeing you all.

With love from Alexis, and your uncle
Henry

From *The New York Times,* Oct. 12, 2008,
New York and Region:

CONGRESSMAN HITS A ROUGH PATCH

Voters in Brooklyn may be forgiven if they find themselves confused by recent events involving their representative of the last sixteen years, Richard Langdon. His constituents are beginning to wonder if Congressman Langdon has been unduly influenced by his twin brother, Michael Langdon, a bond trader and manager of Chemosh Securities, a subsidiary of Wells Fargo Bank. Michael Langdon was recently arrested for forging papers that transferred his mother's funds into his business's account without her knowledge. Chemosh was shut down, and Wells Fargo has issued a statement saying that they are looking into "the last eleven years of investments managed by Michael Langdon for further irregularities." How close have the Langdon twins been? And what influence has Michael Langdon exerted in Washington? When asked, Speaker of the House Nancy Pelosi was willing to say only that "A look at the Congressman's record shows that he has voted for Wall Street more often than he has voted against them." She is right—even apart from the most recent financial bailouts, such as TARP, Congressman Langdon's voting record is more closely aligned with that of the Republicans than with his next door neighbor in Congress, Jerry Nadler.

The word on the street (the street being Flatbush Avenue) is not so much outraged as perplexed. "Yes, I have always voted for him," says Bernice Stein, a lifelong Brooklyn resident and Democrat. "But what's the alternative? It seems like the Republicans just throw their silliest candidates up against him. It's become sort of a race to the bottom."

Congressman Langdon has presented himself for years as aggressively fighting for alternative energy solutions, but evidently to no effect. Vito Lopez, chairman of the Brooklyn Democratic Party, says, "Look, Richard is a decent person and his heart, well, at least he has one, you know? But he hasn't filled Scheuer's shoes, and that's been a concern for all of us for years now. We have to eventually ask, what are we getting from this guy? His challenger looks pretty good this time around, though I bite my tongue before saying so."

Richard Langdon is a twin, younger by four minutes than his brother Michael. Their father was a well-respected defense contractor and World War II veteran. When Mr. Langdon was first elected, in 1992, the outgoing representative, who was a much-decorated veteran and a real power in the House, said that he had

2009

~

J ARED WAS FIDDLING with the espresso maker, his third cup. He lost his temper and smacked the machine (new, De'Longhi) to the floor. He did not bend down to clean up the mess. Instead, he confessed that his company was bust, his employees were let go (had been for two weeks), and the reason was that he had borrowed money against the company to invest with Michael. That was the Friday before Thanksgiving. Janet's first response had been to find herself an AA meeting. She closed the refrigerator door, picked up her car keys from the kitchen counter, and walked out. It was 9:00 a.m. (Thank heavens, Jonah was at school.) She drove around Palo Alto, detesting the eucalyptus trees and their breezy shade as she always did in a crisis, until she finally saw the sign outside of a church. She went in, sat down, waited for the meeting to commence, stayed quiet the whole time, returned home in a daze. Jared was lying on their bed. She said nothing about the fact that he could have at least done the breakfast dishes. She lay down beside him on top of the covers. They were both fully dressed, right down to shoes and socks. Jared had never failed before. He was the reliable one, the sane one, the one who got impatient with her irritability and grudge holding. How he had come to invest with Michael, Janet could not imagine, but she knew she would hear the story, though she didn't want to hear it at that moment.

She had taken his hand, she had come up with the response she wanted to come up with—sympathy, solidarity. Remember when their monthly income was something like a thousand bucks before taxes, when they lived a block from the railroad crossing, when they didn't have a car? Remember, said Jared, when we tried to make our own mozzarella that time the milk went sour and we were afraid to throw it out? They laughed. Now, two months later, that was a poignant memory.

More had to come out, and it did: There was a lien on the house. It was not a second mortgage; the mortgage had first priority, and the mortgage was small, only eighty thousand dollars—he had kept up with those payments.

A day went by. Janet understood that each item of the confession was like a circle on the floor that seemed secure, but could, or would, turn instantly into a hole, dropping her to a deeper, darker level. On Saturday, she asked who had made the loan.

Washington Mutual.

Why hadn't she been told? Why hadn't she had to sign any papers? Her name was on the deed to the house, on the mortgage.

It was a business loan. The loan officer was friendly. He overlooked some of the paperwork. He wanted to make the loan.

Janet said, "Washington Mutual went bust. They were sold to Chase."

"They own the loan now. Or don't. No one is quite sure. I've been talking to them, but everything is so chaotic."

Bad luck—Janet and Jared agreed, he wasn't to blame, just a piece of bad luck.

On Monday, after an amicable two days, Janet broached the topic of Michael. She hadn't known that Jared had talked to Michael, had seen Michael. How in the world could he imagine that—

Then it came out: Michael had set him up. Jared realized that now, but had not realized it in August, when it happened. Did Janet remember when they went for a few days to the Ventana Inn with the Trycks, and Janet had decided not to go with them to the Post Ranch for lunch because the weather was so gloomy?

Janet did remember this—she had opted for a facial.

Michael and some client of his had been there, finishing breakfast in the Sierra Mar. They said they were on their way to Santa Barbara, taking the long route. Jared had been in a bad mood, complaining about business, wishing he could expand. He thought nothing more of it until a few days later, when Michael called him on his cell and told him that, if he wanted to expand, Michael had the investment for him. He was sure to hit it big before the end of the year. If he put in $750,000, he could get several million out, easy as falling off a log, no downside. The client he'd been with (driving a Bentley) was already in—why not Jared? Jared was driving their Toyota Highlander Hybrid, two years old, a car to be proud of, except at the Post Ranch Inn.

Janet swallowed when he said the amount—$750,000. Their house could have eaten that up without gagging in '06, but maybe not anymore. Hard to say. They dropped the subject. Janet had not even said the obvious, "How could you trust Michael for half a second, how could you?" She continued to opt for solidarity, support, getting poor Jared through this, being thankful that they had paid Jonah's school tuition, thankful that Jonah was a senior, thankful that he had not, could not, would never apply to Harvard, Princeton, Yale, thankful that Jonah drove the old Prius and that at his school this was not an embarrassment. Thankful that Emily was enjoying her job at the same Pasadena art gallery where Tina had put up her show five years before, thankful she spent weekends helping Fiona teach the littlest kids, content to ride once in a while, not to aspire to equestrian glory, to talk about someday having a handicapped riding facility, as if this were the form that her rebellion against everything her parents represented would finally take. Janet was in the habit of supporting this aspiration by remarking from time to time that she could never make a living at *that*.

Thanksgiving had been modest, enjoyable. The kids followed Janet's lead in being especially affectionate toward their father and deploring both Richie and Michael—Emily said that a single continent between herself and her uncles was hardly enough. Janet had continued going to AA meetings, listening, remaining silent, cultivating a larger view. Jared's birthday, his sixtieth, had been December 10. Janet made dinner for him, his favorite dishes. He didn't show up that evening, that night, the next morning. The very moment when she was about to pick up the phone to call the cops, it rang, and it was Jared. He was in Minnesota, at his mom's house. He wasn't coming back. He had decided to return to Minnesota as an alternative to killing himself.

If Janet were to look in the drawer on his side of the bed, she would see the loaded gun there. He asked her to dispose of it, very carefully. He did not think it would go off—the lock was on—but you could never be too cautious. He was not coming back to California, to their marriage, to anything. He could not bear it. He hung up. When she called back, no one answered, either then or in the subsequent three days, during which she tried the number seventeen times, and then gave up. It took her several hours to open the drawer. The gun was underneath some folded-up pages from the *Financial Times*. She picked it up the way they did in movies, between thumb and forefinger, and carried it down to the cellar (holding the railing with her other hand every step of the way), and put it into an unused little safe they had bought years before. She locked the door, and in the morning she went out into the backyard and buried the key.

She was surprised at which specifics enraged her, and also at the order in which they arose. First, of course, was that he would have a loaded gun in the house, in the bedroom, and not a shotgun, but a handgun, and many bullets. What if, what if, what if, became a series of steady pops in her brain, day and night, the image of herself and Jonah naïve and stupid, walking around a house inhabited by a loaded gun, making one wrong move and having an accident. That sort of thing happened all the time—some high-school kids in Santa Clara had found a pistol and started playing with it, and one of them ended up shot in the throat. After that, the first notice of late payment, addressed to Jared and to her, arrived. She opened it in a rage and then quailed: no payments had been made on the loan since October, they (she) owed almost twenty thousand dollars, including fees. Twenty thousand that they (she) didn't have. She stopped what-iffing and simply froze—only following her first instinct, which was to go to Safeway and buy lots of beans and cans of stewed tomatoes. In the middle of the night, she prioritized her spending: Bluebird's board and vet bills would come before any of this debt, because a sixteen-year-old former event horse with soundness issues had no hope in the now collapsed equestrian market. But when she went to the barn, she was too edgy to ride; she took Birdie for walks and gave her cookies, and she avoided everyone human.

None of her friends knew that Jared had left. She accepted no invitations of any kind. She told Jonah the barest bones of the story—his dad's company had failed, his dad had gone back to Rochester to get himself together and help his mom move out of her house to an old folks' home (totally made up), everything would be all right. Jonah gave her one of his looks, the one that always said to Janet, "I knew something like this was coming." She told Emily a little more—that maybe she would have to sell the house, that sometimes a marriage was just a marriage, not a love match, and marriages could hit the wall. At least there wasn't another woman, some thirty-five-year-old. Emily said, "Dad doesn't have enough money for one of those"; clearly, Emily was in communication with Jared.

And with Far Hills. When her mother called, she knew all about it, which relieved Janet from having to tell her. Andy hemmed and hawed until it was clear that Janet wasn't ready to confide, then went on to other events—Ray Perroni had died, and Gail Perroni was sure it was because the housing development Michael had funded on the southeast corner of the ranch was such an empty eyesore, rows of prefabs, two stories of rattling plywood bleaching in the sun, weeds everywhere, streets but no sewage lines or electricity. A hundred acres of quite good pasture wrecked. It wasn't much in comparison with the rest of the ranch, but Ray Perroni couldn't stay away from it, couldn't get over it. He keeled over in his truck, heart attack, Gail found him dead and cold, eyes open, hours later. Loretta was not invited to the funeral. She had moved to the house in Savannah—did Janet know they had a house there? Binky was with her. Michael was still in New York, trying to sell the place on the Upper East Side.

Andy's tone was normal for her, the recitation of facts and events, something like a steady hum, nothing like the ups and downs of gossip, absent both Schadenfreude and fear, expressing nothing more than curiosity. All of her money was lost, too, but when Janet said, "Mom, what about you," daring to delve no deeper, Andy only said, "Oh, I have plenty of books I've bought over the years and never read. Chance has simply disappeared."

"What does that mean?" said Janet.

"He might have gotten a job on a cattle ranch in Colorado. Emily heard that through several intermediaries. He doesn't want anything to do with Michael. Terribly shamed."

"I wouldn't have given him that much credit."

"Then you underestimated him, I guess."

Finally, Janet said, "What about Richie?"

"Free at last," said Andy.

And Janet knew this was true.

"And he has a pension."

"How much?" said Janet.

"Oh, goodness, I'm not quite sure," said Andy, "but maybe seventy-five or eighty thousand a year."

After they hung up, this was the thing that enraged Janet for the next four days.

JESSE WAS SURPRISED at how well informed everyone at the Denby Café was—even Julianna, about nineteen, who carried the coffee around and ran the cash register now, had read about Michael Langdon, not quite a local boy but close enough, in the *Chicago Tribune*. He and Jen didn't say much, beyond recalling various incidents they had heard about that served as predictors for some sort of bad behavior. Felicity followed the story in her online subscription to *The New York Times*—she occasionally sent Jesse links and disapproving e-mails, especially when it came out that Michael's fund had been "worth" almost a billion dollars. She had looked for Chance online, but he had closed his MySpace account (who hadn't?), and never responded to e-mails. And his cell-phone number did not work. Every time she tried and failed to contact him, she e-mailed Jesse—"Are you worried?"—and Jesse e-mailed back, "No." He wanted to e-mail back, "Not about him," but then, he knew, she would fire back, "WHO ARE YOU WORRIED ABOUT?"

He didn't dare answer.

The fact was, Guthrie was in the neighborhood: he was spending time, and maybe living, with two friends from high school, Melinda Grand and Barry Heim. Melinda was a nurse's aide at Usherton Hospital, and Barry was a long-haul trucker for the pork-confinement operation that Jesse's father had hated so much. What did Guthrie do? Well, that was a good question. He told Jen that he was taking classes at Usherton Community College, in hotel management, and living on "savings." The house that Melinda and Barry lived in was an old farmhouse north of town, overlooking the river, never good farm country, good for hiding something. Guthrie did not think he would be deployed again; he was glad to be home; he was twenty-five and looked fifty.

Even though it was time to get going on the farm work—at least to be fixing this and that, checking the soil moisture, thinking about seed (or listening to the salesmen give him their pitches)—all Jesse really wanted to do was drive past that dump Guthrie lived in and see what was going on. Except that the dump was located on a very un-Iowa sort of road, not the usual grid, but back up a long drive littered with junk—an old truck, old engine parts, a rusted cultivator, some tires, and that was only what he could see from the road. The roof peak of the house itself thrust up above the treetops, and it looked like it had shingles on it. He knew what people all over Iowa did in those types of houses: they cooked up drugs. Jesse stared up the lane for a few minutes and then drove on to Usherton to the feed store. When he got home in the late afternoon, and Jen told him that Guthrie had called and would be there for supper, Jesse felt anxious and guilty, as if his spying might be found out.

For a week, the weather had been suspiciously mild. Jesse was sitting on the front porch in the old rocker, nursing a beer, and watching the high wisps of cloud to the south turn gold and then pink. When he saw Guthrie's car, a two-year-old Nissan, he couldn't stop himself from wondering if old wreck or newish sedan was more suspect. When Guthrie got out of the driver's side and looked in both directions before proceeding up the walk, he couldn't not wonder what Guthrie was looking at or for. When Guthrie frowned, was that a bad sign? When he then smiled, was it a self-conscious or even a guilty smile? A foot on the bottom step; he looked thin. Was he fit, or was he eaten away? Jesse said, "Hey."

Guthrie said, "Hey."

Everyone said that when a boy went away to a war he came back a man. Guthrie had gone away twice, come back twice—did that double the maturity quotient? Everyone also knew that you could never see the boy in the man: every man looked more like his father and uncles than he did like his youthful self. Guthrie looked like a combination of Jesse's dad and Jen's brother David—which side did the premature worry lines come from? Jesse often missed Minnie, who would tell him. She had moved to the old folks' home, and they hardly ever heard from her. He finished his beer and stood up, but he didn't hug his son. Hadn't seen him in two months, but to hug him could imply something that might offend.

They went in the house.

Jen might also worry about Guthrie, but, as an optimistic, active, fit, and healthy sort, she would almost certainly not have thought of methamphetamine, would only remember the best about Melinda and Barry—how cute they were in fourth grade or whenever—and so Jesse had said nothing to her concerning his anxiety. A scientific type of farmer, he told himself this was an experiment: If and when Jen expressed concern, then his own concerns would be justified, and they could, might, do something. What that would be, no one on the Internet agreed. Guthrie kissed his mom, went to the refrigerator, offered Jesse another beer, took one for himself. Jesse popped the cap. Guthrie said, "Corona? You guys are getting very snooty."

Jesse said, "They just appeared one day."

Jen said, "If you want to know the truth, Felicity left them the last time she was here."

Guthrie said, "I have a hard time imagining Felicity tossing one back."

Jen said, "She sips and savors, as if it were a nice Chardonnay."

Guthrie said, "I believe that." Then, "Listen to this. Grandma called me. She wants me to go with her to the Isle of Skye this summer."

Jen said, "Near Scotland?"

"I guess. She is going for the salmon and the venison."

Jen laughed. "Only Lois."

Jesse said, "Are you going?"

"It is like forty degrees there."

"Nice of her to ask, though."

Guthrie's cheekbones were a little sharp, his eyes a little wide. But he did not fidget. When they sat down at the table, Jesse thought, Please, don't let me count his helpings. But he did—two of the mashed potatoes, one of the meatloaf, one of the green beans, one of the brand-new, spanking-fresh baby spinach from the garden. No dessert. Jen didn't make cakes or pies. Jesse thought that his mom would be sad to know that she had had no lasting effect on their entremets and gâteau consumption; Jen had never opened the Julia Child cookbook his mom had left behind. She was coming here in a week for Easter—there could be leftover crème brûlée and they could maybe persuade Guthrie to get out of town. He leaned back, stretched, and groaned a little, in the great tradition of an aging, slightly overweight farmer, and said, "Anyway, how's it going?"

"I got a job."

"Oh, lovely," said Jen.

"Maybe," said Guthrie. "It's part-time—manning the front desk at the Motel 6 on 330."

"Are you in charge of bedbug patrol?" said Jen, good-naturedly.

"Bedbugs come after exposed wires and clogged drains. I guess new management has a plan, and part of the plan is easing out the eighty-year-old who's checking people in now."

Jesse said, "Then they'll hire themselves some guests."

"It could work," said Guthrie. "At least it's a start."

"A start is always good," said Jen.

Jesse said, "I could use some help in May," but Guthrie didn't appear to have heard him. His absolute resistance to farming remained in place.

Jen began clearing the table. They talked a bit about Felicity, but not about Perky. Jen cast no speculative glances toward Guthrie, made no observations about what he had and hadn't eaten, seemed not to notice his foot tapping the floor. After supper, they watched an episode of something or other in the living room—Jesse felt his distraction and concern beginning to overwhelm him. Guthrie got up to leave; Jen went with him out onto the porch. They talked for a while, and though Jesse did attempt to enlarge his ears in order to hear them, he didn't move from his spot on the sofa. He heard Guthrie's steps, a moment later heard the car turn on and depart, looked at Jen when she came in. She looked back at him. She said, "It's okay if his reintegration is slow. Slow is steady. Slow is stable. He's had a few dates with a girl from the college. She wants to be a chef." Jesse wished he could see Guthrie as Jen did, a system basically sound and stable, just needing a few repairs. He vowed not to drive by that house, that junk, ever again.

FELICITY WAS getting fond of the horse she had to muck out for, who was quarantined at the back of the barn because he had a very contagious ailment called, of all things, "strangles." She gave him hay three times a day, changed his water, mucked his stall out twice, and did everything in a pair of overalls that she had to leave by the door, along with a hat, a hairnet, rubber boots, and a pair of gloves. As long as she was taking care of this horse, she also was not to go into any other part of the equine facility. For four weeks, until the horse tested negative for strangles, that was her job, because there had been an outbreak at the vet school two years earlier, and it had been a nightmare.

The horse's name was Go For It, or Goofy. He was a bay show-jumper, nice-looking, and obviously used to lots of attention. When she came into his little barn, he whinnied to her as if he had been pining for her, and even after she threw down the hay and he started eating, he would keep his eye on her, lifting his head and whinnying if she headed for the exit. She had never thought of horses as convivial, but clearly this guy was as lonely as could be. She began giving him carrots and petting him—she bought herself a whole box of disposable latex gloves in order to pet him.

Now that she was actually at ISU, working at the vet school had succeeded in convincing Felicity that veterinary practice was not her future. When she assisted in the clinic for a semester, she found herself extremely abrupt with the owners of the patients. The turning point was when a woman and her daughter brought in a cat, not very old, with a lung infection from soil-borne bacteria. The woman asked what the vet might do, and Dr. Latham described opening the chest, laving it thoroughly, closing it up—certainly a major operation. Was the doctor sure that would cure the infection? No, could not be sure. Might have to do it more than once. Even looking at the limp, weak black cat and thinking about it made the woman and the little girl burst into tears. They couldn't imagine putting the cat through that. Dr. Latham nodded in sympathy. They decided to put the cat down. Felicity was disappointed, because she didn't much care about the cat, but she was thrilled by the idea of seeing what might happen. She must have harrumphed or something, because, after the woman and her daughter left, her supervisor took her aside and said that she needed to be "more empathetic" if she expected to have a clientele.

It was hard for Felicity to believe that she would turn twenty-one in the fall. By rights, she should be turning twenty-five, or thirty, if only so that people other than her parents would take her seriously. Her parents took her very seriously; she had trained them, with a combination of treats and punishments, to allow her to do as she pleased and express herself, and to pay attention to her opinions. Thanks to Aunt Minnie, she was a researcher first and foremost, exhaustive, organized, and curious. She owed a lot to Aunt Minnie, who had died lying in her bed at the old folks' home, all her possessions boxed and labeled, the day before her ninetieth birthday. Felicity never forgot to leave some locally sourced flowers and herbs on her grave, which was right beside Uncle Frank's. No one had planned it that way—that was where the space was. Aunt Minnie had once told Felicity (after being probed) that, yes, she had loved Uncle Frank, but then he had gone off. Aunt Minnie made sure Felicity understood that Uncle Frank had never loved her back, and Felicity did understand that, so when she laid the flowers on Aunt Minnie's grave, she left nothing on Uncle Frank's grave.

Felicity had four girlfriends, five colleagues/friends who were guys, and a semi-boyfriend, Max, whom she slept with enough so that they were satisfied and not distracted by sexual yearnings. Max was in the math department, and he was not unlike Canute in personality type—INTJ (Felicity herself was ESTJ). She liked to be in charge, and Max liked someone to be in charge of him. She fit beautifully into the world of Iowa State. She liked her job, she thought the campus was exceptionally well organized, and she enjoyed being surrounded by engineers. Her father had taken her once to the spot where Uncle Frank was struck by lightning, and then they looked for the spot where he was said to have lived in a tent by the river for a month, a year, the whole time (Felicity was inclined to think this was family folklore). He had put himself through school with rabbit skins? They had tried to make gunpowder out of cornstalks? And also there was nuclear waste out past the university graveyard? Yes, but. Felicity was not saying that she did not believe these stories, only that she had not researched them, and so could not verify them to her own satisfaction.

What Felicity thought about her family's worries and upsets, she kept to herself. What she felt about them, she also kept to herself.

Her feelings did not seem to be as strong as everyone else's, and the conclusion she drew from this was that her attachment to her family, though sufficient, was not in the upper percentiles. Perhaps, someday, she would regret this, but perhaps, someday, she would not. Her coolness had benefits: Her girlfriends complained more or less incessantly about their parents and their brothers and sisters. Everything any sibling or parent did caused a crisis full of discussions and tears. Max was not like this—he confessed that he often forgot about his parents entirely, and had gotten to be sixteen without ever learning his paternal grandmother's maiden name (he could barely remember her first name). Felicity gave good advice, but she viewed all these upsets as through a window—slightly muffled. Spending so much time tending Goofy had caused her to think; she didn't want to be like Goofy, and she didn't mind hours in the isolation wing at all. If there had been a use for it, she would have listed and analyzed Goofy's idiosyncratic behaviors to pass the time. Instead, she organized her future and reconfirmed her freedom.

IN AUGUST, and not in the Hamptons or Savannah or Nice or Bora-Bora, but lolling on the deck at his and Jessica's condo in D.C., Richie told Michael that he had never been this happy in all his life, and Michael looked right at him, nodded, and said, "Me, too." It was as hot as could be, but apparently only here—Richie was glad not to have to argue with Riley about weather predictions versus climate change and extrapolating from the daily forecast to civilization collapse. Riley had sashayed quite easily from congressional aide ("aide deluxe," as she called herself) into a very well-paid and visible job at a prestigious think tank, and Richie now saw her on television more often than in person. Richie had not sashayed anywhere. He was still too disgraced to enter the private sector visibly. He didn't mind, he didn't worry, he covered the condo payment and let Jessica cover the food and the gym membership.

Jessica let Michael be underfoot; made him do the dishes, did not ask about the state of his marriage, and told Richie not to ask, either. In the meantime, Richie found it irresistible to compare their progress through the aging process. On this very day, they happened to be fifty-six and a half years old, though Richie hadn't mentioned this.

Michael still had the scar on his knee from the accident with that girl before Loretta, where the car key had gone into the flesh, and, Richie thought, he also still had a faint red line in his biceps from Alicia's scissors. What had they been, twenty, when that happened? His chest hair was thick, a little gray in the upper area, not unlike Richie's own chest hair. They were old. He had felt so young for so long that this rather surprised him. Even Leo now seemed older to Richie than he himself was, and Ivy, who took pity on him from time to time and called him, seemed to have outpaced him by a generation. Perhaps this was a side effect of the congressional lifestyle—not perennial youth, but perennial immaturity. However, in accordance with Jessica's advice, once he thought about the House, he redirected his attention—to bellies. His was moderately large, but, he guessed, Michael's was 10 percent larger. They didn't look quite as sleekly predatory as his father had looked at the same age.

Michael said, "Sold the place."

Richie said, "How much?"

"Five."

"What do you think about that?"

"Good riddance." Possibly, Richie thought, including the money, which would have to go to some litigation-settlement account.

"What about all the stuff?"

"The art is being evaluated." In his last four visits, Michael had avoided any mention of Loretta's name, but sometimes Loretta called Jessica, not to complain, or even to confide, Richie thought, but to ask advice about exercise regimens, cleanses, muscle strains, over-the-counter pain medications.

Michael yawned. "If I can ever afford to buy furniture again, it will be IKEA. Jessica can put it together."

"Where are you going to live?"

"I guess we'll find out."

Richie hadn't heard of any financier going to prison, but he hadn't been paying attention, either. He said, "I mean, for now."

"With you."

Richie laughed. Michael's delivery was good—thoughtful, regretful, honest—but there was no comparing notes on this: Michael confided only in him. All of his other relationships that Richie was witness to were polite and superficial. Really, Richie thought, it was like living for years with a huge, aggressive German shepherd, and then having the dog come into your bedroom one night, climb onto the bed, and open up in perfectly good English about his long life of pain and sorrow. The dog still growled at the UPS guy, and no one else in the world knew he could talk.

When he told his mother that Michael had changed, that he was more easygoing, Andy had said, "Your father became very loving in his last few years."

Richie had nearly fallen to the floor.

She went on: "It was like his manner was a shell that was going to be the last thing to change, but inside he was softening. Had softened. We were close. I don't know. There was something about your father. It was as if he had been born old and hard and his task was to regress to vulnerability. I don't know why that was. His parents were like everyone's parents. I was fond of them. You couldn't really know your father and his parents and continue to believe in Freud." Nor did his mother seem to hold her current straitened circumstances against Michael. The two times Richie had broached the subject, she had acted as if she didn't have any idea what money was. Richie wondered if she had ounces of gold stashed somewhere.

Jessica was the boss, or, rather, she did what she wanted, as always, and they went along with it. Sometimes she would need to go to the Smithsonian for a look around, sometimes she would need to go to the 5th Street Market and buy kale, sometimes she would need to hike five miles in Virginia somewhere or take in a movie. But it wasn't like it had been with Alicia—there was no rivalry. Richie and Jessica walked along, holding hands, and Michael ranged here and there around them. When they went to bed, he stayed up watching a movie or reading a book (right now, *Bleak House*). They made love and noise, but he seemed not to notice, except to say, "Glad that part is over for me."

Did he feel regret or shame? Richie had no idea. He himself alternated, understanding that regret was a desire to have lived your life differently, whereas shame was a much more basic, and honorable, emotion. In order of importance, he had five shames: supporting the Iraq Resolution, voting for repeal of the Glass-Steagall Act, not blocking Halliburton in some way, letting the anti–climate-change

forces of big oil roll over him, and not sticking his foot out and trip-
ping Dick Cheney when he had the chance.

He said, "Jessica wants to move to the Catskills and build a hay-
bale house."

"I visited a cob house in California once."

"Built with corncobs?"

"No, it's a kind of mud, including sand and clay, and some straw.
You build it like a sandcastle. It was eerie."

When she found out that Richie was not only still speaking to
Michael, but also had taken him in, Janet had stopped speaking to
him, and, yes, according to his mother, Janet was about done for.
She had gotten enough out of her house to send Jonah down to Santa
Barbara, to the community college, then moved herself and the horse
to Half Moon Bay. No one was invited to visit. She had asked Andy
three times if she remembered that time in Paris, when their father
had called Janet a royal bitch in the middle of the night in the hotel
room. Andy did not remember that incident—she had enjoyed the
trip.

Nor did she know, Richie thought, about the prostitute Michael
had paid to give him a blow job, in a little alcove around the corner
from the hotel, at about two in the morning. First they had dared each
other to escape the suite and hotel, then they had wandered around
until they spotted her, high heels and some kind of fur coat with very
little underneath. Messy hair, druggy look. She knelt down on the
icy pavement while Michael leaned back against the wall. It took
about two minutes and cost a hundred francs. Richie watched the
whole thing.

Richie said, "Riley always said you could grow your own hemp
house in a single season."

"I've read about that. I would do that," said Michael, proving to
Richie that a lifetime together was nevertheless full of surprises.

2010

H ENRY HAD TRIED to avoid but in the end had not been able to resist interpreting the crisis in literary terms. Right when it all came out, he had been reading about the hoard of Anglo-Saxon gold that some average Joe had unearthed in Mercia (well, Stafford-shire), bigger than Sutton Hoo, and that had shaped his response. For Riley and Alexis, it was the long-awaited comic plot-twist: the faith-ful lieutenant promoted to colonel, given charge of her own little regiment of climate-change soldiers, consorting with Bill McKib-ben on a friendly basis, frequently quoted in *The New York Times,* an occasional column in *The Guardian,* and periodically vilified on Fox News, where, when she appeared, she did not allow herself to be interrupted even once. They had not moved out of his house—Riley said that if Henry constituted the sole member of Alexis's village, then that was fine. So Henry spent a lot of time with Alexis, who was almost eight, went to the local public school, but was enrolled in piano lessons and an after-school Spanish class. Henry sometimes read aloud to her (right now, *Black Beauty*), and she sometimes read aloud to him (right now, *Como nasceram as estrelas*) and liked to go on Saturdays to a climbing gym and shimmy her way up rock walls (but she was not yet Charlie: she always scuttled downward when she got about twelve feet off the ground).

Richie was Sisyphus released from his endless task of pushing that stone up the mountain, and every time Henry saw Richie, he saw the relief—no more fund-raisers, no more fake smiles, no more pretending to know what he didn't know, no more listening to the cacophonous demands roaring around him. But Sisyphus had rolled that stone up that mountain for such a long time that he was conditioned to do nothing else. Month by month, Henry had seen Richie slip into pure idleness—go to the gym (well, that tapered off), read a book (never had before), learn to cook (cut himself chopping vegetables, burned himself braising a pot roast), do housework (disorder was not visible to him). Richie's skills were social ones: he was articulate, charming, graceful, witty, self-effacing. He had actually done something for the Congress while he was there in not being obstinate, loud, and ugly, in appearing to be the last remaining representative willing to listen. Sisyphus was going to have to reassemble himself, take on another thankless task, but he didn't know how.

Henry knew that everyone in the family was inclined to see Loretta as the evil queen, staring into the mirror and reciting incantations against her enemies, exercising and expanding her powers so relentlessly that her very own son had to disappear in order to escape the curse, not of being her enemy, but of being her friend. Claire maintained that, though Michael had always been difficult, his problem was impetuosity more than anything else—"Frank without brakes." Whatever intelligence Michael had was a sort of cunning— not introspective, but calculating. Loretta had put his energy, looks, and impetuosity to work for her own purposes. There had been so many girls; why had he picked her? Well, she had picked him—that much was obvious—and then enlisted that priest, what was his name, to keep Michael in line. That was the Catholic way of doing things; Catholicism was about power; there were scandals going back to the beginning of the Church. Claire clucked and clucked. In Chicago, it was all coming out—that choirmaster stabbed in the eighties, the arson at the All Saints church. Andy was not quite so ready to put all of the blame on Loretta. She said, "If she was a witch, then she never cast a spell that worked, did she? No, I haven't talked to her, but how much advice did she ask from me over the years, how to win him, how to persuade him, how to rein him in, how to get his attention? She was always arranging her weapons, making her preparations. I think she was glad he didn't kill and eat the children." Ah, thought

Henry, Saturn. Or, if you preferred the Greek version, Kronos, the most interesting of the gods, who hadn't required that his sons be sacrificed by humans, but simply ate them himself.

His own views were not so mythological, though. In fact, Michael was the one he almost never thought about. He was the accident of nature or the irresistible force that simply had to be endured or avoided. Sometimes, watching Alexis choose a pair of socks or stand on a chair beside the stove making popcorn the old way (she was also allowed to scramble eggs and knead bread), he marveled at how like herself she remained every minute of the day, remembered that his mother had always said he was born already formed and she had had nothing to do with it. So it would be with Michael, testosterone incarnate. And, yes, Henry did remember Michael playing nicely with Tia, singing a song with Chance, tickling Loretta on the top of the head and kissing her cheek, and now he was separated from those loved ones. But why was this not a tragedy, the Story of Michael? Had all of the inner life really gone to Richard, none of it to Michael? There was something about Michael that made that question not worth asking, Henry thought.

As for Janet, well, everyone thought the split was a terrible shame, but there must be some way that she had brought this upon herself. Why had Jared left her? Well, everyone knew she was difficult to live with. Why had she lost the house? She's not the only one; at least she has something to live on. Janet's troubles were an exercise in realism, belonging to her alone. Why did she always flee when something went wrong? Pride, that's what it was, always had been. Head shake, less said about that. Maybe something would turn up. Some deus ex machina, thought Henry, ironically. He did try to call Janet every few weeks. She said that she was fine.

AND MAYBE JANET was fine, since she and Birdie and her new puppy, Antaeus (Jack Russell–poodle mix) were as far west as they could go without falling off the edge of the continent. Thanks to a discussion she had while getting her hair cut the day after the Haitian earthquake, she knew that the chances of the San Gregorio Fault's producing a 6.7 or greater earthquake were considerably less than for the San Andreas. Birdie was living on pasture (and it was pretty green, not like anything Janet had seen in Silicon Valley); Janet was paying the ranch $350 a month and supplying some extra feed. Janet herself was living in a one-bedroom condo in a complex that would probably go into foreclosure, but the laws were so complex that she gave herself six months' breathing room, and at her age, that was enough. The nicest person in her life was Emily. It was Emily who had given her Antaeus, who had taken over supervising Jonah and was doing a pretty good job of it; she drove up to see him in Santa Barbara every month or so, anyway. She had met the roommate, walked around the campus, made sure he changed the oil in the old Prius, and bought him a membership to Costco. She hosted him for a weekend in L.A., where he went to a Lakers game and a show by a band called Steel Panther. He asked after Janet, Emily said.

"What did you tell him?"

"I said you were fine, lying low, he can call you anytime."

He asked after Jared.

"What did you tell him?"

"You don't want to know, Ma."

No, she didn't. It was easier to imagine that Jared was the mess, the one to be pitied, the one who had lost everything, the one who was stuck in Minnesota, where the snowpack was heading for a record. She knew from two letters she'd gotten from him that their marriage had done that thing she had seen with her friends' marriages over the years—flipped from white to black in a heartbeat. As soon as one spouse was ready to get out, then there had never been anything right about it, he had never seen anything in her, she had gotten pregnant and suckered him. This breakup had been coming for a long time. Her flaws turned into impossibilities. Remember the Josephs? Same thing happened, but neither would move out of the house; every day for Laurie Joseph was a lacerating catalogue of not only her character flaws and failures, but her physical defects, too.

The few people she saw around Half Moon Bay and out at the ranch were much more forgiving. At the ranch, they traded funny horse stories or bits of advice. New Leaf, Orlando's, the fish market— she came in with her dollar bills and went away pleased with her sole or her basil or her can of fagiolini beans and bag of spinach. She learned to knit, and the ladies sitting around the yarn shop advised her but asked her no questions—she was becoming one of those silent types, and everyone accepted it so far. What she didn't expect was a call from Loretta. The first thing she said was "How did you get my number?"

Loretta ignored this. She said, "I need you to go to the ranch."

"No. My car is a wreck. It won't get me that far and back."

"I'll rent you a car."

"So—you still have plenty of money. Many of us don't."

"I have enough to pay you to find out whether my mother is still alive."

"You can fly there."

"If it's me that shows up and she's still alive, she will slam the door in my face."

"You deserve it. I know someone who bought one of those houses at the ranch. He made eight dollars an hour, and his wife had a cleaning service. Now they have nothing." Janet did not in fact know what had happened to Marco, but she could guess. And his house was only *near* the ranch, but what was the difference, really?

"I did not give Michael investment advice. I did not know he was shorting the market, or, rather, I did not know what shorting the market was. I did not know he was so desperate for funds. I knew about the development on the ranch, but I didn't approve of it, I thought it was too far from town, I said it was a shitty idea. But no one believed me. I need an emissary. I need someone to find the body. She really would hole up and not lift the phone if she felt ill. She's eighty. She's not like your mom, just immortal. She's got all sorts of conditions."

"No."

"I really will pay you. I know you're broke. I will pay you ten thousand dollars."

"How about seven hundred fifty thousand? Then I can get my house back."

"I can't afford that. I really can't. I mean, he ruined us, too. Don't you know that?"

"I've heard it, but I don't believe it. I'm sure you've given the money you owe me to some Super PAC dedicated to buying Congress." Janet felt herself getting a hot flash—sweat along the back of her neck, panting, waves of heat rising to the top of her head. She put her hand on her forehead.

Loretta said, "Congress isn't that expensive," then, instead of laughing, burst into tears.

Janet tried to imagine this. After Loretta's sobs had subsided a little, she said, "You send me a money order for fifteen thousand dollars, and when it is safely stashed in my bank account, I will go to the ranch. Not before. Your choice." She hung up.

The day she did go was a glorious one—the perfect day to draw her out of her new shadowy landscape and into the sun. There had been plenty of rain, so the hills rose everywhere toward the brilliant sky, wave after wave of thrilling green, as if no water shortage would ever be possible again. Across the hillsides, swaths of lupine had draped themselves, and they shivered in the very breeze that brought their fragrance through Janet's partially open window. Of the fifteen thousand, she had spent fifteen hundred on the Highlander, very practical, and a hundred on eight skeins of bamboo yarn, "Persimmon." She had sent a thousand to Jonah and a thousand to Emily.

She could have passed her old neighborhood, but she went down Route 1 and through Santa Cruz. In Gilroy, she dawdled at the outlet mall, ate a burger at In-N-Out, investigated the Le Creuset store, then made herself get in the car by reflecting that, if she *were* to find a dead body, better to find it when the sun was high in the sky. She plugged the cord of her phone into the charger, in case she had to call someone.

But the fact that Gail Perroni was not dead was the least of surprises at the ranch. The second-greatest was the way Gail threw her arms around Janet when she saw her, and hugged her with considerable strength, and the greatest was Chance, just behind her as she opened the door, also smiling, picking his teeth from their lunch of tamales and spinach salad.

Janet must have looked surprised, because Gail said, "Honey, go ahead and pry."

They stepped back and welcomed her in.

What was Chance? she thought. Only twenty-nine? But years of sun had polished his skin and the angle of his chin. Maybe it had whitened his teeth, too—his teeth practically gave off light. He looked, how to think of this, at home. They led her into the back sitting room, a room she had never been in. It had a series of three French doors facing northwest over a pasture that had been left fallow. It rolled gently upward, lifting its purple wave of lupine with it.

Janet said, "The lupine are amazing this year."

Gail said, "They are amazing every year."

Chance went over and opened one set of the doors, and the fragrance billowed in.

Janet said, "What shall I pry into first?"

Gail said, "After Ray died, I asked Chance to come stay with me and run the ranch for a year while I decide what to do with it."

"Only I know this?"

"My lawyer knows it. The bank knows it. The hands know it. The cattle know it. They run for cover when they see him coming. Ask something else."

"Does Loretta know it?"

"Not so far."

"What if someone were to tell her?"

"Like you?"

Janet nodded.

Chance said, "Please don't, Aunt Janet."

There was a long pause, and finally Janet said, "She paid me to come and find out whether you were still alive, Gail."

Gail said, "No, she can't have the ranch. Not now, not ever."

Janet crossed her legs and looked out the French doors. Finally, she said, "She told me that she was against the development."

"She may have been, but I suspect that she did know that when the fellow paid us for the land we got five hundred thousand, and, we later found out, your brother got a million and a half. That little fact went undisclosed, although Loretta's signature was on the papers."

"I have never understood my brother," said Janet.

"What's to understand?" said Gail. "He is a psychopath."

Janet glanced at Chance, who looked interested but unmoved by this assertion. Clearly, it had been asserted before. Janet said, "Look, Gail. She wasn't putting me on. She sounded worried."

Gail bumped around on her end of the couch for a moment, then said, "I never liked Frank Langdon. The first time, in that restaurant, I said to Ray that he was the coldest man I had ever met in my life. I told Loretta she was making a mistake marrying the son of such a cold man, because someone like that would have no idea, not only how to love someone, but that love exists in this world. Your mother was strange, too. I liked her, actually, but she was more like a plant than a person."

Janet opened her mouth, but she was not the one to defend her father, was she?

Gail went on, "And I for one don't care that your mother has got it together now, and everyone loves her. At the very time when she should have done her job, when those twins were babies, she was missing in action." Then she said, "But weren't we all. However, here we have Chance, and for me, that's the reward." She reached over and pressed her hand into Chance's. He gave it a small squeeze. Where was the wife? Janet thought. Where was the baby? She was uncomfortable enough to sit quietly for a moment or two, then lean forward, saying, "I guess my mission is accomplished, then. I won't say anything, just that you're fine, and not to worry."

Gail said, "I trust you." She held out her hand, and Janet shook it. Chance followed her to, and then out, the door. There was more to say, but she sensed him pulling away, as if fine threads were stretching between them. At the last moment, as he was opening his mouth to wish her goodbye, she said, "Got any new horses to show me?"

"Well, the last horse Grandpa Ray bought was an Appaloosa yearling. Two-year-old now. I've been working with her. Haven't mounted her at all, but she's pretty sturdy. I guess I'll be on her by summer." He headed toward the barn, and Janet followed him.

The filly was in with two other horses, a bay and a gray. They were standing in the far corner of the pen, playing with a plastic bucket. The gray would pick the bucket up and drop it; then the other two would nose it and push it over. When it fell over with a rattle, the Appy and the bay sprang into the air as if surprised, and trotted away, tails in the air. There was whinnying and snorting, and then the three youngsters returned to the bucket and started over. Chance put his fingers to his lips and whistled. All three spun around, and then trotted up. Chance palmed them each a lump of sugar.

The Appaloosa was not like any Appy Janet had seen before— rangy, with a chestnut coat that was overlaid by what looked like a blanket of snow, across the haunches, mainly, but with a splash up the neck, and then around the nostrils. She was a striking animal.

Chance said, "Last thing Grandpa Ray needed was another horse. He paid twenty-five grand for her. Grandma said she was beside herself. I guess they were barely speaking even by the time he passed away."

Janet reached out cautiously to pet the horse, but the horse was friendly. She sniffed Janet's hand and presented her forehead to be tickled. Janet said, "Chance, I don't know that your grandmother should be so, I don't know, blunt with you."

"She doesn't tell me I have to agree with her. She's willing to live with an Obama supporter."

"Oh, for God's sake!"

"You don't have to know what you think about everything in order to get the work done. That's what I think about most."

"You don't mind being stuck out here?"

"I don't mind. Given what I like to do, I'm going to be stuck out somewhere. I like here better than Montana or New Mexico."

"What do you do for fun?"

"We *have* Internet."

"I still think you're too young for this." Then she said, "What about Hanny? Was that her name? You dated her." Janet could not remember if Chance had known anything about the pregnancy or the abortion.

"She's in Phoenix. She's married. She hasn't come around since I've been back. How do you know Hanny?"

So that was the answer.

"She came to look at colleges and stayed with us."

"That was nice of you."

"I liked her."

"I liked her, too. She was a little ambitious for me at that point." He laughed, then waved off the two-year-olds, who wandered back to the bucket but seemed to find it boring. Janet watched them for a moment, then turned to Chance and grabbed his arm. She said, "Chancie, I don't have the feeling that you comprehend what is going on here, what has gone on. Your grandmother loves you, but she's also using you to get back at your mother. Your father is in deep shit. He ruined me! He ruined my life!" Even as she said this, though, she thought that she was not quite speaking the truth—in spite of constant ripples of worry, she didn't mind scraping an existence together in Half Moon Bay. The truth was too complex to speak, which was probably why she didn't talk much anymore. She said, "Anyway, what he did isn't about me. It's about something bigger. . . . Oh, I don't know. Are you still married?"

"Sort of."

That was all he said. In the end, Janet could only shake her head. As she drove home, she thought, a year and a half, and we're all still dazed. We can make the first connection, but not the second one—take the first step, but go no further. And despite all her deep and ancient resentments, she would have defended her own father. Her muscles had twitched when Gail attacked him, even though Gail's observation was right on. "Cold" was the perfect word for him. Here he was, dead for fifteen years, buried, his assets dissipated, his "work," whatever that had been, finished, forgotten. There was a way he'd had of walking through a room . . . and then a scene flashed into her mind, long forgotten and now utterly present: Some summer house somewhere, a little ramshackle, she and her mom coming in the door from shopping, exhilarated by the damp weather and happy with something they'd bought. The twins were sitting apart, each on a sofa pillow, their hands in their laps, not looking at one another. As her mom exclaims, "Hello! We're back!" her father's beautiful head turns. He looks over his shoulder at them, and there it is, revulsion—not dislike or hatred, nothing so conscious—rather, an involuntary shudder, and Janet knows in her deepest being that they should not have come back, they should have stayed away, left for good. She also knows that her mother hasn't noticed, bustling with the packages. She sees her father's face mask over with some sort of fake normality, 1950s male patience. She goes up to him and reaches for his hand, but he avoids touching her, takes one of the boxes from her mother, and the two of them walk away into the kitchen. There is a moment of silence; then Michael reaches out and knocks Richie over. The ensuing brouhaha covers the moment, the look. The oddest thing in the picture in Janet's mind is how young her father is—almost a boy, really. If she had been the age she was now, or even his own age at the time, she would not have taken it personally.

CLAIRE HAD PUT on three parties for the Jaspers, who lived in a stony palatial house on three acres in Lake Forest, a place that would have looked and felt like a tomb if Jed and Caroline Jasper were not the ebullient, generous folks that they happened to be. There had been a fourth party, too—at New Year's—and Caroline had invited Claire and Carl as guests rather than as employees. Claire would have minded losing the business if Caroline hadn't set her up with three of her other friends, five parties there, the most recent a Labor Day bash that had cost the Mordecais forty thousand dollars (10 percent to Claire, a nice addition to the bank account).

As Carl drove up to the Jasper house, Claire looked around—left, right, behind. She did not quite recognize the property. But there was the number, and there was the south tower. Everything else was different; the front yard had become a farm. They pulled into the driveway, and Caroline emerged from behind a stand of sunflowers, be-gloved and be-Crocced, a basket in her hand. She ran over and opened Claire's door, handed her a speckled green tomato. Claire took a bite and gave the rest to Carl.

Caroline said, "Can you believe this? I have almost a bushel of sweet corn, and tomatoes coming out of my ears. I had to invite everyone I knew just to distribute the harvest."

Claire said, "I feel right at home, except that on my folks' farm the garden was out back."

"Not enough sun! My gardener was very adamant. Front yard or nowhere. She was so hypnotic that I just nodded and let her put in the beds."

Carl took another tomato out of Caroline's basket and said, "What in the world do the neighbors think?"

"They are so envious! I mean, I keep them plied with vegetables, and the two kids across the street have emerged from in front of the television to pick weeds and eat raw green beans, and almost everyone is talking about how much they hate grass now. I swear the Carnabys are going to buy goats. Or they say they are."

Claire wondered why she hadn't thought of this herself.

Caroline led them to the eggplants, and, really, Claire thought, they were the most beautiful and impressive, more self-contained and dignified than tomatoes, so densely purple and heavy. She squatted down and let one sink into her palm. Around her, the fragrance of the compost and the straw mulch blended with the damp scent of the plants.

Caroline was saying, "Jed saw one of those little posters—you know, with the phone numbers you tear off—and why he called them I can't imagine. The girl must be forty, but she looks thirty. She is so bubbly, and the boy is darling. They make me feel very old and stick-in-the-muddy." Caroline was fifty-three and looked forty. How did that make Claire feel, seventy-one now, deep into the age where everyone remarked about how well she was holding up? Caroline said, "We can die in peace. The younger generation is going to fix everything. Let's go in. Jed is making mojitos with our very own mint, and he and Carl can discuss building a still for our reserved-label rum in that derelict backyard we've been maintaining all these years."

The Jasper backyard was an acre and a half of beautiful old elms and oaks with a tennis court. Caroline said, "This is a totally locavore meal we are serving you guys, except the rum and the sugar."

And it was delicious. All the way home, Claire and Carl disagreed, in their very agreeable way, about whether a nice raised bed or two would do well in their own backyard. Claire's argument was that Carl needed something to build; he had redone the living-room moldings twice already and rewired the kitchen and put up enough shelves in the basement to last three lifetimes, especially since he was a vocal exponent of getting rid of everything. Once she had a crop, she would add that to her party offerings—seasonal, local, delicious menu—and raise her prices. Carl's argument against was all about deer and squirrels and raccoons and gophers: he had spent years getting rid of the rodents who were turning their yard into a sieve, why go back now, when the deer were finally convinced that there was nothing to be had at 1201 Pine Street? Claire knew what she had to do—order the beams, have them delivered, leave them stacked beside the garage. They would find their way into Carl's hands, and into the yard. She had gotten the name of the gardening girl. She would invite her for breakfast. Angie, too. Angie was working on the South Side, at a youth center. Claire remembered that Angie had even said that she set up some pots in the spring, of pepper plants, tomato plants, onions, garlic, herbs, but her charges, all in their teens, had shied away from touching them—they hated the feeling of dirt on their fingers. Two of the girls had washed their hands over and over after doing a little weeding.

Claire buzzed around with this plan for three days before she realized how it changed her mood, how the last time she had been this hopeful was before Michael's crime hit the papers. When Rahm Emanuel became chief of staff, ambivalence about the Chicago election turned to real arguments—all the Emanuels had a talent for arousing controversy, and liked to do so. Claire had told Carl that she thought she had known despair before the election, but she had been wrong: Should your enemy misbehave, sadness ensued. Should your friend misbehave, desperation ensued, a deep feeling that nothing could be corrected or changed. Carl, of course, had never expected anything to change. But she saw him out the kitchen window, hands on hips, looking down at the beams in the late-fall sunshine. He leaned forward and scratched the wood with his fingernail, brought his hand to his nose, took a sniff. Cedar. Carl loved wood. Then he turned around and gazed out toward the back of the yard, where the most sunlight was, where the deer were worst, where they had let the fencing deteriorate because you couldn't see it from the house. He began rubbing his chin with his hand, then pushed his hat back. He was thinking. Best let him think, say nothing. But she did look in the refrigerator to see how many of those Pink Lady apples she had left. Four—just enough for a galette, a two-person pie. With an oil crust. Some cranberries. She set the apples on the counter.

now, but only short ones); the second was about the food writer's twenty-five favorite recipes (he saved this one for Jessica). After those, he read about the State of the Union address, which would be taking place that night, about how the young man Daniel Hernandez, who had saved Gabby Giffords's life, would be sitting with Michelle Obama. He sighed as he read that. The shooting was as vivid in his mind as if he had been there, though his only interaction with Congresswoman Giffords had been a discussion of bicycle brands back in the spring of '08.

The paragraph about the case against Michael Langdon, of Chemosh Securities, was at the bottom of the business page: the SEC and the attorney general's office had dropped the case, declined to prosecute, no explanation; however, a fine had been levied, amount not stated. Congressman Langdon not mentioned, which was a relief. The fellow who sat in his seat now, a Republican, had squeaked through the 2010 election by two percentage points, surprising both Vito Lopez and himself. He was Jewish, he was unarmed, he didn't mind Obama—the Tea Party target was already painted on the middle of his forehead. You could tell this by the fact that Cantor still didn't know his name, though as minority whip it was Cantor's job to annoy everyone on his side of the aisle. After reading about Michael, he went on to "Sons of Divorce Fare Worse Than Daughters." This was an article that he couldn't bear reading, but did read, curling his toes in his slippers the whole time, and wondering if Leo was really going to fare worse than Chance, something unjust in any conceivable universe. He picked up his landline and dialed Leo's number. Leo's voicemail came on: "'Sup?" Richie said, "Hope you're good, son. Call me." He sounded as awkward as he possibly could. Had he or Michael ever disdained their father? They wouldn't have dared, and that wasn't a good thing, Richie thought. He realized that some kind of anger at Michael was kicking in. He must have deposited his anger with the SEC, and now he was getting it back with interest.

He closed his MacBook Air—lightweight, perfect for him—and looked out the window. It wasn't snowing yet, but it was getting ready to, which meant that Jessica might, indeed, be able to use her much-beloved snowshoes to get home from work that evening, and also that he could make his favorite soup for dinner, potato and leek, the very first recipe in the Julia Child cookbook, and the only one he had tried. There had been lots of snow this month already, though more to the north, of course, than around D.C. Just two weeks before, he had used the big storm as an excuse to dig out his mother in Far Hills—not that she had wanted to be dug out, but it had been something to do, and a reason to give the car and himself some exercise. She had not let him touch the snow on the front porch or the steps; she would go out through the back door if she had to, but having the Hut buried in still-frozen whiteness was a pleasure for her. He had tapped on her propane tank. No echo. It made him feel competent to listen, and then to look at the gauge—40 percent.

He had asked nothing about whether she had been deposed, what she had said. He assumed then that Michael had given her some of the money back, if he had some to give. Now he assumed that Michael had not repaid anything. His mother did not want Michael to be made an example of. If there were other examples, yes, but no one, no one had been prosecuted for anything, not Angelo Mozilo, not Lloyd Blankfein, not Richard Fuld. Why should Michael be the only one? Talking to her about this could raise several sibling issues that he had to discuss with Jessica. He could imagine that his mother preferred Michael. Was the fact that she didn't want him to go to jail evidence of that preference? How often should he fantasize about whether she might want Richie to go to jail had he committed what is normally considered a felony? Jessica would make him walk around the neighborhood until he stopped thinking these thoughts and agreed that he could not experience the feelings his mother had for himself or his brother, and so he could not judge those feelings. Jessica would say that, on statistical grounds, the number of parents who wanted their children to go to jail was far outpaced by the number of those who did not. That's what Richie loved about Jessica: she was sane, and she recognized sanity when it presented itself. He did not go for a walk, but continued to stew.

IT WAS EARLY—before nine—and Jesse was walking the farthest field, up by the Maze, the house where his parents had lived for a while, which was now boarded up. It could be torn down—it was a peculiar house—but it was as sturdy as possible, and Jesse sometimes wondered if he could sell it on the Internet as an antique and have it trucked away. He was carrying his moisture gauges, but he wasn't using them; the years had passed, and he had gotten like his dad, good at instinctive measurement. Sometimes he tested himself, and he was always very close. He walked up the hill behind the house, his own little piece of unplanted prairie, and looked north. The Missouri River floods were two hundred miles away and heading for Kansas; there was no reason for them to spook Jesse, but they did, which was what made him believe that the tornado season had set him up.

Guthrie didn't seem suitably nervous—he showed up one day, as thrilled as he could be with the video he and another employee at the hotel had taken of a tornado touching down just before dusk. For Jesse, it was like looking into the eyes of the demon. But it was reassuring, too, the way the sunlight shone below the clouds, and the thin, brilliant ribbon reached down and down, ever so slowly, as if seeking something. At the last moment, a complementary shaft, also narrow, stretched upward, and the two touched. The sound track was the siren, beginning late, fading away early, reminding Jesse that you had to keep your eyes open, there was never enough warning.

He had been raised on tales of snow and wind and drought and swamplike planting conditions. Farmers always wrested the harvest from challenging weather—that was their variety of heroism, to hear them tell it at the Denby Café. But all he had to do was read the words "rising waters" and he got jumpy. And Guthrie looked worse (Jen agreed); all they'd heard from Perky since Christmas was that his best buddy's dog had been killed by an IED, and the soldier himself had suffered a brain injury. That was two down of the four he and his Dutch shepherd, Laredo, had been deployed with. He got e-mails from Felicity, but they weren't good news about herself or her friends, they were about things like a group of farmers in New York State somewhere suing Monsanto pre-emptively, claiming that Roundup Ready pollination of their cornfields constituted genetic contamination of their crops. She sent updates about the Indian cotton farmers' suicide epidemic—lower yields, higher debt. Or pictures of grotesque birth defects from Argentina, where the glyphosate was sprayed from airplanes. Yes, Jesse was using lots more glyphosate than he had back in the early nineties, and, yes, the weeds were not dying with the regularity they once did. Did she think him a sucker? A criminal? She never seemed to wonder how he would react to these repudiations of his lifework. Did she mean this personally, or was she more like a satellite dish, simply taking in the word "glyphosate" and sending it on? Jen thought it was funny. And, in the end, was he too far down the road to rethink his business model? Bill Cassidy swore that eating Roundup Ready corn had made his hogs infertile—they only gave birth to sacks of water, not piglets. And what about that epidemic at the hog facility, piglets dying in the thousands, no apparent cause, and (they said at the Denby Café) their carcasses being tossed in a pit beside the river? Russ Pinckard said he'd heard that NPPC was going to get $436,000 from the government to clean that mess up. Bill got a little red in the face and said, "Yeah, they should pay me to go organic, but they're always whining that they haven't got the dough." Every time the phone rang, or his e-mail program beeped, Jesse winced, and so it was moderately better to be out in the soggy fields than in the house. Floods weren't the only rising waters; dams and towers of sandbags weren't the only protections that could be breached.

He slept so badly now that Jen had moved across the hall—not all night, but every night. They undressed, chatted, and got into bed as they always had. He turned out his light, and she finished the chapter she was reading or the article, then arranged her pillows and turned out her light. They kissed. He turned on his right side, because his left shoulder hurt, and she stretched out on her back, her hands crossed. He could hear her go to sleep—she was good at that. Eventually, he would go to sleep (when depended on how effectively he fended off all actual thoughts). After that, according to her, he would bundle the covers so tightly against his chest that she could not get them away from him, so she would wake up from the cold. Then he would shift about halfway onto his back, lift his chin, and start snoring. No matter what she did, he kept snoring, but he was working so hard, she didn't want to wake him up, so she slipped out and went across the hall to Guthrie's old room and got into bed there. They always woke up at the same time, but in separate rooms. This morning, he had been rolled so tightly in the quilt that when he woke up he had to unroll just to move his arms. Jen thought talking things through might comfort him, so she tried that once in a while, but just knowing that she shared some of his fears made him more afraid, not less.

There was nothing to the north but clouds—no rain, nothing

swirling. To the west, there was a patch of blue sky; maybe it was getting bigger. Jesse dug his heel into the soil. Certain plants had reappeared on the hillside: a few pale-purple pasque flowers already, and the foliage, though not yet the blossoms, of prairie smoke and phlox. Violets—a few groups of those; what he thought was a trillium plant or two, lost in space, looking for some woods and not finding that here, but maybe protected by the slope. And, yes, wild foxtails, undead. Jesse walked away rather than reaching down and pulling them out. You could get some government money now for a conservation easement, but it was like pulling teeth compared with other subsidies.

At the house, he unlocked the door and pushed it open. The place was dark and chill, absolutely quiet and empty. His mother, of course, had done a superb job of erasing every sign that she had ever lived here or cooked here. Jesse had meant to check the hot-water heater and the faucets for leaks, look at the foundation for cracks, but he couldn't stand it, walked out, shut the door. He looked at his watch; it was nine-thirty. He was wearing thick-soled boots, but he decided to trot the three-quarters of a mile to his own back door, for the sake of his belly.

When he got home, the breakfast dishes were stacked beside the sink, and he could hear the TV from the living room, an odd sound. He called out, then called out again, noticing that his voice shook, though, he hoped, only to his own ears. Her voice came down the stairs—"Here I am!"—and he jumped.

She looked upset, still in her robe.

Jesse said, "What is it?"

She said, "Earthquake. Tsunami."

"Where?" He thought of Janet first, then Emily and Jonah. After that, the New Madrid fault.

Jen said, "Off the coast of Japan. There isn't much on TV—you can turn that off. There's plenty on the Web. I guess three nuclear-power plants are right there. Can I have a hug?" He went up the stairs. Jen was not supposed to react like this. She was supposed to accept fate in good spirits. He said, "Do we know anyone there?"

"Didn't Aaron Cartwright's nephew go teach English there?"

"That was years ago. He's in Davenport now, training to be a chiropractor."

"I guess we don't, then."

She still looked devastated. Jesse put his arms around her and held her for a long, long moment. But he wasn't devastated. He had gotten so small-minded, he thought, that he was mostly grateful that this one disaster, at least, was far away.

AFTER HE PAID his fine, Michael must have had some money, because he bought himself a house in Georgetown that looked like a shoebox on end. It had a yard the size of a deck, square, plain rooms, and almost no kitchen. Jessica loved the sunporch, a tiny room with eight rattling mullioned windows that looked over the alley. The previous owners were in the State Department, leaving to take a position in the embassy in Peru. Michael bought their furniture, and had never, he told Richie, felt so clean and comfortable in his life. And it was true that the whole house, upstairs and downstairs, was painted brilliant white. Jessica presented him with a 36-pack of Zwipes, "to clean as you go." Michael laughed and kissed her on the cheek. A week after he moved in, Andy drove down from Far Hills, and Michael served a meal, admittedly ordered in, but ordered with thought: a Caesar salad for their mom, and a roast chicken with sides of sweet-potato fries and sautéed spinach for the three of them. Binky and Tia came, looked around, and left a few personal items, which also made Michael laugh.

Two weeks later, he showed up in the old way, at seven in the morning, before Jessica had left for her run, before Richie was out of bed. Richie could hear them in the kitchen, talking about the massacre in Norway, how bizarre, how horrifying—how American, really. Then their voices dipped, and he knew they were talking about him. He had been going to get up, but he lay there, staring at the ceiling of the bedroom, until Jessica came in to say goodbye. She put one hand on either side of his face, kissed him, and said, "He's got a plan." Richie took a deep breath. That anger he had felt earlier in the year had seeped away again. Perhaps he was growing up. He said, "Good plan?"

"You decide." She kissed him again, tenderly and with concern. He understood that she hoped he would go along with the plan, whatever it was. He heaved himself out of bed and put a shirt on over his shorts. His breakfast was on the table—a bowl of Special K, a carton of strawberry yogurt, and a cup of black coffee. Michael was reading the paper. He said, "This is what Jessica says you like."

"I like that."

"You're welcome."

Richie took this to mean that it was Michael who had set out the meal. He sat down. Michael pushed the sports section of the paper across the table, and without saying anything, Richie read the article about the north/south rivalry between the Cubs and the White Sox in Chicago. He wondered if their uncle Henry had ever been to a baseball game. He ate his cereal and his yogurt and drank his coffee. Michael said, "First, the haircut."

"Excuse me?"

"You have a ten a.m. appointment at Bang Salon with Umberto. He's level four, very hip. If he doesn't have any ideas, no one will. After that, we'll have a look at Universal Gear, but I'm sure we'll end up at J. Press."

Richie said, "I have clothes."

"Congressmen's wear. No. Time for a change. We don't know what you will actually look like after your haircut, so I'm reserving judgment about the style statement you will end up making. Are you finished?"

He actually stood up and cleared the dishes, not forgetting to fold the paper neatly and set it in the middle of the table.

A little disoriented, Richie put on plain old khakis and a green polo shirt. Better start with a blank slate, he thought. Minutes later, they were in Michael's Acura, heading up 9th Street. That was Monday. It went on like that for the rest of the week; Michael even took him for a foot massage at the Thai Institute of Healing Arts, where they seemed to know him. The masseur was kind, but kept shaking his head when Richie flinched in pain. He was told to come back "at least once a week" and to buy himself a foot roller, nine bucks, something that looked like a miniature of what he had always imagined a medieval rack to look like. They drove around. They went to a matinee of *Mr. Popper's Penguins*, after which Michael told him that he was now making a practice of seeing just about anything, as a way of being more open. Richie would not have said that they talked much during the week, but, then, neither did they avoid talking. It was peculiar and lulling.

It wasn't until Wednesday the following week that either of them mentioned Loretta. It was a short conversation that took place as they were walking down 13th Street, eating butter chicken wrapped in chapati bread, purchased from a food truck.

Michael: "Loretta found out where Chance has been."

Richie: "Where is that?"

Michael: "The ranch. I told her, but she didn't believe me. She never believes me."

Richie: "What is he doing there?"

Michael: "Minding his own business and staying out of the way. Also roping cattle. But Gail was diagnosed with bacterial endocarditis, and Chance got nervous and called Loretta. She hasn't been invited to the patient's bedside, though."

They continued to walk. Richie finished his lunch and wiped his fingers on the three paper napkins he had taken from the food truck, then tossed them into a trash can. This took about four minutes. By that time, he had worked himself up to asking a question: "How long since you've talked to her?"

Michael looked at his cell phone, then said, "Two years, five months, and about four days."

"How do you decide things?"

"She decides, the lawyer tells me."

"No divorce?"

"Not permitted."

They came to the corner of Farragut, and turned toward the park. It was too hot already to run, but Richie was rather looking forward to the walk. Michael said, "Every time I walk in Rock Creek Park, I think of murder."

Richie said, "I can't avoid thinking of massacres, I guess, but I never think of murder," and to himself, he added, "anymore."

HENRY WAS STARING out the window at the two linden trees in his front yard. They were both bright yellow, but the one on the left had red-orange leaves scattered through the yellow, and when the

wind picked up, they fluttered in a pattern that looked like the profile of a face. He took a sip of coffee, and there was a knock that he
recognized—Alexis—on his door. On Wednesdays, her school got
out early. He called out for her to come in.

The Charlie in her was like the red leaves among the yellow ones—
almost but not quite an illusion. Her hair was dark and straight, her
eyes were brown, but she had Charlie's nose and his personality—
inquisitive and friendly rather than doctrinaire, like Riley. She said,
"Today is your birthday."

Henry was genuinely surprised. Yes, October, yes, changing leaves.
But he hadn't celebrated a birthday in so long that it had slipped his
mind. He looked at his watch, but of course she was right—that she
shared with Riley. He said, "Good Lord, I am seventy-nine! What in
the world happened?"

Alexis came over and sat in the chair across from him. She said,
"Tell me about when you were nine." She had turned nine in May.

"I'm sure my mama made me an angel-food cake, which was a
very dry, tall cake with a hole in the middle, and she would have
frosted it with whipped cream, which I would have scraped off and
left in a pile on my plate."

"You were a poor eater."

"That's not a bad thing. Say 'fastidious.'"

She said, "Fastidious. But Mom says it is a waste of good food."

"The thing is to be choosy before you even start cooking or buying. You tell her that you will do the shopping."

"She hates shopping," said Alexis.

"We can do that today. For my seventy-ninth birthday, we can go
buy only what you and I like, and she will have to eat it."

Alexis giggled.

"For the rest of the day, we can do what you want to do. We didn't
do that on your birthday, so we can do it on mine."

"I want to do my homework thing for one half hour."

"Go get it, then. Arithmetic."

Alexis ran out the door. Henry got out the pot and the wooden
spoon.

A boy in Alexis's fourth-grade class had been diagnosed ADD.
His parents, instead of putting him on Ritalin, had decided to train

him like a police horse: while he worked, one parent or the other would march around him, beating a pot with a spoon, and he would have to concentrate to do his work. He gave a report on it. Alexis had come home demanding to try it, but she had her own wrinkle. Since she was taking piano lessons, the pot beater had to use different rhythms—4/4, 2/4, 3/4, 7/8. Quite often the session devolved into chaos since Henry's sense of rhythm wasn't great, but she loved doing her homework now, and usually went from homework straight to piano practice.

She returned and put her arithmetic sheets on the table with two pencils, and Henry set the stove timer for thirty minutes. Then he picked up his pan and spoon. Alexis said, "Ready, set, go!" The song in Henry's head was "Stormy Weather," the Lena Horne version, which had a steady backbeat, one of Philip's all-time favorites: "Can't go on, everything I had is gone." But he had gone on, hadn't he?

Alexis shouted "Beep!" and he switched to "All Out of Love," another of Philip's favorites, 1, 2, 1, 2, 1, 2, a faster beat, a song he had listened to over and over after Philip left him, and then again, over and over, after Philip died. "What are you thinking of? What are you thinking of? What are you thinking of?" His eyes started to sparkle, so when Alexis shouted "Beep!" he went as far back as he could go— "Smoke, Smoke, Smoke That Cigarette," a song that had made him fall over laughing when he was fourteen—every word about something his mother deplored. "Tell St. Peter at the Golden Gate / That you hate to make him wait. . . ." After that, "The Tennessee Waltz," and then Alexis said, "I'm done!" and waved her paper. Henry took a deep breath, set down his instruments, and flopped into his chair. The timer had not gone off. He said, "Seven minutes to spare! You're getting good!"

"Check it!"

He did. Every answer was correct (and when she got to fifth grade, he would have to use a calculator). He said, "Hundred percent! I think you need a birthday present!"

Very seriously, Alexis said, "Can it be not educational?"

Henry leaned toward her and whispered in her ear, "Yes."

....

FELICITY WAS NOT sorry that Max the math guy had faded out of her life, only to be replaced by the much more muscular Jason, who was an education major specializing in kinesiology, and, yes, his coursework included pocket billiards and racquetball, and weren't schools all over the country cutting phys ed? But since she was in her first year of her M.S. in microbiology, she had no fears for her economic future, and he had taught her enough about billiards for her to realize that she had exceptional talents in that direction (he agreed). However, it was one thing to skip your racquetball class in order to Occupy ISU, and quite another to skip both your Insect-Virus Interactions: A Molecular Perspective class and your Foodborne Hazards class in order to join Occupy ISU in a drizzle. But Felicity considered herself even more of an observer now that observing was her vocation, and so she skipped class and went. She even carried a sign she had made out of the bottom of an Amazon shipping box, "We Are the 99.99%" It did not make an iota of difference that the family farm was worth almost six million dollars if you dared not buy a new car and add to the debt because, however much the farm was worth, it was not cash. Felicity knew that, because of corn and bean prices, the value of the farm was bubbling again, the way it had in the eighties. She thought her father should be paid not to farm. Her father didn't want to know what the farm was worth, and her mother didn't care, since it would never be sold. The Occupy movement was not about farming, but if anyone had any sense, Felicity thought, it would be.

They got off the bus at the Union, walked up past Carver. There were about seven people standing by the Campanile, but then Felicity saw the group, maybe a hundred or more, standing on the steps of Beardshear. The wind was blowing from the south, so maybe the protesters were chanting something, but Felicity couldn't hear it. Jason grabbed her hand and pulled her. He seemed excited.

Felicity had not read about any occasions where social action made a real difference—it was, she thought, too hard to organize, and too quick to devolve into self-conflicting actions and arguments. Exactly that thing had happened to feminism, which by rights should have worked beautifully. Felicity believed that viral movements worked better, but Jason was good-looking, Jason was excited, so she was here, skeptical already, but she did have her phone out. She lifted it up and took a picture as soon as she could get all of the occupiers in without their being dwarfed by the building. As she got closer, she read various signs— "Tuition Shooting Up! Jobs Plummeting!" and "Who's the Boss? We Are!" and "What's Your Salary, PreZ!" Felicity knew that President Geoffroy made about $450,000 a year, up every year. It took 112 students to pay the president's salary. Houses *in* Ames were cheap, but there were developments out in the countryside, even to the north, right beside the high-voltage transmission towers, that were a lot more expensive. That was where the administration lived. She wandered among the protesters, smiling, taking pictures, nodding when someone called out, "Post them!"

Everyone looked excited and cheerful, and she and Jason were in the Union by one, eating pulled-pork sandwiches for lunch. She didn't think much about it (though she did conscientiously make up her missed classes) until a month later, when she saw the pepper-spray incident at UC Davis. She had in fact applied to the microbiology department at UC Davis, and gotten in, but she hadn't gotten a fellowship, and the tuition was much higher than at ISU, so she had stayed in Ames. She watched the footage several times, how casually the cop pointed the pepper spray at the kid sitting at his feet, and sprayed him in the face. That might have been her, except—not; would never have happened at ISU. Felicity was a realist above all. She did look up the cop's salary—$110,000. That surprised her. Her best teacher, the Foodborne Hazards professor, wasn't making two-thirds of that; as for Jason, he didn't have a chance, really.

2012

IT WAS the pepper-spray incident that propelled Richie, at long last, into his new job at a think tank—the ReNewVa think tank. Riley found him the spot, but he wouldn't have ended up there without Jerry Nadler, who was conducting an inquiry into law-enforcement malfeasance throughout the Occupy movement, and Michael, who knew Boris Kohn, the ReNewVa funder, from some Caribbean trip and talked Richie up for the job. Officially, he was a "consultant," and he did have an office, but his real job was to be told what to do and say. He still had that TV presence he'd always had, that way of seeming enthusiastic and genuine. As Jerry pursued his inquiry, Richie rephrased what he said and smiled more than Jerry did. Riley insisted that Michael never appear at ReNewVa. Richie didn't have to enforce this—Michael knew where he was welcome and where he wasn't. He spent his time at youth-empowerment programs around D.C., shooting hoops with kids and giving little talks on Focus and Intention.

Michael had opened up to Richie in the last six months. He blamed Loretta for almost everything. Did Richie remember that girl, the artist, Lynne? He'd adored her, bought her that place in SoHo, but she scared him, she was so ambitious and, he thought at the time, knowledgeable. He was wrong. Loretta was the one who should have scared him; she had seemed to agree with him, but she took his every thought or statement a step further. Chance was born, and he said, "This is fun, we should have a flock"—she stopped using birth control, and here came Tia. He said he rather liked Reagan or Thatcher, or whoever, and there they were, contributing as much as possible to Reagan's campaign, offering to go to rallies. He decided to cut back on his drinking, and she had him not only in AA but with a counselor three days a week. He had to agree to whatever she "suggested" just to gain a little bit of freedom. The only thing she left to him was making the money, and so he spent more and more time at work, just to have something for himself. And he wasn't allowed to spend it— she chose the place on the Upper East Side, she chose the schools . . .

When Richie and Jessica went to Michael's place for dinner (and to meet Binky's boyfriend) after the New Hampshire debate, Michael said, idly, "At least Huntsman isn't an idiot."

Richie kept cutting his steak into smaller and smaller pieces. Jessica said, "That depends on your definition of an idiot."

Binky laughed and the boyfriend looked carefully around the table. According to Michael, the boy's family was deeply divided, politically, and dishware had been thrown at Thanksgiving. He was from State College, Pennsylvania, and sold houses on the Internet to investors in China.

Michael said, "What is your definition of an idiot, Jessica?"

"A voice crying out in the wilderness."

Richie laughed and patted her knee under the table, but said nothing.

Michael said, "Well, Romney is an idiot—I know from firsthand experience. You tell him something, anything, and he gives you a sort of blank smile and then looks over your shoulder, I guess for the cue cards. I never met anyone else like him. I always thought he had a condition of some sort."

Richie said, "They can't stop him."

"The voters will," said Michael, decisively, and the boyfriend—oh, yeah, Linc—breathed a sigh of relief.

Michael didn't dislike Obama, never called him by any remotely racist epithet. Michael thought Obama was reasonable in all things, and said that he felt relief just being able to express that opinion out loud. He liked Geithner, he liked Holder, he liked Sonia Sotomayor. Most of the others he hadn't met. It could be said that the only person in the world who made him angry these days was Loretta, who, on the advice of the monsignor (now in North Dakota, where his ministry was profoundly needed), had resolved to be patient. She had even called Richie late one night to probe into whether there was any hope of a reconciliation. Richie, sitting up in bed, with Jessica's hand in his, had told her the truth—no. Loretta had said, "He *will* regret that."

Richie had said, "I don't think so, not in this lifetime."

Loretta had said, "The next one is a lot longer," and slammed down the phone. Then Richie had rolled up against Jessica, kissed her about twenty times, and said, "What do you think happens after we die?" And Jessica said, "Nothing." That thought seemed like a tremendous relief.

As far as Richie knew, Michael was not dating anyone. He never mentioned women, and he told Richie to drop by whenever he was in the neighborhood. Richie did, twice. Not a woman in the place, not a stray item of underwear, no fragrant handkerchief under the sofa. Maybe this was the hardest thing to believe, so Richie did not believe it, but he respected Michael's secrecy skills.

UNLIKE THE HOUSE to the left, their building did still have its roof and shingles, and unlike the building across the street, their front entrance was not blocked by a huge tree that had flipped out of the ground onto two cars, a blue Toyota and a silver Mercedes. Facing east turned out to be a good thing—the only damage was to rooms overlooking the alley, like their bedroom, not to rooms overlooking the street, like their living room. Some junk had blown onto their deck, and the lounge chairs and table were turned over, but, as Michael said when he showed up about five minutes after Richie and Jessica came up from the cellar, where they had spent the night, it could be worse. He had already driven out to Uncle Henry's—trees down, but no real damage; Henry, Riley, and Alexis sent their best. Since he had shoes on, Michael braved the glass-strewn bedroom and brought out some clothes. Power was out everywhere, but his house had a generator— did they know that?—so he would give them breakfast.

The Shoebox was in good shape—the virtue of small windows. Even the tiny little sunporch was okay, since it looked away from the storm. Michael scrambled eggs, made toast and coffee, told Richie and Jessica he had worried about them, been up all night, in fact, though he didn't mind that.

Jessica went to the bathroom to take a shower. Michael talked about the "derecho"—started as a storm cell in Iowa, grew and expanded, eighty-to-ninety-mile-per-hour winds, straight, not swirling, always blew from the northwest. Lots of storms that people thought were tornadoes were really derechos. While he was taking his own shower, Richie managed to come to, and not only from this hard night. He hadn't meant to be so dumbstruck, he hadn't meant to feel so old and sunk in some sort of mental goop, he hadn't meant to be taken care of by Michael, he hadn't meant to let almost four years elapse after his time in the Congress before he got himself together. He hadn't meant to take Jessica for granted, to buy her only a potted hydrangea from the grocery store for their last anniversary. It was a sign of how lost he was that he did love her all the time, turned toward her like a sunflower toward the sun, and yet he let conversations die, occasions where they might do something together pass, opportunities to help her make dinner or do the dishes fall by the wayside. Did she think he was indifferent to her, when, really, he was indifferent to himself? When he got out of the shower, toweled off, and opened the bathroom door, he heard her laugh in the kitchen. She hadn't given him one of those laughs in weeks. Michael laughed, too, exactly in sync. Richie shook his head back and forth, back and forth, loosening the dead particles of brain matter that seemed to be clogging his thoughts. They had done their best to grab his hands and drag him out of the sinkhole. Now it was time for him to exert himself.

Once they put on their clothes, Richie suggested to Jessica that they drive out to Uncle Henry's, partly to see what they could see on the way. And also, of course, to enjoy the car's air conditioning. What they saw was interesting. Their neighborhood was more damaged than most of the neighborhoods in the city, but the suburbs were a mess—lots of detours because of trees and power lines. When they finally got to Henry's, Henry and Riley were out in the yard, raking up debris. Richie pulled in. Were they glad to see him? They seemed glad to see Jessica. Richie started his new life by pitching in, sweeping, raking, picking up debris, dragging the waste containers to the curb, wiping the sweat off his brow with the hem of his shirt, but not therefore tapering off. In spite of the heat, they laughed a lot. Riley kept pausing, looking at Alexis, and smiling. Richie overheard her say to Jessica, "Eight to twelve is the best age! The last time I was really, really happy was when I was in fifth grade." And Jessica laughed and nodded. I'm happy now, thought Richie. I am happy now.

Only two interns and one consultant at ReNewVa were working on climate change, according to Riley. No funds for more. "I could help them," said Richie at supper. "I'm not doing anything else."

Riley said, "Talk to Ezra. He's good."

"He's twenty-three," said Richie. "He weighs six pounds."

"More like a hundred, but he is a vegan. Nevertheless, he's up-to-date. He graduated from Caltech. He has no interpersonal skills. He knows nothing about the Arab Spring, but he can put you to work. Just don't take offense at his air of superiority."

The ReNewVa offices did have power on Monday. He knocked on Ezra's door and said, "So—Ezra! Get me up to speed about climate change."

Ezra looked up from his Diet Coke and burped, then said, "No one ever says that to me."

Richie said, "Good. Then I have you to myself."

"Do you want to work on the Keystone XL pipeline or weather extremes?"

"Anything is fine," said Richie.

Ezra's last name was Newmark, and he was from Roxbury, New York. There was a picture of John Burroughs above his desk. Richie knew this because the words JOHN BURROUGHS were printed on a piece of paper to the left, shaped like an arrow and pointing at the bearded elderly man. Underneath the picture was another piece of paper, cut into a jagged shape, with the words "Marcellus Shale" printed on it. To the right were four pictures of flooding in Roxbury caused by Hurricane Irene, now almost a year in the past. Richie didn't ask if the pictures were of Ezra's parents' house, but he looked at them thoughtfully. He remembered Irene as something of a bust, but, then, a year ago, he hadn't been thinking of the Catskills, or much of anything else. Ezra spoke quickly but with exceptional clarity, as if he had been explaining things to people his whole life. He suggested that Richie write down what he was being told. Richie took his suggestion.

That was his life at work. At home, he avoided looking at the sofa, at the television, at his computer, all lures to sitting down and fading out, including the London Olympics—yes, you could watch javelin and discus and sprints until you fell into a coma. He suggested what might be good for supper, stopped at the market on the way home, bought things like eggplant and leeks. He moved on, in the Julia Child cookbook, from Potage Parmentier to Potage Crème de Cresson, and then he jumped ahead to Carbonnades à la Flamande. Jessica loved it. He bought another cookbook at the supermarket, called *All-Time Best Recipes*. A drain got clogged. He found a wire hanger and unclogged it. The summer, though hot, began to progress with verve and energy.

All the same, he did not take personally the drought in Iowa until Michael brought it up in late August. There was a graphic on the *New York Times* Web site about crops—corn, soybeans, wheat, sorghum. Tiny black dots like a swarm of locusts hovered over the map of Iowa (and Minnesota, and Missouri, and Nebraska), indicating crops that had been declared "poor or worse" and would be left in the ground or turned into silage. Fifty percent of corn, a sixth of the soybean crop. There was also a report that he found somewhere, about river temperatures being almost a hundred, and thousands of fish dying in the water and decaying along the banks. Somehow Michael knew some things that Ezra had mentioned, things that Richie considered rather esoteric—the flow of water down the Mississippi was so lacking that salt water from the Gulf was flowing upriver toward New Orleans; huge soybean plantations were the root cause of the destruction of the Amazonian rain forest. None of these factoids surprised Richie: Ezra had a four-by-six map of the United States with drought conditions penciled in on the wall of his office, across from John Burroughs. What surprised him was that Michael seemed interested, that he knew conditions were worse than they had been in the eighties ("Not the year we were there, but the year after that—'88 was a terrible drought year"), as bad as they had been in the fifties. He was Facebook friends with Felicity. (Did Richie remember her? What was she, early twenties—Jesse's youngest.) She posted about crop reports, even took a picture or two of Jesse's corn (dry, pale) and beans (spare, but not a disaster). She took pictures of the soil between the rows—dusty—and the dust on the west side of the house. Her comments were usually "Could be worse" and "At least a little rain."

Richie said, "What do you post on your Facebook page?"

"Cartoons. Links to YouTube videos of punk bands."

Jessica, who had a Facebook account, said that this was true. She showed Richie: Michael had 932 friends. Jessica had 267 friends. One of Michael's friends was Loretta, but, according to Jessica, she never commented on or liked anything Michael posted.

Richie almost signed up for an account—even Ezra had an account—but in the end, he was too embarrassed.

One day, Michael said, "You know, that place is worth six million bucks now."

"Up from a thousand or something like that," said Richie.

"What do you mean?"

"Don't you remember Dad telling us once that when he was a kid the land was worth eleven dollars an acre, if they were lucky? I don't remember how many acres they had then, but it was probably something like three."

Michael would not even smile. "I can't believe he bought out everyone and gave it to Jesse. That still pisses me off."

"Like we were going to farm."

"I know lots of guys, especially in Chicago, who are in farmland. They say it's a good investment. And if the crops burn up where they are standing, they get insurance payouts. Dad sent him money every year. He never gave me money."

"You were always telling him you were worth more than he was."

Michael scowled and went out on the deck. When he came back in, he talked about shoes—he had found a pair of Edward Greens in a used-clothing store, fit perfectly, perfectly broken in, seventy-five bucks.

It was so disorienting to think of Michael attending to weather conditions in Iowa that Richie was more than thrilled when, in September, he saw an article in the *Times* saying "Drought conditions appear to be easing, says National Weather Service."

FOR EZRA, who had been active in the Keystone XL protests the year before (how had Richie missed that? Well, he had made sure to avoid 1600 Pennsylvania Avenue while it was going on), the election posed a terrible dilemma. Next to the picture of John Burroughs, he now had a printout, in 24-point type, of a quote from *The New York Times*:

"Mr. Romney envisions a nation in which coal-burning power plants are given new life, oil derricks sprout on public lands and waters, industry is given a greater say in the writing and enforcement of environmental rules and the Code of Federal Regulations shrinks rather than grows." On his computer, Ezra had a file of everything Obama had ever said about climate change, including a speech he had made in the spring in Oklahoma, congratulating his administration on circling the world with oil and gas pipelines. Nothing Obama had said subsequently about stopping climate change redeemed his candidacy for Ezra. He thought voting for Romney might usher in the revolution, but, Ezra told Richie (realistically, Richie thought), he, Ezra, was the sort of person who might not survive the revolution. He *could* vote for Jill Stein, but to do so would not sufficiently express his anger at Obama. He was thinking about voting for Jill Stein *and* writing a letter to the White House explaining his vote.

Jessica was voting for Obama as an anti-racist gesture. The cascade of racist remarks about him and the made-up brouhaha about Benghazi offended her almost to the point of anger—a rare point for Jessica. When those soldiers were discovered in Georgia who plotted to assassinate him and had eighty thousand dollars' worth of guns and explosives, she sent in a campaign contribution, resurrected her campaign buttons from 2008, wore them to work. Michael was voting for Obama because Loretta would never vote for Obama, and he was also telling Tia and Binky that they should vote for Obama, as a protest against the Republican Party for offering a roster of candidates that went from bad to worse to worst ever. He didn't believe a word of the Republican yakkety yak about Benghazi, either. For about a week in October, even after Romney won the first debate, he could not stop laughing at an article he read about Romney's body language. The "expert" found his "tilt and nod" gesture ("with eyes wide open") positive and welcoming. Romney's "tilt and nod" was a permanent tic, according to Michael, and had always reminded him of those dolls from the 1950s with dumbstruck round blue eyes, pursed lips, and bobbing heads.

Richie, with his government pension, would of course vote for Obama, but Ezra was getting him worked up. Ezra didn't mind arguing, so he assigned Richie plenty of reading, both for and against the pipeline. When Richie pointed out that the Canadian oil was no worse than oil from California, and that the Canadian oil would get to Texas, and into the atmosphere, no matter what, that the Chinese would not be deprived of the Canadian oil, and that much of the pipeline was already in place and operating, Ezra summoned a pleasant look, then leaned forward and said, "When do you stop? When do you say no? You don't take mistakes from the past and use them as precedents for future mistakes. You say no, try something else—and something else emerges. You get investors to reject investments in oil companies. You use the Internet and crowdfunding. You bypass the Congress."

"Good idea," said Richie.

Michael continued to laugh at Romney—it was one of his greatest pleasures. One day, he said, "Look at me! I am in disgrace! Where's the money? Where's the expertise? But I can't help feeling that I could run a better campaign than this guy. *You* could run a better campaign than this guy!" Michael seemed not to think Richie would be insulted by this remark. And he wasn't. So many remarks over the years had stirred him up, and not anymore. It was strange. He didn't mind it.

In D.C., Hurricane Sandy was like the flipside of the summer derecho—wet and windy, but cold and coming from the east, at the living room, rather than from the west, at the bedroom. Richie tacked a quilt over the windows and stocked up on a few things like Italian tuna packed in olive oil and cracked-wheat bread. He did not expect to be driven from the apartment, and he did expect to stay home—everyone in D.C. stayed home in a State of Emergency. When Jessica went out for her morning run, he stretched himself on the sofa and called Leo, who had an internship at the American Folk Art Museum in New York, thanks to Ivy. He said that he was staying with a friend way uptown, almost to Fort Tryon Park, which was higher ground than his apartment in Chelsea. He sounded calm and moderately receptive to his father's attention. "How about your mom?" said Richie. "She's in France," said Leo. "But her place should be fine. I'm supposed to check it after the storm." Richie said, "Call if there's a problem." Leo said, " 'Kay. Love you." From that Richie knew that Leo was somewhat more nervous than he let on. After Leo, he called Michael, who said he was at Henry's. Richie said, "Are you dating Riley?"

Michael said, "Not yet. I have some tests to pass, and it doesn't look good."

"No surprise," said Richie. After he hung up, he thought for a moment too long about whether this could possibly be true. He called his mom. It was an indication of how immortal he considered his mom that he hadn't called her first. But she didn't seem worried: the Hut was not in a flood zone, and Michael had given her a generator for her birthday and shown her how to use it. If it got really cold, she still had that mink coat from before he was born—she liked to climb into bed and curl up underneath it. Richie said, "What do you have to eat, though?"

Andy said, "Chocolate, dried cranberries, a nice Brie, some Honey Crisp apples, and a big Yellow Brandywine tomato."

He said, "Mom! It could be days!"

She said, "Oh, I doubt that." There was a long silence—she was finished talking. These days, she always finished talking fairly quickly. Richie, thinking of Leo, said, " 'Kay. Love you." They hung up. Richie realized that he had not meant to have any of these calls sound like fond farewells, but they did. That was how big Hurricane Sandy appeared to be.

When Jessica returned, she said that the Smithsonian was closed and groups of Chinese tourists were standing disconsolately at the door. Richie had Jessica's favorite old Steve Martin movie, *Dead Men Don't Wear Plaid,* which she had seen seven times before she turned eighteen, in the DVD player and ready to go. He grabbed her, pulled her down on the couch, and held her as tightly as he could. If he had still been in Congress, he hoped he would have been thinking about the Grand Concourse and Prospect Park. But he wasn't.

And so Sandy ushered in Obama's second term. Michael was on the phone to Richie even as Karl Rove was yammering on in disbelief that, according to Michael, the fix wasn't in after all. "Look at him! Now that blonde is walking through the studio to talk to the numbers guys. What a surprise, except not to everyone outside the bubble. I always thought Rove was a prick!" He started laughing and hung up. Jerry Nadler, of course, had been re-elected, and a Democrat had replaced Richie's replacement. Earnest graduate of NYU, master's in social work, career in nonprofits, idealist, not the type of candidate Vito Lopez would have embraced, but, thanks to feeling up his office help, old Vito looked done for at this point. It was almost midnight. Jessica had fallen asleep on the couch with her feet in his lap. He took off one of her slippers and tickled her. When she opened her eyes, she said, "He won, didn't he?"

"He did, sweetie. He did. The Super PACs don't seem to have bought themselves a thing."

Jessica yawned, and said, "Maybe it's going to be all right, then."

"I think that's up to Ezra and Chance at this point."

Jessica said, "Don't leave out Leo. He's got a lot on the ball."

"That was complete do-it-yourself."

"What isn't?" said Jessica.

2013

EMILY WAS STILL in the ring, teaching a six-year-old boy who could sit on his pony but couldn't get him to turn left or right. Fiona stood leaning against the gate, watching Emily do her best imitation of Mrs. Herman—talk a lot, be encouraging, demonstrate a few things, let the child find his way, but keep your eye out for pony misbehavior. Champ, who was a small pony, only twelve hands, was not as agreeable as Pesky had been, but he was good enough if the instructor carried a whip. The first thing Fiona said when the boy was finished was "What is your cousin Chance doing these days?"

"Ranch work, I guess."

"Get him to come down here. I want to learn something new."

Fiona never said "please" or "thank you"—too many years of giving lessons.

So Emily texted the last number anyone had for Chance, and two days later, he e-mailed her. The first time he came down, he rode four of Fiona's young horses each day for three days; he rode six the second time. Fiona paid him a hundred dollars a horse, offered more, and said the safety factor was worth it. It was interesting to Emily just to watch. One horse, Dulcet, was talented but spooky. She rarely ran, but she often flinched. When Emily exercised her, the flinching was startling and distracting. Emily would worry that something worse might happen. It never did, but Dulcet was not progressing quickly—she was seven now, had never been to a show. Fiona had decided that, at sixty-five, she was too old to fall off, but Dulcet was beautiful and talented. When Chance worked her, he did nothing wild or cowboylike—he just gently solicited her attention over and over, reminded her to trot a circle, or square a corner, or whatever the exercise was. Fiona got on and did the same, and within a day or two, Dulcet was much more relaxed. Just before Chance got into his truck to leave, Fiona hugged him and gave him a kiss on the cheek. She said, "I am going to pretend that you look like Tim"; then she hugged him again and said, "Charlie, too."

The second time he came, Chance worked with one of Fiona's very bad horses, one she'd gotten as payment for lots of missed board bills, who would buck hard and keep bucking. With Chance on his back, every buck led to the horse's quietly spiraling, his back legs stepping over and over, until he sighed and gave it up. At dinner, where Emily talked about it to Chance, where he used words like "mindful" and "redirect," Emily had to admit that she had sort of fallen in love with him, or maybe she was abandoning years of disdain. She could not help comparing him, just a little, with the lawyer she was idly dating, two years older than she was, who shopped only at Whole Foods, always took his shoes off when he entered his house, and chopped vegetables wearing latex gloves. His name was Corey, and Emily had really wanted to find him compelling for six or seven months, but when he rolled his socks together before they had sex, somehow the thrill was gone. She and Chance started idly e-mailing.

Fiona told her that, once upon a time, all the best riding horses came off the track—they were fit and mostly sound and ready to try something new. Those days were gone; Fiona's stable was full of Holsteiners and Hanoverians, most of them bred in Europe, but all old horsemen had a lingering fondness for Thoroughbreds they had known, rangy with lots of bone, nice ones related to Hyperion, Prince John, and Eight Thirty, or tough ones related to Nearco. It was early April. Fiona sent them to the Santa Anita Derby, but she didn't go with them.

Chance knew all about the racing drug scandals and the footing controversy. Both of them had been riding horses too long to be surprised by much, but Emily did say, "That's why I've never been here."

"Why do you expect people to be honest?"

She almost said, "Because Fiona is," but she didn't. Chance might have said, "How do you know?" There was a lot about every aspect of their lives that Emily knew it was wiser not to delve into. Instead, she said, "If you don't expect them to be honest, does that make you honest?"

He said, "So far, never had to be otherwise."

Emily believed him.

They found their seats before the fillies' race, the Oaks, only six horses in the race, and not exciting, because the filly who broke first and went from the outside to the rail just kept running, and the others, no matter how hard they tried, could not get close to her. She had a steady, long stride and a determined attitude that Emily admired. She said, "That was a good race. No drama."

"She's not even three, really," said Chance. "Nicely built."

He acted restless, shifting in his chair as if the chair didn't fit him. Emily said, "Let's walk down by the rail. It looks more fun down there."

When they went through the betting hall, Emily was most impressed by the guys at tables, pencils behind their ears, intently staring at screens, their *Racing Forms* and programs spread out around them. Chance asked if she wanted to place a bet. She looked at her program and said, "Why am I drawn to Dirty Swagg?"

"Who isn't?" said Chance. "But let's have a look at the animals, just to pretend that we know something."

They walked out into the sunny paddock area, Emily behind Chance. She saw people look at him and smile—he did look graceful and horsey, but tall, not of the racetrack. He was not wearing his cowboy hat, just a baseball cap, but he was wearing his boots. A couple of girls scanned him up and down, then looked at Emily and turned away. Emily was amused.

At the rail of the walking ring, her eye went straight to the gray— pale head, beautiful dapples, tall and muscular—Flashback, said the program, the favorite, 6/5 odds. Dirty Swagg was 30/1, but he was handsome. Emily would happily take him when he was retired, and keep his name, which was a good name for a jumper.

Chance put his hands in his pockets and tipped back on his heels, gazing at one horse, then another, in a systematic way. Finally, he said, "I like that chestnut there. He's got a lot of muscle, taller behind than in front, limber stride."

Emily looked at the program—Goldencents, his name was. She said, "Let's bet. I know you have two dollars, because Fiona paid you."

And they did bet, a little nervous about saying the right thing. And their picks, Flashback and Goldencents, dueled it out in the homestretch, neither wanting to give up (Emily thought that, overall, Flashback showed more determination). Chance won eighteen bucks and Emily won three, so she made him buy her a hot dog.

In a year, she hadn't asked him what was going on at the ranch, in his family, with his dad, or his mom. She knew he and Delie had split, but not whether he saw his son, Chandler, who would be almost eight at this point. It was all horses, horses, horses, just as it was with her other horsey pals. Possibly, that was the only space where she and Chance could be friends.

After the hot dog, they wandered through the parking lot to his truck, watching the other patrons scurry here and there. Clearly, some had scored—they gave the valets big tips, and in general seemed to have money falling out of their pockets. Others hunched their shoulders and slinked to their cars—bad day at the races. Emily thought she might come back, if only to keep her eye on Dirty Swagg.

At the very last moment, she said, "What's up at the ranch?"

Chance put his hand on the roof of the truck and looked at her. He said, "Dry. I told my grandmother we had to cull the beef herd— they are scouring the pastures, and the price of hay is sky-high. It's not like over around the foothills of the Sierras—disaster area over there. But we have to cut back. She's not pleased. All the cattle have names."

"They do?"

"Well, not really. But it always surprises me how she remembers their markings, and what that steer was doing last year up there in the north pasture. Anyway. Well." He shrugged. From this, Emily understood that a hundred-thousand-acre ranch was more of a burden than a blessing.

When he dropped her at her apartment, he gave her a tight hug. Corey called her before bedtime to see if he might come over; she told him about going to the races. He was appalled. Every statistic he cited about drugs, about broken-down horses, about gambling addiction was one she herself would have cited the day before, but tonight she only said, "Oh, I know. It's shocking. Okay, well, thanks for calling," and hung up.

THE FIRST TWEAKER Guthrie remembered seeing had been Stephanie Crest's father. Stephanie was in his class at school—what were they, twelve or thirteen? Eighth grade. A slight, hunched man would walk back and forth, back and forth, just off school grounds. No one ever stopped him, even when he grabbed the chain-link fencing and shouted Stephanie's name and that someone was going to kill her and she had better watch out! The other kids liked Stephanie, but there was plenty of gossip that Guthrie overheard and was impressed by: the windows of their house on Kirkman Street in Usherton (a nice street, everyone agreed) were blacked out, her father kept guns in every room, her mother was long gone. Over that summer, Rod Crest went to jail and Stephanie disappeared, maybe into foster care, maybe sent away to her mother. Guthrie never mentioned it at home, and no one gossiped about it—his dad and mom weren't interested in much that went on in town. Five years later, just before his first deployment, Guthrie had seen Rod Crest, out of jail, walking past Hy-Vee, and he had thought, wondered, just for a moment, if the old man was heading into the Hy-Vee drugstore to buy Sudafed, and then he had forgotten about it—tweakers were a different breed, they had nothing to do with him. Even after he got out of the service for good, and started having that one dream about the kid sitting on the hood of the car—Perky's old Jeep Wagoneer—passing through the checkpoint and blowing up just as he lifted his hand to wave to Guthrie, it never occurred to him to touch meth, though he smoked a lot of weed; everyone did. Tweakers were self-evidently stupid; they stole anhydrous ammonia from fertilizer tanks and carried it away in gas cans, they didn't smell the odors emanating from their houses, their houses blew up. If there was one thing Guthrie had learned on the farm, it was that you don't play around with anhydrous. Tweakers never stopped tweaking no matter what, whereas marijuana smokers had interesting discussions about good and evil, then fell asleep.

That was all he needed to know until he ran into Melinda Grand at a Greg Brown concert in Cedar Rapids. Melinda had graduated a year ahead of him from North Usherton High, and had been active in 4-H, though she didn't live on a farm (her cousins had the farm). She had raised pumpkins, brought pumpkins to school for the other kids to carve into jack-o'-lanterns. She was tall and pretty and looked you in the eye. Back then, she had dated Reiner Ohlmann.

Yes, Melinda *lived* with Barry Heim, but they were just roommates—Melinda loved that house, and when it came up for rent, she went straight to the listing agent and asked to rent it. Barry had already claimed it, and the rent was too high for her anyway, so when she ran into Barry in the Cueball, which was right across the street from the crappy apartment complex she was then living in, she offered to move in and help, not only with the rent, but with keeping the lights on and the refrigerator from molding over while he was on the road. He said yes, and for sure he was thinking of getting into her pants, but that fell by the wayside: she was much more useful as a roommate than as a girlfriend. Barry had never dated anyone for more than a month. All this was what she told Guthrie, anyway. It was Barry who was the tweaker, though you couldn't tell—he drove that rig back and forth to Omaha six days a week, and he used the meth to keep himself going.

They both told him that it wasn't like the old days, when tweakers batched their own in the kitchen sink. It all came from Mexico now. Six guys at the pork-processing plant worked butchering hogs five days a week and transported crank a few times a month. If you were making six bucks an hour, you had to have a second job, everyone knew that. Melinda was a nurse—she knew the bad stuff. Part of the relationship, for Guthrie and maybe Melinda, was watching Barry: would he pull it off? He said he knew a guy up by Algona who tweaked for thirty years, had a family and a job; tweaking was his golf or deer-hunting; you could manage it if you had the guts.

A couple of times, Guthrie had been tempted to try it, but he hadn't, nor had Melinda asked him or invited him or tempted him. She was a nurse; she worked long shifts, but she was proud of her degree. She would sit with him on the sofa and laugh and hook her long leg over his and kiss him up the side of his neck, all over his cheek, until he was laughing out loud.

So a dealer from Usherton had been busted in March—Juan Castro, his name was. Guthrie had met him—one of the hog-facility guys. Several pounds of crank had been found taped up into the wheel wells of his ten-year-old Chevy Avalanche. Guthrie didn't think much about it, except to keep his eye on Barry. He was therefore much surprised, toward the end of June, when he was driving up the road toward their house—maybe a half-mile from the driveway— when two cop cars passed him going the other way, and he saw, since there was still plenty of light, that Barry was in the back seat of the first car, and Melinda was in the back seat of the second car. He had the presence of mind to pass the driveway and continue on up the hill, then around the long way past the "lake" and back to his own place. The next day, in the *Usherton Torch* he read that four people had been taken into custody for dealing meth, including Barry, and including Melinda, who had sold it to an undercover agent posing as a low-level administrator at the hospital. The paper said that the "narcotics ring" that had been "broken up" had been operating for several years and dealt hundreds of thousands of dollars' worth of methamphetamine. Guthrie knew what his dad would say: Then why had they never cleaned up the driveway? Why did they furnish the house with junk from JCPenney? Why did Melinda agonize, in her charming way, over a pair of shoes that cost fifty bucks? Maybe Barry was inhaling his profits, but what was Melinda doing? That night, sitting in his own run-down shithole, Guthrie smoked three bongs and still couldn't get to sleep. The fact was, he loved Melinda, he thought he was going to marry Melinda, he thought she was the only girl he had ever met who was steady, pretty, and fun to talk to, the only girl he knew who put her hand up and shook her head when he offered her a hit off the bong.

Or he did get to sleep—since he suddenly sat up in bed at about four and knew for a fact that the cops were heading his way and he had to do something with the bong and the last of his stash, which was in the freezer. That would be the first place they would look. He staggered out of bed, but was perfectly alert by the time he was reaching for his jeans, and five minutes later he was walking down the alley behind his apartment building, looking for just the right trash container—one that had no relationship to him or his building. When he found what seemed to be the right one, he opened it quietly, reached in, pulled out a bag of some sort, oh, McDonald's, and stuffed the weed into a leftover Big Mac. He dropped it into the container, closed the lid, went on. There was no one around. He got rid of the bong by smashing it and shoving it under some bushes, then walked back to his place, about a quarter-mile, still no one around.

The two cops showed up at nine-thirty, pounding on the door and demanding entry. He had actually gone back to sleep, so when he staggered over to let them in, he did look ignorant and helpless, which maybe was the best look. They waited while he put on some pants and a T-shirt.

They questioned him at the kitchen table. Where was his crank? How long had he known Melinda Grand, and how much crank did he buy from her on a regular basis? Who was he dealing to? Other Iraq War vets? Was he buying from Barry Heim and Melinda Grand, or from Juan Castro, known as the Barker? How else did he know Juan Castro? They stared at him as he answered, looking skeptical—he had never taken meth in any form; he had never seen Melinda take meth; he did know Barry took meth, but he didn't know where he got it. They questioned him for an hour, then showed him their search warrant, and he went out into the hall while they went through his things, which took another hour. They did not clean up after themselves. They said they would be over to the hotel later in the day—expect them. And when he showed up at the hotel, he would be watched, so don't try anything. Guthrie promised not to try anything.

There was something about being hostilely questioned by the cops that had an aversive effect, Guthrie thought as he was cleaning the place up, something that put him off thinking about Melinda, made that whole affair seem distasteful and creepy, when he had meant to be faithful and kind and see her through her troubles, whatever they were. Something about those two hours, the cops with their holstered weapons and the bully sticks hanging from their shiny black belts, that convinced him that Melinda was guilty, that her complaints about the long hours and the low pay had indeed persuaded her to go into business, to parrot what Barry often said: Doctors used to prescribe meth. All the ingredients are legal. If you aren't batching, you aren't a danger to anyone. It's my own business—what's the big deal?

When he got to work (right on time), there was someone, not in uniform, standing in the lobby, not looking like any of their usual clientele—truck drivers, homeless people who had saved enough to check in for one night and take a shower, weary travelers trying to make it from Chicago to Denver on a hundred bucks, the occasional talkative former Ushertonian returning home for the weekend. He went in the back room to go into his little locker and put on his tie and his name tag. The hotel was better now than it had been: The pipes were fixed, the electrical wiring was almost fixed, and there was Internet. The grungiest carpets and mattresses had been gotten rid of, and the place where the ceiling collapsed in Room 145, down at the end, in a big thunderstorm (not even a famous one) three years ago, was repaired and repainted. The cop (plainclothes, Guthrie guessed) followed him into the back room and watched him, took note of the number of his locker. The same two policemen showed up half an hour later, talked to his guard, and came over to the counter. "Mr. Langdon?"

"Yes?"

"Let's go have a look."

After that, they went through his locker, through the drawers in the reception desk, through his car, and left. He had no idea what they found, but, standing there, half smiling as people looked at him, then the cops, then him, then the cops, then shook their heads in disapproval, was punishment in itself. His boss drove up, probably called by Lupe, the head housekeeper. He stopped his Dodge Caravan in the middle of the parking lot, opened the door, and sat there in the heat, one foot on the pavement, his khakis scrunched up above his white socks. He said, "What the fuck is this all about, Langdon?"

"I don't know, Mr. Dell."

"You involved with those craphead meth dealers, Langdon?"

"I know them, Mr. Dell."

"That's bad enough." The old man shook his head. "Ah, jeez. I ought to fire you." Guthrie thought, I ought to quit. But he didn't. That afternoon, he checked in a busload of kids from Cleveland on a school trip to Yellowstone. They all looked different to him now— the girls dolled up in push-up bras, glittery makeup, shorts that ended at the crotch, flip-flops; the boys pale and uncertain, already done for, Guthrie thought.

....

FELICITY NEVER KEPT her opinions to herself; she understood that in Iowa she was surrounded by people who muddied the waters by never saying what they really thought. So, when Guthrie stopped in Ames (he didn't *come* for her birthday, he only stopped on his way back from Des Moines) and took her to Aunt Maude's for supper (she had the Onion Creek Lamb Sliders with Radish Slaw, Tzatziki Sauce, and House Made Buns, for eleven bucks; he had the Cajun Prime Rib Sandwich), she waited until they were half finished eating, then pointed out that, by the time their dad was Guthrie's age, Guthrie was a couple of years old, Perky was born, he owned most of the farm, and he was calling the shots about farming it. She admitted that there was some scientific evidence that putting off adult responsibilities was an understandable response to longer average life spans and generally lower economic expectations, but . . .

She made eye contact.

He did not look either shocked or insulted, but she got nervous anyway, while adding the other part she had practiced the night before—the great-and-famous-all-powerful Uncle Frank, whose remains in the form of dusty letters their father kept in a locked box on his desk—and, yes, Felicity had rifled through them and found them mildly interesting for their coyly seductive tone—had been through a war just as Guthrie had, and at about the same age, and, admittedly, all wars were different, but their parents were worried, their mom had talked to Felicity about it for an hour the last time she went home and made Felicity swear on a stack of Bibles that she wouldn't say a word, but since Felicity was a nonbeliever and the stack had not been a stack of scientific journals, she did not feel bound—

Guthrie grunted, ate another bite of his sandwich; she saw that he was going to humor her once again.

She said, "Okay, I am going to tell you what Mom said to me, and this is not necessarily what I think, but you should know what she thinks, and what Dad thinks, because what Dad thinks is about fifteen to twenty percent more anxious than what Mom thinks."

Guthrie said, "Dad thinks I should give up and move back to the farm, live in the old place, raise some goats or heritage chickens, and be content to talk about whether the river at the bridge there on Adams Road is a foot below flood stage or six inches below flood stage, and do I remember when the creek that runs past the southeast field actually had water in it, and the biggest question in life is ethanol. We had that discussion in May. And then we turned to the new interactive tornado map on the Weather Underground site, including the 'historically significant' tornado map, none of which had ever touched down anywhere near Denby."

"No," said Felicity, "Dad—"

"Dad is a saint," said Guthrie. "Mom is a saint."

"Mom knows that Melinda is likely headed for Mitchellville."

"She likely is. I haven't talked to her. I let Mom follow the case."

"Did you love her?"

"I loved the her that I saw. Obviously, there was a lot more to her than I realized."

"Mom says her parents can't believe it."

"She talked to them?"

"Mrs. Grand called her to find out how you were."

"I didn't realize Mrs. Grand knew anything about me."

"Mom said that she always wondered why you never brought Melinda for supper, and then, when the arrests happened, she put two and two together."

Guthrie said, "I saw her at the most three nights a week, depending on her shifts, and I didn't believe it, either. But why would I bring her home when the whole conversation would be about how it's never snowed on the first of May before, and last year we were broiling in the heat and now we are drowning in the rain, and the crop-insurance rates are skyrocketing, and the government used to pay if the yield was below a certain point but now it's privatized and therefore all a gamble? Anyway, the only thing I wonder about her anymore is, where's the money?"

"What about the girl before her?"

"Lisa? Chef Lisa? She has a job in Chicago, making pasta. It was that or sausage."

Felicity imagined the sausage making, the knives, the grinder, the pig intestine casings. Likely Lisa, who would be about Guthrie's age, was making ten bucks an hour if she was lucky. Felicity pondered her possible replies, then said, "At least she got out. At least she got to *Chicago*."

"Where her apartment was flooded out in the spring, and she had to move in with a friend, then get rid of all her stuff," said Guthrie. He ate the rest of his sandwich and wiped his mouth with his napkin.

Felicity said, "Can I be frank?"

"Isn't that your trademark?"

"Yes, but I'm not always tactless. I want to be tactless."

Guthrie made a funny face and said, "You can be tactless for as long as it takes me to eat my Chocolate Toffee Bread Pudding." He gestured to the waitress.

Felicity stayed mum until the dessert was set before her brother. This very morning, at 9:03 Central Standard Time, she had turned twenty-five, the age she had always longed to be. At exactly her birth time, she had stripped off the T-shirt and briefs she slept in and stood in front of her full-length mirror. Eight pounds, four ounces, twenty-one inches long had become five feet, ten inches, 139 pounds, size 9B shoe, thick, dark Guthrie hair, and horn-rimmed glasses. She had an alto voice, a strong jaw, a triangular Langdon nose, blue Langdon eyes, 36C breasts with nice cleavage, and a good waist. She was not beautiful or blond—an advantage. The random act of human breeding had worked in her case, and she was realistic about it, not vain. If success was to be her fate, then every study indicated she had to be built for it, and the metrics were trickier for females than they were for males. Tall, attractive, strong-looking, clearly feminine but reminiscent of the masculine. However, although she had matured on schedule, environmental factors seemed to have interfered with the same process in Guthrie, if not in Perky, who was still in Afghanistan, apparently all set to make the military his career.

Guthrie picked up his fork.

Felicity said, "Almost two hundred fifty thousand Iraq vets have PTSD. I'm surprised it isn't more, frankly, and of the one-point-six million vets, almost seven hundred fifty thousand have filed for disability benefits." Then, nerdily, because she couldn't help herself, she said, "That's forty-six percent."

Guthrie said nothing.

"Have you been to the VA hospital?"

"What symptoms do I have?" He took a bite of the bread pudding.

Felicity opened her mouth to speak, but could not. Guthrie spoke instead. "Am I pissed off all the time? Do I re-experience standing in that square in Sadr City, staring at the women sitting on the curb nursing their babies, while we were peeping around the corners of buildings, deciding if we had to shoot anyone? Do I suspect that my buddy Harper killed himself, since he stopped e-mailing me, and his last three e-mails were about his weapons collection, but I haven't dared to find out? Do I stare out the window of the hotel into the parking lot and imagine a car driving in and blowing up? Was I driving down the street in Usherton a week after they got Melinda, and I had to pull over and put my hands over my mouth to stop myself screaming, because, even though I couldn't see any helicopters, maybe I could hear them? Are those the symptoms you are referring to? Does having these symptoms indicate that I should move to Chicago and try something more productive than a seven-dollar-an-hour job assistant-managing a bedbug hangout on the edge of town?"

"I was thinking about the avoidant symptoms, since you mainly avoid us, and so we don't know about the other stuff."

"Would I feel better if I just got on that tractor and focused on the horizon and drove west, then turned the tractor twenty minutes later and drove east? Maybe I would, even though sitting in the middle of all that noise makes me want to leap out of my skin. If there's noise, you see, then how can you be aware of who might be coming up behind you, just out of your peripheral vision, and you might be so startled that you fall right out of the cab."

He was tense—he stabbed at the last piece of bread pudding, and it jumped off the plate, went down between his legs, and landed on the floor. He said, "Tactless time is up."

Felicity said what came into her mind, which was "Am I the first person you've told about this?"

"Maybe. I can't remember. That is a symptom, too."

He set down his fork, took some deep breaths.

Felicity felt that most therapies she had read about did not actually work: drugs had side effects, Freudian therapy grooved memories even more deeply into your neurons. Since she was basically cerebral, she thought that she might respond best to cognitive therapy—her whole life, in some sense, had been about investigating, understanding, educating. But, as a guy, Felicity thought, Guthrie might do better with exposure therapy. There was no exposure therapist in Usherton, but there was one in Iowa City. She said, "The real question is, why are you stuck in Usherton when you could move here to Ames, or to Iowa City? You don't know what it's like to walk across a campus, or go to the library, or meet thousands of members of your very own age cohort."

"Cohort?"

"So Melinda was the best of the local herd. You're good-looking! You have no signs of a receding hairline! You have deltoids and pecs! You have Daddy's smile! I was supposed to be the pretty one, but you are. Use it!"

He pursed his lips and sat back against his chair, but after they paid the bill, on the way to his car, she knew she had stumbled on the right advice, because he said, "You know anyone in Iowa City?"

She said, "Sure, I do. You do, too."

He didn't say anything more, but he would. She had two months to get him there before the beginning of the spring semester—she thought she could do it. As soon as he dropped her off at her place and drove away, she ran in and called her mom.

2014

Leo's secret was that he was unusually lucky. Over the years, and more than once, he had had the thought, "I need money for the subway, and I left my wallet at home," only to look down and see a dollar bill or a five blowing past him on the sidewalk—never a twenty or a hundred, but just enough. Or he would have a lonely thought—a party he hadn't heard about until too late, or a table of interesting-looking people across the room at a restaurant—and then some friend would text him from the party and tell him he had to come, they were waiting, or someone at the table would recognize him and wave him over; it would turn out to be a guy he knew from freshman year. But the item of luck that he valued the most was that, at the last minute, his boss at the museum, Tanya, had decided last September that she could not go to Venice for the Biennale by herself, and so she would fund Leo to go along and help her see to the return of "The Encyclopedic Palace," which was seven feet by seven feet and eleven feet tall. It had not been his job to dismantle or pack it; Leo didn't know what his job had been, except to stay at the Locanda Antico Fiori for a week, explore Venice as he wished, and keep quiet about the recurring visits of a French sculptor named André to Tanya's breakfasts. The *acqua-alta* flooding had not been as bad as the year before, which was also a piece of luck, because if the weather had been wonderful he would now, in January, be distracted by fantasies of moving to Venice rather than focusing on his present job, which was to help five-year-olds pat together clay figures in the crafts room after their very brief tour of the folk museum.

The crafts room did not have a window, so Leo couldn't see whether the promised blizzard had materialized yet, but of course it did have a door, and one of the three boys (there were seven girls) had his eye on it. He was quick, and his mother was not, so it was Leo's task to interfere with the escape. Having spent years on the run himself, Leo recognized the first shudder of energy—the boy's gaze would flick toward the door; then, before his hand even lifted off the clay, Leo was there, bending down, saying, "Jack! Here you go. Just pat it like this, then push a little." The wet clay seemed to have a natural attraction almost as strong as the door, because the boy dug his fingers into it with pleasure long enough for Leo to praise two of the girls and answer a question about next month's program.

Another piece of luck, Leo thought, was that he had no artistic talent, no musical talent, no literary talent. Every attempt he made was pedestrian and dull; even his mom agreed with that. (When he had showed her two stories that he had written in his creative-writing class junior year, she'd said, "Well, it's early yet, don't give up." So he gave up.) His talent, and a good one for his job, was appreciation. He saw the boy flutter again; that's what it looked like to Leo anyway, a flutter of energy over the child's hands, arms, face. He was on the other side of the room, but he got there in time to take the child's hand smoothly as it touched the doorknob, to turn him back smoothly to the little table, to slide him past the tantrum that might have popped out. "It looks like a truck to me," said Leo. "Trucks are cool. See? We can install the headlights right here." He poked one end of the piece of clay.

Five minutes later, the class was over. The mom waited until everyone had left, and picked up her son. She got right inside Leo's personal space, and smiled up at him. She said, "I am taking Jack to Maialino. Have you heard of it? It's an Italian place in the Gramercy Park Hotel."

"I live down there," said Leo.

"Come with us!" said the woman, and so he did, and so they waited for him to straighten up the crafts room. By three, they were walking into the wind toward the Lincoln Center subway station (no snow yet, but the clouds looked like bags ready to tear open). Leo noticed that the mom was graceful and good-natured, maybe a few years older than he was. He said, "I was a runner. When I was six, my mom had me in San Francisco, at a hotel in Union Square. She went to the bathroom in our room, and I was outside and down to the corner before she realized I was gone."

"It is a nightmare," said the woman. "I'm Britt, by the way. *Not* Brittany."

"Leo. Leo Langdon."

The kid said, "I'm Leo, too."

Leo said, "I didn't know that. I'm terrible with names. I thought you were Jack."

"I used to be Jack."

"When were you Jack?" said Leo.

"This morning." The kid held out his hand. Leo shook it. All three of them laughed.

EMILY DID GO to Gail Perroni's funeral, and she did stay that night at the ranch, and she did have a long talk with Chance, and she did report it to her mom when she got back to Pasadena two days later. The first thing Janet asked was whether Loretta had been there.

Emily said, "No. She sent flowers, but she didn't come. Binky came with her husband—what's his name?—Chris. They live in San Francisco. He said that he put a house in Atherton on the market for four and a half million, and it sold within two days for five. All of the bidders were Chinese, from China, not just half of them."

"Where was it?"

Emily took a deep breath. "Stockbridge Avenue. Near Sequoia. Four bedrooms."

Her mom said, "Where the Cornells used to live, with the fake teahouse?"

Emily hadn't remembered that place, but now she did. She said, "Probably."

"Five million?"

Emily had not felt that she was betraying Chance, telling her mom about the funeral—Chance never said not to talk. But maybe, she realized, she was betraying her mom.

"That's what he said." Then, "Sorry." She pressed on. "Anyway, I guess part of the reason Loretta didn't come, even though they have spoken a few times in the last year, and they met in L.A. . . ."

"Neutral territory."

"Not quite," said Emily. "The Beverly Wilshire, which was more Gail's stomping ground than Loretta's. Anyway, she didn't come because Gail insisted on being cremated and sprinkled around the ranch, and so part of the funeral was a long walk, where we all distributed some ashes. They were put in a bowl, mixed with wildflower seeds, and there was a little scoop, and we took turns."

"I loved the lupine all along that hillside a few years ago," said her mom.

"No lupine this year. The hillsides were already brown."

Silence.

Emily went on: "Anyway, cremation is against Catholic doctrine, so Loretta wouldn't countenance it, and Chance told me that she called him four times, and Uriel, who manages the ranch now, four times, to try and stop it. But Chance said that he was always going to have it the way Gail wanted."

"Isn't Ray buried on the ranch?"

"Well, he is. Supposedly, the little chapel out behind the house is consecrated enough for that. But Gail told Chance that that place was suffocating and she wouldn't have it. Those were almost her last words. No priest would officiate, so they had a funeral director up from Salinas who agreed to do it her way. She'd already set it up with him."

"Please don't tell me she had a horse killed and his ashes mixed in with hers."

"No, but maybe she thought of it. Chance said he helped her go down to the corrals every day. She had a chair there, and she would sit and watch him work the Appaloosa. They call her Ray."

"Oh, good Lord," said her mom. "Now you're going to tell me they think she's Ray Perroni reincarnated."

"She's a nice horse," said Emily. "Chance let me ride her bareback. She was good." And it had been heavenly, Emily thought, bareback, lead rope, perfect obedience. It made every item of horse tack she had ever used seem awkward. She said, "Here's another thing."

"What?"

"Chance says he's going to grow hemp on some of the pasture land. Legalizing it was in the farm bill. It depends on the legislature. I guess he has to get some kind of license. And he's becoming a vegetarian."

"A calf-roping, cattle-raising vegetarian?"

"Well, Gail didn't know this, but the cattle herd is way down—I think less than a hundred—and he might get some bison."

"Bison in California?"

"There are plenty of them. They sell to Whole Foods. And he knows this woman who breeds hogs for restaurants. Her male is a wild boar that she caught as a piglet. With a net. She sells to restaurants in San Fran. He thought that might be a good idea, too."

"Is he even related to Michael?"

Emily said, "Gail would say no. She said no quite often."

Her mom laughed.

"Loretta told Chance that a poll she heard about asked if people thought that there was going to be an armed revolution within three years, and three out of ten said yes. Get this, not only does she agree, but Tia's husband gave a talk at the NRA convention about how to get ready."

Her mom said, "Good Lord."

Now Emily felt she could say, "How are you?"

Her mom said, "Jeez, I was such an idiot. I bathed Birdie with some old Cowboy Magic shampoo, and she got bumps all over her shoulders and across her back. So much hair fell out. Did I tell you about this?"

"No."

"Well, I must have been too ashamed. It's been two months. One woman at the barn said she would be fine, it was like blistering her— you know how they blistered racehorses' legs in the old days, during the winter; nobody does it anymore. But, anyway, the woman said her hair would come back shinier than ever. I haven't ridden in weeks, though."

"How's Antaeus?"

"He killed a rabbit."

"No! I thought he wasn't very predatory."

"It was a stupid rabbit. It ran across his path trying to get to the warren, and he grabbed it and played with it until it had a heart attack. He was kind of disappointed when it died."

Emily said, "He is a strange dog, but so cute."

"He sits on my lap while I watch TV. Makes it hard to knit." Then, "Have you seen Jonah?"

Emily said, "No news is good news."

That was always true with Jonah, who at the moment was pursuing his studies in massage at the Monterey Institute of Touch and living with his girlfriend, whose job was to house-sit a very beautiful estate somewhere back in Carmel Valley so that the owners would feel at home when and if they came to visit for a week or two every year. Jonah didn't even have to mow the lawn—a crew in a truck came and tended the landscaping every week, the irrigation system ran on its own, lights turned on and off, and there were figures in the windows that looked like inhabitants. Her mom said, "How is Corey?"

"Mom, Corey is not in my life anymore."

"He was nice. He stood up to you."

Emily did not say that it was unlikely that she would ever get married at this point, that teaching kids to ride made her not want any of her own, that she valued her vast quantities of free time—even at the gallery, she mostly sat there when she wasn't smiling at browsing tourists.

They did not talk about her dad. It was only after Emily hung up and was running her bath that she realized that, once again, her mother hadn't answered that question about how she was.

THEY HAD STOPPED talking about ISIS and gone into the kitchen. There could be no talk about ISIS in front of Alexis—Riley's rule—because she would ask questions (always did), then, if you answered honestly (have to do that, another of Riley's rules), she would have nightmares. Henry had to admit that he and Alexis had cooked up a bit of a mess, but Richie was good about eating whatever they happened to serve. Now he was holding his plate out for seconds. Riley left meals to Alexis, and with Henry's help, Alexis made the most of her opportunity. This week, they had eaten pasta for four nights, followed by chili, then nachos, now this dish that vaguely resembled chilaquiles. If she wanted a steak or pork chops, Henry was called upon to do the grilling, which he did in the broiler with a grill pan.

He was a better chef now than he had been half his lifetime ago, because Alexis liked to eat, and she was particular. She was only twelve, but she didn't say, "I don't like that," she said, "The flavor isn't very complex, is it?" or "The texture of those potatoes should be lighter. Do you think Mom would mind if I ordered a potato ricer?"

Over the last couple of years, Henry thought, Richie had seemed to sort himself out, to relax. He was a little redeemed, too. His Wikipedia entry said that he had been honest, had worked hard for his constituents through difficult circumstances, was known for his sense of humor. "Now working on environmental issues at an unorthodox nonprofit, the ReNewVa think tank."

Alexis spooned herself another small helping and said, "The fried tortillas could have been crispier. I don't understand that part yet."

Richie said, "Three days a week, thirty dollars an hour, I'll pick you up after school, do your homework for you."

Just a nanosecond of shock passed over Alexis's face before she realized Richie was ribbing her. Alexis had never been teased—maybe a mistake there. But she laughed and said, "I am worth more than that."

Riley said, "Oh, yes."

Henry often wondered what Riley would be like if Charlie had never been on that plane, if that plane had never crashed into the Pentagon. It was like teasing yourself with alternative-history questions: not only what if no Iraq War (they had talked about that on the porch—no Iraq War, no ISIS, said Riley), but what if the Supreme Court had declined to weigh in on Bush versus Gore, and what if Kennedy had backed the CIA on the Bay of Pigs invasion, what if the Nazis hadn't seen quantum mechanics as a Jewish plot, thereby losing the chance to build an atom bomb, but also what if Harold II, the Anglo-Saxon king, had not had to force-march his troops to Yorkshire, to fend off Harald Hardrada before heading 275 miles south to Hastings? Riley might have gotten fed up with Charlie, never told him that she was pregnant, never produced Alexis, and never found that side of herself that could spoil a child, and could also be patient, contemplative, explanatory, yielding. As for himself, his alternative history without Alexis would have been a drying up, a shutting down—his death just a book being closed and put back upon the shelf.

Alexis got up and began to clear the plates. Richie burped, on purpose. Alexis said, "I know that's supposed to be a compliment."

Riley said, "Have you seen the documents from the ICIJ tax-avoidance investigation?"

Henry said, "What's that?" even as Richie said, "Not all of them. There's hundreds of them."

Riley looked at Henry. "Investigating tax avoidance through offshoring and money-laundering schemes. The documents turned up two years ago, but they are complex. Anyway, there's our boy, Michael Langdon. He's got money stashed in the Caymans, Monaco, and, for heaven's sake, the Cook Islands."

Richie said, "I guess that's the part Loretta doesn't know about."

Henry said, "How much?" He didn't know what he was expecting, but when Riley said, "Thirty million," he wasn't startled, hardly impressed.

Richie said, "Well, he bought that house for cash."

Henry said, "How much does he owe Janet, or Andy, or any of his other investors?"

"Who knows?" said Richie.

Henry thought his nephew's reaction was surprisingly mild, almost indifferent. Maybe, he thought, this money was not news to Richie. And never had been.

The conversation moved on to Alexis's music camp in Virginia; she was leaving in four days. Henry couldn't help watching Richie for the rest of the evening, though, just to see. Nothing. Well, he thought, sometimes even academic rivalries died down after sixty years.

THE FIRST PERSON to have lied about Andy's birthday would have been her mother, who wanted her to be off to school and out of her hair, and so she had said she was born in August—August 4, to be exact—and so that was Andy's official birthday all through college, August 4, 1920. Or, rather, that was Hildy's birthday. When she was living in Kansas City during the war, she had gone back to her real birthday, October 3, but she had gotten into the habit of telling people different days—the 4th, the 10th, the 6th—to avoid birthday attention. As a result, perhaps, of that (Frank, she thought, had been truly uncertain, and so had eventually fixed upon the 6th, and maybe he had told the kids that when they asked), she faced no greetings, not

even any communications of any sort, on her ninety-fourth birthday. The e-mails when she opened her account were from Orbitz,
Lucky Brand, Hanes, and Tusk. She clicked on a *Salon* story about
Citibank and Goldman Sachs complaining about the heavy hand of
government regulation under the Obama regime, which, as far as
Andy understood, had not regulated anyone, and had dropped the
case against Michael. Then she deleted all new e-mails and sat staring
at her computer. Ninety-four years old! From the outside, ninety-
four years seemed like quite a lot. Over the summer, she had let that
number intimidate her—although she was in pretty good shape, she
had had her bedroom furniture moved from the upstairs space to
the downstairs former study. She often went upstairs, to open all the
windows and enjoy the breeze.

As she was trying to decide if she had had enough of *The New York
Times* for one day, another e-mail appeared, this one a notification
from eBay—the auction for her size 6 Dior suit from 1948, black skirt
(eighteen-inch waist), white peplum jacket, belted, soft shoulder, was
continuing—up to $6,750 now, depending on authenticity (and, of
course, she still had the sales slip and the receipt). The high bidder was
"TheCollector," a woman who had bought other items, only French
ones, and who seemed to have all the money in the world; sometimes
she outbid the second-highest bidder by 20 or 30 percent. Andy had
never even seen a picture of her; she lived in, or, at any rate, Andy
shipped the boxes to, Dallas, Texas. So far, Andy had resisted dragging the little Google boy to the woman's address and having a look
at her house (in the new version of Maps, he swung from her cursor
like a child on a jungle gym, which made her laugh). Selling off her
designer clothes had kept her in food and heat for six years, and she
had, she thought, the best pieces still in her closet.

Another e-mail came in—"Deposit to your account." At first she
didn't click on it, because she was thinking about the Dior suit, and
that led her to think about the last piece she had sold, a pair of Bou-
cheron crystal earrings for seventy-five hundred dollars, not to The-
Collector, but to a woman in Seattle. But that money had gone into
her account a week ago. She opened the e-mail. The deposit was for
$9,999, a cash deposit. Her first thought was to wonder who in the
world had her account information. But of course it was Michael.
Richie had told her about the found money; it wasn't an item of scan-

dal, but only because so many others who had stashed their money in tax havens were far more famous than Michael. The government was pursuing a rather lackluster campaign to repatriate the money and claim the taxes. As far as she knew, most of the owners of the money and the properties and the corporations whose headquarters were mailboxes in Virgin Gorda had evaded those efforts. Time, she thought, to spend some of it. A birthday present, indeed!

But two hours later, when she got up and went to the kitchen for her English muffin, she saw that she was still the same as she had always been—the shopping was the pleasure, not the buying. She did buy a pair of colorful sneakers from Inkkas, and she did look at Amazon's caviar collection before ending up with white anchovies in olive oil and Australian licorice. You could take the girl out of Decorah, but you couldn't, after all these years, take the Decorah out of the girl. Frank had been that way, too. With their looks, and his ambition, and her addiction to style, they had immigrated to New York, and been taken on, like many immigrants, by kindly natives—the Upjohns. But once the energy propelling the effort dissipated, they fell back to what they had always been, stolid Midwesterners. The phone rang. She looked at the display; it was Janet. She pressed the "talk" button. Janet said, "You didn't think I knew it was your birthday, did you?"

Andy said, "I did not."

Janet said, "Happy Birthday, but I told everyone else it's tomorrow. Expect a flood of intrusive calls and e-mails."

Andy said, "I can take it."

Janet said, "I know you can, Mom. That's one lesson I've learned."

Andy said, "You know, sweetheart, I am so old, I really don't want anything. I think the thing for me to do is give everyone whatever they want, the first thing they think of."

"No!"

"Yes. What is the first thing you've thought of?"

"New tires."

"They are yours. Be sure you get Michelins."

"Fur-lined," said Janet, "with rhinestones."

Andy said, "Don't tell anyone that this is my plan. Just remind them to call me. Say my computer is on the fritz."

Janet said, "Oh, Mom."

On the sixth, Michael sent her a potted plant.

FELICITY'S INSTINCT had proved correct: if you wanted a job, there was nothing like microbiology. You could investigate bacteria and viruses everywhere, including in space, if your specialty happened to be geomicrobiology. She had been much courted, particularly by firms in Des Moines and Minneapolis that wanted her to run laboratories or contemplate milk. She did not get the job in San Jose, but, after three interviews and some nail biting, she did get the job in Boston, at Tufts Medical Center. She did not have the official supervisory experience the job description called for, but her adviser had told her new boss that she had "over twenty years steady practice telling everyone what to do, and she is good at it." The first day on the job, she had suggested a new way of recording results. Now her boss, who was married, seemed to want to date her, but she pretended not to notice. The job was everything that her adviser had said it would be—well paid, and difficult. People were smart and friendly, as if they did not feel that they had been born in a state of original sin, had never conceived of that possibility. She had a tiny apartment in Back Bay, down the street from DeLuca's market and La Voile. She had joined a book club that met in Cambridge. She noticed that the average age in Boston seemed to be twenty-seven, and the average man was good-looking. It was not herself she was worried about.

The guy she hung out with the most was someone she had met on eHarmony, a real assistant professor in the political-science department at BU. He should have been perfect for her, since he was up-to-date about Gaza, ISIS, Ebola, earthquakes related to fracking, congressional dysfunction, and the immigration bill, all of which, Felicity knew, should concern her more than the farm. She did not have to discuss global warming with him, because he wasn't interested in the origins of global warming—that cake was baked. He thought only about possible socioeconomicpoliticocultural responses to global warming, as dictated by historical experience, in particular the effects of climate change (he always called it "climate change") in the seventeenth century, which did not set a good precedent, and so he had several boxes of canned goods in his basement, and, indeed, his parents had stockpiled provisions for Y2K, and they had discovered, to their dismay, that canned goods didn't hold up quite as well as they were advertised to. Felicity suggested that he buy himself a food dryer and a vacuum sealing machine, which he did.

But Gordie was not enough to keep her mind productively occupied, nor was her job or her three nice new girlfriends (UMass, Berkeley, Wellesley); she limited her calls home to one per week, and her calls to Guthrie to one every two weeks. He talked about ISIS, but not Ferguson. Did he do it more than other people she knew? Everyone talked about ISIS and/or Ferguson. Guthrie said that she was obsessing about the farm, because she kept comparing her dad's harvest of corn and beans with the average for the county (beans 2 percent higher, corn 3 percent lower) or checking the markets and calculating in her mind what he might have made for the year, and how that stacked up against the value of the land, which had doubled since 2009 (forty-five hundred per acre to almost nine thousand—not a good sign). And how was he going to sell his crap when it couldn't be shipped because of the railroad cars carrying the tar sands? The harvest was estimated at fourteen and a half billion bushels of corn alone. Her dad would store it. If the moisture content was high, it could crust over. If it crusted over, he could decide to break it up. If he climbed into the bin to break it up, he could sink into it and drown. Though he never had. Felicity truly hated corn. She said nothing about this to Gordie.

Megan from Berkeley said she needed a puppy. Charlene from Wellesley said she needed a cat, and Deanne from UMass said she needed to start running—look around, everyone in Boston ran and ran. She looked around. They did. Once in a while, when she was sitting up in bed with Gordie, both of them busy on their iPhones, she wondered aloud how it could be that, right when you were peaking, you didn't feel the way you always thought you would. Gordie's standard answer was "You feel the way you feel. It's impossible to change that thermostat. I mean, even quadriplegics go back to feeling fairly upbeat, if they were always fairly upbeat." Gordie was a good example of his own observation; every time she brought it up, he mentioned quadriplegics, and so, to avoid this, she stopped talking about it. But as a revelation, the idea that her lifelong project to shape her future had resulted in worry, worry, worry was utterly depressing, and Gordie, the ideal eHarmony male and, according to the algorithm, her perfect mate, had a mole on his upper lip that she didn't like but couldn't help looking at, a subscription to the *Financial Times* (in which he showed her an article about how the sudden drop in oil prices was bad news for wind and solar), and a certain odor that only she could smell—once she had even asked Megan if she could smell Gordie, and Megan had said, "God, no. Compared with every guy I've ever dated, he's a summer breeze." Felicity didn't want to be amazed that, after all her efforts, she was doomed to disappointment, but she was amazed.

2015

CLAIRE KEPT HER EYE on Carl's responses to things in order to gauge whether she was being reasonable or crotchety. This was the current example, where to go after her seventy-sixth birthday. Chicago wasn't unbearably cold, but it was, well, Chicago. There had been torrents of rain in August, then the "bomb cyclone" of cold in November, though, as Carl pointed out three times, "no billion-dollar weather disasters, according to the 'Catastrophe Report.'" Carl felt that they should be pleased that November was catastrophe-less, since each of the previous thirty-three months had seen at least one. "Of course," Carl said, "a billion dollars is only a hundred million in 1960 dollars." 2013 had hosted forty-one billion-dollar events. Carl said "Florida"; Claire said, "Rick Scott makes my skin crawl." Carl directed her to a Web site that rented condos by the week around Melbourne. Claire remained skeptical until the morning after their arrival, when the pleasant weather, the neat furniture, and the well-maintained landscaping won her over, at least for the time being. Her mother had died when she was seventy-four. Seventy-four was quite young these days—she had met a group of seventy-four-year-olds on a plane a few years ago who were going kayaking in Australia. But, really, you lived all your life in the present—memories that accumulated randomly in your mind did not convince you of the passage of time. When your son kissed you kindly on the hair, or your step-daughter spoke extra clearly, that was when you saw yourself as you had once seen your mother. It didn't even matter that the children were hardly children anymore; her automatic response to their getting taller, filling out, sharpening their personalities was much like sitting in a movie theater and watching a film—it had nothing to do with her sense of herself.

The vacation—two weeks—was a break, especially since Claire chose not to bring her computer and they opted to not watch the news. If it wasn't floods in Arizona, then it was drought in California, refugee crises in Italy, algae blooms in the Great Lakes, trains carrying bitumen going off the tracks and exploding in . . .

She tapered off after about an hour, let Carl have some peace, and then watched *Yankee Doodle Dandy* on TCM, casting sideways glances at Carl, enjoying his laughter and his pleasure in Cagney's odd but exhilarating dancing style. When Carl said that if he had been short he might have been a dancer, Claire made him get up and spin her around the living room of their very modest condo, which he did, humming "Singin' in the Rain." She thought, but did not say, that Carl could have done anything he wanted, dancing included. She had said that often enough, and she knew the reason, an egotistical one— she wanted everyone in the world to appreciate him the way she did.

Once they were in bed, in the dark, the condo bedroom was a little disorienting, since the bed, which was against the west wall in their house, was against the east wall in the condo, and if she woke up to use the bathroom, she had to pause long enough to direct herself so as not to walk out onto the balcony and over the railing (she made herself not think this thought). The walls of the bedroom were yellow, which was pretty during the day. Her own walls Carl had repainted four times, finally settling on a restful shade called "Coastal Vista." Nor did she especially like the sheets, which were cotton (hers were bamboo), but the coverlet was perfect—light enough to be cool without air conditioning, and heavy enough to stay put. Finicky. She was so like her mother now. The mattress was a little too firm—

Carl rolled toward her. He put one arm under her neck and laid the other one across her, and she snuggled backward toward him. They sighed simultaneously, and she felt him go to sleep. He always fell asleep before she did, which she found reassuring—it was as if he were the guide, leading her toward sleep and whatever they might find there. As with everything, he went there willingly. She could not say that Carl was never afraid, but he had always approached fear as systematically as he approached laying tile or putting together a cabinet, or, indeed, growing those vegetables in the backyard that he now adored—he would be planting the seeds in paper cups as soon as they got home.

Her own thoughts were more difficult to put to rest. Her knee itched, hair was tickling her nose, her leg jerked suddenly. Who was that who had restless-leg syndrome? Gray's mother-in-law, it was. She took something for it.

Her bladder woke her up, as it did every night. She tried to exit the bed as quietly as she could, made herself turn left rather than right, did not look at the night-light in the bathroom or think about the paragraph in the lease that released the owners from all accidents. She thought she stepped down two steps, which startled her and woke her up—there were no steps. When she got back to bed, the sheets were cool again. Carl was sound asleep, but then he woke up, sat up, blew his nose, lay back again. He groaned softly as he settled in. She tickled the back of his head, which was the only spot within easy reach. She heard him yawn, and yawned herself. He was a little awake, because he squeezed her hand.

Claire always dreamed in the morning; when she woke up, the first thing she thought of was the conundrum in her dream, why had she not made out the bill for her party clients, such a big party, all pink, and her mother's voice said, "Pure laziness, you ask me." Claire stretched and stood up—she hated this part about old age, always heading for the bathroom; it made chamber pots look good. Carl was still asleep. The room was already warm. She looked at the clock. It was nine-twenty-three.

In the bathroom, she washed her hands, blew her nose, took a drink of water. She couldn't believe they had slept so long—hadn't they gone to bed before ten-thirty? But she yawned. She went back into the bedroom. Carl was lying on his side, facing away from her, his arm outside of the covers, his hand resting on his hip. She said, "Sweetie, it's late. What do you want to do today?" When she sat down on her side of the bed, his arm flopped awkwardly backward. He didn't respond. She knew what was wrong—or, at least, her body did, because she avoided touching him, only got up, went around, squatted down in front of him. His eyes were closed; his face looked the way it always did when he was sleeping, handsome, with sculpted cheekbones and a smooth forehead. She ran her fingers through his hair and said, "Sweetie?" His body shifted away from her. She touched his carotid artery, then put her ear to his chest—no movement, no sound.

Claire remained where she was for a long moment. Her immediate thought was, So it's happened again. Of course, the death of her father was sixty-two years in the past, but if all your life was present all the time, then, yes, the two events sat beside one another, proving something. She put her hand on his forehead again, and now she felt its coolness. She kissed his lips, and felt their thickness, their lack of response; that was, indeed, the very thing that convinced her, but also, in a way, reassured her. No need to panic—Carl had gone on ahead. At that thought, the tears began.

Even so, even so, the rest of the world was the enemy now, wasn't it? People would bustle in, push her aside, carry him off. He would then go to the funeral home, after that the crematorium (it was in his will). She continued to stroke his forehead, kissed his beautiful lips again, thought briefly of knives in the kitchen—it might be easy, she could lie down beside him and do it. Why go on, really? But she didn't; she was a good girl. She stroked him for a while, then turned around and sat beside him, her back against the side of the bed, her head resting against his bent knee. He felt present in the room. That was all that mattered.

The coroner's diagnosis was cerebral thrombosis, a blood clot in the brain, often no symptoms ahead of time, came on at night or early morning, when blood pressure was low. No, he would not have felt distressed, would not have awakened. The coroner said he wouldn't mind going that way, compared with what he'd seen over the years. The director of the local funeral home was kind and sympathetic; the owner of the condo let her out of the second week of their lease; everyone was so sorry. Angie screamed and dropped her phone when Claire told her, but called back, still crying, and said she was sorry, how was Claire? When she got back to Chicago, the flowers started coming, the first bouquet from Henry, along with a note that said how much he'd always loved Carl—remember the time in his old place in Evanston when Carl came over to see why the wall in the dining room was damp all the time, and when he cut through the wall he saw that someone had used a piece of garden hose to replace a water pipe? He had to replace the hose with real pipe, the wall, and part of the flooring. Never made a mistake, listened with interest to every one of Henry's ideas about Pope Innocent III, then remarked that he had given up on religion when he was six. Claire kissed the letter.

She let Angie make the decisions about where the service would be and what would be done with the ashes. Angie chose a nondenominational parklike place a little west of her house that had been in the cemetery business for almost a hundred years, and was well cared for; Claire wondered if she would ever visit there. The next day, Claire went into the gardening shed (formerly the garage, and so not terribly cold). Neatly stacked were the cups, the medium, the packets of seed—Red Calabash and Arkansas Traveler tomatoes, Purple Beauty sweet peppers, Dark Star zucchini, sunflowers, parsnips, morning glories. She planted the seeds as she had seen Carl do, three to a cup, made sure they were moist, and covered the cups as she had seen Carl do, with an old blanket. It took her a couple of hours. A week since he died. Oddly, she did not feel terrible; she only felt that he was somewhere—in the back bathroom, perhaps, fixing the toilet so that it would not run, or down in the basement, straightening his tool closet. Wherever he was, he was present; she felt that, and so she wasn't afraid.

AFTER THE IPCC ISSUED its report in October, Ezra taped a quote from it, written in red Magic Marker, just above the head of John Burroughs: "Warming by the end of the 21st century will lead to high to very high risk of severe, widespread, and irreversible impacts globally." When the Republicans took over the Senate, Ezra told Richie that the United States would address climate change by saying, "Fuck you." He told Richie that the interior areas of all the Earth's continents were going to dry up and heat up—125 degrees in Denby, Iowa, in the summer and minus fifty in the winter would become the norm. There were a few safe places to be: Oregon, Washington State, parts of California, New England, Nova Scotia, parts of D.C. (though not Richie's neighborhood—move now, to Columbia

Heights, said Ezra). Richie said, "You sound like my second cousin—well, first cousin once removed. She is a font of statistical information." Ezra, who, when they ate lunch in restaurants, never looked at the girls go by and also never looked at the boys go by, actually made eye contact, and said, "She is?"

"Ezra," said Richie, "she's four inches taller than you."

Ezra said, "She *is*?"

Richie saw that he was going to do some matchmaking. He said, "She's coming in a week, for the spring flowers and to go to some conference at Georgetown."

Ezra shrank into his seat again. Richie would have to give some advice. He was an idiot compared with Ezra, and they both knew it, but Richie had a fine record as a man-about-town—two attractive wives, both of whom remained fond of him, and some old girlfriends who e-mailed regularly (Nadie, of course, the most interesting; she and her wife had each had a child, about three months apart in age, and very compatible). In his two years working with Ezra, Ezra hadn't mentioned a girlfriend, or even, though Richie didn't have the best memory, a date. He stared at Ezra, who was wearing a wrinkled blue plaid shirt, jeans, and orange sneakers. He said, "Wear what you have on, but wash it between now and then." Ezra looked down at his shirt as if seeing it for the first time.

Jessica's faith in Leo, Ezra, and the rest of their generation had only grown over the last few years. After watching Leo with Jack for a weekend, she said, "If I had met anyone like Leo when I was of breeding age, I might have had a kid." Richie admired Leo's skills, too. He kept Jack corralled and entertained while still discussing new exhibitions at the museum—he had a paid job there now, because an anonymous donor had dropped ten million into the museum's coffers "for non–patchwork-quilt" exhibitions. He had declared to Richie (unasked) that hookup culture was over for him, and so he was living with Jack and Britt, who worked at Amazon Publishing on the marketing side. Britt's apartment had a view of the East River. She was older than Leo, but that seemed to be a trend, too. Richie had said once to Jessica, "Do you think he's noticed that Britt is black?" Jessica said, "African American," then gave him one of those looks that said, "I forgive you, because you are old," but that was before Ferguson, before Eric Garner—Richie felt that he was now maybe one degree more sensitive than he had been. As for Ezra, Jessica would take him for walks and he would tell her interesting anecdotes about how he spent his summers when he was in elementary school counting plants, birding, and stalking muskrats. Had he been bullied? she asked him. One year, maybe eighth grade, some kids had stolen his yearbook and written insulting variations on his name inside the cover—"Newfart," "P.U.mark." Ezra had been so out of it that he had glanced over them and not understood what was happening until one of the girls in his class took him aside and apologized for the others. Richie understood without being told that hookup culture had never even begun for Ezra.

Felicity stayed in their second bedroom, but she was out early and back late for the first two days, which gave Richie the ideal opportunity to survey her habits (neat) and her wardrobe (American-made, some Ohio company) before heading to the office for Ezra prepping. He knocked on Ezra's door and walked in.

Ezra literally had his nose in a book: he had taken off his glasses and was leaning forward to make out the tiny type. Richie said, "You remember you're coming tomorrow night for supper? Jessica bought the seitan. She's making spaghetti with seitan Bolognese sauce and chanterelles." This was, indeed, a measure of how kind Jessica could be, that she would cook with seitan. Ezra jumped, and the book fell with a smack on his desk. He looked pale. Richie said, "Ezra, don't panic." Then he had an idea. He went down the hall to Petra Rogers's office. Petra was married and pregnant, but also game for anything. He whispered in her ear, got a laugh, and escorted her to Ezra's office.

It was Richie who directed the play. Petra came in; Ezra got up and greeted her; Petra sat across the desk as across the dinner table; Ezra offered her food and made conversation; Petra showed interest; Ezra suggested they meet at the Natural History section of the Smithsonian later in the week; Petra glanced at Richie; Richie nodded enthusiastically. Then he and Petra critiqued Ezra's performance— look her in the eye, but don't stare until she looks away; don't stand so close; be sure you shower before going to dinner, and *use deodorant;* get your glasses adjusted so they don't keep falling down your nose; after you finish saying something, close your mouth; smile; if you have to shake her hand, do it firmly, *warmly*. Ezra put his forehead on his desk. They gave him a minute, and tried again. Richie had to admit he was a quick study. Maybe, he said to Petra when he walked her back to her office, no one had ever coached him before. Petra said, "Believe me, Congressman, they're all like this."

And then the dinner went off without a problem. Richie gagged down the seitan, not because it tasted bad, but because he couldn't stop thinking about what it was, and Ezra and Felicity hit it off. Ezra was not smooth and eloquent, but Felicity was—Ezra looked at her, listened to her, and lost every iota of self-consciousness. When they were doing the dishes afterward, Jessica said, with a straight face, "She is a Scorpio, and he's a Cancer. That's good, as long as she accepts being the boss."

Richie said, "I'm sure she accepts being the boss. Do you accept being the boss?"

She said, "Some are born bossy, some achieve bossiness, and some have bossiness thrust upon them."

It was only later, after Jessica had gone to sleep, that Richie thought about Felicity's mentioning that Michael had appeared at the farm, allegedly visiting. Her dad and mom had told her about it— Jesse over the phone, Jen by e-mail. Her dad said that Michael had called him from Usherton, said he was passing through. He thought he would come by to say hello, if they didn't mind—it had been so long. Jesse had some free time, since the corn was in and the beans couldn't go in because of a week of steady thunderstorms after corn planting, so Michael came by, wearing his Bogs and his yellow slicker, and they tramped here and there. Jesse thought Michael looked older than he was; must be the worries. It was mildly strange, but then Michael went on to Minneapolis, where he was meeting someone. Jen had written that he seemed friendly, had asked, not about the big house, the nice house, but about the Maze—he had run his fingers over those handmade bricks. After Jesse went back to work, Jen took Michael up there and waited while he looked around—its rooms so small, but charming in its way. Jesse and Jen were not suspicious— who in the world would not want to stop by the farm if he or she was in the neighborhood?—but Richie knew by the way that Felicity had glanced at him that she was suspicious, and wondered if he was, too. He was, of course, but he had said only, "I would like to see the farm. Jessica, we should take a little road trip—visit your mom and see some of the country. Ezra tells me it's going to be a desert in a year or two, so now's the time."

"Not a year or two," said Ezra.

Then he and Felicity talked about how the frackers in California were using and contaminating two million gallons of water a day. And all of that fracking was up in the air now, anyway, with the oil glut. Ezra didn't have much hope. Yes, the overextended drillers might bail on the fracking, but they would leave an epic mess behind them for someone else to clean up—or not. Ezra loved Pennsylvania, had hated to see it sacrificed, thought maybe the lesson had to be learned, but what the lesson was, was constantly changing. After that, they disagreed about water restrictions in California, and Felicity said that it was a mistake to focus on almonds.

Under the table, Jessica tapped Richie's knee with her fingertips. After the two young persons left, she threw out the remaining seitan Bolognese and they dove into some leftover short ribs.

Before Felicity went back to Boston, she ate Indian food with Ezra at Rasika.

The main thing Richie thought about Michael's visiting the farm was, So that's where he's been. He certainly hadn't been around D.C. much, though when he was in the area he stopped by, brought food, helped with the dishes. Sometimes Richie drove past the Shoebox; the lights were on, but that could easily be a timer.

IN THE YEAR since the first deposit, many more had come into Andy's account, all the same amount, $9,999. As far as she could tell by lurking about the Internet, transfers of $10,000 were what banks were required to report. She said nothing to anyone, but she did remove her own funds from that account and put them, about $134,000 altogether, into two other banks, ones that she told no one about and did no business with on the Internet; to make a deposit or withdrawal, she went there in person (she had, in fact, passed her driving test over the summer with an excellent score—the man who tested her guessed she was eighty). Where the leak was, she had no idea—had he hacked her computer somehow? But she knew that, as the money was flowing in, so it would flow out, $460,000 minus $46. Sometime around

Christmas, she'd set about spending it, and she was still spending it—
$10,000 to the local high school's band program, which was about
to be cut, according to the weekly paper; another $10,000 to the
middle school for art-program supplies. She had bought Jonah a used
Honda Civic, paid for Janet to repair her roof when a storm damaged it, bought Emily a Sleep Number bed, a new stove, and a French
saddle. She didn't dare buy Richie anything, but she bought Jessica
a painting they saw one day at a gallery, a watercolor of the Rocky
Mountains, $9,000, which she told Jessica was $900. Jessica seemed
to believe her. She was a little foggy on IRS gift-tax rates, but she
was sure $10,000 was okay. She donated $10,000 apiece to the Sierra
Club, the Save the Children Foundation, The Nation Foundation, the
Smithsonian, and Direct Relief. She donated $15,000 to the Salvation
Army and $5,000 to her local public library. At $100,000, she quailed
for a few weeks—he was certain to find out—but when Richie and
Michael's birthday came round, she'd called Michael on his cell. He
asked how she was, whether she needed anything, had the shipment
of fruit arrived, it was the only valentine he could think to give her.
After talking to him, she knew that he would never say anything,
no matter how much money disappeared, and he apparently wasn't
keeping track—the deposits flowed in regularly, unaffected by what
was paid out. Save the Whales. The Nature Conservancy. The Audu-
bon Society (spring put her in an environmentalist mood). If he ever
challenged her, she thought, she would express complete surprise—
was he not paying her back for the money he stole from her, was this
not her income? The $460,000 was about 3 percent of what he had
taken. And she did declare it, and she did pay her income tax.

In the meantime, she sold a few more items: the pearl necklace
she'd thought she lost that miraculously turned up went for twenty-
three thousand. The pearls were from the west coast of Australia, old
ones, and large. The man who bought it confessed after he paid that
he had gotten it much more cheaply than he expected to. She had
responded, "I'm 95. Value is relative." The world seemed to be awash
in money again. Andy had given up trying to understand it.

Nor did she understand how she had gotten so old—of course,
there was that story about Cousin Gerta, who died at sixty-five of
breast cancer though her mother lived to be 104. Once, when Aunt
Sigrid was ninety-nine (or so Andy's mother had always said), Gerta

came home and couldn't find her anywhere, but eventually she heard noises from the attic—her mother was up there with a flashlight, looking for a frock she'd bought in 1885, so much fabric in the skirt, she hated to see it go to waste; she was going to piece it out for a new dressing gown. The attic stairs were lethally steep, but Aunt Sigrid wasn't fazed. Andy's mother had lived to be eighty; her father, seventy-three; Sven had died young, but he smoked a pipe. The history of the Bergstroms and the Kristjansons was littered with accidents, so Aunt Sigrid might actually have been the norm, not an outlier.

What Aunt Sigrid must have experienced, as Andy did, was the acceleration of the passage of time. She might have been bored, and not only with the news, where the ever-more-childlike newscasters put forth ever-more-childlike theories about passing events. She watched movies, but every announcer, every filmmaker, every actress, every actor she watched on TCM eventually became younger than she was by a generation or more; every writer of every great novel died before he or she learned what he or she had set out to learn. She tried *Dombey and Son,* she tried *In Search of Lost Time,* she tried *Clarissa,* she tried *Ulysses,* which was not as long but much more difficult. As she read these (and she read every word), even the most carefully observed passions and problems seemed to Andy to be those of youth and only fleetingly important. But at least they were there to read; she was endlessly grateful that she had been so stupid for so long, saved some pleasures for these days she had never expected to experience.

Ah, Frank. Vanished without a trace. The picture of him on her bedside table didn't look like him; there was nothing in the Hut that smelled of him or held his shape. Nothing she did in the garden—separating and replanting bulbs, watering, fertilizing, taking in the fragrance of the lavender, the irises, the clematis, the Russian sage, weeding, watering—reminded her of him or of her former self. He was not to be found in books, or in the looks or demeanor of her children or grandchildren. Janet was getting more and more like Andy's own mother; Richie and Michael more and more like Sven; Emily and Jonah, Binky and Tia, Leo, even Chance—whatever Frank had been had receded in them. Always elusive, he had at last eluded her. He was forever young, too, since what she remembered most vividly about him was the contrast between the boy she knew before the war—impulsive, selfish, enthusiastic, passionate, but not hard—and the young man she knew after—wary, ambitious, amorous, desperate. In honor of him, she sent something to Guthrie, an REI gift card for five hundred dollars. It was an involving project, offloading sums of money. It must not result in gratitude or suspicion or objects' making their way into the Hut. She thought of Debbie. She thought of Claire. She thought of Henry and Jesse. Alexis! She had never met Alexis, but Richie spoke highly of her. A little college fund would be nice—say, twenty-five thousand this year and twenty-five thousand next year. After that, they would see.

2016

THERE WERE certain things that no one talked about at the Denby Café, and one of them was who was buying, actually paying for, the machinery that was popping up here and there. Jesse had gone into serious debt for a new tractor and planter six years before, and then, right after that, planters were introduced that could plant twenty-four rows of corn in one pass, and do it all night, because the tractors and planters were equipped with GPS control and bright lights, which meant twenty-four-hour-a-day planting and harvesting, at least if there were enough people on the farm to man the shifts. Jesse recognized that, at last, farming had fulfilled its industrial potential. These huge machines were expensive—delve as he might into his accounts, Jesse could not see how he, or anyone, could make the kind of money that paid for such machinery, and you couldn't buy it cooperatively, since, because the weather was so iffy, everyone had to be planting at the same time. Every year now since 2013 (eleven inches of snow on the first of May followed by fifty degrees the next day, which melted the snow, and then ninety degrees six days later, which evaporated the moisture almost completely; according to Jesse's moisture sensors, the snow hadn't done much to rectify drought conditions from the year before), the pressure had been growing to plant more and more quickly. '14 and '15 hadn't been that bad, but it seemed as though everyone panicked. First it was the Sensordrones that reported moisture levels all over the farm every three hours, and then two more of those giant machines popped up, one at the Whiteheads' and one at a big farm everyone knew was owned by Cargill and was farmed by five Hispanic guys. These days, you would see things in the *Torch* like "As of May 3, 21% of the acres devoted to corn were planted. As of May 10, the number was 78%."

In principle, Jesse should not have been opposed to these changes. Hadn't he always been the one to advocate for the most precise, the most efficient, the most scientific, noninstinctual methods? Hadn't he been very patient with his father, with the stories about the chickens and the hogs and the dairy cows, the oats and the horses, and wetting your finger in your mouth and holding it out in front of you to test the direction of the wind? Hadn't he been a little thrilled when he referred to everything about the farm as "inputs" and "results"? But he was sixty. Maybe every sixty-year-old deplored change, said that things had gone too far, recalled the good old days of whatever? When he complained about something at supper, Jen laughed at him, not with him.

He complained of not having enough land. He had almost nine hundred acres; to make it, you needed a thousand now, or two thousand. ADM and Cargill and other investors were buying up the old farms, putting on them as tenants farmers from California who had lost their properties to drought. At least, that's what longtime denizens said at the Denby Café. How could those folks from Los Banos afford to pay thirteen thousand dollars per acre? And rising, since the High Plains Aquifer was about drained and irrigation was a thing of the past, and so Iowa land had gotten ever more valuable (for the time being, said Felicity, who emailed him photos of glacier retreat and viewed the desertification of the "interior" as inevitable). Who would give a stranger a ten-million-dollar loan? Especially when Ralph Coester, at the Northern Iowa Bank in Usherton, always frowned and shook his head at Jesse Langdon, though even in the drought of 2012 he had never missed a payment. Ralph had given him the money for seed this year, but reluctantly—whereas he had once just signed the papers, and pushed them back across his desk with a smile, this year he'd read them over and over on his computer screen, tapping this key and that key, frowning, clucking. Then he said, "Seed gotten to be a big investment, you know. Gus Whitehead told me he puts the seed in the tanks along with the pesticide, does the job lickety-split, and then takes off. This year he's heading for Chile. Can you imagine that?" No, Jesse could not. Was Ralph bankrolling refugees from the Central Valley? Certainly not. But there were a lot of things that people used to talk about at the café that they didn't talk about now. The place was mostly dead quiet—the only sounds were slurping and chomping.

One morning at breakfast, he said to Jen, "When you were a kid, did you ever imagine living somewhere else?"

She said, "Sure. Didn't you?"

Jesse thought for a moment and said, "I don't think I did. My dad loved the farm so much that he always made it sound terribly romantic."

"But he lived for a while in that house where some uncle killed himself. That didn't spook him?"

"If they delved into the whys and wherefores of that, I never heard about it. Why would it have to do with farming and not with, say, a hopeless love affair?"

"I don't know. I just vaguely remember the gossip."

"You didn't answer my question."

"Well, there was the Miss Kitty fantasy, where I imagined myself living in Dodge City and running a saloon. I think I was five. Then there was the Christine McVie fantasy. We would be living in London. I guess I was eleven or twelve then. Daddy bought me a ukulele after I pestered him enough. I did spend that summer in Washington, D.C., interning for Congressman Leach. Before I left, I imagined never coming home. That lasted a month. What about you?"

"Well, my uncle Frank kept inviting me to New York City. He would send me postcards of various sights we could see. He was all set to paint the town red. Uncle Henry had me to Chicago a couple of times. I don't really mind going to see Annie in Milwaukee and fishing in the lake. But back then, I was sort of afraid of New York, or of Uncle Frank. It seemed disloyal to write to him, to talk to him, to go shooting with him, so visiting him in New York would be a big betrayal."

"Disloyal to whom? Your uncle Frank was like the family god."

"Oh, to my dad. He never said anything, but I knew by the look on his face when he handed me a letter. They papered it over, but they weren't close."

"You know, did I ever tell you about the time I was sitting out on the porch with your dad? It was hot. Your mom was talking all the time about being 'left behind.' So your dad turned to me and said, 'Doesn't she realize that we've already been left behind? Look around—the landscape is empty.' He laughed, but he looked blue."

Now Jesse said, "That's the tragedy of life, I guess—you can only be in one place at a time."

Jen said, "This is the place I chose. I don't mind."

After a moment, Jesse said, "I don't either, baby." And they both knew that, these days, she was the reason he didn't mind.

GUTHRIE LIKED Iowa City. He had a room in a house with two other guys and a girl on East Washington Street. He kept completely to himself. His job was at the mall in Coralville, "Ice Arena Representative." His boss at the mall told him he was to "represent and present" the ice arena to mall customers, so that this "absolutely unique Iowa attraction" would not go to waste. Guthrie, who was a good skater, didn't mind whooshing here and there. Other than "Do you rent skates?," the most common question he got was "What in the world is this?" He would smile and say, "This is a unique recreational opportunity, right here in Coralville. Would you like me to help you?" He would skate gracefully backward, shifting his hips from side to side, smiling his welcome, feeling like a character straight out of Lake Wobegone.

It was an easy job that paid a little something, and, a bonus, he didn't have to feel his dad's worried eyes boring into the back of his head, assessing his "state of mind." Iowa City, everyone said, was suddenly ringed with pot farms—in some bars, they said, you could get high just sitting in your booth, sniffing the air. At the VA hospital, he chatted with several sympathetic counselors about his anxieties. He thought that he got the most out of the Eye Movement Desensitization and Reprocessing sessions. The counselor was a woman about his mom's age, Dr. Kingston, who had grown up on a farm in Illinois. She always wore sensible shoes, but almost at once she noticed that while he was talking he would stare at her shoes, so she made him look at her hand. Which memory kept coming back to him?

Guthrie closed his eyes.

Dr. Kingston said, "No, open your eyes."

Guthrie opened his eyes.

She said, "Tell me the story."

"We were guarding a checkpoint. I guess there were about six of us. The road was clear. So this kid comes down the road with a Coke can in his hand. I'm guessing he was maybe seven, but the kids there acted older, even though they were very small. He was a cute kid; he had sandals on—I noticed that. Maybe a blue shirt. Anyway, he threw the can into the air, and someone shot it; it was like a game for just a second. I guess we thought it might be a bomb; it wasn't beyond them over there to use a kid to deliver a bomb in a Coke can."

Dr. Kingston nodded.

Guthrie cleared his throat. He said, "Anyway, the Coke can broke up and flew into the air, and then someone shot the kid, right in the neck, I saw the blood spurt out on his shirt, into the air; the air was clear. He got this look on his face. We just let the body lie there. We were afraid of it. The longer it lay there, the more afraid of it we got. I kept expecting it to blow up any second. Maybe an hour later, some Iraqis picked it up. It didn't blow up." He shrugged.

"What is the most disturbing image you have? Tell me, but stare at my hand, let your gaze follow my hand."

She put her hand about a foot in front of his face and moved it back and forth. Guthrie stared at her hand, and he could feel his eyeballs swiveling, back and forth, back and forth. After a moment, he said, "I think I shot him."

The hand kept moving.

She said, "Did you shoot him?"

Guthrie thought for a very long moment, then said, "I don't know."

She was well trained. She didn't react or stop moving her hand. She said, "Do you remember lifting your weapon or looking at the boy through the sight?"

Guthrie said, "I don't know."

"Tell me again."

She kept moving her hand.

"I was afraid of the boy. I meant to hit the Coke can, but when the Coke can was shot, I didn't have time to change my aim, the boy jerked forward so fast."

"Keep talking." His eyeballs went back and forth.

"I was afraid of the boy. I had my hand on my weapon, but I didn't lift it. Someone else shot him. I looked around. I didn't see anything except Private Heller. He was the one who hit the can."

"Maybe the same bullet that hit the can killed the boy."

"Maybe we all shot him. It was ten years ago. I have thought about it and dreamed about it so many times that a thousand boys have been killed, and I can't remember what really happened." He did not add his real thought, which was, What's the difference? Or, Maybe I saved that boy from joining ISIS. Or being beheaded by ISIS.

Dr. Kingston prescribed him some Zoloft.

They got into a reassuring routine—twelve sessions. He met interesting women at the ice rink (he didn't dare go into bars, except sometimes for the music and the weedy fragrance), but in fact, he forgot about sex completely. Zoloft was good for that.

Iowa City was a place where people could and did stall out forever. Seated along the bar in the Mill Restaurant was a line of customers that hadn't changed in thirty years, being served by bartenders ten years older than Guthrie was. If you were from Oelwein or Spencer or Denby, you could wash ashore in Iowa City and be so sated with ease and pleasure that you would never move on, which was not the case in Ames. Ames took them in and popped them out. Iowa City took them in and kept them—that was the difference between pain and pleasure, Guthrie supposed. He had been living here two and a half years, and he did feel better than he had at the Usherton Motel 6, but he also felt that he was reaching a point of no return: another year and he would buy a house on American Legion Road and grow a beard to his waist. He was thirty-two now, a disappointment to everyone but himself and Dr. Kingston, who thought she had done a good job with him. He gave himself six months to come up with a plan. If, when he saw Felicity at Thanksgiving, he still hadn't thought of anything, he would put himself in her hands.

THE CORN WAS knee-high on the Fourth of July. This was not a good thing. Jesse had never, even in 2012, seen corn that was only knee-high on the Fourth of July—hybrid seed didn't waste time like that. The June weather had been dry, but not in-the-bottom-five-years-of-the-century dry. After the downpours of mid-May, some farmers had replanted seed with a shorter growing season and a lower yield. Jesse had thought of it, but hadn't dared go back to the bank for more money to buy the "inputs," and so he had ended up doing what his father had always done—hoping for the best. The problem was not the lack of moisture; it was the weeds. In spite of all the herbicide he had used, more than he had ever used before, the weeds were thriving, and not only the velvetleaf, but the foxtail, the thistles, everything. It was evident that they were sucking whatever moisture there was right out of the soil. Weeds always grew fast and produced seed almost instantly. Corn and beans and, for that matter, peas, tomatoes, zucchini, and peppers, were the slowpokes, rather like educated couples who produced a single precious child when they were in their thirties. If the weeds flourished, you had to get them out before their seed distributed itself (his dad, for example, had never allowed the kids to pick dandelions and blow the seedheads into the air; he had gone around the yard when they first came up and pulled them one by one).

Jesse had cultivated the corn once in June, but the soil was so dry that it had lifted off in waves. In the first few days after he did it, he'd thought he might have gotten control of the weeds, but they came up again, flourishing. There was a part of him that expected this to be his worst crop ever. Everyone at the café was complaining about the glyphosate, which had, apparently, given up the ghost at last, overwhelmed by Darwinian selection. And the Monsanto reps were nowhere to be seen, had nothing to suggest. Jen said that they would be too busy offshoring their money to address customer concerns. Jesse got into his truck every morning and drove around Denby and Usherton, even down toward Grinnell and past Ames to Boone, just looking at fields. Some were better, some were worse. He did not feel singled out, but he did feel his scientific certainties dissipating. He almost never opened the computer, not even to read e-mails from Felicity about record droughts in France, tornadoes in Ontario, the collapse of the oil business in North Dakota, locusts in Minneapolis paving the airport runways so that planes were grounded. As always, Felicity communicated these events with a kind of upbeat fascination (lots of exclamation points!!!!!!) that did not seem to indicate fear. She communicated about Ezra Newmark in the same way—no passion, no pain, only detached enjoyment. His mother had hair to the back of her knees! She owned a yarn shop in Delhi, New York, that was mostly mail-order!!!! She had knitted a lace bedspread on size 1 needles! Queensize!!!! Ezra was surprisingly well endowed for a man of his stature!!!! Jesse and Jen got a good laugh out of this one—it was the oversharing they had always expected from Felicity, the girl whose great-aunt gave her a picture book about the nature of reproduction when she was five.

Felicity was fine, Guthrie was fine (or, at least, Jesse and Jen agreed to always say this), Perky was home from Syria, working at Fort Bragg. He was a major now. No one knew what he did, but he was successful at whatever it was. Jesse knew, even though he and Jen never talked about it, that this was all that mattered. Once you were in your sixties, your own fate was unimportant.

He stepped onto the back porch, slipped off his boots, and checked the thermometer. Ninety-eight degrees, nothing to remark upon anymore. It was almost lunchtime, and there would be pork loin from the night before in the refrigerator, but he wasn't hungry yet. He went into his office, opened a drawer, and checked the available balance on his Citicard—$5,987.23. Then he opened the computer, went to the Weather Underground, and checked the national temperature map. All red, just a little orangey-yellow in Maine, the Upper Peninsula, and around Bellingham, Washington. Then he looked at Vancouver—beautiful there, yellow shading to green. The towns in British Columbia had amusing names: Chilliwack, Coquitlam, Squamish. He clicked on Orbitz. There were, in fact, flights from Des Moines to Dallas to Vancouver, daily flights, as if people made that trip all the time. He booked flights for two and a nice hotel for a week, reserved a car, put it on the credit card with fifteen hundred to spare. He had to get away from the weeds and the dust. It felt just then like a matter of life and death. He rummaged around in the desk for their passports, which Felicity had made them apply for in 2009. They had never used them.

The weather was ideal in Vancouver, no fires this year, seventy-five during the day, and congenially sunny, about sixty at night, but they only enjoyed it for one day. Maybe if Jesse had told Felicity where they were going for their little vacation, she would have warned them, but maybe not. There was nothing in the paper the morning of the riots but a notice that there would be a peaceful protest against the Chintar Pipeline beginning that afternoon at one in Jonathan Rogers Park, proceeding from there to City Hall, and then to a "Rock the People" concert put on by local bands in Douglas Park. There was no sign of trouble in the morning. Jesse went out onto the balcony of their room with his cup of coffee. They would go to Granville Island for lunch—there was some kind of famous crafts market there—then come back and watch the rally, then go to the concert. Nothing bad ever happened in Canada; well, maybe in Quebec, but not in Vancouver. Well, maybe about ice hockey. Something bad had happened about ice hockey in 2011. After only one day, it was the best vacation they had ever taken. It made Jesse want to go into the heirloom-tomato business.

When all the people first started running toward them as they were walking down Cambie Street toward the concert venue, Jesse's first thought was "bomb"—that was probably everyone's first thought after the Boston Marathon bombing. There had been no explosion, not even a popping sound. But people were terrified—Jesse could see it in their faces and the handbags and cell phones they dropped as they ran. Rubes that they were, he and Jen kept standing, staring, holding hands. Then they saw the bodies on the ground, at least five of them, and the line of police in helmets, their weapons raised, marching toward them, stepping over the bodies and the signs the protesters had been carrying vowing resistance against the Trudeau government. Felicity would have told them that Trudeau had vowed to get the Chintar Pipeline built no matter what was going on in the oil market, that he had pushed through laws that outlawed protest and imposed draconian punishments on any sort of "insurgent and unauthorized references to so-called climate change." Planes, especially private planes, could not even fly over or near the tar sands, and all analyses of effluents or river or lake pollution were designated as Top Secret; leaking any findings was punishable by years in prison. Felicity did tell them these things when they finally got home. But first, before that could happen, they were taken into custody, handcuffed with painfully tight yellow textile handcuffs, and pushed into the back of a van, where there were at least twelve other people, some of them bleeding. By nightfall, but not before, they were in separate jail cells in separate wings of the Vancouver police station. Late that night, Jesse was ordered over and over to reveal who was behind the protest and who was funding "his" campaign to undermine Canadian national security. Whenever Jesse said that he was just a tourist, he had a farm in Iowa, his hotel was in that neighborhood, his inquisitors laughed. They demanded to see his passport, but they had taken his wallet, and his passport was back in the safe in his hotel. They said, "Why should we believe you, mister?" He held out his hands—knobby, rough, years of grime under his fingernails. They kept Jen for the night, him for two nights, but they lost interest in him—he thought they only kept him for the second night because they had forgotten all about him.

When they got out, they still had three days left. They walked around the city, recognizing its beauty, but in a state of shock. It was as hard to get up and out in the morning as it was to stay in bed, snuggled under the covers. Jesse had never been so simultaneously reluctant to move and restless. They flew home. When they got into their car at the airport in Des Moines, the thermometer registered 105 degrees.

When the call came, three days after they got back (still sweaty hot at midnight, only nine p.m. West Coast time, though), what Annie said seemed like garble to him. Even as he turned over and repeated it to Jen, he didn't understand what he was saying.

"She's dead."

"Who?"

"My mom."

Jen sat up, threw off the sheet. "Oh my God!"

"Annie was locking the car, and lost sight of her, and when she went out onto the beach, Mom had disappeared."

"What does that mean?"

"Something called a 'rogue wave.' They found the body just before sunset."

Even once they were fully awake, this did not seem possible. His mom was eighty-six years old, but when she visited the farm, she seemed unchanged and unchangeable, permanently determined to do what she had decided to do. Once Jesse's dad had told him how they came to marry—all his mom's idea, she was twenty, and it had worked out (here his dad had given him a bear-hug—odd thing for a farmer). It might be that some kids (Felicity, for example) analyzed their parents' marriages looking for signs and symptoms, but Jesse had never done that. The only evidence of Lois's age was her obsession with trying this delicacy or that, and not just at Lunds or Whole Foods, but wherever they were "sourced," as she called it. She had gotten obsessed with smoked oysters, gone to Scotland—there had been a little accident on that trip, driving on the wrong side of the road, that scared the pants off her and the driver of the car she didn't quite hit (a little scrape, knocked off the sideview mirror). She had gotten obsessed with lobster, gone to Maine; gotten obsessed with barbecue, gone to Kansas City. They had joked at Christmas—was she going to get obsessed with tomatoes and go to Hoboken?

And then she had to try abalone before she died—all the items on her bucket list were food. Annie had agreed to take her to Monterey, Jesse had agreed to contribute some money and forgotten all about it.

The next day, there was more information, but none that made his mom's fate less spooky. The beach was called Monastery Beach, south of Carmel. It was notorious for these events—its dangers were frequently underestimated by tourists because nearby beaches were safer. Annie was out of her mind, not exactly at the surprise of it, but at how it fit their mother's personality, just to be swept away like that, doing something she was determined to do.

And Jesse had to ask the question that would have seemed trivial to everyone else in the whole world: "Did she get to eat the abalone?"

"No," said Annie. "She got to look at them, because there is an abalone farm on the wharf, but the restaurant wasn't serving any right then. She loved the sand dabs, though." There was a long silence and then they hung up.

After the service, a week later, Jesse had the box of ashes buried beside his dad's box, as far as possible from Uncle Frank. His mom hadn't liked Uncle Frank, thought he had ruined Aunt Minnie's life.

JANET HAD no idea where she picked up the infection. She would have had a little cut, maybe from stepping on a stone or a shard of glass, and then the cellulitis spread from her instep, over the top of her foot, and up the inside of her ankle, at first only red, hardly swollen, but then red, hot, painful, sometimes as if invisible knives were stabbing her. It was Saturday. Eliza, at the knitting shop, made her go up to Seton Medical Center, which was a bit of a drive in the weekend traffic, and she had to cancel the afternoon dog walk (four dogs plus Antaeus), that was forty dollars down the drain. And then the antibiotic, erythromycin, wasn't cheap, either. The scary part was when the doctor said that if there was no improvement in thirty-six hours she should come back. She did not call her mother, she did not call Jonah, she did not call Emily, because she knew that if she did they would look on the Internet and see what she saw—faces destroyed, legs swollen like homemade sausages, the words "flesh-eating bacteria."

There was no improvement Tuesday morning, and the doctor, whose name she now knew, Dr. Dalal, changed her antibiotic to doxycycline hyclate. It was very expensive, and the brochure included said that it was used to treat malaria, which somehow made her leg, now swollen to the knee, throb. She was to come back on Thursday if there was no improvement, or, to be safe, even if there was improvement.

There was no improvement. In fact, once she was staring at her leg along with Dr. Dalal, she noticed blisters beginning to form under the skin, and when Dr. Dalal touched the largest of them with her gloved finger (it was maybe the size of a BB), it seemed to open up. Dr. Dalal was sending her to Stanford Health Care by ambulance, thirty miles away. While she was telling Janet this (Janet could not drive, because her infection was in her right leg; best not wait any longer, just to be sure), Janet sat there nodding and throbbing, almost in rhythm, and then she texted Mary to please take charge of Antaeus. ("Sure! You off to somewhere nice?") When the two nurses helped her to the ambulance, she could hardly put weight on her right foot, even though she had gotten up, made her coffee, and driven to the hospital without much difficulty an hour earlier. Janet hadn't been to Palo Alto since emptying her house seven years before. She always left the coast through Santa Cruz or Daly City, picturing the ridge that 92 crossed above the Crystal Springs Reservoir as a kind of Berlin Wall that she dared not breach.

The ambulance wasn't screaming, just transporting. It was the kind with a window, a tricked-out Ford truck, so Janet could see the eucalyptus groves. Normally, she hated eucs and never minded going into a diatribe about why they were the worst possible tree to import to California, but now she appreciated, even loved, the sunlight speckling through the branches, perhaps a sign of mortality.

Her leg throbbed the affirmative, and she cried out. "Almost there," said the EMT—oh, Rob, his name was, right there on his shirt. Was she becoming delirious? One thing that could happen with cellulitis was an overwhelming massive infection, foot to leg to liver to heart to brain to grave. She took a deep breath and reminded herself that another of her conversational themes was that she was old enough to die, sixty-eight. The last thing she wanted to do was end up like her mother. She said that all the time.

They came down the mountain and she lay back, watching the reflection of the reservoir ripple across the ceiling of the ambulance.

And then they were flying down 280, and then there she was, being wheeled into the very emergency room where she had nearly given birth to Jonah, and what was the difference, birth, death, a mere twenty-four years, nothing really, nothing at all.

What was different was that, once she was hooked up to the drip and on some sort of painkiller (she ignored everything the doctor said about which antibiotics and which painkiller they put her on, and so what if they decided she was demented), she actually looked around, first at her room, then out the window at the top of one Norfolk pine, several eucs, and the sky. Those three days here with Jonah she remembered not at all, except the sight of Jonah himself, lanky, cross-eyed, darling as could be. And the sight of her own nipple disappearing into his tiny mouth. When the administrative person (not quite human, but humanlike) came in late in the afternoon and asked for her contact information, she gave him Jared's name and a phone number that was possibly correct. He handed her her bag; she gave him her Medicare card. She was lucky to have that; soon, the Republicans would be in control and repealing all forms of Socialism. She scowled at the thought and the doctor scuttled out. She was alone in the room, and, she thought, the thing that was giving her reason to live was that view she had seen through the ambulance window of the light at the crest of the mountain, the trees through the ambulance window, something beautiful that had nothing at all to do with Janet Langdon Nelson.

The hours passed eventlessly but strangely, the pain coming and going randomly, the heat in her leg seeming to flow here and there, the certainty in her mind rising and falling about whether she would lose her leg or lose her mind or lose her life. She had no computer, and she discovered, as soon as she got some time to herself, that her phone was dead. All the better. She thought about Lois, though she hadn't seen her in years and could only imagine her young—younger than she herself was.

Sometime in the middle of the night, she awoke when a nurse was changing her bag. The room seemed hot, and her sheet felt sweaty, and in her half-stupor, she was convinced that they had tied her wrists and ankles to the corners of the bed, that she had been screaming, but she had no memory of any dreams at all. Something came out of her mouth, and the nurse said, "Oh, I am sorry. I didn't mean to wake you up! May I get you some water, or anything? I can help you to the bathroom."

Janet said, "No, thank you," and her hands came up and touched the base of her neck, not tied to the bed at all. That was the worst moment, at least in her opinion.

But the doctor's opinion was different. She might have been lying there, thinking of her old house, trying to calculate exactly how far it was from this bed, or wondering what restaurants were still at the Stanford Shopping Center—was that where she had eaten for the first time at the California Pizza Kitchen—but the doctor said that she had skated on the edge of a real crisis, had she heard of MRSA?

Janet did not say, "Of course"; she only nodded.

Well, she didn't have that, but he had thought she might. It took forty-eight hours to grow out the pathogen, but after thirty-six, she did seem to be responding to treatment. And now look at her: her leg was still red, but almost back to normal. Get up and walk around a bit, let's see how your foot feels. Not bad. Thank your immune system; it really drove him bananas the way everyone had turned antibiotics into candy over the last fifty years; he was a vegetarian himself, but what good did it do you? The damage was done. He'd lost a fourteen-year-old boy ten days before, wrestler on the team up in Belmont, lesion on his forearm.

Janet kept quiet. She did not say, "I wouldn't have minded going instead of him." It would not have been a lie.

But she was glad when Mary picked her up and drove her home, when Antaeus jumped into her lap and licked her face, when Emily called and asked her why her phone was dead. Four days, not such a long time.

LATE IN AUGUST, Jesse got a letter that said that his mortgage had been sold to a company based in Delaware called Piddinghoe Investments. He was given instructions about how to go online and order a payment booklet for his payments. His payments would now be due monthly, not, as before, when the harvest was in and sold. He told Jen that had its benefits; he wasn't going to complain about that. His official level of debt was $356,893—not much, he privately thought, compared with the value of the farm. The letter actually left him feeling not bad. At 5 percent interest, his monthly payment wasn't even fifteen hundred. He thought that would be no problem; the crop was poor, but 125 bushels an acre would be enough to get them through the year, and the beans, at least, were better off than the corn. He followed instructions, sent off for his booklet, went about everything with his usual method. He also called Northern Iowa Bank and asked to speak to Ralph Coester. Ralph had left, he was told. Taken a job in Chicago. Ted Kugelhaupt was the loan officer now. Jesse had never met Ted Kugelhaupt, or even heard of him. He said he would get back to them. On August 28, he mailed in his payment and forgot about it.

The first foreclosure notice came in mid-November, a week after he sent in his third payment, a week after he sold his crop, a week after he breathed a sigh of relief because the corn yield was 135 bushels even though the weeds had been a nightmare and an eyesore, causing the harvest to last an extra two weeks, a week after the disastrous presidential election (but he was too distracted to care about that). What he would do in the spring he had no idea, since there was no real replacement for glyphosate, and the Monsanto reps were still scarce on the ground. But that was months away. He went to the Piddinghoe Investments Web site and looked through all the options. There was one, "Have a Problem? Contact a representative," that gave a phone number (877 877-6543), a chat option, and an e-mail option. He tried the phone number three times and never got through to a "banker." He tried the chat option, and wrote back and forth for a while with "Kathy," who said that she would look into the issue and get back to him within twenty-four hours. He e-mailed the manager, the repayments department, and the customer representative. Nothing. Finally, he drove into Usherton and spoke to Ted Kugelhaupt, a nondescript thirty-year-old who sucked his lips and nodded his head the whole time Jesse was explaining his problem, then said that the bundle had been sold, two bundles had been sold, that was all he knew about it, there was no recourse through *this* bank. And he knew nothing about Piddinghoe Investments—had Mr. Langdon sent his checks by registered mail, and had the checks cleared? Yes, they had. Must be a paperwork problem, then, said Ted. He should try that angle. Otherwise, Ted—suck, suck, nod, nod—couldn't help him. And he didn't know where Ralph Coester was. Maybe Cleveland? He had heard something about Cleveland. When Jesse got home, he realized that since Northern Iowa Bank had sold the bundles of mortgages the paperwork problem was theirs, but when he tried to call Ted Kugelhaupt back, Ted could not be reached.

It was rather like the week in Vancouver followed by his mother's death—it took Jesse and Jen a very long time to assimilate what was happening, ten days for them to go from "Maybe we should call a lawyer," to calling the lawyer, then another five days to get an appointment. The lawyer had another case with stacks of discovery to be done. Better for Jesse to sort through the paperwork that he had in his files, and refrain from paying the December payment, sending along by certified mail a notice seeking all paperwork appertaining to the mortgage. After that, silence. Jen said, "Well, no news is good news."

They went to D.C. for Christmas. The day they left, Jesse got a letter stating that their "complaint(s) was being looked into. We request your patience." Guthrie couldn't go with them because the mall's busiest season was Christmas, but he promised to come on the 26th. Perky said he would be there, but then his leave was canceled because of the new crisis in Ukraine. They all knew that this might be Uncle Henry's last Christmas. It turned out that he had had what he called "a mini–heart attack" right around his birthday in October, and only Riley knew about it; even Richie didn't hear about it until he and Jessica went there for Thanksgiving. Henry wrote everyone a letter saying that he was fine and not to worry; then Richie wrote everyone a letter saying that Henry was not fine, and Christmas in D.C. was the best option. What with deploring Lois's "accident," meeting Ezra for the first time, making their way around D.C. in the ice and snow, and trying not to seem alarmed about Uncle Henry, who smiled a lot but never got out of his chair, there were enough spurs for general anxiety. It was difficult enough to relate the tale of Vancouver two times too many oohs and ahs and jeezes: the foreclosure problem seemed to have subsided enough to go unmentioned. The interesting thing was the pile of presents from Andy—they dwarfed the tree. Among them were a new MacBook for Felicity, a new piano for Alexis, a beautiful brown shearling coat for himself, and the most stylish black Gucci boots for Jen that he had ever seen. Felicity allowed as how Andy had requested sizes, and Felicity of course knew them. Felicity said, "She buys all sorts of presents, but she told me the most expensive ones go to the youngest recipients." That, Jesse thought, explained the piano, which was a baby grand, a Yamaha.

After Christmas, they were stuck in D.C. for an extra two days because of ice, snow, and hail at both O'Hare and Hartsfield-Jackson.

way people got through the winter in the countryside, all the way until the 1950s, had been a sort of hibernation—sleeping from sunset to sunup (some fifteen hours) saved heat and food. For three days, they were really cut off—no Internet, no TV, no recharging the cell phones, no mail. Sun came up after seven-thirty, went down before five—not quite as bad as France. Jen decided to read *Middlemarch,* and Jesse went through every *New Yorker* that Felicity had stacked in her room. They ate mostly out of the pantry, put the cuts of meat from the freezer in a box sunk into the snow by the northwest corner of the house, where, in spite of the fluctuation in temperatures, it had a chance of staying chilled. It was Jen's idea to surround the meat with bags of frozen peas and beans as a gauge. They talked fondly of Lois, who would have cooked every roast and stew the first day before burying them outside—not just survival, but gourmet survival.

The morning after the blizzards had stopped, the electricity came back on and the road was finally plowed. The full results of the November election still weren't announced; after eight years of Obama, everyone was certain there'd be a Republican sweep, and it looked like the Senate and House were going dramatically in that direction. But even the presidential tally wasn't in. Because of the twenty-three-state Election Day power outage, there was no telling how many votes were lost, or worse. Rumors abounded that the grid had been hacked, since the polar vortex alone could not have caused the complete electrical shutdown—in, say, Los Angeles.

There was a knock on the door. It was Sheriff—what was his name?—Bill Jenks, standing on the front porch. Jesse thought that there must be some disaster, that the county was sending people out to see if everyone was okay, so he opened the door with a smile, and Sheriff Jenks handed him a paper: Request for a donation? Tickets to some fund-raiser? But it was a copy of a notice of sale, and the property being sold was this very farm—Jesse recognized the parcel number. Sheriff Jenks said, "Shoulda given you this ten days ago, but no one could get here. You can appeal that, and put off the date." The sale date on the paper was February 1. Jesse didn't say anything, he was so thunderstruck. Sheriff Jenks handed him a pen, and for a moment Jesse thought of refusing to sign, but he did sign—intimidated by the uniform, no doubt. Sheriff Jenks said, "Well, then," and made his way carefully down the icy steps and over to his vehicle, which still had three inches of snow frozen on the roof. But the sky was clear, brilliantly clear, almost blinding, in every direction.

Jen was in the kitchen, enjoying the hot water, humming to herself. He set the paper beside the sink and walked out the back door. It was freezing cold and he didn't feel a thing, he was so enraged. Moments later, the door slammed open behind him, and Jen said, "Is this what I think it is?"

"If you and I both think it is a notice of foreclosure, sale, and eviction, then we agree on what it probably is."

"How can that happen?"

"I think the real question is, how can it happen this fast, without any response from goddamned Piddinghoe Investments, or the bank."

"Can we get into town?"

"Not until Monday." It was Thursday. "There's no point going tomorrow, because the state and county offices are on four-day weeks. I'm not sure we would get there tomorrow, anyway. The sheriff's car had chains. We don't know what the roads are like." Jesse called the lawyer there, but there was no answer.

It was a difficult weekend. Winds were so strong that they blew the TV dish off the roof of the house, and Jesse had to cover the west windows with plywood. No branches broke through any part of the roof, but they did fall all around, littering the surface of the snow, which, even after melting and freezing, came as high as the porch floor and drifted much higher in some spots. What had seemed to be an amusing adventure now became a test of patience, and since the upstairs was closed off to save on heat, there was no escape from one another, either. They agreed to blame Ralph Coester, for lack of anyone else, but Jesse felt blameworthy, too, though he didn't know why: For going in debt in the first place? For not being a good enough role model to be able to bring at least one of his sons into the farm? For priding himself for so long on his clear-eyed and unsentimental approach? For not going into something else, anything else, and getting out when the getting was good? Even for marrying into a farm family instead of into, say, an engineering family? But Jen was the only girl he ever truly loved. There was another girl he'd asked out, but he now could not remember her name. So he was not going to blame himself for that. On Sunday morning, they had a spat about bacon grease—she had let the grease can get too full, Jesse spilled some when he went to dump it, and then she burst into tears, and he burst into tears, and that was that for rage. On Monday, right after breakfast, they went together into Usherton, to the county courthouse. The results were not good: the paperwork was there, filed by the county attorney on behalf of Piddinghoe Investments, signed by a judge. The old way of having a hearing was gone now, as of last July 1, because the state couldn't afford to have a judicial hearing about every foreclosure; it took too long and clogged the system. If the papers were in order and the evidence went against the mortgage holder, that was that. As for putting off the date, the snow was an act of God, no provision in the law—the sale of the property would go forward as planned. Jesse asked what his recourse was, and the county clerk asked him if he had a lawyer. He named his lawyer. The county clerk said, "I'd get someone else, if I were you."

The days progressed both slowly and quickly. Jesse did get another lawyer, and the lawyer was upbeat at first, but after Jesse had called him the fifth time to see what he thought, he got irritable, until he finally said, "Look, I am doing what I can, all right?" In the meantime, Jen started going into closets and opening drawers and getting boxes from a box store in Usherton (the roads were fine now). She was packing up to leave before Jesse had even admitted that they would have to leave. They said nothing about where they might go. Jesse went out to the machine shed and ran his hand over the tractor, the planter, the cultivator, the rest of the machinery, old and new. He stood and stared for a long time at the lister, which his grandfather had dragged along the rows of corn; once the plants got a foot tall, the machine would mound dirt along the stalks, supporting them. It was like looking at a hatchet and contemplating a wood stove.

After the sale went through—to Piddinghoe Investments—they were given a month to depart. The new owners would be doing the fertilizing and the planting. Jesse was not to go into the fields for any reason.

HENRY COULD NOT help brooding on the loss of the farm, though he hadn't been there in decades. It was surprising how sharp the images and sensations from his childhood were. He had to keep reminding himself that the house he was in when he closed his eyes no longer existed; the house Jesse and Jen were losing was the Frederick place, not the Langdon place. Even so, that sense of lying on his back on the sofa, holding his book (which in his mind was *The Bride of Lammermoor*), seeing the sunlight cross the page in a triangle, moving the book, shading his eyes, thinking about his aching hip simultaneously with thinking about Edgar Ravenswood, who looks like Frank crossing the moor, and what is that, something like the back field. His mother is in the kitchen, talking to Claire and snapping beans for supper. He is planning his getaway. He turns his head and looks out the front window at the two leafy oak trees out there, and the rustling cornfield beyond. It is summer. The corn tassels are undulating in the breeze. He is idle, a pleasure.

He opened his eyes. Really, he was in his own chair, about eight feet from his bed. Through the doorway into the living room, he could hear Alexis playing the piano—she was practicing "Pictures at an Exhibition." She was supposed to perform the whole thing in a recital at the end of May, and she had been practicing assiduously, which, it had to be said, drove Riley out of the house, but Henry didn't mind—he liked the way the pattern of the notes was engraving itself on his brain. He did not think that Mussorgsky had intended his suite to be soothing, but Henry found it so.

The loss of the farm had been so quick that no one could believe it. Jesse had said nothing at Christmas, had seemed fine enough, considering the experience in Vancouver and Lois's amazing end. He had complained only about the weather, but complaining about the weather was the friendliest complaint a person could make. Riley kept Henry fully informed about the blizzards in early January; Riley no longer talked about global warming or climate change, only "climate disruption." Henry knew that she thought her career had been a failure, a beating of her head against the brick wall of capitalism. Often after she looked at Alexis, she looked away. How had she, of all people, invested in a future she knew would never happen? She even showed Henry an article on her phone that some archeologist had written about civilization collapse. The gist of it was that everything a civilization congratulated itself upon ended up precipitating collapse. Yes, Henry thought, Rome, Byzantium, Zapoteca.

Henry listened to the low throbbing accompanied by the melodious tune—da dah di da da da da; doo doo. Alexis was doing a mournfully good job with the music. Then the pounding chords of the next section; Henry didn't remember what it was called. He imagined the Louvre, great halls of columns, marble, light, paintings. He imagined himself walking slowly from one painting to another. He wished he had bothered to go to St. Petersburg and visit the Hermitage. There were many things he had forgotten to do.

Now the tune started high and quickly deepened—the essence of being Russian, maybe. Who was that, Greg Stein, who had specialized in nineteenth-century Russian lit, lectured his students in a booming voice audible from the corridor, sounded and wrote as if he were six five and heavily bearded, but was actually five six and slight. Loved Gogol above all. He had quite a handshake, too. When Henry congratulated him on getting tenure, he had nearly broken Henry's hand, his grip was so strong. Philly. He was from Philly.

People from cities hardly remembered the houses they grew up in. Greg Stein had kicked off the dust of Philadelphia and never looked back—Harvard was where he was born, at least in his own mind. Henry had tried that, but here it was. Every other memory was of the farm now. Walking to school at four with the adored Lillian, ten, wearing his mattress-ticking outfit, holding Lillian's hand, looking up and closing his eyes, feeling her kiss him gently on the lips, hearing her say, "Don't ask every question that you think of today, Henry. Just every other one." Himself saying, "I promise."

Now the finale, loud and a little discordant, drove all other thoughts out of his head. Bom bom bom bom bom. It was beautiful. Loud, then soft. Henry closed his eyes again.

A few minutes later, the Mussorgsky came to a measured end, and there was silence. He heard footsteps. He opened his eyes, and Alexis was standing in the doorway. Henry said, "Beautiful, darling. It's almost there."

"Maybe," said Alexis. "Can I get you anything? I need to go through it one more time."

"I'm fine," said Henry. "I might get up today."

Alexis smiled. She was so built like Charlie that he might as well have been in the room.

"Do it again, then we'll see," said Henry.

She turned, and disappeared.

He heard the bench scrape the floor; then there was a pause. A siren came and went in the distance. Henry shifted in his chair and licked his lips. He should have asked her to refill his water glass. He reached for the Kleenex, and the music began again, those simple notes at the beginning, then the chords, which always seemed so promising and patient, maybe the best opening measures of any music he knew of. That was when the pain came, a sharp but short pain. Henry writhed, clenched his fist, then relaxed, opened his mouth for a little air. The music swelled. Da da da da.

IF FELICITY AND EZRA had been getting along better, they might have uncovered who was behind Piddinghoe Investments more quickly, but every time they got together, at least in person (Felicity was *not* moving to D.C. and Ezra was *not* moving to Boston), they would argue, not about the election (they agreed that the election was a bald-faced power grab by the Corporatocracy), but about an organization called Deep Green Resistance. Ezra hadn't joined DGR, and how did you join? There were no dues or meetings. But he was infected (Felicity's word) by DGR's manifesto, and the infection caused argument outbreaks. It also festered in Felicity's brain, giving her migraine headaches. Even at Uncle Henry's funeral, they'd had a vicious whispering argument in the living room, when Ezra pointed his finger at the light switch as if to shoot it. Felicity knew that her least developed talent was a sense of humor, but still could not help herself.

The theory propounded on the Deep Green Resistance Web site and in books by the DGR founders was that the only way to save a modicum of civilization was to systematically destroy the energy infrastructure right now, and maybe right now was too late; 2013 might not have been too late, but the world had dithered itself into four more years of climate collapse. Felicity's problem with these ideas was that she could see the logic of them—if the world were forced to go local by the destruction of airports, roads, oil and gas pipelines, transmission towers, banks, harbors, the Internet, then, yes, there would be a war, or many wars, but the population would decrease, and the humans who were left would be forced to live the best they could in the environments they found themselves in. Abstractly, Felicity understood the necessity for population collapse of humans in order that other species might have the ghost of a chance, but she thought Ezra skated around the deaths of millions, and seemed to imagine that the items of infrastructure to be destroyed (including windfarms) would be manned only by jerks and assholes who deserved to die. Had there not been a day care in the building that the Oklahoma bombers blew up in '95? Well, yes, said Ezra, but . . . And then he would spout the perfectly logical argument against non- or partial resistance put out by DGR: As energy supplies diminish and get dirtier, one society after another is going to be taken over by ruthless dictators, determined to preserve privilege. The entire world is going to turn into Haiti or Pakistan, and not only will more people die in the end, more overall destruction will be wrought, so that the planet will not be able to recover. The boil of civilization had to be lanced *right now*. Of course, Ezra didn't even have a gun, much less a store of fertilizer, and he didn't kill flies or spiders—he always wanted to see what they would do, so he followed them around his apartment and then opened a window and shooed them out. Felicity considered herself the cold one—the coldest one. Her first thought when her parents lost the farm was "About time." Hadn't she told her dad to switch to organics in 2013? The market was there, and the links between conventional farming, obesity, starvation, and habitat destruction were unequivocal. But how could he afford to take the land out of production for the three years it would take to clear out the chemicals (maybe more)? The farm bill didn't pay for that.

Her second thought was "Why am I crying?"

Nevertheless, they did uncover the primary shareholders in Piddinghoe Investments, and right at the top of the list was Michael Langdon.

ANDY KNEW IT all along, simply by the ebb and flow of money into her account. She kept track. On May 1, there were three deposits right in a row; on May 6, three more; and so on, all through May. As fast as she could, she sent it away—to school districts all over New Jersey and New York, to the New York Public Library, and to all the disaster-relief organizations she could find: floods in Maryland, Norfolk, England, and Denmark; hurricanes in Mexico, the Florida

Keys, and Texas; earthquakes in Russia, India, and Italy; drought relief in Arkansas and Oklahoma; research into enterovirus D68. When Richie told her that the farm had been sold to Cargill for fifteen thousand an acre, about thirteen and a half million dollars, she had pretended to be shocked, but she hadn't been. However, she had stayed up all night writing checks. She kept no records, gave little thought to the IRS—that little thought being, Come and get me, I am ninety-six years old. Her own accounts were down, though, so at the end of May she sold her best item, a Dior gown from 1957 that she had worn to some Upjohn gala for the New York City Ballet. It was cream-colored, with beading at the tiny waist and a silk band that wrapped around the shoulders, highlighting the face, the upswept hairdo, and, as she remembered, the sapphire necklace she had borrowed from Frances Upjohn. It was a beautiful piece, it still fit, and she sold it for forty-six thousand, throwing in the white calfskin elbow-length gloves for free. Michael hadn't called her in a year, but he did send smoked salmon, champagne, and chocolates for Mother's Day.

MICHAEL WAS ELUSIVE, indeed. No more dropping by Richie's condo with bags of take-out, no more laughing with Jessica in the kitchen, no more unsolicited advice about how to get his act together. Their last real conversation had been about the election. Michael's theory was that the Supreme Court had acted wisely—the right was much better armed than the left, so, although deciding for the Republicans had led to roiling protests, they were relatively peaceful. Deciding for the Dems would have triggered a disaster, "if you consider disunion a disaster," which Michael did, at the moment. Then he shrugged, as, Richie had thought, a man with a flat in the Greenwich Peninsula development in the southeast of London might do. A nearby spot was called "Isle of Dogs," which did give Richie a laugh. But as far as Richie knew, Michael still owned the Shoebox. No "For Sale" sign, and the furniture was still there (Richie peeped in the windows). He did not think that he, Richie, was being actively avoided; he thought Michael was back in business, but it was a new sort of business, more adventurous and piratelike, no longer based in having a respectable domestic establishment on the Upper East Side of Manhattan. As soon as Ezra told Richie that Michael had somehow foreclosed on the farm and kicked Jesse and Jen out, it all clicked into place without Richie's even pondering it—first and foremost, that look of rage every time Michael talked about inheriting only a hundred grand from the old man and then finding out that the portion of the farm that Jesse got was worth six times that, then the intermittent teeth-grinding references to Jesse he had made over the years, that the "kid" (Jesse was two years younger than they were) was making all kinds of mistakes, as if Michael knew the first thing about farming. That time—say, two or three years ago—when Felicity mentioned at the table that her dad had refused to try organics, Michael had actually blown his stack and gone on at length about the free market, and if the free market was on the side of Whole Foods, well, so be it—he had no more allegiance to Monsanto than he did to Pan American World Airways. It was the same with feminism, with nuclear power, with solar, with anti-virus vaccines. The truest gauge of the way forward was the free market. Jessica had said, "But the free market is always so late to the game, isn't it?" and Michael had laughed out loud.

At first, the theft of the farm (for that's what it was) didn't bother Richie all that much. But he kept thinking about it. Jesse and Jen had moved in with her brother; he was helping with the farm work, she was looking for a job. They could end up anywhere. The thing Richie wanted most was to hear Michael's side of it—not some slogan about "what's done is done" but the details, what he thought when he was pretending to be broke, how he got off scot-free from the forgery, why it all happened, how he fucking felt now, whether he had been lying about every single thing—but Michael was nowhere to be found. Their mom hadn't heard from him in over a year. Janet sometimes mentioned Chance, since he and Emily were good friends, but Richie couldn't imagine Michael showing up at the ranch and having some tender father-son moment with the cowboy. Frankly, if Michael had ever felt anything for Chance, Richie thought, Loretta had put a stop to it, claimed him for her own until her mom took him away.

It went this way through the summer, into September, into October. Everyone was distracted by the Pakistan/India skirmish, but the president did what Richie thought he should do—he sat on his hands until the Chinese premier, Ji Ling, who was younger than Richie by twenty years, stepped in and told both the Pakistanis and the Indians that China would do the retaliating if a single atomic weapon was deployed, even by accident, since prevailing winds over Beijing were from the west. After the Chinese had disarmed Iran in December, they became the de-facto peacemaker of the world, but peace was getting harder and harder to make; even Richie could see that (they hadn't disarmed the United States, had they, and Vice-President Cotton was still arguing for war).

Of course, Michael showed up at 2:00 a.m. Of course, he was banging on the door to the condo; of course, Richie jumped out of bed, his heart pounding, and ran out to quash the noise. He closed the bedroom door. Jessica was still asleep.

Michael was happy, bouncy, and cheerful. Drunk? High? Not evidently. Flat-bellied and in good shape, neatly bearded—Richie noticed even as he invited him in that the white pattern in his beard was quite similar to Richie's own.

What he wanted to talk about was not the farm; he had forgotten about the farm. Fact was, he was getting married again. Richie hadn't even known that he and Loretta were divorced, and were they? Unlikely, Richie thought. When Richie said, "Why did you bother with the fucking farm?" Michael looked blank, genuinely blank, then said, "Shit! That was a sweet deal. Cargill and ADM were falling over each other trying to get that place."

Richie said, "Do you know what an asshole you are? I've always wondered."

"Do *you* know that land is a commodity, just like anything else? What do you care? It isn't your farm. You never cared about it. I don't believe you care now."

Richie ignored this and said, "I know you did something underhanded." He hadn't known this a moment ago, but now the conviction flooded him. "Or illegal."

Michael shrugged.

Assent.

Michael said, "I did not go looking for the fucking farm."

"Actually, you did go there. I found out. Why did you go there?"

"Oh Jesus, Richie, I was in the neighborhood anyway. Look, irrigation is a thing of the past. The world population is eight billion. If we don't have a vertically integrated food-production system, our kids are done for. There's about three spots left on the planet— well, of course I'm exaggerating—where the food is going to grow, almost, but not quite, no matter what. Why should a bunch of guys go out every February and scratch their heads and say, 'Wale, what'm Ah gonna do this ye-ah?'"

Richie clenched his fists. He could feel the back of his neck heating up. He said, "That isn't Jesse. Jesse isn't a rube, never was. He knows more about farming than you."

"Well, so what? However smart he is, he isn't equipped to do economies of scale. It's no big deal. I, we, bought two bundles of mortgages from that bank. They weren't the only ones, that wasn't the only bank, and I am not the only investor. I was scrolling through the list, and there he was." He shrugged again. Then he put his hand on his shoulder and cracked his neck and moved his jaw left, then right. There was something about this set of movements that told Richie that Michael was sure he would get away with it.

He said, "You foreclosed even though he had made all the payments."

Michael said, "It's been done before."

"Remember that time at the farm? You were screaming about subsidies and how you, as a taxpayer, shouldn't have to subsidize incompetence or stupidity, or whatever you—" Richie felt his back teeth grind together.

Michael smiled his old smile, the sly one. He didn't need his own lobbyist in Congress, or his own bought-and-paid-for flack on the SEC; all he needed was chaos, and there was plenty of that to go around. The smile was still there, the smile that said, "You don't care, really. Your loyalty is to me, really. I know it and you know it."

Richie stared at Michael, then faked a yawn. After a few beats of silence, he said, "Who are you marrying?"

"Do you remember Lynne? She came to your wedding." Michael smiled again.

"The decorator? Your mistress who was just daring Loretta to ask her why she was there?"

"Repurposer. Those days, it was lofts, but she's done all sorts of things. She likes to find architectural gems from certain periods, mostly modernist, and put them back together. She's done three

Frank Lloyd Wrights. With the flat roofs and all the windows, they tend to deteriorate." He palmed his iPhone and handed it to Richie. Plain woman, glasses, gray hair, practical look. No resemblance to any model or movie star ever. Richie stood up and said, "Get the fuck out." He handed back the phone; then, softening, he made it sound like a bit of a joke: "It's three o'clock in the morning, for Christ's sake."

"Fuck, yeah!" said Michael. But he hoisted himself out of the sofa, grabbed his jacket, and left, not forgetting to yank the door open so hard that it hit the wall and knocked into a framed photograph of Jessica and her brother and sister on the day Jessica graduated from high school, gowned in white that reflected in her face, her hair in a shiny bowl cut. Michael thumped down the stairs.

2018

AFTERWARD, Richie didn't know what to think. He hadn't seen Michael for months, nor did he hear from him, call him, e-mail him, or drive past the Shoebox. If Jessica was aware of that visit in November, she said nothing about it; she was such a sound sleeper that she could easily not have heard a thing. There was a part of him that had forgotten about it, the part of him that reveled in Leo's Thanksgiving visit with Britt and Jack and their baby, Mona. Jack was ten now, and it looked as though he modeled his every word and gesture on Leo. Even Britt laughed that she could ask Jack if he wanted cereal for breakfast or eggs, and the first thing he did was look at Leo. Leo appeared to feel comfortable with being adored; he was affectionate with Mona, who at nine months was grabbing table edges, pulling herself up, and crowing ecstatically. Jessica would sit on the sofa and set Mona astride her knees, and within moments, they would both be laughing. When Richie described how Leo was as a toddler, everyone laughed at that, too. Maybe all that resistance had been funny, and Richie hadn't had the sense to see it.

But there was a part of him that didn't forget Michael, or, at least, that was how he reconstructed it after the fact. He looked up that girl whom they once left floundering in the freezing water down the road from their house in Englewood Cliffs—older than they were, bulky and contemptuous, Donna Fitzgerald then. On Facebook there were four, one of whom had once worked as a steamfitter. No way, with a girl who might have married, to find her and ask what she remembered about that incident. There were fourteen William Westons—which one had supplied the hammer that Richie had slugged Michael with when Michael sneered at his tent-erecting failures? Alicia Tomassi—there were eight of those on Facebook and seven on LinkedIn. None appeared to be an artist, though one looked rather like the old Alicia, who, he remembered, put it about that he and Michael both attacked her. "And lucky for her" was what Michael said. And so, if he could line up the witnesses, how would they testify? Would his congressional colleagues remember Richie's bike leaning against Michael's Ferrari? Would Jerry Nadler remember giving him the oh-yeah-I-get-it-now look a week or so after Richie voted for the Iraq Resolution, and Nadler saw them walking side by side out of a restaurant? Nothing had rankled quite so much in that article in the *Times* as the line about Richie being the younger twin. He had crushed the paper and thrown it against the wall—they called themselves reporters! How often had he thought about these things in the intervening months? How often did he tell himself the past was past and he was over it, and for that year, Michael *did* take him in hand, did make him get his act together. Did *not* tease him about how he might sleep with Jessica (his thoughts lingered over this one, and Leo entered the picture, only to be consciously banished). Did these thoughts form a pattern, or just appear to form a pattern in retrospect?

And why was he out after midnight, why did he wake up with a raging headache and lie there beside the person he cared most about, and, after finding no ibuprofen in the bathroom, decide that right now he had to go to Safeway and get some, that his head would burst if he didn't? He got dressed and went to his car. The evening was warmish and foggy, so that the air was full of light and the streets were shining, and he didn't have his watch, he'd forgotten it, and he drove rather aimlessly because of the headache—he had to make himself think how to get to Safeway, although the hardest thing in the world was thinking. The streets were empty, so empty, and there was a man in a smooth leather jacket that caught the light, jaywalking, holding up his hand imperiously, looking at him, and he realized that it was Michael, though why he was there at that moment, Richie could not understand. Michael recognized him, grinned, and gave him the finger; and

Richie felt himself press down on the accelerator, press down hard, and then Michael grew to enormous size, and there was an impact, and a bump-bump as the car went over the body, and he drove home without looking back and without any headache, and he went to bed and slept like a rock until Jessica came into the room (it was bright daylight) and said, "Honey, someone is here from the police." She looked upset, and all the cop said was "Congressman, I have some bad news for you. Your brother was the victim of a hit-and-run sometime between three-thirty and four-fifteen this morning, and, I am sorry to tell you, he passed away, and his body is at the morgue."

Richie said, "Oh Jesus, you are kidding me," and the cop frowned regretfully, and Richie said, "Any clues about the perpetrator?" and one cop said, "Not many, I'm sorry to say. The surveillance cameras in the area seem to have been down for maintenance."

"Which area?" said Richie.

"Delaware, almost to M Street, sir. Southwest?"

It seemed to Richie that he didn't even know where that was.

After they called his mom and Janet to give them the news, and Jessica left for work, he went out and looked at his car, a nondescript silver Toyota. No dents, no scrapes, no hairs caught in the grille. At dinner, he said to Jessica, "I have been tired all day. I feel like I was up a lot last night."

She said, "You know me, I sleep through everything, but I have this vague memory of you going to the bathroom. You groaned."

He didn't ask anything further.

Surely, Richie thought, this is all a hallucination, not something he remembered but something he had fantasized about for so long that it had now sprung into his head, a movie he'd finally bought the ticket to. He did not go to the morgue, and when the funeral director suggested a closed coffin, he agreed at once.

Janet called Chance and Loretta; Loretta called Binky and Tia. Claire said that she would come to the funeral, but Jesse and Jen didn't think they could afford it—they did know about Piddinghoe Investments, because Felicity had told them. Loretta came; she was obese now, looked terrible in an autocratic way. Chance and Emily went to the Hut and got Andy. The obituary included the part about Michael being the victim of a hit-and-run, that the case remained open, but left out Piddinghoe Investments, the offshored millions, everything Richie had never told anyone about Michael's small cruelties and invisible (to others) sneers. No one invited Lynne, and it turned out that, according to Loretta, she and Michael were not divorced, but Richie wasn't sure exactly how Loretta meant the word "not." Claire came—the last original Langdon. She gave Richie a hug and said that she couldn't imagine what he must be feeling. She was right: she couldn't. He would not say that he grieved, he would not say that he didn't grieve. He thought maybe, if you had spent your entire life suffering from serious pains in your leg, and then that limb was amputated, those particular pains were gone, but other pains replaced them—that was the best way to describe how he was feeling. Jessica knew he was freed, but he said nothing to her about the regret, fear, anxiety, the sense of being lopsided and perhaps fatally out of balance. He looked around the service and saw tears—Tia and Binky for sure, Jessica because she was a kind person, but also Janet? Chance maintained his stoicism, Emily stuck close to Chance and squeezed his hand every so often, Leo explained the concept of death to Jack, and Britt walked around the room and out into the corridor hand in hand with Mona, just to keep her quiet. Felicity stayed away, Guthrie had to work, and Perky was in Moscow. After chatting with his mom and giving her a hug, Claire came back and stood next to Richie, put her arm around his waist, and leaned against him just a little bit. She said, "When you get to be my age, the deaths get quicker. It's making me kind of crazy. Not only Carl and Lois and Henry, and now Michael, but three friends of mine in Chicago." Richie said, "Felicity would say, Get used to it," and he spoke in such a cold voice that Claire turned and stared at him. Then she said, "Well, I do know what you mean," and moved away.

He did not dare spend any time with his mom. He felt like she would know the answer to his conundrum, and she would tell it to him in a single enigmatic phrase. He preferred to wait for the police to come up with something.

Loretta had the body shipped to Savannah, where she interred it in a family plot she had purchased. Richie thought that she had caged Michael at last, and no doubt the tombstone would read, "Loving husband of."

....

CLAIRE WOULD HAVE put on a better funeral—more to eat, because you had to give the mourners plenty of time to get comfortable with one another. And you had to lay the food out in stages, so that they would eat plenty and feel their endorphins kick in. Strawberries dipped in dark chocolate, baguettes and an array of cheeses, ambrosia—her mother's old standby (with sliced oranges, coconut, and chunks of banana)—small squares of bacon-Gruyère quiche, champagne. You had to bring it out and offer it around with a sympathetic look on your face, and people would take it and feel better, and then they would start to talk more openly, and stories would come out about the person who had died, and all of those stories would be funny or affectionate, and by the time the food was gone, everyone would have a positive feeling about the corpse. But Richie was in shock, and Jessica, lovely woman that she was, was never offended by reality, and so never thought of changing reality for the better. As they were driving back to the hotel from the funeral, Janet said, "That gave me the creeps."

Claire said, "Worst I've ever seen. Chicago gangsters are buried with more affection."

"Michael aroused passion, I suppose, but I doubt if he ever aroused affection, or even wanted to."

"But," said Claire, "you are supposed to paper that over at a funeral, or the death forever afterward seems to be roiling in anger and resentment."

Janet said, "A fitting tribute, then."

She stopped at a red light, and they exchanged a glance. Claire said, "So why did you cry at the service?"

"He was a cute baby. I was only three, but I remember that. I think I was crying for all the cute babies."

Claire reached over and squeezed her niece affectionately on the knee. They were practically the same age now, weren't they? The eleven years that separated them had dwindled to almost nothing.

Claire was dreaming that their hotel was attached to a hospital, and that she had gone into one of the hospital rooms and gotten into bed with a gray cat. She was snuggling up to him and thinking that the hospital bed was much more comfortable than the hotel bed when

Janet woke her up, saying, "Do you think that we've lived through a golden age?"

Claire's eyes opened on the clock face, which read "10:34"—she had been asleep for maybe seven minutes. She took a deep breath, then said, "Why would we think that? No one thinks that." What she really thought was, Why would you think that, with everything that you've been through? She turned on her side. Janet's gray bob was pale in the light from the hotel courtyard. Janet said, "Believe me, I never would have—my conviction that we as a species have fucked every single thing up is the most lasting thing about me. But I was looking at my mom open her handbag for a Kleenex, and that handbag is truly vintage—"

"Green vinyl," said Claire. "I saw that."

They both laughed.

"Anyway, I remembered telling her that I wished I had been born in 1787 and died in 1860, because there weren't any wars then, so I must have been in sixth or seventh grade, because that was when we first studied American history."

"Nineteen sixty?"

"Sometime around the U-2 incident. Francis Gary Powers shot down spying in the USSR. I wonder what ever happened to him. Jeez. It was like I learned what death was and that it was imminent at the very same moment. But it never happened. We're still alive."

"I know what happened to him," said Claire. "After they traded him back from Russia, he got a job for some TV station, and he was doing fire recon in California when his copter crashed. I don't think it's been a golden age."

"How long have I been convinced this country is doomed? I always thought it would be fossil fuels, corruption, guns, and climate change, Frank Langdon's legacies. I thought racism was like a giant tapeworm, horrible and disgusting, that we just had to live with."

"I never heard Frank make a racist comment."

"After the people were murdered in that church in Charleston, I said to myself, That's what's going to destroy us after all."

"No," said Claire. "That is what will make it so that no one in the world will care if this country is destroyed."

"A golden age, though," said Janet. "In comparison with what's to come. Golden ages are always in the past."

Just then, Claire had a small memory, maybe from the nineties? She was sitting in her window seat, waiting for takeoff at O'Hare. They must have been at the edge of the runway, and for some reason, she saw something she had never seen before—planes approaching in the twilight, their headlights on, appearing in the distance, tipping slightly upward, then floating downward. As soon as one landed, another appeared, so silently, so rhythmically, so cooperatively. And then darkness fell, and a few stars glimmered, and a three-quarter moon. She didn't relate this memory to Janet, but she did think right then that all golden ages were discovered within. No one would ever know that her father, Carl, the endless Iowa horizon, a pan of short-bread emerging from the oven, and her grandchildren laughing in the next room had indeed made her life a golden age. She glanced over at Janet, who gave a little snore. Dreaming, Claire hoped.

GUTHRIE SOMETIMES TALKED to Perky, now known as LTC John Perkins Langdon (he had added the "John" himself because as "Perky" he had been incessantly harassed during training and he didn't like "Franklin"). LTC John Langdon talked like an army train-ing manual—clipped, ruthless, impatient. As far as Guthrie was con-cerned, Perky's way of dealing with his own PTSD was to embrace it. He had seen action not only in Afghanistan, but in Yemen, during the crisis, and in Greece, when the EU called in American forces to put down the uprising. When Perky was in the States, he was stationed at Fort Hood. He complained a lot about the heat and said there were rumors going around that Fort Hood was no longer sustainable—they might reopen Fort Ord, out in California, just for the weather. The way he talked now was always sharp, irritated, military, never "perky." What John would do when they retired him, Guthrie could not imagine.

One day, at the noodle shop in Iowa City, Guthrie overheard some people talking, talking about Seattle, about Pike Place Market, Bain-bridge Island, and, most important, how far Seattle was from every-place else in the world—"almost like Perth," said one of the girls. Of course, this was not true. You could see on any map that Seattle was close to several cities: Portland, the nightmare that was Vancouver. But he got up from his lunch, disposed of his bowl and his utensils, and placed his tray on the stand, and that afternoon he left. He took all of his cash out of the bank ($846), packed a single suitcase, filled his car with gas. He stopped at the mall, gave his letter of immediate resignation to the supervisor of the skating rink, picked up his skates, and bought four new decks of cards, just to pass the time. He headed west on 80, not intending to see the farm, but at 63 he turned north after all. Late in the afternoon, he drove past it, then looped around the section. The big house was still there, but the old Maze, the windbreaks, and the barns were gone. Even the Osage-orange hedge was gone. Equipment was parked beside the hill. The hill still sported a small jungle of weeds, trees, wildflowers. Possibly that had been his dad's favorite place on the farm, but possibly not. He drove on, through Sioux City up to Sioux Falls, where he stopped and spent the night in his car. It was then that he decided not to head straight to Seattle, but to see a few things. He thought twice about this when he woke up just after dawn and all that was visible was dust (he could taste it, too, even though the windows and the vents in the car were closed). He sat up sweaty from the heat, and looked at his watch. Only 7:00 a.m. He put up his seat back, blew his nose (dust) a few times, and made himself wake up. He could turn around. But he knew perfectly well that Iowa City was death for him. No one saw that but Guthrie. Even so . . . and, anyway, he had resigned from his job. These days, that *was* like committing suicide.

He drank some water and pulled out of the parking lot. South Dakota was strangely different from Iowa, even this close to the border. Already in May, the former farm fields were brown, the parking lots had no cars parked in them, and the abandoned buildings they surrounded had lost their names. It was spooky. He pulled onto I-90. By eight, the dust had settled, and he could turn on the AC, which might be, literally, a lifesaver. He remembered from school that the Ogallala Aquifer had never stretched this far north—it was mostly in Kansas and Nebraska. There must have been some aquifer up this way, but he couldn't remember the name of it. It was gone now. The landscape was moonlike, except for the quality of the road (excellent) and the remnants of former towns that he passed along the way. The Missouri River at Chamberlain was almost dry—the bridge soared above it, and the former bed of the river was a dusty stretch of dirt with a thin, shiny greenish line running through it; there had been so little snow out west that it hadn't flooded in five years. His dad had always been strangely anxious about floods.

He was to the Badlands by lunch; he stopped and had a hot dog and a Coke at a bar in Wall, then drove south into maybe the strangest landscape he had ever seen. His car thermometer said ninety-eight outside, eighty inside. He took off his shirt and shoes, and drove barefoot. The Badlands came upon you gradually, but then there they were: you were driving along the edge of steep cliffs that fell away from the plains, rather than rising above them. The land was so dry that it looked rather like rock. Things got more and more desolate; after a while, he was among the cliffs, and then past them. A house here and there—abandoned ranches, no doubt. The switchbacks meant that he had to drive slowly, so it was dusk when he stopped, parked by the side of the road, and rustled up a box of crackers and another thermos of water. He thought it was perfect, in its way, that he would spend the night here, in the bleakest spot he had ever been in, bleaker than Iraq. Iraq was dry and forbidding, but you knew from ninth-grade history that every square foot of Mesopotamia had been walked over and thought about for thousands of years. Here, that did not seem to be so. Even though Native Americans had lived here, they seemed entirely vanished now, as if, Guthrie thought, the world had ended. But it was cooler than Sioux Falls. He slept fine, and was in a better mood in the morning. He detoured over to Rapid City and ate three fried eggs, an order of bacon, and a slice of cantaloupe. His car was saving him a lot of money. It got fifty miles to the gallon and was comfortable enough to sleep in—that was a hundred dollars a night in hotel costs.

He knew three guys who had disappeared into the North Dakota oil fields—Jake Sharp, in 2012, Randy Case in 2014, and, the most desperate, Lundy Mitchell last year, when he lost his job at the Iowa City Veterans Administration, and left his wife and three kids on South Lucas Street. He sent back most of his paycheck from Williston, where he, too, lived in his car. But the oil business wasn't what it had been five years ago. According to Tracy Mitchell—who had never wanted Lundy to go, but what else was there to do, especially since their four-year-old was battling liver cancer and needed a transplant—the best fields ran out in about a month.

The weather cooled off a little as he drove north, but as soon as he crossed I-94, he felt the anxiety coming on. Even though he was alert about his triggers, he at first didn't understand that it was the huge tankers rumbling by, shaking the road and buffeting his old car, that were giving him headaches and making his palms sweat. And the sunlight was blinding—or it seemed blinding to Guthrie—another trigger, because whenever he remembered Iraq he remembered squinting into the desert, barely able to make out where the danger was coming from. Finally, he saw a rest stop and pulled over. It was a nice rest stop, with aspen trees and a bit of a lawn, obviously built in the last few years, but the former oil fields encroached upon it—four dead derricks within a quarter-mile of the lookout, and another one in the distance. There was some sort of old holding pool nearby, and where there might once have been prairie grasses (and even wildflowers, at this time of year), there was now just dusty, gravelly earth. He imagined George Armstrong Custer sitting here on his horse, thinking he had been transported to Mars. On the highway, beyond the little break of trees, brakes squealed and two horns blared, a whining car horn and a deep, aggressive tanker horn. There was no sound of a crash (Guthrie didn't turn around), but Guthrie's heart was pounding anyway, as if the gunfire and explosions would commence momentarily. He went into the men's john—rather luxurious—and sat there in the coolness for a long time, going through his exercises. Maybe, he thought, what worked in peaceful Iowa City would not necessarily work in oil country. He went back to his car, rolled down the windows, and stayed there for a while, practicing his card tricks. By one o'clock, he felt calmer, and also hungry—hunger was always a worthy distraction. He pulled out of the rest stop.

But he couldn't tolerate the highway. Every driver seemed predatory. So, at the next turnoff, he took a small road into the wildlife refuge, and it was like entering another world. The rough hills were marginally greener than the plains; deer stood by the side of the road as if they enjoyed observing passersby. Most important, the park was quiet and nearly empty: empty hills, empty roads, empty cliffs, empty valleys, empty enormous sky. He took some deep breaths, and found his box of crackers again—almost empty. He did not drive far into the park; it was pretty apparent that the roads were narrow and treacherous, it would be easy to get lost. But he got himself together here, so that when he headed back to the main road, even though it was now dusk and he could see the gas flares on the horizon more clearly, and smell the oily scent that pervaded the countryside as it came through his ventilation system, he was okay with it, more willing to think about his imminent hamburger than his imminent death.

He half hoped to run into Lundy Mitchell—he didn't—but he did run into, of all people, Scott Crandall, who had been in his unit in Iraq, and whom he hadn't thought of once in the interim. He was sitting at a bar in Williston, and when he heard Guthrie order his burger and onion rings, he turned around and said, "Shit!"

He looked so belligerent that Guthrie prepared himself right then to be cold-cocked, but the guy smiled (not many teeth), flexed his enormous biceps (years in oil country, setting rigs), and said, "Langdon, shit, man, what the fuck!" and threw his arms around Guthrie and squeezed. Guthrie was six feet tall, 190, but Scott—or, as he was now known, "Croc"—was two inches taller and forty pounds heavier, all muscle. Even his enormous belly was as hard as a rock. He was bald, had a tatt on his cheek and another on his forehead, and took Guthrie back to his man-camp room for the night. Which would have been fine, considering they both got pretty drunk, but Croc wanted to talk and talk and talk. He hadn't been away from Williston in ten years; he'd once made plenty of dough, but he played a lot of poker, too; and he wanted Guthrie to know every detail of how his best friend in Williston had been crushed to death when a tanker rolled backward into a drilling rig—the screaming lasted ten full minutes, and they couldn't do a thing about it. If Langdon thought Iraq was bad, he should stick around in Williston for a week. Anyway, that scam set up by the big oil companies and the Arabs, the one where they dropped the price of oil to fifty dollars a barrel and kept it there for a year, had worked—put most of the drillers on the Bakken out of business. Croc finally passed out (twelve Coronas and a bottle of vodka; Guthrie remembered him getting so drunk in Iraq that he set his duffel bag on end and shot it full of holes, laughing the entire time). Guthrie was out of the man camp and to Billings, Montana, by noon.

He had $346, and wasn't halfway yet. He was getting fifty miles to the gallon; he had eight hundred or so miles to go; so at $8.90 a gallon (the price of gas was back up now), it would cost him $150 just in gas. There was a part of him that wanted to arrive in Seattle with a dollar in his pocket and a new name—let's say "Sage" (maybe, with effort, he could live up to that)—but it was a stupid part of him. There was no speed limit in Montana, so he could get pretty far in twenty-four hours. That was what he was thinking. It would also be smart to plug in his phone, now dead, but he realized that he had left the car charger somewhere—it wasn't under the seat.

He filled up in Coeur d'Alene, happy to have gotten that far. He was a man of the plains, so the switchbacks over the mountains in the dark, the way the guardrail loomed into the light, spooked him and made him jerk the wheel. He did think many times about how one of the effects of PTSD was not that you were suicidal, exactly, but that death was such a familiar concept that it seemed like a reasonable alternative to, not fear, but shock, suddenness, the unexpected. Eventually, a person got very tired of those shots of adrenaline that didn't stop firing. Your body itself became the enemy that could never be placated. At a place called Moses Lake, he turned off into Potholes State Park (how could he resist?), and pulled into a shady spot. The weather wasn't terrible here—he only had to crack his windows a little. He was hungry, though. That was his last thought before he fell asleep.

The blow against the window that woke him up was followed by the blow that cracked the window. The third one shattered it, and the glass poured into his lap. A face was right in his, the face of a teen-ager. The face was snarling, and behind it were more faces, three or more. Everyone was screaming. Guthrie jerked back, and the kid leaned in, saying, "How much money you got, fuckhead?"

Guthrie had no idea, but he said, "Hundred bucks, maybe." The kid said, "Hand it over. Hand me your wallet."

Guthrie hesitated, not out of fear—that hadn't kicked in yet—but just out of surprise, slowness. The kid lifted his gun. Guthrie recognized it; it was an old Ruger. It came through the broken window, and Guthrie felt the muzzle touch his cheek. Instinctively, he turned his head.

2019

A LAWYER DID COME to the Hut. It wasn't anyone from the IRS—he was working for the Loretta Langdon Family Trust. He had a Southern accent, and Andy, though she wasn't getting around very well, invited him to have a seat and offered him a cup of mint tea, which he took. He had a briefcase with him, but before he opened it, he complimented her on how "charming" her place was. He said, "This is a lot like my grandma's place, that I remember from a boy. It was up in Asheville? I used to love to go up there. My father's mother. My mother was from Savannah; my word, she turned up her nose at the hillbillies on my dad's side, but I did love them best, I have to say."

Andy said, "I take it your grandparents are no longer living?"

"No, no. They died pretty young. I think Grandpa was sixty and Grandma was sixty-four."

"That is young," said Andy, and he stared at her, at the life she had made herself by contemplating death so often and so thoroughly for as long as she could remember, training herself not to let death come unexpectedly, to step aside or look over her shoulder at every tire squeal, to note every slippery patch, every dangling wire, every scent of gas, every sign of infection. Frank had been alert, but never quite as alert as she was to the skull within the beautiful visage. Finally, the young man said, "You look in excellent health, ma'am."

Andy said, "I can't complain," and for some reason she laughed, and then he laughed. He took a deep breath and embraced his briefcase, as if to fortify his resolve. Andy sipped her mint tea. Her hand was just bones now, but no arthritis, at least.

He opened the briefcase and pulled out some papers. He said, "It does appear, as we look into Michael Langdon's estate, that he was making deposits into an account that is in your name. I am told by Mrs. Langdon that these were support payments to you."

"Or, perhaps," said Andy, "restitution. His antics in 2008 cost me eighteen million dollars." She grabbed this amount out of the ozone—her clearest memory of the Uncle Jens fund was from about 1955, when it hit a hundred grand because of real-estate investments Frank had made with that Mafia type they met at Belmont Park.

"Mrs. Langdon said nothing to me about restitution."

Andy said, "How about money laundering? When the cash started being deposited was when all those offshore accounts were being investigated. Possibly he was stashing his money in my account to hide it, so I paid my taxes." She smiled politely.

"As you will remember, Mrs. Langdon, it was decided by the Supreme Court that offshore accounts are entirely legal, and that it was in the public interest for corporations to follow uniform international tax laws as set up by the Trans-Pacific Trade Agreement, and so there was no actual reason for Mr. Langdon to, as you say, launder any money."

"After 2017."

"True, that decision did come down a year and a half ago. However, that is neither here nor there from Mrs. Langdon's point of view. She would like an accounting of the money you received from your son."

"I can send you the bank statements."

"And, if you don't mind, can you estimate how much is in that account right now?"

"I believe a hundred and six dollars."

Now the young man looked taken aback. He said, "Mrs. Langdon estimates that Mr. Langdon deposited at least a million dollars in that account."

"In the end, more, I would say."

"And you felt that this was your money, so you spent it?" He looked around the Hut in amazement. His gaze paused at the wall oven, as if she might have put the cash in there.

Andy said, "I wouldn't say that I spent it, though it undoubtedly has been spent. I gave it away."

He licked his lips.

"Ma'am, have you kept a list of the persons or organizations you gave that money to? And do you have your tax returns from the last six years?"

Andy said, "Oh, my goodness! You will have to subpoena me for those! But it isn't going to do Loretta any good. That money is gone, as well it should be. If the IRS wants to put a ninety-eight-year-old woman in jail, they are welcome to do so." She again gave him her best, most radiant, and, she knew some would say, skeletal smile. He looked taken aback.

Andy said, "I didn't give a penny to the Catholic Church."

He didn't say anything to that. He took another sip of his tea. She said, "Will you tell me something?" She made sure she sounded wheedling, kind, and decrepit—she even got a little bit of a shake into her voice.

He said, "What's that?"

"What has happened to the ranch in California? What was it, the Angel Ranch."

"The Angelina Ranch has been donated by Mr. Chance Langdon to the California Rangeland Trust, and he has moved to ten or so acres somewhere around Santa Ynez. Since the ranch sits square on the Monterey Shale, he thought maybe the trust was in a better position to preserve it, should fracking become viable again. Of course, there is the drought aspect as well."

They both shook their heads regretfully.

"Mrs. Langdon has no quarrel with her son's decision."

"She has her good points," said Andy.

The lawyer said, "Yes, ma'am. She does."

WHEN, after a year of on-and-off suspense about Michael's "accident," Richie told Jessica over breakfast that it was he himself who had killed him, run him down in the Toyota because he laughed at Richie and gave him the finger, she lathered some pear jam on her toast and said, in her straightforward Jessica way, "I don't believe that."

Richie pushed his plate away, even though he'd hardly touched a thing. "I tell you something that it has taken me a year to confess, and you don't believe me?"

"I believe that you think that you killed him, but I don't believe that you did." The toast was so crisp he could hear it crunching. Jessica did so love to eat.

"You think I have dementia or something?"

She set her elbows on the table and leaned toward him. "Darling, don't you realize that you ask me certain things over and over, like whether we've watched *Crystal and Cooper* already this week, and why isn't it on the DVR?"

"I do ask you that?"

"Yes."

"Why isn't it on the DVR?"

"Because we watched the latest episode Monday night and then you deleted it."

"Do I know how to operate the DVR?"

"You do."

"Did I enjoy *Crystal and Cooper*?"

"You seemed to." She shook her head. She thought he was joking, and maybe he was, a little. He said, "I am sixty-six. My mom is almost a hundred. Aunt Claire is eighty. Everyone in our family is sharp as a tack."

Jessica said, "I know that, sweetie."

He let the subject drop, but every so often, he called the investigator who had been put on the case at the beginning and asked him if there was any new information. The investigator was sympathetic—he had cousins who were twins, very close—but he never had new information. Finally, after the fifth call, he said, "Congressman, I would like to pursue this, but we are so low on funds that I would have to do it on my own time, and there are other cases that seem more important to me. Not to mention the backlog in the courts. There are a few retired investigators you might contact to see if one of them would do it—but it's a boring case. It's a hit-and-run. It's more or less meaningless. Now, you were telling me about that young man you knew, who was shot out in Washington State?"

"Cousin," said Richie.

"Yes, sir. Well, that is more interesting in its way, because those gangs of kids that they have in certain places—there in Washington State, but also in Kansas and Wisconsin and Oklahoma, and a lot of places where the economy has simply vanished these last years, they are a real symptom of the times we live in. They don't care if they murder, they don't care if they die. They've got nothing to look forward to, so, as with your cousin, they kill for a twenty-dollar bill. We thought those types were a third-world phenom; well, look where they are now. At least they got those boys, and they're in jail. Sixteen people had to die before they got 'em, but they got 'em. That's all I have to say."

"Thank you for your help."

"I wish I *could* help, Congressman, but you've got to accept the fact that whoever killed your brother got away with it."

After that call, Richie thought about those kids in Washington. Some had been fourteen (the most ruthless age, in Richie's estimation), though the apparent killer was eighteen—he had been living at the park for three years. His father had been a migrant from Amarillo, Texas. He farmed for ADM for a year, but couldn't support his family doing it. The son began stealing, was kicked out of the house; the wife died mysteriously (domestic violence was no longer investigated, as a policy to save money); then the father shot himself in the mouth. The other four kids had similar backgrounds. It was the same in Oregon, the same wherever there was still water, still even the smallest hope of making a living. The boys drank from the river, shot and ate animals, ambushed passersby. The sixteen bodies (Guthrie had been number fourteen; fifteen and sixteen were a local couple, the boys' biggest mistake) were left under bushes for the vultures and the crows to take care of them. Two of them drove Guthrie's car to a local town, where they spent his last $38.56. Then they left the car in a parking lot and hitchhiked back to the park. Until the death of the local couple, people in the town had thought they were "harmless," figured they couldn't "do nothing about them—gonna ship them back to Texas?" Was he like these boys? Since he had done what he did, why did what they did fill him with horror? Sometimes he allowed himself to believe that what he had done had a certain justice to it, or, at least, a certain practicality. Other times he thought he had fulfilled his destiny—you name which one, psychological, mythological, political, masculine. But no one believed he had done it. No one believed that Congressman Langdon (D-NY) had the balls.

CLAIRE'S HOUSE WAS big enough for Jesse and Jen to feel almost comfortable. It was certainly well equipped—Jesse only had to think of a tool, walk into Carl's old workshop, and find it ready to hand. They had moved in originally for Claire's sake. Jesse's job was to maintain the gardens and the property, sell vegetables at the city market when they were harvested, and keep the place up, though Carl had been so careful that only the most routine maintenance was needed. Jen's job, unspoken, was to keep an eye on Claire. The very first evening, Claire had looked at them across the supper table and said, "I am eighty. I will never leave here, because I feel Carl's presence here," which meant, Live here, take care of me, I will bequeath you the house. It seemed like a decent bargain, not least because Claire had almost no sentimental attachment to the farm: I love it here; look at these vegetables; and to think, you can weed the garden, then take the train to the Field Museum and pick up some pomegranate balsamic on the way home. She didn't insist that they view their eviction as a salvation, but she set the example.

After Guthrie's car and then his body were found, though, Claire became the caretaker. It was a parent's worst nightmare—first he disappears without a word, as if he just can't take you anymore, and then his remains are found somewhere you've never been or he's never been, until now. Guthrie, the riddle; Guthrie, the boy who smiled no matter what, and deflected all questions, all looks of concern; Guthrie, aged thirty-four, the boy who was always about to get it together. Guthrie, who died before you could look him in the eye and say, "I told you not to enlist, I told you not to be a sucker." But he hadn't told him, and look at Perky, "John"—it had all worked out for him.

Jesse did not think that Jen would recover from this. She had lost twenty pounds, she cried all the time, she refused antidepressants. He had never, never seen her not bounce back—even when they moved off the farm, she had truly seemed to believe that the opportunity to get rid of a lot of junk outweighed the injustice and the dislocation. She loved Claire, she loved Chicago, she loved the city market and the people she was meeting. Until. Now she could not look at Jesse; he looked too much like Guthrie. She spent her time with Claire, and Claire allowed it, comforted her over and over. Some nights she slept in Claire's room, and Jesse could hear them through the heating vents, talking. It didn't have to be about Guthrie—they talked about their childhoods and the news and knitting sweaters for Claire's grandchildren.

Sometime after dawn, he woke up to find Claire in her robe, sitting on his bed. He jerked upward, and Claire took his hand. She said, "It's all right. She's asleep. It's me that couldn't sleep. I thought you might be awake already."

"Aunt Claire, those days are gone. Even when I was farming, I never got up before eight."

"No cows to milk," said Claire.

"Nothing to love at all," said Jesse. "What good was it?"

"Ah," said Claire. "Hmm. What did I love? I think all the scents. Mama's lilac trees, and the wild iris in the fields, and rain on the breeze on a hot day. Apple and pear blossoms. The hay just cut. The mix of odors in the barn when the sunlight was shafting through the cracks in the boards, heating everything up."

Jesse said, "I liked a big harvest, but I didn't love it. Not like my dad. He would put his hands into a bin of corn kernels and let them flow through his fingers, and he would pick up the cobs and sniff them."

"Joe was a very sensuous man, and I am old enough to say that! Oh, I loved that house, the Frederick house. I remember, when I was six, so it was right around the end of the war, I used to ease out whatever door Mama wasn't near and walk over there. It seemed like there was such a hill between our house and theirs, but it was just a little rise. I would walk in the weeds along the edge of the big field, and then I would just stand there, looking up at the row of windows, and the upstairs porch off the back; then I would walk around and look at the ripply glass panes in the front door. It was painted a minty rust-green then. I thought the color was very appealing. Whatever Mama didn't like, I liked, that's for sure."

"She was a character," said Jesse.

"And characters don't always make the best mothers, but, with a little distance and Henry's help, I came to appreciate her."

Jesse did not say what he was thinking, that because, according to the police report, Guthrie probably felt no pain—the bullet went straight through his brainstem and cerebellum, then lodged in the headrest of his seat, and so he had lucked out—he had no worries anymore. If you were not religious, then you could imagine him at rest; and if you were religious, you could imagine him released, redeemed, reborn. Sometimes Jesse thought of this as his father had (redemption in the soil itself, in compost, in the memories of those who loved you), and sometimes he thought of this as his mother had, redemption in the arms of the Lord (and she had always told him those arms were wide open, no matter what certain pastors might say). You could grieve the strange horror of Guthrie's demise, and what that meant about the world they lived in, or you could grieve Guthrie's loss, or you could grieve your own loss. Or you could condemn yourself for bequeathing this new world to your children. He put his hands over his face, and his aunt Claire patted his knee. She said, "Oh, Jess. I don't know what to say."

THE BARGAIN THEY MADE was that Ezra could plan the wedding, and Felicity would plan the honeymoon, and each set of plans would be secret from the other person. Felicity thought that it would be very difficult for Ezra to plan the wedding around a rally or a march, but if she gave him the honeymoon, he would have a field day, and, as usual (in her experience), she was right. He put off and put off, and then, when they went to Britt and Leo's place for Halloween, there was the Officiant, and there were her parents, looking spent but better than they had in the summer. Britt and Mona were wearing matching outfits, Leo and Jack were in suits, and Ezra had bought her a dress—beige, not white—and it fit perfectly of course, and looked good. Ezra was nothing if not precise. Emily and Jonah were there, too. Jonah was doing graduate work at Cornell, in Chinese, and if he wasn't going to work for the NSA, Felicity would be dumbfounded; but at the moment, he was writing his dissertation on the violent end of the Ming Dynasty. Emily had with her a present from Tina, who had become a potter "as a retirement gesture." It was a beautiful six-quart stoneware casserole that looked as though a peacock feather had been draped over it. Chance had been unable to come, but he had sent along his and hers cowboy shirts made of old feed sacks, which Ezra's mom liked so much she said she would sell them in her shop. She had knitted Ezra a black vest and Felicity a white lace shawl. Felicity could tell she had been planning their marriage maybe longer than she and Ezra had, because the shawl and the vest were intricate and time-consuming. Felicity loved Ezra's mom—in Roxbury, you did not have to hide your hippie origins or feel any embarrassment about all your friends who still lived in Woodstock. Ezra's dad brought the Lamoreaux Landing Finger Lakes sparkling wine, a case.

She hugged her mom for about five minutes, she was so happy to see them, happy they looked okay, happy that Ezra had talked them into it, happy that her mom and Ezra kissed as if they really liked each other. But the fact was, everyone in the family liked Ezra; they thought she was lucky to get him. She did, too. Uncle Richie couldn't come—he was in the hospital for an emergency cardiac procedure. All through the wedding, everyone tried not to be worried about him, tried to talk about Guthrie instead, what a sweet young man he had been, but at least six people, including Leo, said, "He just hasn't been the same since Uncle Michael got killed." When, before the ceremony, they said a prayer for Guthrie, they included Uncle Richie. As a rule, Felicity stared straight at the wall when anyone said prayers, but because it was for Guthrie, and her mom was standing next to her, holding her hand, she bowed her head this time. And so it was a big wedding, and so Ezra had pulled it off, and so the onus was now on Felicity to make something of the honeymoon.

Ezra had never been west of State College, and he had only gone there when Wolf was inaugurated as governor in '15, to protest fracking. A honeymoon in late November was always a risk, especially since Ezra did not like sports but didn't like any other sort of leisure, either. There had been no snow, however, so Felicity decided that a road trip, first to Chicago to visit her parents and Aunt Claire and sample the wares at the city market, and then on to . . . Well, that would be the surprise. Ezra might think that she was setting up an inspection of the Illinois coal mines and oil fields that he would like to blow up, or perhaps the old nuclear-waste site on the Missouri side of the river down by St. Louis, which had become such a scandal.

There was really nowhere safe to go on a honeymoon anymore—not Florida, or even the Caribbean, since the hurricane season had gotten so wild. This was, perhaps, a bad omen for a marriage. Nevertheless, Felicity hadn't been to the farm in four years. They would drink a bottle of real champagne in their room at the Days Inn in Ames, and that would remind them of who they were.

Felicity did the driving. Eleven hours through Maryland, Pennsylvania, Ohio, Illinois, Ezra staring out the window and noting roses blooming here, jonquils blooming there. As they drove, Ezra checked his phone for coordinates, and kept a list of what he saw. Only two years ago, monster snowfall, and now this.

Aunt Claire's house was an oasis of beauty and order, her dad still seemed mournfully relaxed, and her mom was beginning to resemble her old Guthrie self. She took Felicity and Ezra to the city market— tables of products from Illinois, Wisconsin, Indiana, even Michigan. Organic pulled-pork sandwiches, and on your ticket was the name of the hog you were eating (in Ezra's case, "Dennis"). Tomatoes that were fresh off the vine in the last week. Baby asparagus. One of the sellers said, "Yes, the weather is crazy, but as long as we are deploring it, we have to take advantage, and produce as much as we can, for the compost, and also for the dryer. We are on our own now." She was from Racine. Ezra took down her name. Felicity bought five skeins of lamb's wool, undyed, cream, gray, and dark gray. That night, she was almost happy when she lay in bed, in spite of what she knew was coming.

They left at 7:00 a.m., with six of Aunt Claire's scones in a bag and a small jar of pear jelly. They were through Cedar Rapids and on the Lincoln Highway before noon, and Ezra said, "You are taking me to the farm."

"Just for the afternoon," said Felicity.

The weather remained sinisterly sunny. It was strange to crack her window so late in the year because the interior of the car was so warm, strange to see . . . Well, she kept her eye on the road.

The farm was entirely flattened. You could loop around it, as you had always been able to do, but if you didn't know the numbers and names of the roads, you wouldn't know where you were. The houses were gone, the barn was gone, the butternut trees were gone, the little hill was gone, the old creek bed was gone. Some kind of machinery had been used to plane the surface of the land so that it was as flat as a table, and slightly raised, and over it the owners had spread acres and acres of black plastic sheeting, no doubt to preserve the moisture. Between the rows of sheeting, there were long, deep ditches with slanting sides, fake creeks that stored the rainwater and, Ezra thought, let it seep, by means of some sort of capillary system, into the adjacent "soil." On the southwest corner of the farm, where the old house had once been, there was now a double-wide trailer. After Felicity and Ezra had been standing beside their car for a few minutes, its door opened, and a man stepped out onto the tiny porch. He was holding a Bushmaster. Ezra waved, and they got back into the car and drove around to the other side, where he wouldn't be able to see them. Felicity wasn't exactly afraid of guns, and the man hadn't lifted his, but she was happy to drive away. She said, "One more thing."

Ezra said, "Measuring the depth of the soil."

"Exactly," said Felicity. They pulled over where maybe the hill had been, the hill her dad had never wanted to plant, just west of that, where the soil had been deepest and most fertile from years of manure. She didn't have a tool, so she used the spoon they had used for the pear jelly. She dug. She came to subsoil.

"Two inches," said Ezra.

"It was twelve or fourteen a hundred and fifty years ago," said Felicity.

"And it's very fine, like sand or dust. I guess that's the reason they cover it with plastic."

Felicity rubbed a bit between her fingers. It was gray, just grit.

Ezra said, "You know, it took the Mesopotamians thousands of years to destroy their soil base."

They got back into the car and drove to Ames. That night, Felicity did not feel like drinking champagne.

WHEN ANDY WOKE UP, she thought it was the new year, but the clock on her phone read "11:55." Her eyes opened wide; she was not sleepy, and she was looking out the window of her room. Maybe the moon had awakened her, so bright that it pierced her eyelids. The surprising thing was the quiet weight in bed with her—behind her, causing the mattress to dip. She knew who it was, and so she didn't roll over. Out the window, the moon had moved upward; the light it cast was a shimmering film—over her golden yard and the glittering hill beyond, into the darkness of the trees, so that they looked bejeweled, across the sky, so that it was a deep cerulean. There was no wind. The fox that was crossing her yard paused, waved its tail, turned its head. They exchanged a glance, and what came into her mind was "Now. Right now." Then it happened again—she saw her world through the eyes of the fox. It was more monochrome, but also more distinct—it was as if she could see every blade of dry grass, note the ones that were quivering with life. A squirrel on a branch, a rat under the porch, the earth undulating in every direction, the sky far above. She did remember that fox in Iowa: same fox? A different fox? And now she knew that that fox had come to get her, and that she had sent him away because she'd had more lessons to learn. This time, she would not send him away. The weight in the bed shifted. A warmth lifted off him. She closed her eyes. He took her into him, Frank.

Acknowledgments

I would like to thank Barbara Grossman for plenty of support and advice. I would like to thank the members of the U.S. Congress for being so easy to satirize, and I would like to thank my own personal perfectionist, Robin Desser, for her patience.

13 WAYS OF LOOKING AT THE NOVEL

In her inimitable style—exuberant, candid, opinionated—
Smiley explores the power of the novel, looking at its history and variety, its cultural impact, and just how it works
its magic. She invites us behind the scenes of novel writing,
sharing her own habits and spilling the secrets of her craft.
And she offers priceless advice to aspiring authors. As she
works her way through one hundred novels—from classics
such as the thousand-year-old *Tale of Genji* to recent fiction by Zadie Smith and Alice Munro—she infects us anew
with the passion for reading that is the governing spirit of
this gift to book lovers everywhere.

Literary Criticism

DUPLICATE KEYS

Alice Ellis is a Midwestern refugee living in Manhattan.
Still recovering from a painful divorce, she depends on the
companionship and camaraderie of her tightly knit circle
of friends. At the center of this circle is a rock band struggling to navigate New York's erratic music scene, and an
apartment/practice space with approximately fifty key-
holders. One sunny day, Alice enters the apartment and
finds two of the band members shot dead. As the dou-
ble-murder sends waves of shock through their lives, this
group of friends begins to unravel, and dangerous secrets
are revealed one by one. When Alice begins to notice things
amiss in her own apartment, the tension breaks out as it
occurs to her that she is not the only person with a key, and
she may not get a chance to change the locks.

Fiction

GOOD FAITH

Greed. Envy. Sex. Property. In this subversively funny and genuinely moving novel, Jane Smiley nails down several American obsessions with the expertise of a master carpenter. Forthright, likable Joe Stratford is the kind of local businessman everybody trusts, for good reason. But it's 1982, and even in Joe's small town, values are in upheaval—not just property values, either. Enter Marcus Burns, a would-be master of the universe whose years with the IRS have taught him which rules are meant to be broken. Before long he and Joe are new best friends—and partners in an investment venture so complex that no one may ever understand it. Add to this Joe's roller coaster affair with his mentor's married daughter. The result is as suspenseful and entertaining as any of Jane Smiley's fiction.

Fiction

MOO

Nestled in the heart of the Midwest, amid cow pastures and waving fields of grain, lies Moo University, a distinguished institution devoted to the art and science of agriculture. Here, among an atmosphere rife with devious plots, mischievous intrigue, lusty liaisons, and academic one-upmanship, Chairman X of the Horticulture Department harbors a secret fantasy to kill the dean; Mrs. Walker, the provost's right hand and campus information queen, knows where all the bodies are buried; Timothy Nonahan, associate professor of English, advocates eavesdropping for his creative writing assignments; and Bob Carlson, a sophomore, feeds and maintains his only friend: a hog named Earl Butz. In this wonderfully written and masterfully plotted novel, Jane Smiley offers us a wickedly funny comedy that is also a darkly poignant slice of life.

Fiction

ORDINARY LOVE AND GOOD WILL

From Jane Smiley, author of the Pulitzer Prize–winning novel *A Thousand Acres*: a pair of novellas chronicling difficult choices that reshape the dynamics of two very different families. In *Ordinary Love*, Smiley focuses on a woman's infidelity and the lasting, indelible effects it leaves on her children long after her departure. *Good Will* describes a father who realizes how his son has been affected by his decision to lead a counterculture life and move his family to a farm. As both stories unfold, Smiley gracefully raises the questions that confront all families with the characteristic style and insight that has marked all of her work.

Fiction

PRIVATE LIFE

Private Life tells the powerful and deeply affecting story of one woman's life, from post–Civil War Missouri to California in the midst of World War II. When Margaret Mayfield marries Captain Andrew Jackson Jefferson Early at the age of twenty-seven, she narrowly avoids condemning herself to life as an old maid. Instead, knowing little about marriage and even less about her husband, she moves with Andrew to his naval base in California. Margaret stands by Andrew during tragedies both historical and personal, but as World War II approaches and the secrets of her husband's scientific and academic past begin to surface, she is forced to reconsider the life she had so carefully constructed. A riveting and nuanced novel of marriage and family, *Private Life* reveals the mysteries of intimacy and the anonymity that endures even in lives lived side by side.

Fiction

In the aftermath of the 2003 Academy Awards, Max and Elena—he's an Oscar-winning writer/director—open their Hollywood Hills home to a group of friends and neighbors, industy insiders and hangers-on, eager to escape the outside world and dissect the latest news, gossip, and secrets of the business. Over the next ten days, old lovers collide, new relationships form, and sparks fly, all with Smiley's signature sparkling wit and characterization. With its breathtaking passion and sexy irreverence, *Ten Days in the Hills* is a glowing addition to the work of one of our most beloved novelists.

Fiction

A THOUSAND ACRES

A successful Iowa farmer decides to divide his farm between his three daughters. When the youngest objects, she is cut out of his will. This sets off a chain of events that brings dark truths to light and explodes long-suppressed emotions. An ambitious reimagining of Shakespeare's *King Lear* cast upon a typical American community in the late twentieth century, *A Thousand Acres* takes on themes of truth, justice, love, and pride, and reveals the beautiful yet treacherous topography of humanity.

Fiction

ALSO AVAILABLE

The Age of Grief
The Greenlanders
Some Luck
Early Warning

ANCHOR BOOKS
Available wherever books are sold.
www.anchorbooks.com